THE
ISLAND
HOPPER

A novel

MICHAEL HILLIARD

authorHOUSE®

AuthorHouse™ LLC
1663 Liberty Drive
Bloomington, IN 47403
www.authorhouse.com
Phone: 1-800-839-8640

Cover design: Chester Baldicantos
Author photograph by Heather Crowder

This book is a work of fiction. People, places, events, and situations are the product of the author's imagination. Any resemblance to actual persons, living or dead, or historical events, is purely coincidental.

Published by AuthorHouse   12/04/2013

ISBN: 978-1-4918-2927-1 (sc)
ISBN: 978-1-4918-2926-4 (hc)
ISBN: 978-1-4918-2925-7 (e)

Library of Congress Control Number: 2013919088

Any people depicted in stock imagery provided by Thinkstock are models, and such images are being used for illustrative purposes only.
Certain stock imagery © Thinkstock.

This book is printed on acid-free paper.

Because of the dynamic nature of the Internet, any web addresses or links contained in this book may have changed since publication and may no longer be valid. The views expressed in this work are solely those of the author and do not necessarily reflect the views of the publisher, and the publisher hereby disclaims any responsibility for them.

For my home team:
Kimberly, Chase, Summer, & Brayden

PROLOGUE

February 14
Seven Mile Beach
Negril, Jamaica

I knew I was going to die. I didn't need to see the knife in my killer's hand. The malice in his eyes left little doubt.

At first I deflected a few of the higher arcing slashes, but my attacker was faster and stronger.

He had the added benefit of forethought and planning.

Soon I was overtaken and unable to fight against the deeper cuts that sliced into tissue, muscle, and bone. Over and over I was stabbed like a pin cushion and I felt each targeted strike, though my senses were reeling in the moment.

I felt my lungs fill with blood and smelled and tasted its copper-like tang. As my killer stood over me, he peered into my eyes. He even smiled as he followed my feeble, erratic hand movements as I tried to cover my puncture wounds.

But the blood kept coming and I felt my soul being poured out within it. I tried to call out but my breathing became increasingly labored. Air became harder to grasp. I convulsed and coughed, as each violent jolt forced more blood into the sand.

In my final seconds of life I became cold, even as I turned my face toward the hot sun. My wide eyes remained open; and although I stared directly into the bright light, my sight grew dim and eventually faded to black.

My last thoughts were of disbelief and rage, but also curiosity that was not long lived.

Would anyone catch my killer?

Could they ever unravel the reasons why I died so violently on such a beautiful beach; and in my wedding dress just an hour before the ceremony?

Tom Brightwell—the father of the bride—stood on the hotel balcony, welcoming the sun on his face. Jamaica was a total departure from his life in Chicago and he was still acclimating to the care-free attitude of the island.

He couldn't believe it was summer in the middle of February!

He wore relaxed shorts and a loud orange shirt. It wasn't the outfit he'd thought he'd wear for the wedding of his only child, Kelly, but he wasn't complaining.

Tom sucked in the salty air and stretched his arms, feeling the effects of his morning exercise. He'd turned fifty the week before and instead of lightening up, decided to add one more repetition and another mile to the arduous workouts he'd enjoyed since high school.

His ultimate goal was to be the healthiest man he could be; to be there for his wife and daughter for as long as they needed him. If he had any weakness, it was the unconditional love he felt for the two women in his life, and that vulnerability only grew as time went on.

Inside the room, his wife was making last minute additions to her make-up; a process of application and removal that took entirely too long but was certain to achieve the best look possible. Jessica was, after all, the *mother* of the bride, and even though the day's events spot-lighted the bride and groom, she was no doubt going to look her best.

Looking inside, Tom glanced at the long-stem red roses he'd given her the day before. They were her favorite flower and he'd been bringing them to her since high school.

Then he stared at his wife and best friend, still in absolute awe of her. Her long, dark hair flowed down her slender shoulders and framed her delicate features: her small nose, wide smile, soft brown eyes, and porcelain skin.

Although hurried, she exacted a charm and confidence that left him speechless. Jess was his *everything* and he still wondered what the woman had ever seen in him.

He was a simple homicide detective in Chicago's Beverly neighborhood. A job he was exceedingly good at, but not without consequence. It was getting more difficult; not only from the volume of cases that he mauled through each week, but from the caliber of hate the job revealed.

He couldn't believe what one human being was capable of doing to another, and it was starting to take its toll. As he aged, or as he liked to think, *evolved* as a person, he'd been pondering his own existence, his role in humanity, and his job. Why was he subjecting himself to murder scenes? Was this what he was destined for?

He smiled—as he always did—at the realization. *Because I'm good at it. Because it's the right thing to do.*

But he'd been thinking about retirement and the privilege of spending more quality time with *his* bride. They were planning to move to a quiet country club community in Florida and live a slower life. She was excited to become involved in several social organizations and meet new people, and Tom was eager to play golf and go fishing year-round.

Turning away from his wife, he palmed the balcony railing and again peered out at Negril's famous Seven Mile Beach, regarding the listless bodies that dotted the sand. He saw the gazebo that would see his daughter married and smiled at the stargazer lilies that decorated the balustrades.

Though it was a beach wedding and a far cry from the traditional, Kelly's favorite flower was something that was not up for negotiation. They would be there and they'd be fresh, eye-popping, and in abundance.

Tom had thought out the day's events many times, more in an effort to numb the helpless feeling of release. Today he would give his daughter away so she could find her way in the world. He just prayed that his baby would be okay.

But then he saw Kelly walking near the beach; which was odd, considering that the wedding was just an hour away.

She ambled slowly, as if not seeking a specific destination.

He understood her body language and immediately knew she was troubled. But before he could call out, he saw an arm reach out from the dense tree line near the beach. Almost like a tentacle, it wrapped around her small waist in a moment's time and her entire body disappeared into the brush. A black gloved hand was raised, showing a long knife, and it came down repeatedly.

If gravity allowed, he would've thrown himself over the third floor balcony and run to his daughter's aid. If he'd had his gun he would have shot into the trees. If he could've found his voice he would have screamed for help.

Instead he was silenced and a nauseating feeling of helplessness eclipsed him.

He went into shock and fell hard, hitting the floor with a terrible thud that caused his wife to look over.

TEN YEARS LATER

AUGUST

CHAPTER 1

The killer revved his silver Maybach 62 Landaulet convertible as he entered his gated compound and eased up the long cobblestone driveway. He stopped under the large portico and nearly leapt out with anticipation.

He was expecting an email.

The final piece of the puzzle.

He entered his considerable home and locked himself inside. With a spring in his step he glided down the stairs and into the basement; a huge modern space that mirrored the taste and ambience of the three floors above it.

He moved past the theater room, the long granite bar, game room, fitness center, wine cellar, and sauna. At the far end, he arrived at a small utility closet, which seemed ordinary, even innocuous, in every way. Then he unscrewed a large panel and carefully slid behind it and into a very small room.

A flipped switch illuminated a single light bulb that hung from a wire above. The tiny area was unfinished, with concrete flooring and exposed wood and dry wall. The furnishings were just as plain, with a small wooden desk, an old file cabinet, and a worn swivel chair. Still, this was his area—his lair—and it was as precious and comfortable to him as the twenty-thousand feet of home that enveloped it.

He powered up the computer with giddy excitement. He impatiently waited for the screen to come alive by regarding the surrounding walls and the scores of pictures on display. His eyes washed over each of them as he revisited The Plan, just a few days away. He'd spent so much time in its development and to think the game would start so soon!

The computer lit up and he mechanically typed in his passwords to allow for total encryption.

Then it was there. A simple email that both confirmed and denied several pieces of critical information.

The final piece of the puzzle.

He had been communicating with a group he personally called The Organization, but he had no idea what they called themselves. It started with a casual conversation with one of their top handlers when he was on business in the Philippines. The man said he managed a large group of contractors that could deliver anything at any time, with total discretion, for a price.

Intrigued, he'd begun an exploratory and completely confidential dialogue.

They promised to do *any* bidding for a fee. The legalities weren't of importance and morality wasn't for them to question. They were professional operators that assured results and complete anonymity.

It was simple outsourcing, really, but at the highest level. They were paid through a network of offshore, clandestine, and untraceable bank accounts. They communicated through a web of highly encrypted systems. All text was completely erased within moments of appearing on screen and then scrubbed from the system's server. It was more secure than the 256-bit encryption applications of late and similar to what the NSA used.

They were his invisible right hand man and their tentacles stretched everywhere. Completely veiled and dedicated, they had always proven their proficiency.

But now it was time to really challenge them.

He read the email with delight, as his smile widened and he erupted into a laugh. Then his eyes drifted to the top of the screen, where the first words of the email disappeared down the black hole in the system's defense system. One by one they vanished forever, never to be retrieved again.

Soon the message was gone, but the final piece of the puzzle was complete.

Now he had to get to Grand Cayman.

Satisfied, he looked to the wall and to a picture of Tom Brightwell. *It all started and now will end with you,* he thought.

And the killer wondered what the man was doing at the moment.

CHAPTER 2

Morgan Park
Chicago's South Side

Tom Brightwell moved the Colt Python revolver into his mouth and closed his eyes. His hands shook and his teeth clanked against the gun's unforgiving solidity.

His senses peeked. He heard the distant ticking of a wall clock. He smelled the remnants of spent sulfur.

This had become a familiar exercise over the past week. But *unlike* any time before, he pulled the trigger at least half way into the gun's trigger pull; tempting fate and even apathetic to the outcome.

Earlier he'd spent considerable time handling the .357 Magnum; studying it for what could have been the last time. It was his favorite in his collection and there was no doubt as to why.

He'd admired the ribbed barrel, six-chamber cylinder, and frame-mounted firing pin. He'd moved his fingers across the smooth steel and felt the indentations of the rapid colt emblem.

But then he lowered his head and let out a groan, with his hands trembling even more. Then the tears came and he put the Colt down.

Tom had been drinking since early morning and was more inebriated than usual.

It was typical since cancer had taken Jessica four years earlier.

Thinking of his deceased wife and murdered daughter, he stepped clumsily across the bedroom and passed out in his un-made bed, sleeping well into the afternoon.

The heavy metal music cut through the hot air and into the open window, awakening Tom Brightwell with a jolt that forced his dampened pillow to the floor.

He reached across the bed but only found another pillow. His wife was not there and would never be again.

The reality always hit hard.

He'd just been safely asleep and immune to the pain of his life. But now he was awake and the angst slowly set in. The cutting perspective between the two worlds was never as hard as the first waking moments.

Although it took a few seconds to gain perspective, his headache was immediate, as was the acrid taste in his mouth. But he was used to hangovers and the constant feeling of nausea.

He lay still for a few seconds, but then realized that his bed was completely soaked with sweat. It had been hot and humid, and like many times before, he was too drunk to wake from the discomfort.

With a clouded mind, he moved his bulk and planted two heavy feet on the floor. He cradled his head in his large hands and rubbed his eyes, forcefully.

There was a glass of stale water and an assortment of medications on the nightstand; and in practiced movements he downed eight-hundred milligrams of Ibuprofen and let out a satisfying belch. It would do the trick, just like always, numbing his senses and calming the banging in his head. Then he moved through his heart and cholesterol medications and casually looked around the room.

It was the same space he'd shared with Jessica for over three decades, though its appearance had dulled since her passing. What was once a warm, colorful, and nicely decorated dwelling had deteriorated into the absolute wreck he called a home.

The walls seemed to be sweating from the heat, and the once vibrant colors had long faded. The blinds and window coverings were dusty and worn, and litter and debris had become a permanent fixture.

The lonely resident simply didn't care anymore. He could hardly muster the energy to walk through with a trash bag, much less push a vacuum.

Jessica had been a meticulous housekeeper and clutter had not been tolerated. Before she passed, Tom often mused that their home looked more like a museum or a fancy hotel. The beds were made to perfection and decorative pillows were placed carefully over the perfectly-tucked sheets.

After her death, he tried to duplicate her efforts. But as the days passed, the duties became harder to fulfill. Things would be skipped, other tasks would be forgotten for days, and doing a fair job became precedent. Things compounded and he became increasingly indifferent. He hated letting her memory down, but he just couldn't do it and guilt joined grief in his mindset.

There was an absence—a void—in the house that was unsettling.

He'd speak with her spirit at times, feeling the pang of enlightenment and joy. But when reality set in, his thoughts would turn just as quickly and he would feel more alone than ever.

The teenagers next door were now revving their car engines and shouting encouragements. A steady breeze found its way into the room, and it carried the fragrant smell of freshly-cut grass. Affording a deep breath, Tom's senses awakened and his lazy, dry eyes adjusted to the light.

He stood with a grunt, silently cursing himself for drinking so much. Of all days, this was the one he'd tried to remain sober and alert. It was Jessica's birthday and he was going to visit her and Kelly at the cemetery. He ached at the thought of what used to be. But as hard as he tried, alcohol couldn't fade the memories and time couldn't deaden his feelings.

He moved to the bathroom with significant effort, relieved himself in the toilet, and stepped on the scale as a matter of routine. In the last few years he'd ballooned more than a hundred pounds, and even for his six-foot height, he didn't carry the weight well. He still had a thick crop of graying hair, but his reddened, chubby cheeks and lined face forced a look much older than his sixty years.

He looked into the mirror. For a moment he saw a younger version of himself, as he considered his pale-blue eyes. Jessica had always said she'd found comfort in them, but now Tom saw nothing in his dull stare. He shook his head in disgust and looked away.

Tom felt like a prisoner; with his waning body the holding cell. Why did he keep living when everything he cared about was gone? Why didn't God just take him?

But the biggest question was why his daughter and wife had to die? He felt guilty when he thought of how much they'd appreciated life. They were robbed of theirs and he now took his for granted; living a vacant existence and seeking comfort in the bottle.

He considered death more than he should. He thought about it several times each day, and his gun play was becoming routine. What would it be like? How he yearned to be free from his addictions, demons, and constant hollowness.

He was only happy when he thought of the past; his future, he knew, was just a continuation of the hapless void he lived in. Even if there *was* nothing on the other side, at least the pain would end.

Tom was more alert now, and just like always his first *real* thought was of his late family. He was instantly in Jamaica ten years prior, and he frowned as he delved into the past.

He remembered little after witnessing his daughter's murder, and though he was a homicide detective, albeit on vacation, he was no help in the shoddy investigation that followed. There were no leads and the only suspect, Kelly's fiancé, was eventually cleared. Jeremy was seen elsewhere at the time of the crime, and appeared as horrified as everyone else. The interviews that followed turned up nothing of consequence.

The only clue left behind were the two, twelve-sided, one-cent aluminum Jamaican coins that were placed over his daughter's eyes. But they just added more questions about the murder.

Physically they were wiped of any identifiable markings that could allow for a trace, so Tom had researched the cultural significance. Even after a decade, it was still an absolute mystery to him.

Then he thought of his wife. Their relationship had degenerated the moment they lost Kelly. The flight back from Jamaica was in absolute silence, and the ensuing communication was hard. They turned their anger, grief, and frustrations inward; trying to be strong for each other, but it only forged continued isolation.

Then Jessica was diagnosed with melanoma.

Although they became closer with her terminal condition; with a broken spirit and a heavy mind, her small body was drained and unable to fight. She was gone in a matter of months and Tom's body and mind went into steady decline.

Alone, he quietly retired from the police force, became fractured from his small grouping of friends, and withdrew to his modest home in Morgan Park. He turned to alcohol, stopped exercising, and ate poorly. He neglected everything around him and the empty days and months turned into years.

He drank greedily from a tall glass of water as he waited for the shower to warm up. Then he moved into the basin where the targeted spray moved over his weary body. Afterward, he spent considerable time shaving and combing his hair, and stepped into the only suit he owned.

On the way out the door, he grabbed a few cookies and a Coke and walked to his Oldsmobile. The late afternoon sun was muted behind a thick hazy sky, but the humidity seemed to clamp his clothes to his body.

Soon he was driving to the Saunoris & Sons Floral Shop on West 111th Street to pick up the very important long stemmed red rose and stargazer lily he'd ordered the day before.

Realizing it was almost five o'clock, he again cursed himself for his ignorance. It was already evening and he was just beginning the day, hung over as usual.

CHAPTER 3

The Holy Sepulchre Cemetery is located near the Worth neighborhood on Chicago's south-west side. It isn't the area's largest or oldest memorial park, but *is* a favorite in the Irish Catholic community—especially the working class—and is also the final resting place for Chicago's longest reigning mayor, Richard J. Daley.

The impressive green gates were open and Tom drove up to the large circled area that separated into seven smaller roadways. He turned right past the two cement trumpeting angels and into the inner, manicured workings. Soon he arrived at a spot he knew all too well; the general area that was marked only by a small sign displaying the number fifty-seven.

Climbing from his car, he stepped onto the fresh-cut grass and into the maze of tombstones that lined the expansive lawn. The landscape rose and fell around him, and the sunlight cut jagged shadows against the different burial markings.

He saw others walking and standing in the distance, and noticed the familiar trance-like, detached stares that could only come from pure loss. The other mourners walked casually and thoughtfully, treading on the thick lawn in silence. Tom knew their mindset well, having made the trip several times each year; first with Jessica to visit Kelly, and then alone after *her* passing to visit them both.

He stepped to Jessica's grave first and rested the long-stem rose at the base of her modest tombstone. Kneeling before it, he kissed the cool marble and lowered his head in reverence.

"I'm sorry for what I've become, Jess," he started, his words thick with emotion. "And I'm sorry we couldn't talk about Kelly. I guess even now, I wouldn't know what to say other than 'I'm sorry I couldn't protect her.' I wish so much it had been me instead."

His voice cracked and he wept, lowering his head further.

"I'm sorry that terrible event separated us. We should have been stronger and we weren't. *I* wasn't. I'm *still* not."

Tom looked at Jessica's grave through the tears. Living alone, and especially the way he did, he realized that meaningful conversation, although one-sided, was a rarity. Hearing his own words lent him comfort. This was as close as he could be to his wife, and he was struck with a rare moment of self-content.

He spoke slowly, recalling how they first met and the trepidation that was all his. Throughout high school, he'd been popular with his friends, smart in the classroom, and a hero on the football field. But when Jessica transferred from Mother of Sorrows and into Morgan Park High School in their senior year, he had only one interest.

She was beautiful, smart, and witty; and after he fumbled through their first conversation and walked her home one day, they were inseparable.

He let out a controlled laugh as he thought of their first Valentine's Day. He'd spent his entire allowance on a bundle of long-stemmed red roses. He didn't see her until lunch, and had to carry them longer than he would've liked, which drew a lot of attention and shellacking from his friends. When he finally saw her, he'd promised to bring them to her for as long as she'd have him, and he'd never broken tradition.

They were married a few years later and moved into an ordinary home in Morgan Park. They were blessed with the arrival of their only child, Kelly; and after several years Tom was elevated to detective at the police department.

A couple of easy decades passed, forging happy memories and seeded optimism. Then Kelly met Jeremy and *everything* changed.

Tom stepped to Kelly's grave and gently placed the stargazer lily at the base of her tombstone. Then he sat for several minutes, catching his breath and gathering his thoughts.

"Kelly," he began through lumbering gasps. "I'm sorry I wasn't there for you when you needed me. And I'm sorry I never caught your killer. Maybe someday—"

He cut himself off and was immediately disgusted. To lie to his daughter, who was dead in her permanent bed below was deplorable. He knew he could never find her killer. He couldn't even care for *himself!* He was just a shadow of the man he'd once been; a used up drunk on a path to nowhere.

He frowned and began thinking of happier times, which was always easier. He saw her as the little girl that grabbed at his leg; that pushed her small hand into his at the slightest sign of discomfort. The shy girl who was scared at the start of each new school year.

Then he remembered coming home from work. Upon hearing the unmistakable misgivings of his old car engine resonate down the street, she'd run from the house and greet him in the driveway. She'd jump into his open arms with a smile that melted him. She had been so precious, and the memories flooded him as he sat smiling and crying.

The perimeter lighting of the cemetery showed in the distance and he noticed the sky had turned a cool blue. To the south-west he saw the town of Alsip's large water tower, colorfully painted orange, white, and blue. Then, he gazed north-west to see the town of Worth's tower, a less majestic white with red trim. He remembered when they were both erected, and could recall nearly every color they'd been painted in the decades in between.

With effort, he rose to his feet and took a deep breath. He'd spent all the time he could and his body and mind couldn't take any more. A dull pain had gathered in the front of his head, and he wasn't sure if it was from alcohol withdrawal or emotional distress.

He took turns looking between the graves of the two women in his life. Then his eyes darted left to the area he'd been trying to ignore. He saw a definitive patch of undisturbed grass where he would be buried someday. It used to be less noticeable, but as time passed and more tombstones were added, his final resting place had become more pronounced.

With no family or real friends, he wondered who would even be at his ceremony. But then he grimaced. He didn't deserve a funeral. He'd been living a selfish life that was drowning in excess; too weak to deal with the mounting feelings of self-pity and guilt. Worst of all, he'd let down his wife and daughter when they needed him most. He was *still* letting them down with every drink he took.

He moved to his future grave and knelt, eerily casting his large hand over the long, prickly blades of grass.

Then he heard a car horn on Ridgeland Avenue and was thrown into the present. After all, although he felt oddly comfortable among his dead loved ones, he didn't belong there yet.

"Soon," he said, softly.

Then he walked to his car with a frown.

"But probably not soon enough," he added, under his breath.

Driving slowly through the cemetery he came to the stop light at Austin Avenue, where he should have turned right and gone home. Instead he turned left and immediately right into the parking lot of the Grove Sports Bar & Grill.

He parked in front of a large White Sox sign, and noticed that all of Chicago's major teams were displayed, save the Cubs, a product of the north side.

With a deep breath he walked the stamped green concrete that led to the double doors. He settled into a bar stool near the brass tap at the center of the wooden bar. There were several muted televisions on display and he took notice that the White Sox were tied in extra innings against the Orioles. On the right the Bears were beating the Vikings in a pre-season game.

There were only three others at the bar. Tom acknowledged them all with a small nod and continued looking around the room. To his right, a couple in their mid-seventies danced slowly to the sounds of Tony Bennett, as they moved on the black and white checkered floor, oblivious to everything around them.

Tom turned to the bartender. "A double gin and tonic, please," he said, sheepishly.

Then he again regarded the older couple, watching them move gracefully. The song was one of his favorites; one that he and Jess used to dance to.

"Once upon a time—"

His drink arrived and he smiled, reaching for a memory. For several moments he contemplated the past as thoughts flooded his mind. But then the song waned, the couple headed for the door, and Tom emptied the swill.

He thought ahead to nighttime, when the alcohol would own him and his emotions would rule. Would he play with his Colt again? Would everything end tonight?

Another cocktail arrived and he shook his head, trying to dismiss the thought.

He drank it in no time.

Then he ordered another and they kept coming until close.

CHAPTER 4

Georgetown
Grand Cayman Island

With only minutes to live, the man spent his time pouting like a dejected child. He was leaning against a stone wall outside one of the many shops that hugged the cobblestone roads of Georgetown. He held the packages his wife had accumulated thus far, and wasn't happy about it. He clearly wanted to be somewhere else and it showed in every exasperated breath he took.

Sitting on a bench on Fort Street near the Town Hall, the killer eyed the people in their pathetic trances. It was actually hilarious—beyond compare—to see them stumble along without thought or premeditation. They walked here and there, unaware of whom was watching them.

What was watching them.

It would be easy to take one out, but he couldn't decide until he saw the man with the packages. He would do well.

The killer called it ownership, this little game of cat and mouse. He scrutinized everyone. Deciding if they were worthy of the kill; worthy of his time.

He owned them all.

He'd been in Grand Cayman for a couple days now. It had, in his opinion, the best snorkeling and SCUBA destinations in the world, not only due to the underwater visibility, but because of the variety. The night dives, cliff dives, and different reefs and sunken ships were unparalleled.

And although a little busy for his taste, he loved Stingray City. It was a specific spot where fisherman had cleaned their catches for centuries and still attracted the stingray today. The office of tourism now controlled the feeding, and it was the largest and most docile accumulation of stingray in the world. People came from all over to touch and swim with them in the open sea. With a floor of about twenty feet, it was the only time he favored snorkeling over SCUBA diving.

After this murder, he was sad to have to stay away for a while. So he'd played tourist; renting a moped and riding past the natural blow holes and Stingray Brewery, all the way to North Side and Rum Point. There he sat in the surf, soaked up the sun, and sipped frozen daiquiris while revisiting the game plan.

How funny it was, he mused, how the people all around him were enjoying their vacations, while he was planning what was sure to become one of the most mysterious string of murders the world had ever seen.

He loved the thought of it. The charge it sent through his entire being.

The day before he'd gone to the *biggest* tourist trap on the island: the tiny destination called Hell. There wasn't much there; and if it weren't for the small post office bearing the town's name, the place wouldn't even be on the map. He'd sat under a tree sipping a bottle of water from the only convenience store and enjoyed the solidarity of the moment. The future, he knew, would be much more chaotic.

Then he went to the turtle farm, only a short distance away. He'd eased his moped through the residential neighborhood and quiet streets, until the large circled tanks came into view.

He'd always liked marine life and enjoyed holding the baby turtles in his hands. He eagerly walked the raised pools, admiring their transformation and development. As he left, he stuffed several thousands of dollars of neatly folded and cleaned bills into the donations box. It was sure to create another mystery, but it wasn't meant to be that way. He loved nature and everything about the sea, and it was just a silent thank you for the care of the turtles.

But now his stay on the island was over and it was time to move on. His agenda was full and time was a definite factor. His choice was perfect in every way. The man looked to be in his mid-fifties, dressed too warm for the weather; with high navy socks ending just under the knee, and a light V-neck sweater.

As if the killer had willed it, the man lit a cigarette and walked into a side alley, blowing a cloud of smoke from the side of his mouth. Palming a thin white cord, the killer sprang into action and crossed the street, applying gloves and checking the two shiny coins he carried in his pocket.

They were almost as important as the kill itself.

It was just another mystery the authorities would never figure out.

CHAPTER 5

The body was discovered by a store clerk on break. The police were notified and nearly every one of them hurried down from Elgin Avenue.

The scene was surreal.

By the time the police captain arrived, hundreds of people were scattered around. No one could believe there could be a murder in paradise.

Captain Arrangio bullied his way into the middle of the crowd. He briefly regarded the body before snapping his officers to attention. He wasn't accustomed to crime scenes—especially ones with corpses—but his inexperience didn't show. He assumed control and started barking orders.

The perimeter was expanded and people were disbursed. The medical examiner was contacted and the search was on for witnesses. Non-uniformed officers were ordered to the outer reaching of the crowd to study the curious onlookers; hoping the killer had an ego that forced him back to the crime scene.

From a distance the body looked normal. The man's legs were slightly parted, with his arms at his sides and his head turned to the right. But upon closer inspection, his purple tongue fell from his mouth and a pained look preserved his last moments. The ligature mark on the man's neck revealed the obvious cause of death, and the captain knelt to observe the thin red line that had cut into his skin.

But then Arrangio noticed something else. Perfectly placed on the man's eyes were two ten dollar Grand Cayman coins.

He'd never seen anything like it.

And it had happened on his island.

The killer was not at the crime scene.

Not physically *or* mentally. After boarding his Hinckley 70' sloop, he hadn't given the murder a second thought.

The veteran sailor left the Cayman Islands to his stern, as a fresh seventeen-knot trade wind filled in from the north-east, and the seas swelled four to six feet. Smiling at his good fortune, he eased the main sheets and loosened the outhaul. The boat settled into a comfortable broad reach and eventually achieved its maximum hull speed at over ten knots.

He'd been under sail for several hours, heading south-east and carrying a full main and genoa; completely attuned to the momentum of the sea. The conditions were perfect; with the rail in the water, perfectly trimmed sails, and the bow cleaving through the waves with precision. On his current tack, barring any change in the weather, he knew he'd reach Aruba ahead of schedule, easily achieving two-hundred nautical miles per day.

The killer sucked in the salty air and enjoyed a natural high. To be alone on the open sea with these conditions was euphoric. Nothing compared to the pureness of it.

Looking at the placement of the sun, he knew it was about three o'clock and Jamaica was far off to his port side. He smiled at the irony. That was, after all, where everything had started ten years before.

But he wouldn't complicate things by thinking of the past. He'd be in Aruba soon enough.

Once there, things would only get more interesting.

CHAPTER 6

18° 33' N; 80° 12' W
The Caribbean Sea

That night the stars blanketed the sky, spanning the 360 degree horizon. The moon glowed orange and appeared painted on the earth's high black dome. Looking larger than usual, it supplied the only *natural* light in every direction.

The trade winds were moderate, so the killer set the sloop's autopilot for an easy beam reach to Aruba. It allowed him to relax and sip his Chivas Regal.

His mind was at full speed, touching on scores of memories that spanned his entire life. Some thoughts were happy, others sad; some details were colorful enough to illicit a smile, while most were mere glimpses and not worthy of deliberation.

The most vivid and painful memory was one of his earliest, when he was six years old. His mother had an unplanned pregnancy and had given birth prematurely. The boy survived, though he was underweight and sickly for the first several months. Still, his parents chose their social life over family, and both children were cared for by the ample house staff.

As a young boy he remembered being excited to have a baby brother; an eventual play mate and confidant. At home, he embraced an innate feeling of responsibility and instinct. He would sleep outside the baby's room, sneaking up to make sure the infant was okay. The caregivers were not as responsive and would only tend to the child sporadically.

The baby would generally be alone on the third floor of the massive home, two flights of stairs from the servant quarters, and six rooms away from the nearest stairway. The young boy would hide in the adjoining rooms, acting out games with himself, and looking in on his baby brother. He would run away when anyone drew near and then spy on them.

He had appointed himself guardian.

But one hot day, the servants didn't come by as much as usual. The baby stopped crying mid-morning, which cast an unnerving silence in the empty halls. Like always, the young boy had entered the room unnoticed and crept to the crib without a sound.

Peering in he saw the baby lying eerily still, and even for his young age he knew what it meant. The blue coloring on the infant's face and the blank stare was unmistakable. The baby had died from what the medical community would later call SIDS.

The boy remembered feeling stripped of everything. But when the anger and grief subsided, one strange emotion remained. He harbored a sick curiosity about death that had never been satisfied.

The killer's thoughts moved forward to his early days in the classroom, when the hired help would deliver him to school and he'd be forced to listen and learn like the other children. But he was never like them. They had parents that cared; that saw to their well-being and even spent time with them. *His* caregivers depended on who was employed by the family.

Holiday memories were scarce. His father was usually absent, closing some deal in another part of the world. His mother was always somewhere else, but usually sneaking drinks from the bottles she hid across the capacious estate. Still the staff looked after him, more out of pity than obligation; though no one really spoke to him at any length for the better part of his adolescence.

He felt nothing when his parents died in a car accident. All it did was shake things up. A forgotten uncle—his mother's brother—appeared and did what he could, providing for his nephew in the most basic ways.

The man made sure the boy was fed, clothed, and well-groomed; attended school, church, and the other obligations fitting of a youth. But his uncle was a homosexual and had his own life in California; and it wasn't long before the unrelenting responsibilities of being a guardian grew tiring.

At eighteen, when he *officially* became a man and was granted access to his trust, he made a deal with his aging uncle. With hundreds of millions of dollars at his disposal, the uncle was paid a hefty sum to just go away. Then the young man went to college to study mechanical and electrical engineering.

But the classes proved boring. Although he negotiated his studies with a natural ability of absorption and understanding, he became jaded and restless. Even the parties, sporting events, and random sex couldn't hold his attention.

He was attractive, easy going, and had no problem making friends; but he grew bored of discussing academics with others he thought as inferior and incompetent. He also didn't identify with the trust fund kids that bragged of blowing their parents money on material things and recreational drugs.

He quit after four semesters with a perfect grade point average, but he didn't regret the experience. The time allowed him to dissolve his parent's tangible assets and consolidate his financial position. He was also able to feed his natural curiosity about wiring and frequency.

At twenty years of age he was an island to himself. He was motivated and financially-enabled to do what he pleased.

So he'd turned to the sea, deciding to explore the world like the sailors of old. He purchased several boats of various style and size and scattered them throughout the world.

He loved the feeling of complete contentment; the oneness he felt with the open sea. As a master sailor, he relied on natural markings as much as modern instrumentation, and took great satisfaction in experiencing the water just as it was centuries before. How he would've liked to be one of the original mariners, navigating the unknown in search of natural wonder!

A shooting star shot across the blackness and displaced his thoughts.

The killer silently toasted his success in part one of The Plan, savoring the cutting taste of his favorite scotch.

Aruba was three days away.

After that, he knew nothing would ever be the same.

CHAPTER 7

Savaneta Beach
Aruba

The killer arrived on schedule, just after nightfall. He anchored off the south side of Aruba, very near the small town of Santo Largo and just south of the Balashi brewery.

In planning *this* kill, entering near Savaneta Beach was a must, as it was only nine kilometers from Oranjestad and usually vacant at night. By day the local waterman owned this stretch of beach, and it was packed with SCUBA divers, snorkelers, and fishermen from the Lago reef to the Kantil reef.

Sometimes there were pockets of teenagers or a few bums milling around, but he hoped that wouldn't be a factor.

It was the only dynamic he couldn't account for. But although he wanted to hunt only *one* tonight, it didn't mean he wasn't capable of killing more. He simply hated uncalculated action. Deviation from The Plan was not something he took lightly.

He had contemplated killing a random person at Savaneta beach, but had decided against it. Only locals frequented the area after dark and they were less likely to draw the attention he needed.

He wanted an intimate kill that would be reported immediately. He expected to make the world news before reaching Bonaire early the next morning.

He threw his back pack and bike into the dingy and started rowing to shore. His thoughts were lost in the motions; his movements masked under the cover of near darkness. At about three-hundred yards from shore, he could no longer see his boat, so he concentrated on the perimeter lights on the 1B that led to L.G. Smith Boulevard. He grasped the oars tighter; rethinking what had been so long in the making. He could hardly control the excitement that was welling up inside him!

Minutes later, the sea seemed to gather momentum as the shelf rose and the water became shallow. He crashed sideways onto the sand and moved the dingy under a tree, covering it in the brush. Soon he was biking north on the snaking one-lane road to Oranjestad. Anticipation washed over him as he welcomed the night air on his face.

The street was as dark as the night itself and the separation was hard to identify. He felt as though he was riding on black air, a strange sensation that only added to his enjoyment. He liked the small eccentricities of life and living every moment to the fullest. Riding a bicycle in the dark night to commit a murder was certainly one to remember.

The drawback to his plan was that Aruba was one of his favorite islands, and he wouldn't be able to stay for long. He frowned, knowing he'd miss the brick-oven pizza from Casa Tua, but smiled at avoiding the hazardous spiral stairway that led to the restaurant's second floor.

He thought about the butterfly farm across from the Phoenix. He always gave annual donations to care for the butterflies. How he enjoyed bringing in a cup of strong coffee and sitting on the bench next to the smaller pond to watch them fly around him.

He arrived at the first cluster of buildings in Oranjestad and paused at the long front of the Talk of the Town hotel, with its obnoxious mustard coloring. Cars whipped around him, just a few feet away on the 1B. Like him, they were all heading into town, which was so close he could hear the distant thumping of music.

Looking north, he envisioned the busy casinos, restaurants, bars, and stores that made up the area. Oranjestad was his destination, and it would be at the center of every national news story the next morning.

He closed his eyes and opened his senses, taking in the smells and sounds of the night. A determined and dark look came over him, as the final details of his plan came to the forefront of his mind.

In a near meditated state, he was a picture of concentration.

His immediate mission was the only thing that mattered, and he would think of nothing else until it was executed to perfection.

CHAPTER 8

The Iguana Cantina was packed. With two cruise ships in port, less than a thousand feet away, tourists and townies alike settled into the famous bar to eat, drink, and be merry.

The high ceiling fans cooled the crowd and the bartenders tried to stay ahead of the drink orders. Every seat was taken and people were spread across the second floor bar, even pouring outside to the porch area. The DJ was banging out a Jay-Z/Beyonce hip hop tune, as everyone—with drink in hand—swayed to the music.

Craig Binderman, in from Missouri on his first cruise, was tapping his right leg and taking in the scene. He had never experienced anything like it. As much as he loved Aruba's weather and beaches, he was fascinated by the strangers around him. Huddled around a pub table in the corner with his wife, he looked everywhere in silent wonder.

The girls wore snug-fitting, low cut jeans that flaunted their lower abdomens and bikini lines. The young men had close-cropped spiked hair and tight shirts that accentuated the tattoos snaking up their thick arms.

Finishing his third daiquiri from a large, neon souvenir goblet, he kissed his wife and motioned toward the bathroom. Then he maneuvered through the crowd, crossing the worn, wooden floor and moving past the escalator. The alcohol lifted his spirits and he seemed to glide across the room, feeling much younger than his fifty years and giving into the excitement that abounded.

He entered the bathroom just as another man exited. He looked at the urinals to the right and the more fortified, private stalls to his left. He decidedly moved to the far toilet, gently shutting the door behind him.

Relieving himself, he let out a deep breath, as he felt the last of his tensions leave him, almost as if they were being dispelled in the urine itself. His lazy eyes looked over the graffiti markings on the wall, before settling on a picture of the California Lighthouse.

Then he felt a slight pop in the back of his head and saw a bright stain of blood and bone spray onto the wall. For a moment his body was numb; his thoughts paused in time. He blinked twice, with his mouth open but unable to speak the confusion he felt. Then he fell to the right and into the close wall. Everything went dark, even as his glassy eyes remained open.

He didn't feel the coins being placed on his eyes or see the killer lock the stall door and athletically snake underneath. He certainly didn't hear the latest offering from the DJ, or the crowd respond as the volume was increased in the adjacent hall.

Instead, his body lay undisturbed for several minutes, enough time for many men to use the urinals on the far side, and a few others to use the neighboring stall just inches away.

But eventually a stream of blood came into view and the Iguana Cantina played a role in the latest of Aruba's high-profiled murders.

CHAPTER 9

The FBI arrived in Aruba late afternoon in the form of Special Agent M. Jackson Seargant and his five-member team.

They'd been briefed en route on all available information, but there were more questions than answers. An American citizen was murdered in a crowded bar and there were no leads or suspects. It was too coincidental that another tourist was killed days earlier in Grand Cayman.

Though the FBI had no jurisdiction in Aruba, the victim *was* a U.S. citizen, and with the Natalee Holloway debacle not far from everyone's thoughts, the Dutch authorities had granted the FBI's request to help with the investigation.

As far as they were concerned, *tourism*—not homicide—was their specialty, and if the FBI was going to donate their services to get things back to normal, then it was fine with them.

Seargant was an impressive looking black man in his mid-forties, standing well over six feet tall and very physically fit. He was more athletic than muscular, choosing a varied routine of running, swimming, and group sports over more targeted weight lifting. Still, he *was* in the gym several hours each week, and it showed in his toned muscles.

When he wore shorts and a T-shirt he still looked like the star wide receiver he'd been at Ohio State over twenty years before. When he wore a suit and tie, he held the chiseled and eye-catching look of any male model in the world of high fashion.

His head was shaved and he sported a thin goatee that outlined his handsome face. His overall appearance conveyed cleanliness and efficiency, and it was reinforced in the way he carried himself and treated others. Unassuming in almost every way, he was a true example of a gentlemen.

He was smooth, calculated, and fair; a straight shooter who was highly respected by his team and superiors. His work ethic was unsurpassed, and he would often be on the job for several days at a time in multiple time zones.

A twenty year veteran of the FBI's BSU, Seargant had hunted and captured—along with a team of many others—more than a dozen classified serial killers; and solved scores of other cases in the more traditional vein. An analytical man, he was always interviewing murderers of *all* types, engaging them in deep, probing discussions to understand how they operated.

He'd worked with most of his collars, except the two he'd personally killed, developing a careful bond. It was hardly a friendship, but it *was* a relationship that he respected for the sake of saving others.

A car was waiting for the FBI on the tarmac and within minutes they entered Oranjestad. The downtown area was bustling with activity, with the happy tourists and shoppers out for another day in paradise. The market place came into view, and they took a left on Main Street to the crime scene, parking at the end of the street.

The media was already camped out and their arrival had attracted a crowd. The FBI men emptied the vehicle and an older man in a tan suit approached.

"Hello gentlemen," he began, with both arms extended. "My name is Gerard Von Buren. I'm the chief of police here and you are invited guests of the Dutch government."

When the introductions were complete, Von Buren eyed Seargant, who stood in the middle of the group.

"I understand you have read the rules for your time here," Von Buren started. "While we appreciate your help, I will *not* accept any deviation. I believe that this was a one-time, horrific event, and that there were other circumstances that we've yet to uncover. Personally, I have no idea how you found out so quickly or why you've come so fast, but so be it."

Seargant smiled, humbly, studying the man that was trying to assert himself and bully his men. But everyone remained silent and the chief continued.

"If you uncover *anything*, you'll bring it to us straight away. You will not discuss this case with anyone, most definitely the media, and you'll be as indiscernible as possible."

"Agreed," Seargant said. "Can we take a look at the crime scene?"

The Iguana Cantina was closed, but amazingly there were employees scattered about; restocking the bar, arranging tables and chairs, and mopping the floor. The air smelled of beer and cleaning products. Looking at the worn floor, Seargant could only guess how much beer had made it through the small cracks of wood and into the very foundation of the building.

Taking a slight right, they moved up the stairs to the second floor. Seargant eyed every detail, committing it all to memory. At the bathroom, the group stopped and Seargant looked to the police chief.

"We removed the door to make it easier to get the body out. It's a tight place and we needed space to work," he said.

"The body has been removed," Seargant said, his tone more statement than inquiry.

Von Buren became annoyed, speaking curtly. "It was brought to the street to await the ambulance, then to the hospital as a matter of procedure. When the victim was pronounced dead, the body was moved to the morgue, where—"

". . . it was dressed and taken out for ice cream?" an FBI agent interrupted, jokingly.

This drew a harsh look from Seargant and the man was silenced.

"Again," the chief began. "We have our protocols and I ask that you respect them."

Seargant moved into the bathroom and studied the space for a long moment. A dark red splash of dried blood was sprayed on the wall above the toilet in the far stall, with more on the floor. A crude outline of duct tape tried to delineate where the body had fallen. Then he looked into the toilet, and saw that it remained unflushed.

Seargant moved closer and scrutinized the wall from a few inches away; then he knelt and examined the floor and the tape, the stench of urine filling his lungs. He flushed the toilet, the sound emphasized in the small, crowded area.

"No reason to smell that," he said. "I'm estimating a single shot above the left ear using a .22 with a silencer. Judging from the splatter it was close range. The man collapsed to his right. This was a very contained and immediate episode."

"Exactly what our investigators have determined."

"Did you find two coins on the victim's eyes?" Seargant asked, looking to the chief for the first time in the exchange.

Von Buren just stood there, his face showing more emotion than any words he could have spoken. It was clear there were coins on the eyes and that Seargant knew more than he'd let on. The FBI-man didn't loosen his grip as he squared against the man, awaiting a response.

"Yes, there were two Dutch coins over the eyes; and they have been inventoried, along with the deceased's other personal effects."

"I'll need to see them if it's not too much trouble," Seargant said.

"Look, I don't want any interference. This is our happy little island and I will not have you destroy our reputation as such."

Seargant frowned. He already knew Von Buren all too well and opted for another route. Instead of engaging him, Seargant turned and walked downstairs and outside into the sunlight.

The bright day was at opposite from the grungy bar, and he hoped it would lighten the mood and afford some degree of increased cooperation. His men automatically followed, as did Von Buren, who was starting to regret the visit.

Seargant looked to the right to see the large bow of the Crown Princess, ironically the cruise ship the victim had arrived on. Then he peered up the one-way street to see several members of the media under the blue and white sign for Kildare's.

Agent Hartley, who had stayed with the car, perked up as he ended a conversation on his cell phone. He stuffed it into his suit jacket and approached Seargant with a grim face.

"Sir, there's been another one, this time in Bonaire. Coins on the eyes, no witnesses, no suspects. Discovered about twenty minutes ago."

Seargant showed no emotion as he took in the information. Once more he regarded the media and pockets of people at the perimeter. The murder of an American in Aruba was more than newsworthy, and everyone had showed up accordingly.

"Call our pilots and get a flight plan," Seargant said. "I'll be right back."

Hartley followed Seargant's gaze. "Are you sure you want to do that?" he asked, almost to himself.

"It's time to pick a fight with this son-of-a-bitch and I can't think of a more direct way," Seargant called out, not looking back.

Hartley smiled, knowing his friend and colleague all too well. Decisiveness was the man's gift, and even though Seargant often led with emotion, the choice was always the right one.

"You know you're going to piss off the Dutch authorities," Hartley yelled. But Seargant was unresponsive and even quickened his pace.

Seargant deliberately moved to a CNN correspondent, a pretty young woman who knew exactly who he was and what it could mean. She straightened and stood to greet him, as a cameraman instinctively moved behind his machine.

In no time Seargant was giving an impromptu and unauthorized press conference to the world. There wasn't a podium or a backdrop. Just the bare essentials he needed to accomplish his goal.

He knew that millions of people would be watching, either live or in the near future via a replay on any number of channels.

He could only hope the killer would be one of them.

Seargant wanted to send a very clear message and most definitely introduce himself.

CHAPTER 10

Seargant stared straight ahead, leaning into a handful of microphones and looking to the cameras. Then he began a slow and meticulous dialogue.

"My name is Special Agent M. Jackson Seargant with the FBI's Behavioral Sciences Unit, and I have a brief statement concerning a recent incident here in Aruba.

"I will confirm that there has been a murder of an American citizen. I will not go into detail about the victim until the family has been properly notified, but there are similarities to a killing that was discovered in Bonaire within the hour and another in Grand Cayman several days ago."

He paused to glance at the reporters that hung on his every word, and the throng of spectators that were inching closer.

"I will *not* go into specifics about the crimes, other than to say that there appears to be an active serial killer in the Caribbean. My immediate message is precaution. I want to alert the public and ask that you take appropriate measures, as we are not quite sure *what* we are dealing with at this time."

"Sir," a reporter cut in. "Is there any evidence as to what this 'Island Hopper' may look like, or what type of victim he is most interested in?"

Seargant was caught off guard but recovered easily. When he spoke, his delivery was much slower and well-pronounced than before. The words were emphasized with emotion, and there was no doubt he was speaking directly to the killer.

"This *thing* is a selfish coward that attacks his victims when they are completely vulnerable in an unfamiliar environment. I know that at least two of them were on vacation. He seeks an advantage because he is weak, and probably kills to satisfy some depravation that's been eating away at him since childhood. He is not a monster or someone with super powers. Do not build him up as anything but a sick human being that will be caught and face justice."

Seargant paused and again looked to his small audience, before returning his focus to the camera. "That's all I have right now."

The reporter tried to sneak in another question, but Seargant was already several yards away. His stride increased, even as Von Buren hurried over, red-faced and angry.

"I told you no media interviews!" Von Buren screamed, trying to block Seargant's path.

But the larger man sidestepped him easily. Hartley looked to his boss and winked. It was a time-tested gesture that Seargant knew well; a silent communication that his # 1 did when a task was completed. Seargant got the message. The jet was ready with a cleared flight path to Bonaire.

Von Buren rushed the group, not wanting to let go.

"You have deliberately violated my wishes and are no longer welcome here. I ask that you—"

"It's okay, chief," Seargant interrupted. "I apologize for offending you but I'm looking at the broader picture. If I can just see the coins that were left at the scene and then look at the body, we'll be out of your hair and off to Bonaire."

The private jet landed in Bonaire with the sunset. And like in Aruba several hours earlier, the Dutch authorities had a car waiting for Seargant and his team.

But this time the police commander was genuinely concerned and grateful for the help. Bram Janssen was a stout, serious man; with short, curly red hair and wire-rimmed glasses that sat atop his large nose. He had a warm smile and a firm handshake, and after some rushed introductions, they were on their way to the crime scene, near the salt mines.

Janssen sat beside Seargant in the back of a SUV, as they bounced along the narrow, windy road. He appeared agitated and nervous—but focused—talking non-stop to his guest.

He reviewed what little information they'd gathered, and informed Seargant that the FBI would have every resource at their disposal.

Janssen said he'd seen Seargant's press conference and was impressed by its form and content. He was shocked at the murders and even more so that one had occurred on his island. Shaking his head in disgust, Janssen stopped only to peer out the window and regroup. Then he turned and again chatted up Seargant, adding that his department just wasn't equipped to handle a crime of this kind.

"What should I do about the media?" he asked, rhetorically. "Surely they'll arrive soon and probably camp right outside my window! How do we stay them off?"

Seargant appreciated Janssen's candor and his admitted shortcomings. He probably ran an efficient and diligent police force and felt frustrated that he was suddenly out of his depth.

"Don't worry about the media," Seargant said, flatly. "I'll handle them if you'd like, and sometimes they can even be helpful."

Janssen let out a deep sigh and smiled for the first time. "Thank you for coming," he said.

Then the vehicle came to an abrupt stop and everyone spilled out.

But Seargant couldn't have been prepared for what he saw.

They walked to the top of a hill and stopped. The salt mines could barely be seen to the east. The Caribbean Sea, which was now deep blue against the darkening sky, expanded to the west.

Before them was an eerie wooden structure, standing about ten feet tall. It looked to be crude in both design and constitution, but there was no denying its effectiveness.

A body was laid out at the base. The victim's hands were tied behind his back and his legs were splayed out at an awkward angle. A severed head was a few feet away and staring up at Seargant were two shiny coins that gleamed off the beam of his flashlight.

Seargant moved closer, assessing the scene, the victim, and the instrument of death.

He was looking at a guillotine.

The killer laughed, heartily.

With the boat pivoting peacefully at anchor, he was relaxing under the Bimini; eating an apple and listening to yet another replay of the news from the television down in the salon.

He was dressed comfortably, wearing white cotton trousers and a blue button-down shirt. Both garments moved with the warm night wind that cut over the light chop and washed into the mahogany-rich cabin.

He didn't have a care in the world. He was a picture of absolute calm.

The killer wasn't offended by the FBI agent's insults or accusations; instead he was curious and even entertained. His slayings were pure and nothing was personal. He expected the chiding that would come from the simpletons that could never understand the *why* that set his plan in motion.

A strange smile formed as he contemplated the greater design, and how he could add the FBI agent to his well-formulated equation. Surely there was room to accommodate a man like Special Agent M. Jackson Seargant.

The killer was looking forward to meeting him.

Killing three people in five days had been exhausting but well worth it. If nothing else, he had a new name. He was now the Island Hopper and he liked it!

But he didn't have time to revel in the thought or celebrate the victory.

Another one of his headaches suddenly hit him and it was the worst one yet.

The pain was severe and he was unable to see or even form a coherent thought. He tried to endure the pain, which felt like lightning flowing through his entire being, but he was impotent in its grip. Though his eyes were open; purple, yellow, and green shades were all he saw, and he watched the kaleidoscope of colors as he collapsed.

He hit the decking forcefully, unable to break his fall. He was knocked unconscious and laid there unmoving until the morning sun warmed his face.

CHAPTER 11

Morgan Park
Chicago's South Side

Cookies and muffins were the topic of conversation, when Tom Brightwell arrived at Captain's Pub. He came into the discussion late, but bar talk was always easy, and soon he was part of the exchange; his opinion even being solicited on the matter at hand.

Eighty-four year old Olly Freshwater was staring down eighty-two year old Elmer Betts, who was alternating his attention between a draft beer and the peanuts he was throwing into his mouth.

Both had been sitting at the long, U-shaped bar for most of the afternoon. The argument was just another example of the countless things they'd sparred over in their sixty-year friendship.

"All I'm saying," Elmer managed in mid-chew. "Is that I was making chocolate chip cookies yesterday and I forgot to add the chocolate chips. They turned out great anyway and I have therefore discovered the classic cookie. It's simple, without any added stuff and it still tastes great!"

Olly fired back. "It's not a classic cookie. It's a chocolate chip cookie without the chips. It's a mistake."

Elmer was unfazed and pushed on. "The closest thing to this type of invention is the sugar cookie; the only extra ingredient being the sugar on top. You can change the coloring to fit the occasion, but it's still simplistic in nature. I'm sure it came about in a similar way."

Elmer was smiling as he took a quick pull from his beer and clawed at the peanuts. He eyed Olly, who was taking the conversation much more seriously.

"Then what about the classic muffin?" Olly asked. "Couldn't you just withhold the blueberries from a blueberry muffin? What do you think, Tom?"

Tom had quietly slid into a worn bar stool, a few seats away from the others. With his hands flat on the bar, he made a slow circling motion on the smooth, wooden surface. His demeanor was unengaging—his look pensive—and for a moment Olly wasn't sure if he would answer. But then Tom forced a dry smile and faked an expression of deep thought.

"*Everyone* knows the classic muffin is the corn muffin," he said. "It's perfect in the morning or in the evening, with soup, plain, or with butter."

The men enjoyed a quick laugh. The bartender appeared and slung a couple of drafts to Elmer and Olly, whom were easily distracted. Then she looked to Tom, expectantly.

"Gin and tonic, please," he said.

She moved to the bottles behind the bar and filled a tall glass with ice. Tom studied the woman who'd been behind Captain's bar for as long as he could remember.

"How are you, Peggy?" he added, softly.

"You know. Same old stuff," she said, placing his drink on a coaster and pushing it to him.

Peggy was a fixture at the place and was even said to be one of the original bartenders. None of the patrons knew her age, but it was somewhere between seventy and eighty-five, and even for her small frame, she was usually the toughest person in the place. She dyed her shoulder-length blonde hair, wore entirely too much make-up, but was courteous, compassionate, and always ready to lend an ear or give a little advice. She was usually over-extended in her duties, but was great at multi-tasking and kept the pub running smoothly.

The bar was originally established by a retired police captain in the mid-1970's and named after his only daughter, Lana. But with so many cops frequenting the place over the years that followed, and out of respect to their retired captain, the locals had nicknamed it Captain's Pub.

When it changed owners it was *officially* named Captain's Pub. In the heart of Chicago's south side, it was a sanctuary for the working class; a frequent stop between work and home that still offered a burger, fries, and a beer for a reasonable price.

Tom was usually not one for conversation, and the people who *did* know him, or more exactly his *plight,* respected it. But Peggy was a good friend and had spent many nights after close with him, either waiting for him to be sober enough to leave, or helping him into a cab. Thankfully, the bar was less than a mile from his home, and weather-permitting he could usually make the walk.

Elmer and Olly were fixtures at the pub as well. Like Tom, they were widowers, but even in their eighties, they had a brighter outlook on life. Both had experienced life-threatening injuries in the Vietnam War, married upon their return, raised children, worked hard at the stockyards, and were now enjoying the downward slide of life. Simple in every way, they would spend hours each day drinking, reminiscing, and quarrelling over the pettiest things. They had each other and they were usually good for a few laughs.

Tom was feeling nostalgic and in rare need of conversation, especially after being so emotionally drained from another cemetery visit. He knew that Olly and Elmer would be at the pub and sure to provide some interesting speak.

But before Tom could raise his glass to the others, the door flew open and four hoods in their early twenties entered. Tom's senses peaked.

The ex-cop knew they weren't interested in drinking, because each took entirely too long assessing the area, and a couple of them were already agitated. Tom took the man in a red hooded sweatshirt as the leader. The others fanned out but stood behind him, waiting for something to happen.

Tom studied Red from behind his drink, taking a small sip and crunching on an ice cube. The bulkiness in the young man's pocket suggested at least one weapon; and the layered clothing in his mid-section appeared too big, judging from the punk's tight, thin face.

Thankfully, he wore black sweatpants, which appeared to not have pockets, so Tom focused on what was inside the sweatshirt. Tom's stare moved to the others, whom stood defiantly. He knew they weren't active participants in whatever was about to occur, so he looked back to Red.

Peggy picked up on the tension and eyed the group, using a damp towel to work the bar counter. Olly sensed it as well and thought it a good time to leave Elmer and head to the bathroom.

"What can I get for ya?" Peggy asked.

"First of all," Red started. "You can put on some good music. Not this slow, boring shit. And it looks like a funeral in here," he added, looking over to Elmer, who shrank into his seat.

Tom grinned. He hadn't even noticed the music, which was also very telling. If he couldn't have heard it over the last several minutes, how could the hood have in mere moments? Tom decided that Red had an agenda and it was time to figure it out and even catch him off guard.

Tom snickered, looking to the group in total.

"What are you laughing at, old man?" Red screamed, zeroing in on Tom.

Tom glared back. He hated people that disrespected and bullied others, and the anger mounted within him. He was also devoid of any normal feelings of self-preservation, and figured an uncaring attitude and disregard for common reaction could only help.

"Shouldn't you boys be at the playground?" Tom asked, smiling wide.

The other young men looked to Red, who rushed over to Tom. He was about to say something when Tom launched off the bar stool and clocked him with a right hand punch that laid him out flat. His friends ran over but stopped short, as Tom straightened and cocked back his arm again.

"I can do this all day boys," he said evenly, without a hint of anxiety. "This is how it was when I was your age and I guess I'm still good at it."

Red got up, feeling the side of his face swell, as he fumbled for his middle pocket. Tom saw the movement and didn't pause. He swiftly kicked Red in the groin and punched him again in the jaw, hearing an awful crack. Tom was on him in no time and found a switchblade knife, which he threw onto the bar.

Peggy scooped it up, handled it for a moment and the blade snapped up. Then she picked up the phone, punching in numbers and glaring at the hoods. Her eyes spoke volumes and for a moment, Tom thought she would physically haul them to the dumpster.

"The police will be here any minute," she said.

The men ran to the door and Tom returned to the bar. Peggy put the knife in a drawer, Elmer grabbed the bowl of peanuts, and Tom withdrew into himself.

Tom didn't like the man he'd just become. But what concerned him most was his indifference toward the potentially fatal situation he'd thrown himself into. His actions came so easily and his pulse hadn't even quickened. The confidence to take them all felt so overwhelmingly comfortable. Had he no restraint left? Did he have no regard for his personal safety? Or maybe he was just a born cop and such things didn't just vanish upon retirement?

But then a harsh thought crept in. Did he unwittingly *want* to die and be with his wife and daughter? He knew he had no fear of death, but was it a sin to seek it? It had been almost a week since he'd last put his Colt in his mouth, and that was another disturbing consideration.

"On the house," Peggy said loudly, breaking Tom's concentration and shoving another drink in front of him.

"I'm so sorry, Peggy," he countered in a small voice. "I'm not sure what came over me."

"Are you kidding? You're the great protector," Peggy shot back.

But then she recoiled, thinking about what she'd just said and how he might take it. She moved closer, looking him in the eyes, but he turned away.

"*That's* a joke," he began, somberly. "I couldn't even protect the two things I loved most in the world."

There it was, she knew. He held himself forever accountable for things that were out of his control. And now, he over-compensated by standing up for others.

"What happened to them wasn't your fault, Tom. You weren't responsible."

Suddenly a hand touched his back. Olly had returned from the bathroom and quickly sat down. He looked alternatively between Elmer and Tom.

"Can I ask you guys a personal question?" he asked, feigning seriousness. "After all, we've known each other for several years."

"Sure," Tom said. "What is it?"

"Do you guys have urinal allegiance? I mean, if it's available, do you use the same pisser every time?"

The men laughed, which eased the mood, and Peggy raised the volume as the Rolling Stones sang "Play with Fire." She thought it fitting as she regarded Tom.

"I'm not kidding," Olly continued. "They say that 68% of men have urinal allegiance and only 8% of women. I guess we take it more seriously."

"Speaking of dicks," Elmer began, chuckling. "Did you hear about Grady O'Malley?"

"I know him well," Olly said. "He sold his business for six million, married his private nurse—who's half his age by the way—and now he plays golf every day."

"That's true," Elmer said. "But did you hear she made him get a vasectomy? I mean the guy's gonna be eighty next month and she pulls that crap on him!"

Tom and Olly laughed again. Elmer always enjoyed an audience and he continued with pride.

"But that's not even the funny part," Elmer persisted. "After the procedure, they told him to rest and put peas on his balls. And Grady's so dumb he used *canned* peas instead of frozen!"

The banter continued, as Olly, Elmer, and Tom recalled the past and discussed current events. Peggy tended to their drink orders and the hours flew by.

But when Elmer mistakenly started talking about his children and grandchildren, Tom grew silent and withdrew from the conversation. The alcohol had long set in and the familiar feeling embraced and held him for the remainder of the night.

CHAPTER 12

Tom perked up in a moment of clarity. His mind was clouded, his vision blurred. His mouth felt like a cotton ball. He was slumped against the bar, but for how long he couldn't tell. Elmer and Olly were gone, as were most of the other patrons, and a stale drink stood untouched in front of him.

His watch showed it to be well past midnight and the ceiling lights were brighter than they'd been all night. Peggy was sweeping the floor and stacking bar stools, and a couple of guys were playing pool at the far end. The music still played, but Tom couldn't make out the song from the dull pulse of the speakers. He suddenly felt uncomfortable and out of place, so he threw a fifty dollar bill on the bar and peeled himself off his seat.

Still, he eyed the drink on the bar, not recalling how long it had been there. The ice was nearly melted and the glass was wet with condensation. Without hesitation he swigged it all and returned it to the bar top, causing a loud crack that made Peggy look over.

"Are you gonna cab it, Tom?"

"I'll walk, Peggy," he said, studying the floor.

He was completely drunk and incoherent as he took his first wild step and almost crashed into the wall. Regaining his balance, he moved clumsily to the door with his head down, shamefully.

Outside, Tom felt like he was in a cartoon. After hours of binge drinking, his body was numb. His gestures and thoughts were in slow motion. A leaden drone resonated in his head, which now seemed heavier on his shoulders.

The night air did little to clear his mind, but it was a change of scenery and he was thankful for it. He walked into the parking lot as a cool breeze found him. Then he looked to the moon. Seeing it glow against the blackness of the night sky calmed him. He moved past his car, starting home.

Just him and the moon.

But with his wild stepping he tripped on a concrete pylon and fell hard. He hit his head on the asphalt and blood gushed from a long, jagged cut on his head. He struggled to move but his mid-section felt on fire. He tried to yell but the words couldn't get past his swollen tongue. Instead, he curled up and held his head. With the blood loss and his drunken condition, it didn't take long to lose consciousness.

Peggy finally found him, and after checking for a pulse and calling 911, she sat on the asphalt beside him. He never regained consciousness and didn't feel her holding his hand, brushing his hair away from the open wound, or singing to him.

In the dark, calm night, they waited for the ambulance. She looked down at a broken man; a friend that she hoped would find the inner peace he deserved.

CHAPTER 13

For the first day, Tom was close to comatose. He tossed and turned, in and out of deep sleeps, muttering incoherently. His side was taped, with his ribs packed tightly, and a thick bandage covered his head. Small cuts spider-webbed across the right side of his face and he had a horrible black eye, with a purple bruise that extended to his temple.

When he *did* awake, there were no flowers or cards, and no one even noticed. Looking around, he saw that he was in a sterile, white room, with close draperies that enveloped him in a semi-circle.

He heard distant sounds and voices and realized he was in the hospital. He felt tubing around his mid-section, and moved slowly to get his bearings. But a sharp pain overtook him and he paused, closing his eyes and lying still.

The clearer things became, the more uncomfortable he was. His head throbbed, his side ached, and he was consumed by a thirst he'd never known. Feeling his ribs, he afforded a small cough to clear his throat. Then he yawned through dry lips and smelled his own harsh stink. Why did he have to wake up? Things were so peaceful just a few moments before.

A nurse appeared and Tom was embarrassed by the thought of what he must look like. She was in her mid-twenties, up-beat, and presented herself well. Her smile was genuine and it put him at ease.

"Where am I?" he managed.

"Cook County Hospital," Mr. Brightwell. "It seems you had quite a fall a couple night's back. Welcome back to the world. Is there anything I can bring you?"

"Water, please. And could you get the doctor? I'd like to discuss my injuries."

"Certainly," she said. And she was gone.

Dr. Mattingly stood at the foot of Tom's bed, reading a chart and staring down at his patient. The man made no attempt at polite bedside manner or idle chit chat, as he let out a sigh and looked at Tom with disdain.

Being a retired cop, Tom knew the doctor's mindset well, having dealt with his own fair share of human waste. Tom had always read people well and the man's disposition spoke volumes.

The good doctor looked to be in his late sixties, probably a manager of sorts, and most definitely a man of respect at the hospital. His gray hair was neatly trimmed and combed to the side, and he wore a smart-looking white lab coat over his suit and tie. He was a picture of professionalism, but his narrow eyes burrowed into Tom.

"Well, Mr. Brightwell. You had a real good time didn't you?"

Tom just blinked, not wanting to engage the man in a debate of morality.

"You have three bruised ribs on your right side that will be tender for the next couple weeks, but should mend on their own, provided you don't go to any more fraternity parties."

The doctor peered at Tom, who held his tongue and absorbed the comment. Tom was craving information and knew the best route to that resolve was silence.

"I'm going to keep you for a couple more days because you have a concussion. The initial CAT scan didn't show any bleeding, but I want to make sure you don't develop a subdural hematoma or swelling of the brain. But what's more concerning is that you came in with a blood alcohol level of 2.9, which is almost five times the legal limit to drive and very close to alcohol poisoning.

"I also ran a comprehensive metabolic profile. You have elevated liver functions, which suggests liver disease, cirrhosis, or a half dozen other afflictions. Your blood pressure is one-eighty over one-hundred and five and I bet your cholesterol is through the roof. What's more is your blood sugar is over two-hundred, which means you're also diabetic."

Dr. Mattingly broke from his commentary to check on Tom, who was following the man's words intently, and even trying to prop himself up to appear more engaged. The doctor relaxed and put his clipboard on Tom's bed.

"Look, Mr. Brightwell. Medically you can be treated for all your ailments, and honestly I've seen much worse. I see from your chart that you were brought in by your friend Peggy Wisniewski. She said you are a widower and an ex-police detective. I don't want to assume what brought you to your present condition, but I would suggest you consider rehab, A.A., or counseling to seek a different perspective on life. Alcoholism is a choice and you owe it to yourself."

Tom broke his silence, cutting the man off and looking past him to the television on the wall.

"I owe nothing to myself, Doc. I've accepted who I am and what I've become. It's my lot in life."

"Not good enough, Tom," he countered, moving closer. "You're not dead yet. I know what it looks like and I can still see a spark in you."

Tom regarded the doctor for a long moment. He garnered a greater respect for him, judging that he genuinely *did* care. Still, a lecture on how he was living his life was not something he wanted.

Tom noticed the increased sounds of the television and saw a couple of nurses watching a news repost, intently. He had no idea about current events, but suspected it was important.

He looked to the doctor with soft eyes. "I know what you're saying and I appreciate it. I really do. But for now could you please turn that TV up?"

Dr. Mattingly turned to the television with remote in hand, as a CNN correspondent came on screen. She was wearing shorts and looked more relaxed than a typical reporter. The background appeared to be warm and balmy. If the CNN logo wasn't there, Tom would have thought she was on vacation.

"This is Stacie Espionzo, reporting from the tiny island of Bonaire. It's been a horrible week in the islands. The serial killer known as the Island Hopper has struck again, claiming his third victim. We don't have information on the deceased, but have unconfirmed reports that there were coins placed on his or her eyes."

In an instant, Tom forgot about the pounding in his head. *Did she just say coins on the victim's eyes?* He stared intently at the screen, learning about the series of murders that had gripped the Caribbean.

When he looked away, his eyes were dry and he was more tired than he'd ever been. The doctor was gone and Tom was clutching the side rails of the bed with bright, white knuckles.

Three murders in the Caribbean? Coins on their eyes?

Tom leaned back in bed and stared at the ceiling. His thoughts turned to Jamaica ten years earlier.

He pictured his murdered daughter curled up in the sand. Her still hands clutched her chest. Her wedding dress was soaked with blood. Her face was twisted, showing the final moments of her forced death.

Then he saw the coins on her eyes.

Two questions screamed for answers inside his weary mind. Was this the same killer that took his daughter? And was he prepared to hunt him down?

But soon his mind couldn't process anymore and his body surrendered to the sleep it so desperately craved.

CHAPTER 14

Kralendijk
Bonaire

Seargant stood next to a nervous Bram Janssen on the front steps of the police station. It had been two days since the body was discovered and they'd promised the media an update. There were also several tourists, some with drinks in hand, moping around and waiting for anything interesting to happen.

Agent Hartley walked over to Seargant and whispered in his boss's ear. "I have something that you want to know about."

Seargant politely excused himself from Janssen and moved away. "Go on."

"A little over ten years ago there was a murder in Jamaica. A young woman named Kelly Brightwell, who was about to be married. I mean she was *literally* in her wedding gown. It's unsolved. She was stabbed multiple times in broad daylight, not fifty feet from the water's edge in Negril. When they found her, she had coins on her eyes."

Seargant perked up in complete surprise, catching the attention of several reporters nearby. As they looked on, he began a slow walk, with Hartley at his side. Seargant's mind was spinning with thoughts about the case. Was the killer the girl's fiancée? Where was he now? What evidence was left behind?

But he only asked one question. "Where's the file?"

Hartley nodded, knowing his boss all too well. "I've already talked to the Jamaican authorities. They're couriering it over right away.

"But that's not all. The *father* of the bride witnessed the attack."

Seargant was surprised again and there was no hiding it. "There was a *witness?* What did he see?"

"It gets better. He was a Chicago homicide detective there to see his only child and daughter married."

Hartley handed Seargant a note. "This is his phone number and name. He's currently at Cook County Hospital and I'm told he should be *very* eager to speak to us."

"Why's he in the hospital?"

"It's nothing life-threatening."

"Set up a call as soon as this is done."

Then Seargant walked to the podium. He placed his large hands on both sides of the heavy wood and peered into his audience. His mind was racing with the recent developments in Bonaire and the information from Jamaica a decade earlier. But most of all, he felt contempt and bitter anger for the person responsible for these heinous acts.

Seargant got a reassuring nod from Hartley and turned to the cameras.

He knew the Island Hopper was watching.

CHAPTER 15

Cook County Hospital
Chicago, Illinois.

After two days in the hospital, Tom was going stir-crazy. Though he was allowed short walks in the hall and to the waiting room for a change of scenery, there were none of the conveniences of home. He wanted to take a long, hot shower. He wanted to plop down on his sofa.

But he also had a new focus.

The murders in the Caribbean overtook every news channel, and Tom couldn't absorb the information fast enough. He would watch the news in his room and then explore the different waiting areas in search of newspapers.

Although his head still hurt, he was alert and sober for the first time in years. His mind was analyzing and strategizing about what should be done as the lead investigator. Although many would label him a used-up drunk, he *was* an ex-homicide detective, albeit many years removed, and those skills were still at his core. He couldn't shake the interest, especially with the possible ties to his daughter.

The latest development was in Bonaire and Tom was waiting for a planned news conference. He'd seen the first one from Aruba several times and liked how Jack Seargant had conducted himself. The man exuded both confidence and empathy, as if he were personally invested.

Tom looked to the television as Seargant acknowledged the small crowd.

"I am very sorry to be here today, speaking from the beautiful island of Bonaire. I can verify that there has been *another* murder and it's the third of its kind. Again, it appears to be the work of a serial killer, who the media has named the 'Island Hopper.' We are currently gathering evidence and looking for witnesses."

A reporter chimed in. "We've heard that the victims had coins on their eyes. Is that true?"

Seargant straightened, thinking things through. "I can tell you that all three had coins placed over their eyes."

"How were they killed?"

"They have all been males so far, but that's not to say that females shouldn't be careful. Fifty-six year old Jeffrey Kincannon was strangled in Grand Cayman, Forty-three year old Craig Binderman was shot at close range in Aruba, and twenty-eight year old Campbell Wendleton was murdered here on Bonaire."

"How was the latest victim killed?"

Seargant looked pained as he looked down in contemplation. "I will not go into detail about that. My goal here is two-fold. First, to share information to the masses in hopes that someone may aid in our investigation. And second, to urge that you become vigilant and alert."

Seargant looked to the faces and cameras, sensing the intense focus of the hundreds that were physically watching him and the probable millions more that would do so around the world. Blood rushed to his cheeks and he felt flushed, but the raw emotion didn't come from nervousness or discomfort. It was a feeling of rage that was aching to get out and it was aimed at the Island Hopper.

Seargant glanced at the piece of paper Hartley had given him about Tom Brightwell. He had an overwhelming urge to talk to the man.

"There's one more thing, and this speaks directly to the animal behind this. You *will* be hunted, captured, and put down. And you will be shown as the coward that you are. This I promise you."

In his hospital bed Tom smiled as he watched the FBI agent step away from the podium. The camera swung a little to the right as a reporter came on screen, but Tom was fixed on Seargant in the background. He watched him pull out a cell phone and poke at it several times, finally bringing the device to his ear.

Several moments later the phone rang on the table next to Tom.

"Tom Brightwell," he stated, calmly.

"Mr. Brightwell, this is Special Agent M. Jackson Seargant of the FBI, and I was hoping to have a few words with you."

Tom looked to the television to see Seargant move out of view of the camera.

"I couldn't agree with you more. I really liked your briefing just now and I can be in Bonaire by tomorrow night."

CHAPTER 16

Early the next morning, Tom left the hospital and returned home. The decision to go to Bonaire was rash and unplanned, but the more Tom thought about it, the more it made sense.

The murder of his daughter had stopped his life; and when his wife died six years later, he went into rapid decline. He didn't feel the progression of time. He felt invisible and inconsequential. As he watched others go about their busy lives with fervor and optimism, his was in decay.

But it was time to do something about it.

Since he'd spoke to Jack Seargant, Tom had become even more focused. He'd also had further interaction with Dr. Mattingly, which had motivated him further. Tom felt alive and purposeful for the first time in years.

Arriving home, Tom told the taxi driver to wait while he readied himself. It took more time to find his old suitcase than pack it. Then a couple more minutes to prepare the house for an elongated departure, empty the refrigerator, and take out the trash.

He called Peggy and offered a quick thank for getting him to the hospital. He told her about his plans, where he'd hidden the house key, and she'd agreed to check on things a couple days each week. A quick phone call to Midway airport confirmed a flight out in the next few hours to Bonaire through Miami.

Soon he sat in the open waiting area of B11, waiting for his flight to be called. Although it was mid-morning, laughter erupted from a bar nearby, and Tom fought the urge to get a drink. It had been several days since his last and the minutes seemed like hours as he contemplated it.

He grew fidgety, and then out of boredom, began a slow walk over to Millers' Pub. He saw the two large television screens that flanked the bar's red and green sign, and then stared at the four beer taps that seemed to call him. He sat on a large leather stool, as his hands fanned across the smooth green bar top.

A bartender threw a napkin down, looking to him expectantly. But Tom closed his eyes, frowned, and quickly retreated. Moving away, he dodged the travelers who were both exiting and entering the moving walkway, and then paused to study the monitors on the wall, perusing the flight schedules. His departure was still an hour away, so he wandered left toward the eatery.

He bought a thick slice of sausage pizza and ate it near the large windows, looking out to watch a plane rolling in. Then he heard the indistinct chatter of people at the nearby Reilly's Daughter bar. Several people filled the high pub tables, as the sounds of the televisions rose and fell all around them.

He felt compelled to walk over and order a large draft beer. He licked his lips as he thought of the cold glass in his hand; the head of the brew moving to his mouth.

But instead he closed his eyes and forced the thought from his mind. He finished the pizza and left the area, eventually finding a gift shop and buying a couple of news magazines.

Finally, his flight was called and he smiled; happy that he didn't have a drink.

It was a small victory, but how long could he remain sober?

CHAPTER 17

Kralendijk
Bonaire

Things were getting interesting for the Island Hopper. His plan was completely on schedule; and everything—from the media attention and budding investigation, to the murder count and time line—was progressing just as he'd hoped.

So he'd settled into a large room at Harbour Village. It was arguably the nicest and most stylish resort on Bonaire and he'd been relaxing inside all day.

The bathroom and kitchen were constructed in granite and marble, the large white tile flooring had European accents, and the considerable furniture was light oak. The décor was not overdone in any one area, and he appreciated the various sculptures, rugs, and artwork that created the warm ambience. Overall, the room had a comfortable yet elegant feel, and it was just what he needed after being at sea.

The killer had been watching the news channels all day, enjoying the coverage just a couple miles away in Kralendijk. He alternated between napping in the four-post over-sized bed and spilling onto the large terrace that allowed a breathtaking view of the sea. He ordered room service every several hours and enjoyed sampling everything on the menu.

He wasn't in a hurry and The Plan didn't call for anything for the next several days. This was intended, because he wanted to enjoy Bonaire. It wasn't as commercial as the other islands, with their high-rises, franchises, and cruise ships in port. Bonaire had just enough nightlife to make things interesting, without the crowds and wretched tourists. And although he liked to gamble on occasion, there were only two main casinos, and they were quaint and well-managed.

But he also liked the island itself, literally, and respected its physicality and how it was created. Bonaire was formed much more recently, in absolute terms, than the earth, and was the youngest well-populated atoll in the Caribbean. With the slow movement of the continental shelf, large masses of rock were forced up; and as the ocean covered the surface, coral grew across the top. When the waters receded, the coral turned to the limestone deposits that still covered the island's surface.

The killer liked Bonaire's unspoiled expansiveness. He enjoyed searching the hidden coves, hiking up the hills to the salt mines, and examining the coral skeletons sunken into the land. It was almost like walking on another planet and he liked the exploratory and historical significance.

His stay had been relaxing, but the small repose had a more serious undertone. He'd been hurting more than ever, with his headaches coming more frequently, lasting longer, and with more concentrated pain. He knew he needed to stay on land for a while, drink more water, eat well, and build his energy.

But there was the FBI investigation and he couldn't shake the excitement. Although he needed to rest, he just *had to* take a short ride to town to spy on things.

Maybe tomorrow, he thought, as he finished off the remainder of his water bottle and took one last look to the sea. Then he closed the balcony doors and walked back into his air-conditioned room, dimming the lights.

He eased himself into the large bed and watched the ceiling fan blades whirring above him. With a dull pulsing in his head, he drifted away into a deep sleep, still thinking of more excitement to come.

CHAPTER 18

Tom Brightwell arrived in Miami Dade International Airport just in time to hear that his connecting flight to Bonaire was delayed.

After eating a better-than-expected hotdog, he found himself in front of another bar. But instead of going in, he stood in the middle of the foot traffic, paralyzed in indecision. With his days-old sobriety, his perspective was starting to normalize.

Tom studied the people all around him and slowly inched closer. Many were laughing with friends and hoisting tall draft beers. Others spilled out in front to watch the televisions that covered the walls.

On the left Tiger Woods was teeing off somewhere in Arizona; on the right the Rays were trailing the Twins. The middle television was muted, but it was a Texas Hold-em tournament and someone had just flopped a straight.

But nothing could distract Tom as he focused on the shiny, glass bottles behind the bar. So when the bartender smiled and asked what he needed, he instinctively sat down.

He felt a pang of guilt, but robotically ordered a gin and tonic and a shot of whisky. Surely he could have just a couple drinks to pass the time before his flight to Bonaire. Was he really a full blown alcoholic like the doctor suggested? This would be a test, he decided. If he could simply have a few drinks and then hop on his flight, he'd be okay. He just needed to ease his mind and let his stress dissipate.

Tom felt better when the bartender swiftly moved to fill his order. Then he looked to the televisions, feigning interest.

After downing the shot and taking more time with the rail drink, he settled in and thought about things. His mind turned to the logistics of it all. He'd stay at the bar for a couple of hours and unwind. Then he'd board the plane to Bonaire and meet the FBI. He'd get to his hotel, visit some stores to buy the proper clothing and toiletries, and then get down to business.

The alcohol hit his system and opened his mind. Soon he was contemplating his past life as a homicide detective, and the details of several cases came to mind.

There was the "Snow-side killer," who had murdered four prostitutes in the Chicago area. He dumped their bodies in wooded areas in the north-west suburbs, always beneath a pile of snow on a hill.

Whether it was because the snow would cover the bodies or its melting would help erode any evidence, Tom never knew, but he grimaced at the thought. The killer had always walked backwards at the scene, wore shoes three times larger than his own, and had stabbed each victim with his left hand to throw off the authorities.

Then there were the two cases that would haunt him forever, no matter how much he drank. Both were simple homicides and easy closes, but they were so cutting in their senselessness.

The first involved a young father. He'd been waking up with his infant daughter each night to change and feed her, before gently rocking her back to sleep. He never drank alcohol or used drugs. He worked very successfully for a consulting firm and was active in the community and church.

With no outward signs of paranoia, depression, or disparity, one night he strangled the tiny child. In the morning his wife found him still cradling her dead body, as he gently rocked and sang to her. He was not able to speak afterward, and in the months that followed was found to be insane. Even several years later the man was rocking from side to side in a hypnotic stare, singing to his empty arms in a psychiatric ward.

The second case was at Woodfield Mall in Schaumberg. It happened out of Tom's jurisdiction, but he was sent to consult. A man positioned himself just outside the third floor area near JC Penny's, very close to the stairway and escalators. It was a Saturday afternoon in mid-December and the place was packed. The man backed against the railing, watching and waiting.

Witnesses later said they'd felt the man's stare. Others said he seemed to be in a trance-like state, with his dark eyes glassy and wide. He was a large, white man in his mid-thirties, and had been a starting lineman in college.

Suddenly, he started grabbing people and throwing them from the railing and ranting in a language that no one could understand. Nine people of different ages, sexes, and races were killed in the two minutes it took bystanders to subdue him. Still, he was able to get free long enough to leap to his death from the same spot.

After his sixth drink Tom felt sick. While his mind embraced the charge of the alcohol, he was still weak from the head trauma.

He swiftly paid the bill and left to find his gate. But when he rose, he became light-headed. Whether it was the combination of alcohol and his pain medication, or even his dilapidated state he didn't know, but he was in serious trouble.

The numbers on the gates appeared blurry and he fell completely numb and out of control. Fumbling in his pocket, he found his flight number and worked his way to a large electronic board. A terrible feeling gripped him as he realized that he was in danger of missing the plane.

He went to the bathroom, vomited, and peed. Sweating, he moved to the sink and splashed cold water on his face.

Looking in the mirror, he shook his head in disappointment.

"What are you doing to yourself?!" he asked angrily, as others looked over.

But he didn't see them and didn't care. He just peered at his reflection, despairingly.

"Pull it together. This is your last chance!" he yelled.

Then he wiped his face with a paper towel and stormed out.

He shuffled through the airport, clutching his bruised side and falling into a modest gait. As his breathing became labored and his chest hot, he stopped again to check his flight's status.

He could only hope to get to his gate on time.

But he knew he didn't deserve any favors.

Chapter 19

"**I** love you more than anything," Susan Seargant said, softly.

"Not because you have to?" he countered.

Seargant could hear his wife's muted laugh and picture her pretty smile as she bobbed her head, playfully. He heard her relaxed breaths and knew she was content, even though he was almost two-thousand miles away in Bonaire.

There was no doubt that Jack Seargant loved his wife and he knew she felt the same. Even after being together for so long, it was the same way they'd ended their conversations since college. Their relationship was still fresh and was ripened with every quick snippet he called out and every smile she gathered.

But he knew their life wasn't as full as it could be. There was something missing; a crucial ingredient—a child—and it was becoming a source of tension between them.

Seargant knew it was weighing on Susan's mind. It usually did when he was away and the loneliness set in. She loved her man unconditionally, especially his work ethic and moral integrity. But it was a double edged sword. It was those same traits that kept him away for weeks at a time and always on the job. Susan was a casualty of his tenacity; held at bay and sometimes ignored for the benefit of catching the bad guy. She'd been a faithful companion and wife and now she wanted to be a mother as well.

Still, she let it go for the man she loved, because she knew why he did it. The twelve-year old boy was still inside him; the one that witnessed his father's murder during a convenience store robbery. It was the one case in his life that still remained unsolved and she understood that no matter how many perps he caught, there would still be a hunger to do more.

But time was moving on. They had spoken of having children, when dating so many years ago and the thought of an unwritten future was so far away. Now Susan's maternal clock was ticking very loudly and the pressure was mounting. They still made love several times per month, but a pregnancy had eluded them.

He reflected on their talks in college, when they'd agreed that having children would complete their perfect union. He remembered the whispered conversations in their dorm rooms at night. They would come home after a party or a football game and talk until the sun came up. They would dream of their future lives together and wish for everything to be perfect.

But a tendon injury disallowed his entry into the NFL and he chose a career in federal law enforcement. And after years of trying to become pregnant and countless visits to fertility centers, it seemed that their ideal future was fading. Every birthday was more of a reminder than a celebration. Another step closer to losing her dream of becoming a mother.

"So you're okay?" he asked.

There was a long pause and he could picture her fighting off tears. But there was nothing he could do, except try even harder to find this killer.

In doing so, he could also get home to his wife.

CHAPTER 20

Seargant decided to meet Tom's plane personally, leaving his team to work on other matters. After the emotional phone call with Susan, he appreciated the night air and the time alone. He needed to reflect on his *own* life and gain some perspective on the case.

Bonaire International Airport, or Flamingo Airport, is one of the smallest in the Caribbean. It's also one of the more colorful, with the long main building painted bright pink and royal blue. Hosting exactly one airstrip, it is fully capable of receiving international flights, but more frequently gets the shorter ones to and from Aruba, Curacao, and Saint Maarten.

With his clearance, Seargant was allowed on the tarmac when Tom's plane came in just before midnight. As the passengers walked away from the aircraft, Seargant saw the familiar expressions of the weary travelers; all thankful to be at their destination, but looking uncomfortable as they shuffled across the concrete.

Tom was the last to exit and Seargant sized him up right away. The FBI profiler saw a man that was unfit in both appearance and mind. Physically he was overweight and unshaven, with unruly hair and wandering eyes that suggested uncertainty and confusion. The man held his side and clumsily grabbed at the railing as he limped down the stairs.

Seargant immediately questioned his decision in inviting Tom Brightwell to Bonaire. He'd read the ex-homicide detective's file and spoken to his former superiors. But he couldn't believe that the man lumbering toward him was that same super-star cop. Seargant knew Tom had lost his daughter and wife, and that he'd taken to the bottle, but this was even worse than he'd imagined.

When Tom saw Seargant, recognition flashed in the older man's eyes. Tom stood straighter and his gait quickened.

Seargant moved with efficient stepping and outstretched his hand to accept Tom's. "I'm Jack Seargant with the FBI. It's a pleasure to meet you Mr. Brightwell."

"Please call me Tom."

"Okay, Tom. You can call me Seargant. How was your flight?"

"It was fine," Tom said, becoming impatient. "But we're not here to waste time with idle pleasantries. Can you take me right to the crime scene?"

Seargant smiled, appreciating the man's bark. "I think we should get to know each other before I discuss the case."

Tom started to walk and Seargant moved with him.

"You mean you want to size me up, maybe catch me off guard. Get an idea if I'm still emotionally and physically able to help your investigation."

Seargant stopped and squared himself against Tom. For a long moment the two men looked at each other, not knowing what would happen. Seargant was cool and engaging, and Tom was on edge after his travels. But both sought the same resolve; a possible partnership to catch a killer.

"I appreciate your candor, Tom, but to be direct, I smell alcohol on you. Are you even in the right mindset to help?"

Tom frowned. "I *do* drink, but I promise it will not affect our relationship or impede you whatsoever. I am fully committed."

"If I'm to share information with you, you need to stop drinking and *always* be alert. I know you're here as an unpaid guest and I have no authority over you, but the more I trust you the more I can share."

"I completely understand and I'd be apprehensive too," Tom said, softening. "I'll stop drinking to help find my daughter's killer. You have my word."

The mood lightened but Seargant persisted. "I still must be frank," he said. "What are your motives here; what *do you* hope to accomplish?"

Tom nodded, thoughtfully. "I want to catch this son-of-a-bitch, perhaps more than you. And I'll do whatever it takes."

"That's what I'm talking about," Seargant said. "What do you mean *exactly*?"

Tom looked around and saw they were alone. The other passengers were inside collecting their luggage and the airplane's engines were now silent. Tom hadn't planned on what to say to Jack Seargant. He also didn't think their initial talk would be on the tarmac, but he was open and honest.

"I will not spell it out for you, but being who you are, and who you know me to be from the file I'm sure you have, I think you have an idea. I have nothing to lose and nothing to look forward to. This is my last and possibly *only* chance to catch the thing that killed my little girl and I will do *whatever* it takes to be a part of the equation. I consider myself expendable."

Seargant was thinking about how to use Tom. He began a slow walk as his mind deliberated. The man was a used-up drunk, but had a lifetime of experience and would be working off the record. Certainly Seargant could use an asset like that.

They moved past the other passengers and Seargant waved his badge to get to the front of the line at customs. Soon they were at the car and Tom turned to Seargant.

"I want to see the crime scene before you take me to the hotel," Tom said, flatly.

"It's after midnight Tom; let me—"

"I want to see it. I could tell at the press conference that you were rattled. Something was definitely different about this one. I'm intrigued and want to have something to ponder through the night."

"Have it your way Detective," Seargant said, starting the car and turning left out of the lot. "But I must say you'd sleep better if you didn't see it."

CHAPTER 21

The terrain turned rocky, the road narrowed, and the car jumped along the uneven path. Driving the curving roadway at night felt eerie, but the ride didn't take long.

A brilliant light showed in the distance, and it grew brighter as they approached the salt mines. Seargant parked at a distance and they walked up a long hill to the source. A large utility light lit up the area. Two policemen stood to greet them, but relaxed when they recognized Seargant.

"Can you give us a few minutes?" Seargant asked, and the officers moved down the hill to their vehicle.

Tom couldn't believe what he saw as he approached. He was looking at a mechanism about ten feet tall, made of wood with a shiny blade at the bottom.

"That's not a guillotine, is it?"

Seargant nodded, maintaining his silence and watching Tom make an initial assessment. First Tom looked to the edges of the perimeter, then to the sky and distant horizon. Then he took out a compass and walked the scene several times.

"What direction were the other bodies facing? Were they pointing to the previous or subsequent murder?"

"We're already on that angle," Seargant said, flatly. Then the FBI-man cleared his throat and spoke softly. "Tom, there's no easy way to say this so I'm just going to get into it."

Tom looked up. "Go on; I'm an open book and here to help."

"That's good because I need to talk about Kelly, as hard as it may be."

Tom walked a few steps away, looking into the black expanse that fell all around them. "I know," he said.

"This guy is placing coins on his victim's eyes. Kelly may have been his first, even though it was over ten years ago. Can you talk about what happened?"

Tom was direct. "Jess and I were in Jamaica for the wedding, and it was troubling me. I'm not sure if it was because I wanted more for my daughter, or that I didn't like my future son-in-law, but it just didn't seem right."

"How so?"

"I'd only met Jeremy a couple of times and both were unsettling. He supposedly had no living relatives and Kelly had only met a few of his friends; none of whom were at the wedding. I'm used to frank and honest talk, so I pressed him on all fronts, but he had well-rehearsed responses that were exhausting and off-putting."

"What did Jessica think?"

"I raised my concerns, but she said that nobody would ever be good enough for my daughter, and I couldn't disagree. I also over-discussed it with Kelly, which forced awkward silences and heated arguments. She just wanted us to let her be happy. Jeremy was *her* choice so I had to let it go."

"What about Jeremy? What was your take-away?"

"He was hollow and distant. He was self-employed, traveled often, and was a supposed genius with computer software. That's really all I know."

"In your gut do you think he did it?"

"Yeah I always thought so, but he had an alibi for everything."

"And then your wife was diagnosed with cancer and your whole life was turned upside down again."

Tom nodded but remained silent. Then he again looked to the sky and into the distance, before approaching where the body had been. He knelt, regarding the area in complete concentration.

Seargant knew what Tom was doing. Homicide detectives would often spend considerable time at the exact place of death, either trying to gain a perspective of the victim's last moments, get an inroad to the killer's mindset, or even find a clue that could unravel the entire thing. Tom leaned in closer, to within inches of the guillotine blade, which was dulled and stained with a mixture of dirt, blood, and human tissue.

Then Tom sighed as he turned to look at Seargant. "He's getting more intricate and deliberate. He has a clear agenda and he's marching forward. I think we have a major problem."

"What's that?"

"I think he's testing death."

CHAPTER 22

"Go on," Seargant prodded, crouching next to Tom.

"Let's see," Tom began, incredulously. "We have a killer using different methodologies, operating in different places, and doing it with ease. I've never heard of it before."

"Tell me more."

"Each murder has been different. You've got strangulation, a gun-shot, a guillotine, and if you want to add Kelly, a stabbing. And they've all been in uncontained environments, which is *certainly* not out of convenience. I mean look around. This is the most elaborate crime scene I've ever seen. Just imagine the planning and *patience* that went into this."

Seargant looked at the two guards in the distance and waved them off.

"Take a couple hours off, guys. We need to be alone up here."

The men nodded and soon Seargant was watching their red taillights bob up and down in the night, before disappearing around a curve.

"You know I read your jacket at the CPD and spoke to your former Captain Gilmore in great detail."

Tom laughed, shrugging his shoulders. "What did he have to say?"

"Several things. You were the most tedious, deliberate, hard-working, and dedicated cop he'd ever known. You always put yourself last. You have a very good moral compass; almost like a 'what would Jesus do?' mentality. And you are honest and straight-forward."

"Really?" Tom asked, visibly confused. "I didn't think he liked me."

"He *didn't* like you. He was very clear on that. He thought you were also arrogant, inflexible, and entirely too independent; but to his own admission, usually correct in your judgment calls."

"How's he doing?"

"He retired a year ago, and now he and his wife are living in Florida, playing golf and living the slow life."

Tom smiled as his mind painted the picture. It was the life he and Jess wanted but could never have.

Seargant picked up on Tom's sudden detachment. He gathered a couple of chairs that had been brought for the security team.

"Have a seat, Tom. I figure we should get to know each other, seeing as we may be colleagues for the time being."

They both sat, but neither spoke for a long moment. Instead, they took in the warm air and considered the terrain that fell around them.

Tom was the first to speak. "So tell me something about yourself."

"Like what?"

"First of all, what's the 'M.' stand for in 'Special Agent M. Jackson Seargant?'"

Seargant laughed. "It's Maurice. I was named after my uncle. And 'Seargant' is French and should be pronounced 'Seer-Gaunt,' but everyone says it like the military rank. I've never corrected anyone and don't mind."

"Okay, now what's something you like and something you hate?"

"Interesting question," Seargant said, taking a moment. "I hate when I see milk left out on the countertop. It has to be in the fridge as much as possible. Definitely the last thing I buy at the grocery store and the first thing put away at home."

Tom smiled. "I can see that. So what do you like?"

"That's easy. Look around you."

Tom obliged and the two men took in the landscape and the blanket of bright stars above.

When Seargant spoke again, he was more relaxed. "The natural wonder that makes up this planet amazes me everyday, especially the things that haven't changed in thousands of years.

"I like standing on the beach just before sunrise, watching the first glow of the sun as it rises; the natural orange, reddish coloring that chases the night sky away. I like the sounds of the waves crashing at night, and then in a moments glance, seeing hundreds of thousands of stars so many light years away."

"So you're a nature freak, then?" Tom asked.

"No, I wouldn't go that far. I don't know the names of any constellations, the timing of the sunrise on any given day, or even the names of any vegetation. But I *am* appreciative and definitely aware of my surroundings. I think it makes me a better law enforcement officer. You know, understanding the bigger picture before concentrating on things locally."

"I know what you mean," Tom said. "Like when you see a picture of the earth from space, it looks so peaceful. Just a happy mixture of bluish-green. You can't see the man-made problems, the unnecessary wars, and violence."

"Exactly," Seargant said. "So what about you, then? What do you like and hate?"

"That's easy," Tom said. "I hate disorder, especially when it's out of selfishness. I hate bullies or people who intentionally inflict pain. I wish I could magically be there to stop it every time, especially when kids are involved. And speaking of kids, the *only* thing I love is my family."

Seargant nodded, respectfully. He had read Tom's entire file, but it went further than that. The Chicago FBI office sent a team to learn more about Tom Brightwell and interview people at his former workplace and favorite hangouts. Still, Seargant needed to engage him further.

"I should say the *memory* of my family," Tom added. "They are the only ones that keep me going, until I see them again."

"Are you okay to talk about it?"

"Sure, though I've rarely spoken about it. But for some reason on a hilltop in Bonaire, alone in the warm night with a guy I just met, it seems like a good time to open up."

Seargant laughed and Tom joined in. The moment eased, and both men settled into their chairs, each looking to the sky once more.

"I'll tell you what, Seargant," Tom started. "If you really want to know me, I can break it down very easily. I'm not sharing this because I have an emotional need to, and it's not like I have something to get off my chest. I'm a realist and like you I'm definitely aware of how I fit into the greater picture."

Seargant remained quiet and Tom gathered his thoughts. The older man's eyes softened, his body relaxed, and Seargant knew Tom was speaking from the heart.

"It's like my current life can be compared to staying at a party too long. All of a sudden it's hot and crowded. The music is too loud and unfamiliar. Everyone is better dressed, younger, more attractive, and I'm surrounded by strangers. My days are like maneuvering around this endless, uncomfortable void. My thoughts are always interrupted by the distant memory of better times. I know I've reached the time when life stops giving and starts taking. Metaphorically I see the door, which would be like dying, but sometimes I fear there's nothing on the other side.

"I remember my childhood and everything leading up to meeting Jess, and it was amazing. Things were going so well. I enjoyed my job and felt challenged every day. Financially, things were good and she completed everything that I was lacking.

"When Kelly was born, it was as if my heart could burst each day. Those two women controlled me at every level and I enjoyed every moment of it. There was absolutely nothing I wouldn't do for them. They held my heart and the problems of the world couldn't penetrate our lives.

"And then Kelly was murdered and Jess died of cancer. Since then, I'm sure you know, I've been mentally and physically broken, and I'm just a wasted shell of the man I used to be."

Seargant grimaced. He no longer wanted to assess Tom's mental state or needle him any further. Rather, he wanted to reach out and console the man beside him.

"I must say, Tom, that I just witnessed two completely different things from you. You're talking about how beaten up you are, but when you assessed this scene just now, I saw a seasoned detective that was completely alive. I think you have a lot left to do and can really help us here. But I must ask, do you feel sorry for yourself?"

"Absolutely not," Tom said, emphatically. "It's God's plan, I'm sure. I'm not overly-religious, but I was raised in the Catholic Church and believe there's a greater design. I just don't know what mine is."

"You said something interesting. You feel your current situation is uncomfortable? Do you have a death wish?"

"I would *die* to catch my daughter's killer and be fine with it. But not being afraid of death and wishing for it are two different things. Let's just say that I wouldn't hesitate to rush into a place in pursuit of her killer. Some call it adrenaline; I call it pissed off. If this guy shoots me, I'm gonna be too angry to die. I'll run right through him and worry about dying later."

"Well I guess I can't question your work ethic," Seargant said.

Tom didn't respond. When Seargant turned, he saw a stoic man that was pensive and serious.

Tom was peering into Seargant with hard, determined eyes. "When it comes to Kelly, no one can *ever* question my work ethic."

And Seargant couldn't disagree.

CHAPTER 23

Seargant and his team—which loosely included Tom—were staying at the Plaza Resort in Kralendijk. It was an obvious pick, due to its proximity to the airport and police station, but it was also one of the nicer hotels on Bonaire.

Tom awoke the next morning well-rested and alert. He gently moved out of bed, feeling the tenderness in his bandaged side. Then he shaved and took a quick shower, dressing in a pair of shorts and a loose-fitting button-down shirt.

The room was wall to wall red tile, with modest furnishings and tasteful wicker furniture. It was simple, clean, and comfortable; and suited Tom just fine. He moved onto the balcony and leaned against the railing as a feeling of tranquility came over him.

The sun was bright but still low in the sky. It cast a long, jagged shadow over the pool area below him, and it expanded all the way to the beach. Beyond that, Tom looked to the sea, which showed eye-catching pockets of bluish green all the way to the horizon.

Below and to the left, Tom saw the entrance to the fitness center and he perked up. It had been several years since his last workout, but he recalled how he used to love it.

He'd always been a student of health, though one would never know it now. In high school, he'd taken an elective in health and human anatomy. He enjoyed understanding how the body operated and then designing various workouts to achieve his physique. He coupled his targeted exercises with proper dieting and it allowed him to be in great shape well beyond his early years.

Then he frowned as he remembered his *last* workout in Jamaica. It was the day Kelly was murdered. He took another look at the gym and made a mental note to visit it later.

Regaining focus, Tom thought about his conversation with Seargant the night before. They had communicated well and Tom sensed a friendship was forming. He knew they shared an affinity for police work and an ethic for justice. But as they spoke, the hardened layers of their inner-most selves seemed to fold away, revealing two men that just wanted to live good lives and help others along the way.

The exchange was also revealing. Tom clearly realized he'd been living a void existence, but a spark had lit within him. The hint of a better life had shown through. Moreover, he'd made a promise to stop drinking and he took his commitments seriously. It was a precious first step to reclaim his life, but it was also essential to gain Seargant's trust.

Tom's first priority was to buy clothing and toiletries. Seargant had provided a car and a cell phone, but instead of driving, Tom decided to take a stroll in the morning air.

The walk was surprisingly easy on him, though he felt the dull pressure of his bruised ribs. His head was clear and he remained focused on his destination. Surprisingly, his ankles and knees didn't bother him, and he married steady breathing with a measured walk. Smiling at those he saw, Tom began to feel a sense of belonging.

Arriving at a small breakfast shop, Tom found he was more famished than he'd thought. He ordered an egg sandwich, coffee, and a bowl of fresh fruit. After a few hurried bites, he settled into his chair and began reading a brochure on Bonaire.

There was a map on the back and he began planning the day. He chartered out where the police station was and the other sites he wanted to see. He also made a mental list of what he needed, if he were required to stay in the Caribbean longer than expected.

Tom finished his food and let out a satisfied breath, testing his injured right side. Although his stomach was content and his body mending, his mind was troubled. The ex-homicide detective had an overwhelming sense of foreboding.

Tom just *knew* the Island Hopper was still on Bonaire; and was certain the killer wasn't finished.

But Tom had no way of knowing he was correct on both counts.

Or that the killer was even *closer* than he could imagine.

CHAPTER 24

The Island Hopper found Tom Brightwell amusing.

The last time he'd *physically* seen him was in Jamaica, though he'd certainly kept tabs on him since. He knew about his wife's death, his retirement from the police department, and the drunken lifestyle the idiot had fallen into.

Now he studied Tom lumbering down the street, watching the man cast easy smiles and wave to everyone he came across. But the killer couldn't believe what he was seeing. Tom had gained so much weight and in the last ten years seemed to age at least twenty!

At one time, he knew Tom Brightwell was a talented investigator. But in his current condition, both mentally and physically, maybe he should be put down.

Say hello to your wife and daughter. Have a nice trip.

But the killer didn't like straying too far from his design. No, Tom was close enough to the action and would be a welcome participant, even if he wasn't up to par.

The Island Hopper followed him along a sidewalk. Tom disappeared into a store and the killer found a bench to relax and ponder things. It was the thinking that he enjoyed the most. He loved allowing his brilliant mind to wander. Sometimes he'd be in such deep thought that he'd be oblivious to his surroundings and would "awake" much later. He thought of everything; but most of all The Plan, which was well on its way.

For now, though, he contemplated himself. He wondered if he was indeed a sociopath or even a psychopath. How he hoped he was the latter. There was so much more excitement involved!

He remembered an old talk show that delved into the human psyche. A well-known psychologist had lectured that no one ever thinks they're truly bad. They are just exponentially more selfish than others and put their desires—however perverted, unjust, or inhumane—above others.

Was that the answer he sought for himself? Was he just narcissistic to an extreme degree? He knew he didn't value human life, not even his own, but was that the answer to the question he pondered so often?

He had read books on serial killers and had always found them intriguing. He even laughed out loud at the thought of being labeled one. But he wondered if he fit the stereotype. Yes he was Caucasian and fit the age category; was intelligent and self-serving. But there was no sexual element to his style.

He was a hunter.

He was well-liked, active in the charitable community, and known in the social scene. He was polite, honest, and deliberate. His physical characteristics were agreeable; with calming green eyes, thick dark hair, and an engaging smile. He kept in top physical condition and was taller than most. He had no problem with the ladies, and with his care-free demeanor, confidence, and charm, even the men were easy to befriend. Having near unlimited money at his disposal only helped his cause.

Still, he knew that although many saw him as outgoing, he was extremely introverted and content to dwell within the contents of his own mind. Solitude was his best friend. Being alone and in control was freeing.

He decided that he was more curious than anything. He forward-thought to the impossible: being caught and put on display in a packed courtroom of his so-called peers. Then he laughed at what he would say to the judge. *I was just curious to see them all die. And the actual murdering part? Of course I enjoyed it! I mean, who wouldn't?*

But then his wide smile evaporated. His head suddenly felt like it was exploding in the frontal lobe. It was like he was plugged into an electrical socket. In an instant, his nerve endings were on fire and the pain shot through his head, paralyzing him.

He was used to the agony. It was the timing he could do without. The spells would hit several times each day and then subside for hours, only to happen again at the worst time. The doctor told him they would be sporadic, frequent, and more protracted as the Glioblastoma tumor grew in his brain.

A GBM is one of the worst kind brain tumors and is *always* fatal. His had begun like every other, similar to a tiny closed fist that was inoperable. Then, as time progressed, the fist became bigger and finger-like tentacles began growing outward and taking permanent hold.

Shaking, he clumsily reached into his pocket for two morphine pills, which he stuffed into his mouth and swallowed. He couldn't make a scene, so he closed his eyes and pretended to rest. He couldn't see, so he watched the colorful blur of fantastic colors swirling in the foreground. His brain was misfiring because the tumor was affecting the normal brain patterns. He just had to wait it out.

Then the pain eased long enough to allow a free thought. He opened his eyes to see Tom Brightwell exiting a store with several large bags.

But the Island Hopper couldn't follow his target. Instead, after nearly an hour, he rose on wobbly legs, mounted a moped, and headed back to his room, where he slept well into the next day.

CHAPTER 25

Tom unpacked his purchases and placed them neatly into drawers. Then he took a bottle of water from the refrigerator and walked to the balcony. The sun was high above him now and the pool was filled with excited children.

Time had passed easily. Although the shopping trip was necessary, Tom was eager to find Seargant and get updated on the investigation. He drained the rest of the water and left his room; eventually finding the FBI team in the conference room off the lobby. They were all in careful review of the paperwork that was sprawled out on the table.

Making a faint knock on the door, Tom was surprised at the greeting he received. Each of the FBI agents rose to meet him with polite handshakes and affectionate nods.

"Any new developments?" Tom asked, casually.

"Nothing," Seargant said, frowning. "We *did* bag everything and send it to Quantico for any traces of DNA or fingerprints. But now we're cooling our heels and I'm sad to say, just waiting to see where this guy will take us next."

Tom looked to the map on the table, which was an extensive look of the Caribbean. There were several highlighted areas and different colored markings. The FBI was not just looking at where the killer had been, but where he might go next.

"I imagine you're trying to plot his course," Tom said, almost to himself.

"Do you like hockey?" Seargant asked.

"Not as much as I should, being from Chicago. Why?"

"One of the game's greatest players was Wayne Gretzky. He always said that he was never the biggest guy on the ice, or even the best skater. But he went to where he thought the puck was going, not to where it was. I'm sending people to several places that we deem highly plausible."

"Are you going, too?" Tom asked.

"I'm staying here with you. I think we should pick each other's brains and get to know each other a little more. But I'll have a jet standing by."

The others emptied the room; off to their respective places, along with scores of others coming out of D.C. Soon it was just Tom and Seargant sitting around the table.

"You weren't totally up front with me on two counts," Tom said.

Seargant shrugged. "What's on your mind, Detective?"

"You wanted me out of the way today, so you could have a few hours alone with your team, which is fine. You never have to baby sit me, just tell me the parameters."

"And the second item?"

"You didn't finish your thoughts about family. You mentioned how important it was, but then diverted to your wife."

Seargant sucked in a deep breath and stared blankly. Tom knew he had touched on something that made the man genuinely uncomfortable. But then Seargant broke the tension by rising and moving a few empty water bottles to a recycling can.

"It's time for an early dinner," Seargant said. "Courtesy of the FBI."

They ate at Sassy's in Kralendijk; a quaint two-story structure, just like the other brightly-colored colonial buildings around it.

They spoke about the investigation, the profilers back at the Behavioral Science Unit at Quantico, and Seargant's immediate field force.

There were no leads or trace evidence, and all possible scenarios were being examined. How did the killer travel between destinations? Was it one killer or several? And the theory of terrorism, albeit doubtful, was also being examined.

But the men spoke more about themselves than the case.

Later, they returned to the hotel and sat poolside, drinking strong coffee and taking in the night air. Although they'd just met the night before, a deep respect was being forged, both personally and professionally.

Seargant appreciated the natural good at Tom's core; and although he sensed Tom was at rock bottom and could even be suicidal, Seargant knew he wasn't a waste. He'd seen the flash in Tom's eyes and felt the fire within him. There was much more the man could do and the investigation could not only save others, but maybe even Tom as well.

Tom was impressed by the pure efficiency of Jack Seargant and how he led his team. He spoke *with* them not *at* them, and never put himself before others. He sought direction only after deep consideration and led by pure ethic.

They sat by the pool, contemplating each other. They were an unlikely pair, but they sensed they could be great together.

"So Tom," Seargant began. "You mentioned that I didn't answer your question about family. I'm not sure exactly where I'll go with this. I've never spoken about it to anyone but my wife and some doctors, but with you being so forthcoming, I feel compelled to open up.

"Susan and I are having trouble conceiving. My job takes me everywhere, and though she would never pressure me, I know it's grating on her that I'm not home as much as I should be. Many of her friend's husbands travel, but they're home on the weekends, cutting the grass or tending the grill. I always seem to be chasing some bad guy."

"It's in your blood. You can't just turn it off."

"I know. But maybe I should get a desk job and be closer to home."

"And someday you may, if that's what you want. I imagine you have a lot of pull."

"I would never ask for any special favors. I go where my team goes, and the bad guys aren't in an office."

"You're right about that. They're everywhere, living among us."

"You know what gets me, too, Tom?"

"What's that?"

"We were at a fertility clinic and spoke in detail with a doctor about statistics. Did you know that the average sperm count is about thirty million?"

Tom smiled, not knowing where Seargant was going. "I counted three-hundred once, but got bored and gave up."

Seargant laughed, continuing. "But seriously, we all won the lottery by even *being* here. We were that one in thirty million that became *us*. Then consider that we were born at the best time in history, with the greatest technology, health care, and comforts; and that we live in the best country in the world."

Tom nodded. "I guess I never thought about it that way. What's really scary is if the sun was 1% closer or further from the earth, we probably wouldn't be here either."

Seargant was in total agreement. "Or that if one of your grandfathers hadn't met his wife somewhere long ago, you wouldn't exist."

"Actually you know what's really scary about that?" Tom asked, rhetorically. "My family was originally from Minnesota. And sometime in the late 1800's, my great great great grandfather, Wilbur, was living in St. Paul and married to a woman named Elizabeth.

"Anyway—and here's the scary part—the circus came to town and she was enamored with one of the young male performers. One morning she was gone and left Wilbur with a note and two kids. As cliché as it sounds, she *literally* ran away with the circus and was never seen again. So he remarried, had my great great grandfather and the rest is history. If the circus hadn't been in Minneapolis that summer I would never have been born."

"That's crazy," Seargant said. "Is that a true story?"

"Yep. My father told it to me several times. I'm also lucky because I was born to older parents. My mother was fifty-two when she had me. My father was sixty and they'd almost given up trying."

Seargant sat back and exhaled. "Life really is a precious gift and people are killing each other over stupid arguments, a pair of shoes, or just for sport, like the guy we're tracking."

Tom and Seargant spoke for several more hours, until both men decided to turn in. Tom looked at the exercise room as they walked by, and asked Seargant to join him in the morning.

"What time should I meet you?" Seargant asked.

Tom suddenly felt very good about things. He successfully completed day one of his sobriety, he'd become fast friends with Jack Seargant, and was charged with a desire to begin his workouts again.

"I'll be there first thing," he said.

CHAPTER 26

True to his word, Tom began his morning stretches before sunrise, testing his agility on a bench outside the fitness room. After several minutes, he began a light walk with a modest incline on the treadmill, before using the free weights to work every muscle group. He felt the reducing tenderness in his side and was confident his ribs were mending.

This was his first workout in several years, and although excited and eager, he held no ego on what to expect. He was careful not to place too much stress on his body. Getting hurt was something he couldn't afford.

A couple hours later, Seargant appeared in the doorway. He smiled and shook his head in admiration.

"I thought morning still meant around seven o'clock. How long have you been here?"

Finishing with some free weights, Tom secured the dumbbells and rolled off the bench, eyeing Seargant.

"Not long. Wanna spot me over here?"

Seargant followed Tom to a bench press and moved behind him.

"I'm doing a ten, five, ten set."

Seargant's large arms moved with Tom for the first several pumps, but then he backed off. Looking around, he saw that Tom had fitted each of the ten stations for a pre-determined workout. Seargant smiled and gained a stronger appreciation for Tom's natural drive.

Putting the bar in place, Tom sat up and followed Seargant's stare around the room.

"Yeah, I'm sorry about that. I wasn't sure when you were coming so I customized everything."

"No that's fine. Let me work the room for a while."

After another hour, Seargant and Tom were breathing heavy and thick with sweat. They exited into the morning light as a light breeze found them. Then they sat on a bench and drank from their bottled waters, greedily; each feeling the burn of the workout.

Tom spoke first. "I have something I'd like to tell you, Seargant. It's really nothing, but I've never told anyone and it's really important to me. It's something about Jess that I never really understood until recently."

Seargant nodded, waiting for Tom, who suddenly looked pained and unsure.

"Jess was a wonderful person, very full of life. She was intelligent, funny, and caring; and to this day I'm not sure what she saw in me. But thank God I had her."

"I think you're selling yourself short, Tom," Seargant quipped. "From what I know of you, I could use the same words to describe you."

Tom waved off the compliment and continued. "There was one thing that she could never remember, for whatever reason. It even became an inside joke between us."

Tom smiled, shyly, and Seargant studied the man to his side. Tom was opening up again and Seargant felt honored to be a trusted confidant.

"She would get excited when the thirty-first would come, when she thought there were only thirty days in that given month. She'd get surprised a couple times a year and treat it like an extra day of life. She'd get her nails done, do a little shopping, and we'd sometimes go out to dinner and have the best time. She acted like that day technically shouldn't exist and it was one more day to enjoy life."

"I bet leap year was especially fun."

"Yep; same principle."

"That's a nice story, Tom. Thank you for sharing it with me."

"I just want you to know how much passion Jess had for life, and I never really felt that way until right now. It's not just the sobriety or the workout, or even this great weather. I feel reborn and my only focus is to catch this killer. I haven't felt this free since—"

Tom suddenly thought of his last workout, just before he walked onto his hotel balcony in Jamaica to witness his daughter's murder. Seargant looked over and saw the anguish in Tom.

"—since I lost Kelly."

"I'm here Tom and I hear you, man," Seargant said.

"I loved my wife more deeply than anything, until Kelly came along."

Tom looked to Seargant. "I don't want to offend you by speaking of children, because I know you're having difficulties. But loving a child is something that you can't understand until you have one. And when that child is taken away—"

Tom's voice fell off. He cradled his head in his hands and the tears flowed freely. Seargant put his hand on Tom's shoulder.

"I would love Kelly no matter what she did. She will forever be the little girl who stared into my eyes as I fed her a bottle, or tugged at my pant leg as a toddler. The one who squeezed my hand whenever she was scared, and ran after my car when I left for work.

"And call me crazy but I would love her even if something had cracked deep inside her and she pulled a gun on me. I'd love her even more if she pulled the trigger."

Seargant was shocked. "Why even *more* if she shot you?"

Tom looked to his new friend. "Because if things ever got *that* bad, that's when she would need me the most."

Tom was spent and suddenly felt the need to break from the conversation. Changing his demeanor, he rose and looked to Seargant, thoughtfully.

"Same time tomorrow?"

"Absolutely," Seargant said, grinning. "By the way, I have a conference call with my men at noon and I'd like you to be there."

"Thanks for including me," Tom said. "I'm gonna walk to the store and pick up some fruit, yogurt, and water."

Seargant watched Tom go. "You know that store is about two miles away, right?" he yelled.

Tom didn't slow, but looked back and waved. "Then I'll take a long walk."

CHAPTER 27

Phillipsburg
Saint Maarten

The Island Hopper stood in the bright morning sunshine, studying the red brick under his feet. With three cruise ships in port, people of all types hurried around him; dashing in all directions and eager to start another day in paradise.

The colorful vendors were out in style, as were the cabbies and street performers. All were more than ready to greet the tourists and the fresh money that came with them.

He smiled at it all, wondering which one of these unfortunates he would choose to play with. It humored him, the disparity between real life and the media's coverage of things. For almost two weeks, he'd been watching the news—just like everyone else—about the maniacal happenings in the Caribbean islands. There was a senseless killer on the loose and everyone was at risk!

He'd seen footage of the crime scenes and the commentaries from law enforcement in each jurisdiction. He'd listened to the FBI's speeches and promises, and even watched as the reports expanded to the home towns of the victims. The media had even compared him to Jack the Ripper—a title he actually appreciated—due to the killer's brazen ability and his confidence in operating in public places.

But what humored him most was the dark outlook and absolute terror the media portrayed. It was as if the entire Caribbean was under attack. It was a death trap, with evil lurking around every corner.

But to physically be in the islands and take the pulse of the Caribbean, with all of the excited people spilling into the seaside market places, it was still a bustling paradise. No one had a care in the world.

The disparity only worked in his favor.

Were they that naïve or just ignorant? Don't they know that they all belong to me? Do they really think they are safe just because the temperature is in the eighties and the relaxing sounds of steel drums are being carried through the air?

Suddenly the killer felt a tug on his shirt and was startled to see a local teenage boy looking at him. The Island Hopper jerked back. He'd been in such deep thought that he hadn't heard or even felt the boy's presence, and now the two just stared at each other.

"Sir," the boy began. "Three beers for five dollars?"

The killer studied the boy and looked at the large plastic pails he carried. There were several bottles of Heineken and Amstel Light peeking through a domed covering of ice.

"It's a little too early," the Island Hopper said, politely, reaching for his wallet. "But here's a few dollars for the effort."

"Thank you, sir," the boy said, studying the money. Then he walked away and the killer's eyes followed him. The boy joined several others who looked over.

Not wanting attention, the Island Hopper moved with the crowd, eventually pausing at a plaque for John Philip Frederick Craane. He read with interest about the man's life, his devotion to boating, and his part in the island's history.

Then the killer continued past the long tan buildings with their orange roofs, finally entering the heart of Phillipsburg. The paths narrowed, neatly outlining the shops and restaurants, and he turned left toward the beach.

Removing his shoes, he fell into a state of calm. He felt the sand between his toes and enjoyed its cool, abrasive touch. The waves splashed a few yards away, and he treaded thoughtfully on the hardened, wet sand.

He looked up and to the right to see the high green hills of the island interior, before looking to the sky. A group of low clouds hovered over Great Bay and he could see the thinner ones dissipating right before his eyes.

He outwardly laughed. *Maybe the tourists were right. This is paradise and what could spoil it? What could possibly go wrong here?*

Of course he knew the answer, but as eager and capable as he was to deliver, it had to wait.

Feeling a pang of hunger, the killer looked to the casual eateries that hugged the waterfront. He saw Pagano's Bistro and the Big Wave Beach Bar, but finally stepped into the Harbour View Restaurant.

It was built on covered decking and was nothing special to the passing glance, with its bright red awning and simple atmosphere.

But fifteen minutes later, he was delighted to enjoy the best ham and egg omelet he'd ever tasted.

Swallowing a savory bite, he drank fresh orange juice and looked to the shoreline, where a handful of local boys were chasing a wayward chicken. Taking another flavorful bite, he closed his eyes as their excited laughs filled the air.

He ordered a bottled water to go, left a generous tip, and walked the beach to the Sonesta Great Bay Beach Resort.

Once there, he stood at the pool area and looked across the bay and to the arcing path he'd just walked. The people looked like ants from afar, and he again pondered who would be the lucky one.

But that was a day away and he still had much more to do.

Saint Maarten is one of the more unique islands; if nothing more because of the dichotomy between the Dutch and French sides. While he enjoyed the city-like markets, casinos, and laid-back feel of the Dutch, he also respected the French for their cuisine, shopping, and nude beaches. He was hoping to carve out some time to hit his favorite spots, but with all the planning for the next day, he wasn't sure if he could.

He could hardly contain himself through the excitement he felt.

The Sunset Bar and Grill is located at the base of Saint Maarten's Princess Juliana International Airport, huddled to the side between the runway and the Caribbean Sea. With a full menu of island food and drinks, it is one of the most remarkable outdoor bars in the world.

It also happened to be the Island Hopper's favorite.

A local guitarist had just finished his interpretation of Jimmy Buffett's "Pirate Looks at Forty" and was on break. So the only sounds were the water crashing onto the beach below, the traffic on the road nearby, and the cheerful banter of the patrons that were spread across the picnic tables.

The killer sipped a Heineken and studied the board that posted the incoming flights. There were nine listed, but only one held importance to him. It was one of the most crucial parts to the overall plan and he was eager to watch the aircraft arrive personally.

So far things were working perfectly. Everything was on schedule and all his pawns were in play. But his main concern was afloat at the Palapa Marina behind the Rancho Steak House, about a mile away.

Finishing the beer, the killer walked to the taxi line at the casino next door. As much as he wanted to celebrate his victories, he had to rest and prepare for tomorrow.

He would awake precisely at 2 a.m.; and that would begin a sleepless period of no less than twenty-four hours.

The next day would be a personal first for him.

The Island Hopper was, after all, going to murder three people in one day.

CHAPTER 28

At six o'clock, the morning had just started, but the Island Hopper had been working for several hours.

He'd already left a special surprise next to the police station in Phillipsburg. She was in a trash can in the adjacent alley; hidden by brush and a discarded cardboard box. He knew the trash collection schedule. She wouldn't be found for another day and that was all the time he needed to complete his next task and make a clean exit.

The killer was on St. Bart's and had been since 4 a.m., arriving by boat on the north-west side under cover of darkness.

The rocky shore meant less development, and it was quiet and vacant in the early morning. But he knew there would be a certain jogger passing by at a specific time at an exact stretch of beach.

Just as she'd done every Saturday, she jogged alone; wearing size-zero spandex shorts and a tight-fitting athletic top. Her iPod fit snug to her waist and she'd be listening to Hip Hop.

The Island Hopper was hidden within a rocky enclave and unseen as she ran by. He took a quick look around and then emerged, running hard behind her. He overtook her easily and brought her down hard on the sand.

Her first reaction was complete shock, as she opened her mouth in an empty scream. But this only helped him. He quickly pushed a soaked cloth of chloroform and ether into her mouth and waited out her kicking feet and flailing arms. She was physical but he was much stronger, and with her heavy breathing, she was unconscious in moments.

He gently placed her head on the sand and unpacked the carefully-labeled syringes. There were three in total, and he noticed the pancuronium bromide was still cold from refrigeration. He first injected her with five grams of sodium thiopental and then sat back to watch, imagining the chemical racing through her blood stream.

Within seconds her body relaxed and her breathing slowed, so he administered one-hundred milligrams of the pancuronium bromide. Next he picked up the syringe of potassium chloride but paused, wanting to watch the effects of the Pavulon before ending things.

This was what he was waiting for; the result of delaying the third drug! The pancuronium bromide had no sedative effects, but it also prevented her body from displaying pain, and he was eager to see the polarity of the two. He was also *very* aware that the Pavulon would eventually prove fatal by paralyzing her respiratory muscles and lead to death by asphyxiation, even without the potassium chloride.

Though unconscious, he noticed her eyes were open, so he sat back and watched the bulging, blood-shot balls that looked dead against the early morning sunlight. Her pupils were mere pinpoints; and although fixed, he could sense her body's compulsory need to react. Her lips remained pursed and were now turning blue. Her skin suddenly looked ashen and even seemed tightened against her body.

He was enthralled by the sudden transformation.

Satisfied, he injected her with potassium chloride and within seconds it was over. Her body relaxed, though her facial expressions were fixed in horror.

The Island Hopper sat back, staring at his specimen. "Goodbye Heidi," he said, reverently. "You did great."

Then he positioned two French Francs on her eyes, slung his backpack on his shoulder, and moved to the shoreline. He swam to his thirty-five foot Chris Craft just a hundred yards off shore, started the engine, and headed due north.

His next victim awaited him on Anguilla.

He took his time on the way over, noting that he had several more hours to prepare for his next kill. In the galley, he made a ham and egg omelet, though it didn't compare to the one the day before. He washed it down with fresh orange juice as he perused the world news stories.

Then he settled in behind his lap top and checked on the next part of his plan.

That afternoon the Island Hopper walked the powder-like sand of Anguilla's Shoal Beach, before pausing in front of Uncle Ernie's BBQ.

The temperature was balmy and the refreshing breeze thwarted any real humidity. Steel drums played in the distance from Mac and Hanks and the air carried the fresh smell of jerk chicken and ribs being cooked right on the beach.

Happy hour had long been under way, and everyone was enjoying their frozen rum drinks, as the immortal sounds of Bob Marley played.

The killer continued past the Ku Hotel and Elodia's, where the beach curved and defined the area between lower and upper Shoal Bay. It was an isolated stretch, boasting a point that allowed a view of both ends of Shoal Beach, but also a perfect place for the duty at hand.

The bend disallowed a visual to the busier eastern end and offered the extra degree of anonymity he sought. He looked up and down the shoreline, smiling at how perfect the spot really was.

He considered the sea and enjoyed a moment of contentment. He smiled at the sounds of the water lapping at his feet; watching as the short waves were thrown onto the sand with one more push from the sea.

He looked out at the fluorescent blue water that seemed to lift to the horizon. Then his eyes drifted to the sky, where the sun now favored the west and forced sparkles on the water as far as he could see.

Even *he* couldn't believe the horror that was about to unfold against the backdrop of such beauty.

He casually turned to see the woman he'd chosen to play with. She was in her late sixties, physically fit, with long silver hair that was tied in a pony tail. She wore a white floppy hat, black sunglasses, and a simple red one-piece bathing suit. She was walking the beach a couple hundred feet away and *definitely* unaware of her predicament.

The Island Hopper grinned as she started back to her beach chair. So he moved under a few palm trees and waited for the kill to happen.

Literally.

The poison had already been delivered and was mixed into the water bottle that was peeking out from her cooler. He was just waiting for her to take one small sip and it would all be over.

The excitement washed over him and he fought to remain calm. But as thrilled as he was, he felt impotent being a voyeur in his own game.

It was an interesting scenario for sure. His other kills were so personal, with each of his victims so close before they'd died. Some gasped, while others fell silent. Some soiled themselves, while others just seemed to accept their fate. He wondered what this one would do. How would she meet her end? What an interesting thing to watch!

He'd always been fascinated by death, but what was most interesting was watching someone die when they had no idea they were about to. One second she'd be enjoying herself; the next she'd be gasping for her last breath.

The Island Hopper saw her plop down in her chair. She threw her legs into the sand and dug her feet in to get comfortable. Then she turned to her cooler, picked up the tainted water bottle, and moved it to her lips.

She took a large gulp before withdrawing and throwing the bottle down. The killer knew her entire mouth and throat was burning and the sensation was growing exponentially faster than her mind could process. He only hoped that she didn't go into shock because that would ruin the fun.

Throwing herself from the chair, she lurched onto the sand and clutched at her throat, spitting wildly. Her body convulsed so violently that it looked like her skeleton would burst through her skin. Her mouth opened and although she moved to scream, nothing came. He studied her from afar, watching as her innards erupted in turmoil.

Does it really taste like burnt almonds, sweetie?

Finally she drove her body into the sand and stopped moving.

He looked in every direction. No one was coming to her aid. No one had even noticed.

But the waves still came and the birds continued to call out from the brush. The sun still shined and nothing had changed in the immediate episode.

Strike three. You're out, he thought, as he looked to the coins in his gloved hand and moved to the lifeless body.

CHAPTER 29

Kralendijk
Bonaire

Tom Brightwell studied Seargant as another conference call entered its third hour.

Seargant had been on his feet the whole time, pacing the room and dictating orders, methodically. He was wired into over a hundred others that were either embedded on islands throughout the Caribbean, or in the many FBI hubs that supported their efforts. Tom was the only one physically with Seargant.

In the week since they'd met, Tom and Seargant had become quick friends. But Tom had garnered an even greater respect for the man as an investigator. He likened him to a maestro leading a great orchestra, and was fascinated at how he controlled the flow of information.

Seargant was talking to Otto Varatek. He was the FBI's most senior profiler and had been at the Behavioral Science Unit since it was formed in 1972.

"So Otto," Seargant began. "What are your thoughts? What do your five decades of experience tell you?"

Otto's voice was loud and crisp. "As with most serial killers our guy is deliberate, intelligent, and patient. He's also demonstrated extreme confidence and a total narcissistic mentality.

"But what really concerns me is that he's capable of killing in different ways and is successfully maneuvering in different *places*.

"These islands have barriers of entry, with varying cultures and infrastructure. Typically serials stick to the same manner of killing within a general geographic area to maintain a better level of control. In my opinion this is the most talented killers I've ever investigated."

"What's he like? Who does he resemble?" Seargant asked.

It was a typical inquiry and Otto was expecting it. Investigators always wanted to get a baseline read on a suspect and draw on history for anything that could help.

"Again, this guy is different in many ways, but to cut to the chase BTK and the Zodiac Killer come to mind. He's probably got the cunningness and intelligence of Bundy as well."

"What about style?" Seargant inserted.

"What's interesting is there is no sexual element, so you can throw out Ridgway, Cunanan, Gacy, and Gein. But he may have a hint of the Hillside Strangler. Not the sexual part, but the possibility that there may be more than one of them. He's not killing children so you can discount Mughal and Chikatilo; and I don't think he's psychotic or cannibalistic so you can eliminate Dahmer, Chase, Fish, and Berkowitz."

"You don't think he's crazy?" Seargant called out, almost shouting into the phone.

Otto cleared his throat. "Actually I don't think he's crazy at all and I define it in the truest sense of the word. What I mean is I don't think he's *psychotic* and hearing voices like Albert Fish or Son of Sam. I agree that all killers are sick, but this guy is way too deliberate. Must I remind you that he built a working guillotine?!"

"He's just a man, Otto."

"I know but he may be a different *kind* of man."

"What do you mean?"

"I'm almost sure he's a white male, because most serials tend to stay within their own race; but the composite is contradictory because he's only killing men and there's no sexuality in his style."

"So what's that tell you?"

"That he's a pure hunter, which is the worst kind of serial."

"Tell me how we're gonna nail him."

"Unfortunately Seargant, I think we'll have to either get lucky or he'll make a mistake. I think he resembles BTK because he's stalking his vics and the coins are a form of taunting, which was what got Dennis Rader caught.

"But I'm afraid he may resemble the Zodiac more, due to the pure patience and intricacies, and *he* was never caught. We may have to wait until he strikes again and hope one of our agents is on-site. Obviously he's moving with great ease, so I'm sure you're checking out the possibility of multiple killers?"

"Please hold, Otto," Seargant said, flatly, tapping a button on his display as another analyst joined the conversation.

"Dave Kush, bring me up to date on the entry points."

"Flamingo airport is shut down and every marina is wrapped up tight. We have our guys interviewing every boat captain or owner—commercial or otherwise—that have been out in the last couple weeks, and passport files have been pulled going back three months. Helo's have been in the air, spanning out and covering a one-hundred mile area, but we think it's futile."

"Thanks Kush, but stay on it. And I want us to control birds in every major island and have them ready to go."

Seargant again tapped his screen and Otto came back on line. "What about the murders themselves and where do the coins come in?"

Otto sighed, as if pained. "I think he has an over-fascination with death, as if he respects it more than life itself. All of the kills thus far have been very personal; meaning that each victim came in physical contact with him. Then the killer even stays with the victim post-mortem to place coins on their eyes."

"Where are we with that angle?"

"I've spent a great deal of time on what we refer to as signatures and posing. I really think it's just a game he's playing. It doesn't mean anything; just something to keep us thinking.

"I'm almost convinced it's a dead end and will not be a factor in stopping him. The only way it would be helpful is if there was a finger print left on the coins or some other traceable factor."

"Still," Seargant began. "It means a great deal to him so treat it with a little more respect. Perhaps put one of your guys on it for me."

"I actually have Ken Silverman on line. He is the authority on this exact topic and I'd like to yield to him."

Seargant heard the clicking sounds as Silverman was brought into the mix. "Good day Agent Silverman. What do you have for me?"

Silverman fumbled at first, but quickly recovered as he spoke about the historic meaning of placing coins with the dead. He sounded as if he was just out of school, but there was no doubting his knowledge on the subject.

"There are many derivatives as to where it started," he began. "Some say it's an old Magyar custom to close the eyes of the dead with silver because if they remain open, the living can see their *own* death captured in the eyes of the deceased."

Silverman paused before continuing.

"But most say—and I agree—that it's based in Greek mythology. In that culture, Charon was the ferryman of Hades, and carried the souls of the dead across the rivers Styx and Archeron. They believed these rivers divided the world of the living from the dead. A coin—typically an obolus or danake—was placed in or on the mouth of the dead as payment to Charon. It was believed that those who could not pay had to wander the shores for one-hundred years."

"I thought it was on the *eyes*," Seargant interjected.

"That's what most people think, because there have been movies showing that. But there is no historical truth suggesting placement on the eyes. It was in or on the mouth, or even in the hand of the deceased."

"And this was only with the Greeks?"

"Actually the practice continued into the Roman era, where the coin was usually bronze or copper; and even in Germanic burials, but we know they had a preference for gold. The custom is also evident in the Jewish culture. Though they would never have placed coins with the dead, because it would be idolatry, there have been instances of Jewish ossuaries containing a single coin and boats are sometimes depicted on the walls of Jewish crypts. In fact Charon's obol also appears in tombs throughout Scandinavia and even in Christianity starting in Britain with—"

"Okay, okay," Seargant interrupted. "What's the *significance* of it all?"

"In Latin, Charon's obol is sometimes called a viaticum, which means 'provision for a journey.'"

Seargant sighed. "So what's the *relevance?*"

There was an extended pause and Agent Silverman let out his own deep breath.

"I believe there are only three conclusions we can draw and none help us. First, it may be a sign of respect, as if he's sorry for the kill and feels compelled to send off the vic with a token of appreciation. Second, it's just a signature that allows him to take credit for each killing. But I really think it's the third reason."

"Which is?" Seargant prodded.

"To waste time and throw us off. To send us on a wild goose chase and make us over-think it. Quite frankly this conversation is exactly *why* he's doing it; to throw resources in the wrong direction while he embeds himself in his next venture."

"I understand but just keep on it. Otto you mentioned 'posing' as well."

Otto came back on line. "There's a difference between staging and posing; the latter being present only in serial killings and in less than 1% of all murders. Staging is moving the body to cover the crime scene or mislead authorities and is almost always done by a disorganized and opportunistic killer. Posing is done post-mortem to satisfy the whims of the killer. I want to be clear that it is in no way designed to cover up the murder, but rather exploit and celebrate it."

"So what are your conclusions?"

"I have found absolutely nothing of significance. I'm with Silverman here."

Seargant's cell phone buzzed. As he was thanking Otto, he glanced at the caller ID and picked up.

"This is Seargant."

"Sir, this is Dillon in St. Barts. There's been another one."

"Go on."

"I'm on my way to the crime scene and will call you within the next several minutes."

"I'm coming to you now, Dillon."

Seargant looked at Tom and then tapped his monitor, creating an open channel to everyone on the call.

"There's been another one, people. This time in St. Barts. I'm en route and I'll upload my report to the main for your view by day's end. We'll continue this call at the same time tomorrow."

He disconnected and then looked to Tom, grimly.

"Ever been to St. Barts?"

CHAPTER 30

Tom held his breath as the small plane jerked downward over the rocky hillside, before descending aggressively into the airport on St. Barts. Terrified, he grabbed the chair armrests and peered out the tiny window, certain of an impending crash.

But as steep as the decline was, he heard the constant moan of the engines, and saw the brown terrain beneath him give way to asphalt and the inner-workings of a small airport. He couldn't believe that the runway was literally carved into a valley. Suddenly he felt the thump of the touchdown and was thankful when the plane slowed and eventually stopped.

In the cabin, Tom watched Seargant receive word of yet *another* murder on neighboring Anguilla, and he'd had taken the news badly.

Tom studied his new friend and partner, trying to read his mindset. It was clear they both felt the same sense of helplessness. There were now *two* more dead bodies and they were no closer to finding the killer. They felt like they were just trailing a murderer; always one step behind. Were they just voyeurs within their own investigation?

Still, Seargant remained on task. He didn't seem to notice the harrowing landing that almost made Tom throw up his breakfast.

The plane hadn't even come to a full stop when Seargant rose and moved to the exit. He was the first one in the waiting van and was barking orders at the driver before Tom had even left the plane.

The drive took ten minutes. Once there, Seargant made another hasty exit and darted to the crime scene. His dress shoes looked awkward on the beach but did little to slow him. Tom followed, carrying some evidence bags, and finally caught up as the crime scene opened up before them.

From what they could see, the victim was a very physically-fit and pretty thirty-something female, with long blonde hair in a ponytail. Her eyes were open, frozen in terror, but there was no blood or outward evidence of trauma.

Agent Dillon rushed over to Seargant. He'd been designated to St. Barts.

"What do you have?" Seargant asked, kneeling next to the body.

"Sir, this is Heidi Bradley. Age thirty-three, married for six years with no children. She's from northern Europe, I believe Finland, and her husband is standing behind you at the perimeter."

Seargant didn't turn around, not wanting to break from the flow of information. Instead he eyed Dillon, keenly.

"The body was found by a jogger who notified the police. She's here as well. The vic hasn't been moved and as you can see there are coins on the eyes. We are very aware of the tides, but they will be low for another couple of hours, which will give us plenty of time. The coroner is here, as is the local police chief, and both are yielding jurisdiction to you."

Seargant nodded solemnly, looking to the others. "I want three copies of pictures developed, categorized, and documented in three identical files. Take the body to the coroner for a complete autopsy and I want the results ASAP.

"Interview the husband and put that in the file as well. Find out if they were getting along. From here on out, with the media coverage gaining spirit, we must be aware of possible copycats as a means to an alibi.

"We'll meet in Saint Maarten this evening to review this case."

"Understood, sir," Dillon said, nodding.

Seargant rose and took a step back so that Dillon, Tom, and he were in a small triangle.

"What do you see, Tom? Talk to me."

"It looks like it happened at daybreak and this was probably a daily routine for her. He may have tracked her for some time and may not be as opportunistic as we think. He was either disarming to put her at ease or very physical."

Tom paused and looked around. "I bet he was hiding in that enclave over there," he added, pointing.

Seargant nodded in agreement, scanning the beach. His eyes settled on the helicopter that had been provided by the local authorities.

"Let's go, Tom. We're off to Anguilla."

CHAPTER 31

Phillipsburg
Saint Maarten

By early evening the FBI had taken over the main conference room of police headquarters in Phillipsburg. Since them, Tom, Seargant, and a dozen other FBI agents were pouring over every detail of the murders in neighboring St. Barts and Anguilla.

Saint Maarten was in view of both islands, and because it was larger, had an international airport, and more infrastructure, it was deemed perfect for a central command post. The Dutch authorities had also become overwhelmingly more supportive and had insisted on it.

The call came in from the main operator and was transferred into the conference room, where Seargant placed it on speaker.

"This is Seargant. Go ahead."

"This is Ruthi Walker from the coroner's office and I have the results for both of your victims."

"Go ahead, please."

"The one on St. Barts had a combination of three chemicals in her system. There were traces of sodium thiopental, pancuronium, and potassium chloride, and three needle punctures in her arm. This is suggestive of a formal lethal injection execution."

Seargant was listening intently, absorbing everything. "Are they difficult to obtain?"

"They are not available at the corner store, but it would be naïve to think that a motivated person couldn't acquire them over time."

"Where are these chemicals generally found? Can they be traced?"

"I doubt they could be traced, because they're available all over. PC can be used to make fertilizer, as a means for general water treatment, in heat packs, and as a fire extinguishing agent. Medically it's used to treat hypokalemia, as an electrolyte replenisher, and in cardiac surgery. The other two are almost *always* used medically; sodium thiopental as an anesthetic and pancuronium as a muscle relaxant. But come to think about it—"

The coroner cut herself off.

"What is it?" Seargant asked, quickly.

"It may be nothing, but there was a serial killer named Efren Saldivar who used a lethal dose of Pavulon, using the compound pancuronium, back in the States in the late 1980's. He killed at least six people under his care. There was also a guy named Richard Angle or Angelo who killed using Anectine. It could be something to look into."

Seargant was scribbling notes, furiously. "We'll look into that, but talk more about this style of execution."

"It's generally painless when done properly, but the victim had significantly more than the normal dosages in her system."

"What's that tell you? Was he sloppy or going for overkill?"

"It could mean several things, really," the coroner started. "But I don't think it was accidental. The high level of sodium thiopental was probably used to save time in bringing her into a coma-like state in a matter of seconds instead of almost a minute. I cannot determine the exact levels of PB due to the time lapse, but the amount of PC was *definitely* excessive."

"Could he have wanted her to suffer more or make sure of her death?"

"It's actually a good thing that he administered more PC. She would have easily died from the PB and the PC just sped it up."

"What about the second victim?" Seargant asked.

"Sixty-five year old Lori Frank voluntarily consumed a mouthful of cyanide. She drank from a tainted water bottle, but there were coins on her eyes, so the killer was close before and after death."

"And it was cyanide?"

"Potassium cyanide. It's not as available as the others, but certainly attainable and even simple to manufacture, given a respectable knowledge of chemistry."

"So does this guy have a medical background?"

"That's difficult to say. The needles on Heidi Bradley's arms were not professionally administered, but that may be a function of a struggle or his abbreviated time frame. The dosages were not accurate with either victim, but again that could have been to save time as well."

"So this guy wasn't fooling around."

The coroner sighed. "No Mr. Seargant. I'm afraid he knew *exactly* what he was doing."

CHAPTER 32

The Sonesta Great Bay Beach Resort & Casino sits on a high cliff in Phillipsburg, Saint Maarten; and hosts a spectacular view of the Caribbean. It's about a mile from the police station and was a perfect place for Seargant and Tom to stay.

With the pastel-colored buildings of the downtown area hugging the interior of Great Bay, and the shimmering aqua water swelling outward, it was the most incredible view Tom Brightwell had ever seen.

But Seargant and Tom were not discussing the sights or the balmy weather. They were sitting at a table in the far corner of the patio, brainstorming about the recent killings and discussing how to prevent others.

They both knew that it wasn't a matter of if, but when.

"So what's your gut telling you, Tom?"

"I think the key is mobility. How's this guy moving around so easily? Is it by private boat or plane? I just can't believe there are multiple killers."

"I totally agree," Seargant said.

"I also don't think he'll ever be satisfied," Tom added. "His desire to kill is insatiable and he's a unique kind of animal. Your profilers are spot on. I mean, not only does he kill in different ways but he demonstrates great confidence in different locations. I agree with Otto that we're gonna have to get lucky. You may want to alert the media like they did with the Unabomber. Just to see if anyone knows someone that could be our guy."

"But that also ushers in the crazies, yielding thousands of leads and wild goose chases. I'm just not ready for that yet."

Tom raised his hands in mock surrender. "This is your deal Seargant and I know I'm just here for the ride. But you're dealing with a killer that actually built a guillotine; and then successfully used it to kill someone, only to disappear with ease and leave no clues! Again do you understand the *patience* and *forethought* that went into that?"

Seargant remained stoic. "How are *you* doing so far?"

Tom was taken back. He wanted to maintain the current train of thoughts, but respected Seargant's want to end the conversation.

"I'm okay."

"That's not what I meant. By my calculation, you haven't had a drink in over a week. How's it been?"

Tom looked at Seargant and saw the man eyeing him, skeptically.

"I don't bullshit, Tom. I don't have time for it and it doesn't do any good. I respect you and to be honest I *need* you. If you don't want to talk about it that's fine, but an open dialogue is always better."

"No, it's okay. At first it was hard, but with my daily workouts and the focus of the investigation, I have a renewed energy and outlook. I don't miss the alcohol and I thank you for that. I'm already down fifteen pounds and feel five years younger."

"Well let's hit the gym, then. It'll get our minds off things for a while."

"Fine with me," Tom said.

But when Tom stood and looked around, his face paled. He swung behind Seargant, grabbing his arm. Seargant's momentum carried him for a few feet, until both men were behind a large pillar.

"What the hell are you doing?" Seargant yelled.

"See that man?" Tom asked, pointing to the second floor terrace.

"Yeah, I see him. What's up?"

"That's Jeremy."

Seargant was taken back. "You mean *the* Jeremy; as in the one that almost married your daughter?"

"No the Jeremy that was *going* to marry my daughter but probably killed her instead."

Tom's hands went to his face as he fought a multitude of emotions. Seargant too, was surprised by the sudden exchange and development. He shifted to take another look at Jeremy, who had disappeared from sight.

Seargant turned to Tom, finding him red-faced and breathing erratically. Still, Tom's eyes peered directly into Seargant's.

"And you know what else?" Tom asked through short gasps. "If he's here I think he's probably the Island Hopper, too."

Jeremy was in a hurry.

He sped through the hotel lobby with a couple of light-weight bags. Dashing around people like a seasoned running back, he kept his head down and focused on getting through the lobby doors. His face was flush and sweaty from the movement and his demeanor spoke volumes. He was clearly agitated and in no mood to waste time.

Moving outside, he looked at the long line of people and the short supply of taxi's and openly cursed. The nearby tourists looked over and a young mother covered her son's ears, but Jeremy remained defiant. Exasperated, he took out a wad of cash and pushed it to the bell captain, before moving to a taxi and hopping in.

Anger in the crowd swelled, but Jeremy shoved even more cash in front of the taxi driver and ordered him to drive. The taxi leapt forward only to screech to a sudden halt.

In front of the car with his gun leveled, was Seargant.

The cabby held up his hands and Jeremy sunk into his seat in open disgust. Tom opened the car door and violently yanked Jeremy out and to the ground. Then the larger man placed his heavy knee into Jeremy's back and moved his head around so Jeremy could see him.

"How are ya, Jeremy?" Tom asked, sarcastically. "Remember me?"

Recognition flashed in Jeremy's eyes. But then the younger man showed his strength by snaking his body sideways and kicking Tom to the side. Jeremy was free, but just as he stood, Seargant tackled him and Jeremy went down hard.

In no time, Jeremy was cuffed and led back inside to an open office. Tom sat on a bench in the lobby, catching his breath and trying to make sense of what just happened.

Did they just apprehend his daughter's killer?

Did they just catch the Island Hopper?

CHAPTER 33

Jeremy was slumped over the table in the police interrogation room. His body was folded over the bolted-down steel table. His arms were at his side, with his legs stretched out underneath.

It had been seven hours since he was brought into custody and six since he'd had anything to eat or drink. Sleep, he was told, would be a distant luxury. He knew nothing about Dutch law, and although he'd requested an attorney and a phone call, neither wish had been granted.

Seargant had been unforgiving—even robotic—as his dark eyes burned into Jeremy. Even after hours of incessant questioning, the FBI-man seemed content and even eager to keep going. Seargant had stood the entire time, choosing to tower over Jeremy and pick him apart.

It was after midnight as Seargant peered down at his dejected prisoner.

"We've been to your hotel room, Jeremy." Seargant said, sharply. "We've also been on your boat here. Over a dozen agents are pouring over every inch of your life as we speak. Your wife is being questioned, as are all of your business associates, and a search warrant for your homes and offices are being prepared.

"Again, I have three very specific questions. Why were you in the Caribbean when you told your wife you'd be in London? Why were you checked into the hotel under an alias; and where did you get all of the fake passports?"

Seargant threw three passports on the table and eyed Jeremy as they slid in front of him. Jeremy withdrew in his chair, sighing loudly.

Seargant's large hands were flat on the table as he leaned down inches from Jeremy's face. Then Seargant's cell phone chirped, and he looked down to read a text message. He nodded to a guard and excused himself.

"I'll be right back, Jeremy. Believe me; we still have *plenty* to talk about."

Three doors down, the conference room was buzzing with activity. Seargant walked in and was greeted by several enthusiastic team members.

"What's up?" he asked to no one in particular, sensing the excitement.

Agent Hartley came to his side. "We went underneath his docked boat and found two air tight bags, connected to a submerged rope. The contents have been photographed and catalogued. Everything's in the next room and here's a print-out of what we found."

Seargant read the sheet, shaking his head. It was a list of chemicals, guns, knives, and an array of other weapons and supplies that could be used to commit murder. There were also coins from many of the Caribbean islands, more passports, cash, maps, and several pre-paid cell phones.

"Book him into the custody of the Dutch and put him to bed," Seargant said. "I've got to talk to the Attorney General about extradition. Let's meet back here at 6 a.m."

Seargant looked over to see Tom sitting in the corner with his head in his hands.

Seargant walked over and Tom perked up. "It looks like we got him, Tom."

CHAPTER 34

Seargant was literally staring at the phone when it rang.

Lying in bed, his mind was racing. He was unable to sleep and was watching the hotel phone/clock display it to be 3:55 a.m.

The phone didn't ring twice before Seargant sprang to attention.

The news was alarming. Another body with coins on the eyes had been found, and she'd been left in a trash can outside of the police station that he'd just been at!

Several thoughts fought for control. Did Jeremy kill her just before being arrested? Was that why he was in such a rush to leave the day before? Was it pure coincidence that he and his men were so close to the latest murder?

Within minutes, Seargant, Tom and a handful of FBI agents were in cars, snaking down the narrow roadway into Phillipsburg. Tom sighed as he regarded the small homes and simple lean-to's that edged the crumbling asphalt. The front car slowed suddenly to avoid hitting a chicken and the movement only added to the tension.

The short entourage eventually turned left into a parking lot. Tom looked to the police station, which was a simple white block-like structure with small rectangular windows across the second floor. Then he walked behind the others, as they joined the assembly of local police at the crime scene.

But Tom couldn't have expected what happened next. The discussion he walked into was not about the dead woman on police property, directly to their right.

They learned that Jeremy had escaped.

And he probably had a lead time of at least two hours.

CHAPTER 35

It wasn't even 6 a.m. and Seargant felt like he was halfway into a busy day. After the excitement of apprehending and interrogating Jeremy the day before, they were dejected to learn of yet another murder and their suspect's escape.

The crime scene had been photographed and the body removed to the coroner's office. Local law enforcement and a handful of FBI agents were canvassing the area for clues and eye witnesses, but no one was optimistic.

Seargant looked over to Tom and frowned. "I can't believe it either," he said, guessing the man's thoughts. "It's my fault for booking him into custody, rather than keeping him at the interrogation level. I didn't know it meant a different wing with less security."

Tom nodded. "I spoke to the chief. He said they're not set up for long-term holds. There were only three in-house officers overnight and a door twenty feet away from Jeremy's cell led directly outside. It was locked, but every cop holds that key. They're sure it's an inside job."

"I still feel horrible. We had him."

Tom spoke evenly, trying to hide his frustration. "At least we caught Jeremy by surprise and now he's on the run and making important decisions without the benefit of time, money, or thought. He'll make a mistake and we'll get him."

But Tom was surprised at how optimistic he sounded. In truth, he was seething and barely able to maintain control. But he couldn't let Seargant know. He had to be level-headed to stay on the team and make a difference.

But Tom was not only reeling over Jeremy's escape and yet another dead body. He was totally unprepared to see him. The man who almost certainly killed his little girl.

Seargant turned to Tom. "Our guys are taking over the investigation of escape. Why don't you take a break and we'll meet after lunch at the hotel?"

Tom spent the next several hours in isolated contemplation. He walked back to the hotel and went straight to the fitness center. After a quick shower and a light breakfast of fruit and strong coffee, he sat at his hotel room desk and started writing some ideas about the investigation.

He created time lines, analyzed key points, and sharpened his own evolving composite of the killer. In deep deliberation, the hours passed and it was almost noon. He suddenly felt the need for fresh air and a change of scenery, so he decided to sit by the pool.

With his feet sprawled out and a large umbrella overhead, he stared at the pool in the near and Great Bay in the distance. The tranquility consumed him. He felt like he was in an invisible bubble and he cherished the alone-time to regroup. He'd always considered himself a loner, and although he welcomed teamwork and synergy, he often was most productive alone.

It had been ten days since he'd joined the Island Hopper investigation, but things had changed so much. He thought of his life in Chicago and smiled at the disparity. It wasn't just the physical differences in location, but his mentality and perspective as well.

He'd stopped drinking, bettered his diet, and begun a detailed exercise regimen. The busy investigation had forced him to flex his mind and he'd even found a new friend in Jack Seargant.

Tom had already felt the efforts in his waist and in his mental agility. His energy level hadn't been as high for a long time, and he'd been waking early each morning with a sense of purpose and clarity.

So for three days he continued his routine, with early morning work-outs and healthy breakfasts. While Seargant and his team were busy with their duties, Tom would read their summaries and feed it into his own working composite.

Now he again sat in a pool-side lounge chair and reflected on the latest victim.

The coroner had worked hard and fast to complete the latest autopsy, and it confirmed what Tom had already hypothesized. She had been dead for at least twenty hours before being discovered and well before Jeremy's arrest. Although there were three killings in one day, and even though the third victim was discovered last, she was most definitely the first murder of the three.

This meant the killer was on a specific time table and didn't want the latest body to be discovered until much later.

Why was that, though? Tom thought. *To keep the authorities away from Saint Maarten and concentrated on Anguilla and St. Barts? To buy time?*

He switched his line of thought to the methodology used and the victim herself. Twenty-two year old Claudia Ramjon was a local prostitute and sometimes drug-user that ran with a questionable crowd. She hung out on the beaches and walked Phillipsburg making money any way she could.

There were no outward signs of struggle or bruising on her body, which meant she had trusted the perpetrator. There was no DNA under her nails or trace evidence of her killer.

Tom closed his eyes, remembering the crime scene. It was far simpler than any of the others. Folded into an over-sized trash can, along with some clutter, was the latest victim, with two guilder coins on her eyes. Several feet away there was a large bucket of water and the coroner confirmed she'd died from a forced drowning.

But what intrigued Tom most was that she was so haughtily placed next to the police station.

The Island Hopper was most certainly testing different ways to die, but was he now making statements?

Tom could only hope that an ego was forming.

CHAPTER 36

"Don't do it," the woman said, looking over at Tom Brightwell.

"Excuse me?" he asked, politely.

"I know that look all too well."

She was sitting alone at the outside tiki bar, swirling an icy pink concoction and looking him over from several feet away. A bubbly red-haired woman in her mid-fifties, she was naturally pretty, with a polite southern manner that called to him.

"What look?" Tom asked, playing along and closing the distance between them.

"I saw you come down about two hours ago and once you saw the bar, you stopped in your tracks. You've been milling around here as if the drinks were calling you. I don't mean to offend you but my late husband was an alcoholic and I know that look."

"It's that transparent?" Tom asked, looking down and shuffling his feet.

"I don't mean anything by it. I just hope you don't give in. How long has it been?"

"May I?" he asked, taking the empty stool to her left. "It's been almost two weeks."

She nodded, thoughtfully. "I'm Dannie Sullivan," she said, shaking Tom's hand. "It's actually Danielle, but being the only child of an Irish father and the 'Oh Danny Boy' song, I became Dannie pretty quick."

"I'm Tom Brightwell."

"I know who you are and believe me I'd consider a drink or two if I were you."

Tom was perplexed and it showed on his face. But before he could ask, she explained.

"I've been here for a week and you've been on the news."

The media had done their research. They'd quickly learned of Kelly's unsolved murder in Jamaica a decade earlier. They knew there were coins on her eyes and inferred that she was the Island Hopper's first victim.

Even as Tom repeatedly declined their interview requests, they'd aired a comprehensive news story a couple days before. They filled in the blanks with their own opinions and even showed recent coverage of Tom working with the FBI. It was why Tom hadn't been working with Seargant as closely as he did on Bonaire.

"I'm so sorry about what happened to your daughter," Dannie said. "And I don't mean to pry."

Tom frowned and looked to the bartender, ordering a bottle of water. Then he glanced at Dannie, considering her for a long moment. She was direct, but there was no malice within her. No hidden agenda. He found her disarming and easy to be with, and was enjoying the interaction.

"I never mind talking about my daughter. Just because she's gone, doesn't mean she's erased from my memory. Even if it's in the past tense, I still enjoy speaking of her."

Dannie smiled and placed her hand on Tom's arm. "You are a very warm man, I can tell. You deserve every bit of happiness."

"Tell me about your late husband," Tom said.

"James was an amazing man and I miss him every day. But you have to live your life. It's like that Brad Paisley song. I picture him waiting on a bench for me in heaven and someday I'll pass on and we'll see each other again."

"I'm sorry I don't know music very well but that's a lovely image."

"Me either," Dannie said. "But my youngest daughter played it for me. James worked his whole life for his family. There was nothing he wouldn't do for me and our two daughters.

"He started his own plumbing business right out of high school and worked sixty-hour weeks. He took pay cuts and worked longer hours during the lean years so he never had to lay off an employee. He eventually took on a few partners and expanded into distribution. Then he sold it off and was able to retire in comfort. But then he started drinking more. He was able to kick alcohol for the two years before he died of a heart attack."

Tom regarded Dannie as she focused on something in the distance. She was a strong woman and he was entranced by her. She had pretty blue eyes that flashed when she spoke, and a presence that communicated both zeal and compassion. She was wearing a light cover-up over a one-piece bathing suit, but he could tell she was in great shape for her age.

Tom took a drink from his water bottle. "So you have two daughters?"

"And a granddaughter," Dannie answered, enthusiastically. "They are the light of my life and they're all here with me. Abby is thirty-five; her daughter Sara Ann just turned ten last week, and my other daughter, Cindy is thirty-two. Just four girls in the Caribbean having fun."

"Where are they now?"

"Today they went shopping on the French side. And they have a lot of excursions planned that aren't for an old lady like me."

Tom shook his head. "You're hardly an old lady. What are you, twenty-nine?"

"Slow down there; I'm actually the speed limit. Fifty-five."

"Really?" Tom asked, rhetorically. "Forty-five is also a speed limit and I think it's better suited for you.

"You're sweet," Dannie said. Her smile was contagious.

"So you're having a good time?" Tom asked.

"Absolutely," she said, with a quick wave of her hand. "I mean look at this view."

"What's the occasion?"

"My husband died three years ago this month. So every summer we take a vacation to celebrate him. This year it's two weeks in Saint Maarten."

"I'm sorry to bring it up; I'm sorry about James," Tom offered.

"It's fine," Dannie said, turning to him and holding his arm.

But then she softened. "The four of us were *everything* to him. He treated us like princesses and we didn't want for anything. And though I miss him, I just imagine what he'd say if he were an angel beside me."

Tom was enthralled. "What would he say?"

"Knowing James he'd say something like, 'I'm sorry I had to go but I'm in a better place now. Please let yourself be happy and take care of our babies. Don't stop living. I love you and you all make me proud every day.'"

Tom nodded in admiration. "You have thought a lot about it, haven't you?"

"Every day for the last three years. In the shower, late at night, driving in the car, in the supermarket, daydreaming while watching television. As cliché as it sounds, he really *does* live within my heart. Although I cannot see him in the physical, I feel him within me and in that capacity he's not gone. We were each other's best friends and he still guides me."

"I guess I never thought about it that way," Tom said. "I'm a widower and I always thought that Jess is gone and I'm selfishly living my life."

Dannie straightened. "It's good that you cherish your wife's memory, it really is. But we are *all* individuals on this earth; and even though marriage unifies us, we're still just independent souls working together. When we meet The Lord to stand judgment, we all do it alone."

"It's just hard. I feel so terrible that I'm here and she's not."

"What if it was reversed, then? What would you want *her* to do upon *your* death?"

"That's easy. I had plenty of life insurance that would pay off the mortgage and my pension would've taken care of her. Hopefully she'd live on and flourish; go out with her friends and find happiness. I guess *I'd* be on a park bench waiting for her, like that song."

"Are you chauvinistic Tom?"

"Not at all," Tom said defiantly, soured by the accusation. "She was my *world* and I catered to her every wish!"

"Then why wouldn't you allow Jess the same perspective? Why won't you let yourself live on in happiness?"

Tom moved his lips to say something, but fell silent. He looked down, avoiding eye contact and in a few brief moments, realized that Dannie was right. Still, he felt uncomfortable in his realization and took a quick drink of water.

"I've just never been disrespectful or dishonest with my wife, whether it was during her life or in regard to her memory. I guess I just need time."

Dannie smiled and patted her new friend on the back.

"That's the most important thing you've said so far, Tom. Time is a friend to us all. Whether you think it goes too fast or too slow or don't like what happens. Everything occurs within the scope of being alive between two ends of time; and being a good, thoughtful person is the most important thing of all."

Tom felt Dannie's warmth, both physically and mentally, but was compelled to change the subject.

"So where are you from?" he asked.

"Alabama. A beautiful place for sure, but nothing compared to this."

"I hear you," Tom said. "I love Chicago. I've been there my entire life. I didn't know places like this even existed."

He made a point to stare out to the Caribbean from their perch at the bar high above.

"Look at the sea from here," Tom began. "Doesn't it look fake, with all the different shades of blue?"

Dannie was bobbing her head in agreement even before Tom finished the words. "It's like God took a paint brush and spilled the most beautiful colors throughout the Caribbean."

Steel drums sounded from the far corner and Tom looked over to see two musicians banging on them, each smiling and swaying to the beat. Soon the place found its own pulse, with people dancing on the pool deck and moving in their bar stools.

Several hours passed and the conversation remained fluid and engaging. When the sun started to fade and the perimeter lights came on, both forgot they'd skipped dinner.

They were too wrapped up in each other to notice.

CHAPTER 37

Seargant frowned when he spotted Tom at the pool bar.

He was sitting comfortably next to an attractive woman. Both were smiling and laughing as they enthusiastically talked about things he couldn't hear. But Tom had no business anywhere near alcohol and Seargant walked over, purposely.

But then Seargant saw the water bottles and his mood lightened. Still, he needed to speak to Tom immediately.

"Tom," Seargant began, firmly. "I am *very* sorry to interrupt, but can I steal you away for a bit?"

"No problem," Dannie said, smiling. "I'm almost done with him."

Tom laughed, rising. "I'll be right back."

They walked to the hotel lobby, with Seargant guiding Tom to an empty bench.

"We know how Jeremy escaped. There were ten police officers on duty that night in Phillipsburg and three confirmed inside the precinct when it happened. All of them have been interviewed and cleared except one. Officer Willy Adamar is missing and so is his airplane."

Tom shook his head in disgust.

"I know," Seargant said. "He's a licensed pilot and has a small twin-engine plane. But it gets worse."

"How?"

"All of the Dutch islands—including this side of Saint Maarten—share the same prison system, with all the *real* criminals doing time on the south end of Aruba. It seems that Adamar was a former prison guard at the Aruba facility years ago, and he was a source of narcotics for the inmates there. Aruba is only seventeen miles off the coast of Venezuela."

"So you're saying this guy used to make drug runs into Venezuela?"

"He has ties to one of the major drug cartels. We think he's sought sanctuary there. He obviously knew Jeremy was worth hundreds of millions of dollars and took him along."

"Any family members we can talk to?"

"The kid's twenty-six years old. No wife; no siblings. He's not close to his parents, but he has an uncle in the local government here. I imagine he suppressed the prison drug thing and got him on the police force here. Of course he denied everything."

"So what are we gonna do?" Tom asked, breathing hard.

"We are already working with the State Department to try to get into Venezuela. But in case you haven't heard, Venezuela is hardly on good terms with the United States."

"Then we go in under the radar as civilians, right?"

Seargant shook his head. "Do you know anything about Venezuela, Tom? The cartels and dirty politicians run everything. It's practically an unchecked dictatorship. The cops are glorified henchman and the civilians live in fear. If Jeremy has any support, he'll melt into society and eventually rebuild a life. Hell, in five years he may even be married and be fluent in their language!"

Tom became openly angry thinking of the image. His face reddened and he spoke through gritted teeth. Seargant put his hand on Tom's shoulder, trying to ease things. Then he spoke calmly to his friend.

"I share your frustrations. Let's see where we get with the diplomatic route and we'll meet in the gym tomorrow morning."

Tom shook his head. "With all due respect, Seargant, you *do not* share my frustrations. You didn't have a daughter who was murdered while you watched helplessly, only to have the killer get away from the law twice."

"You're right, Tom. I'm sorry."

For a moment the two men sat and avoided eye contact. Tom was stewing in emotion, faltering amongst anger, helplessness, and frustration; while Seargant felt immobilized. He hadn't told his friend the extent of his conversation with his superiors. Especially that there was no possibility the FBI would be allowed in Venezuela. Or that the timeline alone suggested that Jeremy was already well within Venezuela and most likely being protected by the cartels in the south.

So Seargant looked to Tom and said the one thing he was thinking. "I *do* have some ties with the CIA. I can probably get us in by the end of the week. But it'll be off-the-books, very dangerous, and definitely illegal."

Tom looked over and for the first time in the exchange, he smiled.

CHAPTER 38

The next morning Seargant entered the gym to find Tom already deep into a set. This wasn't uncommon, but he was surprised to see who was with him. It was the woman from the bar the night before.

Dannie's hair was pulled into a pony tail; and she was dressed in a pink jumpsuit, matching headband, and stylish Brooks Adrenaline running shoes. She was stepping off the treadmill when Seargant entered, and he moved over to her.

"Hello," he said. "I'm sorry I didn't formally introduce myself last night. I'm Jack Seargant."

She accepted his hand and shook it with a smile. "I'm Dannie Sullivan," she stated in a sweet southern drawl. "It is so very nice to meet you."

Seargant liked her instantly. She was warm, charming, and confident. She was engaging and exacted a presence he found trusting. As he retreated to the far wall and began stretching, he paused to peer over at them. Dannie was helping Tom with some freestyle weights and they both looked genuinely happy.

Seargant couldn't help but smile. The night before, Tom had explained that Dannie had also lost a spouse, and Seargant was warmed by the thought of them healing each other.

Dannie pointed the remote at the flat screen television on the wall. The voice of a news anchor echoed in the small confines, as he reported the latest developments of the Island Hopper case. Seargant was on screen, speaking to a CNN reporter. Tom and Dannie looked over to him, but he was more focused on the free weights than the report.

He sensed their stares. "You might as well turn it up. It'll save me the time of telling you what I said."

". . . And where do you think the suspect is right now?" the reporter asked.

Seargant was visibly irritated, though his voice remained steady. "If I knew that, I would personally be there to take him down."

"Do you have a general *feel* of where he is?"

"It's an active investigation."

The reporter paused and Seargant changed the subject.

"My heart goes out to the families of these victims. That's all I have at this time."

Dannie turned the television off and apologized.

Tom and Seargant looked confused, so she went on. "I just feel awful for the families of these people, and for you having to be thrown into it all."

"We'll get him," Seargant said, flatly.

Dannie frowned. "I just hope no one else gets killed."

Then she looked over at Tom, compassionately. "And I really hope nothing happens to you."

CHAPTER 39

For three days Dannie and Tom were inseparable. They met at the gym for early morning workouts and grazed at the breakfast buffet. Then they would ready themselves for the day and hop into Dannie's rental car to cruise around Saint Maarten.

Tom had briefly met her two daughters and granddaughter, but they were busy with their own day trips.

Dannie's youngest daughter, Cindy, was very shy and had barely spoken. The older of the two, Abby, had been cordial but aloof, but *her* daughter Sara Ann was a ball of excitement.

The ten-year old girl shook Tom's hand formally and talked non-stop about everything she'd done on the island. She had a tall, thin frame and long dark hair. She was well-spoken, polite, and had large almond eyes that grew wider as she spoke. She was the most charismatic child he'd ever met and even reminded him of his Kelly at that age.

Tom didn't know if it was wise to spend so much time with Dannie. But the investigation was in a stall. Seargant and his team were working the three recent murders while trying to track Jeremy, but everything was a dead end.

No evidence, no witnesses, and a ticking clock.

With the recent developments, new personnel were flown in; and with the increased press coverage, Seargant told Tom to keep an even lower profile. But Tom didn't like sitting idly by. His mind was always teeming and churning out ideas about the case.

He'd awake at odd hours with thoughts that he'd scribble into his working composite. Though not visible, he was still connected to the investigation, and his FBI-issued cell phone gave him constant access to Seargant. He hadn't heard anything more about getting into Venezuela, but he also knew the FBI wasn't keen to the idea.

Still, Tom's respite from the case allowed him more time with Dannie. Their talks were therapeutic and energizing; and the more he got to know her, the better he felt about himself.

Their conversations were easy. One moment they'd be talking about their lives and delving into personal issues; the next they'd be laughing about something completely cosmetic. He appreciated the interaction; with the light-hearted conversation laced into the more serious speak. It was as if every conversation held a life lesson and he was starting to see things differently.

Tom had rarely spoken about his wife and daughter, and though sometimes tepid and even withdrawn, he trusted Dannie completely. So he told her everything, and in doing so became more emotionally attached to her. She reciprocated, and in only a few days it was as if they'd known each other forever.

The first day they'd biked along the deserted Cay Bay coast and around the Belair Pond to Fort Amsterdam. While walking the high grasses and touring the old canons, a sudden downpour swept across Little Bay and sheets of rain came down for several minutes. They left their bikes under a tree and crouched next to the short crumbling stone walls, before running to the chapel house for cover.

But the doors were locked, so they rushed back to the tree and knelt against its trunk. When the rain let up, they were drenched but laughing uncontrollably. Then they rode their bikes to Divi Little Bay Beach and enjoyed a casual dinner at the Toucan Café.

The next day Tom surprised Dannie by taking her horseback riding at Coralita Beach. For two hours they searched the winding trails adjacent to Great Bay and galloped in the surf. Then they sat on a blanket and enjoyed a light picnic of fruit, crackers, and cheese.

After another enlightening conversation, Dannie snuggled up to Tom. They held each other in silence and listened to the surf, not twenty feet away. The fine, white sand felt good between their toes and the warm air washed over them as evening drew near.

Tom felt the urge to speak, but with Dannie in his arms there was no need.

To their right, a family made their way to the beach and laid down several blankets. There were three small children, a man and woman in their forties, and an older couple, probably the grandparents. The kids ran to the water and photographs were taken. A bonfire was lit and they began toasting marshmallows.

Tom followed Dannie's line of sight as she regarded the group with a broad smile.

"Isn't that beautiful, Tom? I hope they know how lucky they are."

Tom nodded, massaging Dannie's arm and hugging her closer. "It certainly is," he said.

Then silence ruled as they watched the fire grow.

"Do you want to get a toasted marshmallow?" Tom asked. "When's the last time you had one?"

But Dannie was withdrawn, still looking the family over. "No," she said. "Some things should be left alone. Besides, there's nothing better than this moment."

The next day they walked Orient Beach, something that Dannie's daughters had chided her for. It was the largest nude beach on the French side, and although Dannie and Tom were rooted in morality and traditionalism, they both had a sense of spirit, adventure, and curiosity.

They remained clothed—as did more than half of the beachgoers—but the nude bodies offered little distraction. The new couple was more intent on each other.

They held hands as they walked the shoreline, then found a quaint beach bar where they sat and drank lemonade.

Fully content, Tom turned to Dannie to find her watching him. The setting sun cast an orange glow on her face and lit sparkles in her deep blue eyes. Her hair moved gently in the breeze and an easy smile showed her perfect teeth. Her skin was porcelain and seemed to light up against the darkening sky.

He took time to examine her, marveling at her beauty, both inside and out. He was amazed at the dramatic effects she'd had on him. He never thought he'd feel so alive again.

"What?" she asked, playfully. "What are you looking at?"

"The most beautiful thing in a long time," he said immediately.

The world seemed to dissolve around them as they looked into each other's eyes. And it was in that simple wooden lean-to, on two uneven bar stools, that Tom casually moved over to Dannie and they had their first kiss.

It was slow and easy, but charged with the emotions the last few days had cultivated. When they withdrew, they just peered into each other's eyes.

"Well Mr. Brightwell," Dannie said. "That was very nice."

Tom moved his lips but fell silent.

Sometimes words weren't necessary.

On the way back, Tom's cell phone rang.

He looked at the display, knowing it was Seargant. "This is Tom."

Seargant's voice was low and direct. "If you're still serious, I found a way into Venezuela, but we have to leave in the next couple hours."

Tom received the information with a smile. Then he looked to Dannie, who was driving the car. Though he hated to leave her; he'd never been so sure of anything in his life.

"I'll be ready," he said.

He was going after Jeremy.

CHAPTER 40

It felt like something out of a spy movie. But reality set in when the door of the Gulfstream IV shut tight and the low hum of the jet engines swelled.

Tom sat in the back row and counted six passengers plus a crew of three. He knew most of them from the investigations on either Bonaire or Saint Maarten, but a few others were new to him.

They all knew about him.

Tensions were high and there was no denying the uncertainty of the mission. Most were looking out the window into total blackness; no doubt contemplating what brought them to this place and time.

Everyone, it seemed, wanted to be somewhere else.

But Tom was excited about the possibilities. Would he finally confront his daughter's killer? Although ecstatic about the idea, he wanted to better understand the plan. Seargant had briefed him earlier, but the conversation had been hurried.

But a few things *were* clear. Seargant had managed to gain entry, albeit illegally, into Venezuela, and Tom was told to pack very light. More importantly, he understood that their mission was not sanctioned by the U.S. government, and Tom would be operating completely without their support. Few other details were available.

Tom craned his head to see Seargant at the front of the aircraft, consulting with the two pilots. The FBI-man had discarded his typical suit and tie, and now, like Tom, wore casual shorts, an un-tucked polo shirt, and sandals.

They were studying what appeared to be a map. After a hushed discussion, the captain jabbed his finger at the paper and nodded in angst. Then he moved into the forward cabin and started flipping switches. The co-pilot and Seargant glanced at each other, sharing a moment of concern, before moving to their respective seats.

The take-off was easy and uneventful, and if it weren't for the ambiguity and danger involved, Tom would have enjoyed every moment of it. At ten-thousand feet, the lights dimmed. The persistent moan from the engines was hypnotic and Tom fell into a well-needed sleep.

It wasn't until they landed south-west of Barinas that Tom awoke and looked out the window into complete darkness. The tiny, rapid flashing lights at the extremities of the jet wing were the only thing he could see.

When the plane jerked to a stop, everyone rose and moved to the exit, where a set of stairs unfolded into uncertainty. A bag of flashlights was sitting on a seat and each man took one.

Stepping down, Tom was hit with the humid, nighttime air as he walked where his flashlight pointed. He had no idea what to expect, so he treaded lightly, as if walking on an alien planet.

As he moved the flashlight to where the jet had come in, and the light stretched into the darkness, he outwardly gasped at the airstrip.

From what he could tell, it was no more than a narrow band of dirt road, cut into dense forestation.

But the coordinates were correct and it was more than adequate to handle the Gulfstream IV. When the jet took off and waned out of sight, Seargant, Tom and two FBI men hiked north for a half mile.

They eventually found the small hunting cabin that was promised, and some of the tension eased. Inside was an assembly of blankets and supplies on the wooden floor. There was also a lantern, some matches, a loaf of bread, and an empty pitcher; with instructions about the well outside. Thankfully, the generator was already working, and it lit a single light bulb and powered a coughing air conditioner against the only window.

The men went to work quickly, unpacking and arranging things.

Tom felt encouraged. But he also knew this was just the first stop in a journey that would be the biggest test of his life.

CHAPTER 41

The next morning Tom awoke with clarity and purpose; which he thought odd, considering the sleeping conditions and his current location.

The sun was just rising and Tom felt energized by its budding glow. The others were still asleep, spread across the hard floor, so he rose quietly and stepped outside.

Shutting the door gently, Tom moved away from the cabin to regard the area in total. He was looking out to a valley, flanked by flowing green hills that seemed to leap off the flush land. He saw old, broken fencing that suggested they were on the perimeter of a forgotten farm. In the distance he saw a few wild goats milling around.

He stretched and sucked in the fresh air. In his solace he heard the natural sounds of a stream and he made his way over, peering into the rushing water. A few small fish scurried away and he smiled at the encounter. Then he took out an energy bar and ate a small breakfast.

The sun shined on the grassy dew and the sounds of the flowing water relaxed him. But even with the natural beauty that abounded,

Tom concentrated on the next leg of the mission. Was Seargant really going to equip and enable him to go after Jeremy?

But then his thoughts were cut short. He froze at the sound of a cocking gun behind him. Then he heard deliberate footsteps closing in.

"Stop right there," Seargant said.

Turning, Tom was relieved to see his friend. But the feeling was short-lived when he saw Seargant's gun leveled at a man about twenty feet away.

The Venezuelan was middle aged, with peppered hair and a thin mustache. And although he had an AK-47 dangling from a long strap across his chest, he had a compassionate look that was disarming.

But Seargant held his aim, his eyes burning into the stranger. The FBI-man's stance was rigid and there was no mistaking his ability or resolve.

The man held his arms up and smiled. "I'm Emilio. The guide your friend arranged."

Seargant held his stance. "What's the password?"

"Pineapple."

Seargant relaxed and moved over, offering a quick handshake. The other FBI agents spilled out of the cabin and everyone looked to Seargant, wondering the next course of action.

"I have a truck, fully fueled and ready to go," Emilio said. "I understand you want to go to where the cartels are?"

"That's correct," Tom answered eagerly, which drew a swift look from Seargant.

"Señor," Emilio began with a thick accent. "Your friend said to take you to the south, but I must inquire why. It is just not safe, especially for men such as you."

The men remained silent.

"Can I at least ask why, then?" Emilio added.

Again Tom answered. "We are looking for a white man. An escaped killer. We think he has ties to the cartels."

Emilio sighed. "Then he is gone."

"What do you mean?" Seargant asked.

"The cartels are black holes, my friend. Once you are in there is no way out. There are no laws there. If they see you, you will be in great danger."

"Then we'll be in the right place," Tom said.

Emilio shook his head, conceding. "Okay, then. We'll be on the road until evening and then make camp off-road. The cartels run everything down there and are the only authority. I will take you as close as I can, but I will not stay."

Tom looked to Seargant. "This is it, then," he said, extending his hand.

Seargant accepted it and looked into Tom's eyes. "Can I talk to you for a few minutes?"

Then he turned to his men. "Load the truck with everything from the cabin."

The men left and Tom and Seargant were alone, standing next to the stream.

"You know this is probably a one way trip, right?" Seargant asked.

Tom looked down. "Yes. But I'm fully prepared."

Seargant continued. "Before we landed last night, I received a couple of confirmations. First, Jeremy and that guard *did* flee into

Venezuela along the route that we thought. Second, as you probably have guessed, our government is not pursuing him, so we can't come with you."

"I figured that," Tom said, flatly.

"Emilio will provide all the weaponry and supplies you'll need. I know you're trained and I don't question your ability, but are you certain you want to do this?"

"I have to. I've never been so sure of anything in my life."

Seargant shook his head and they regarded each other for several moments. Neither spoke, but each knew what the other meant to say. Something stirred within them, as if they didn't realize how strong their friendship had become. The silence was tense but not uncomfortable, and both men embraced.

Seargant spoke first. "If things get bad I want you to shoot first."

Tom nodded and broke away.

"And another thing," Seargant said, waving Tom's passport. "I took the liberty of borrowing your passport. The less anyone knows about you the better."

Tom nodded, starting a slow walk to Emilio.

"Give me a call when you come back," Seargant called out, sounding more optimistic than he felt.

But he was certain he would never see Tom Brightwell again.

CHAPTER 42

The pick up truck was nondescript in both age and model. It had likely been bright red several decades before, but was now dull orange in color. A generous amount of rust, dirt, and dents covered it from bumper to bumper, and Tom wondered if it would even run.

But soon Tom and Emilio were lumbering along the narrow, bumpy trail that led to the main road. Dense forestation and root systems edged the path, and low tree branches reached out and scratched the sides of the truck. The old vehicle groaned with each deep pocket and crevice it championed, but it somehow managed to keep going. Emilio seemed indifferent and stayed focused on their forward progress.

When they emerged from the woods and started south on the main road, the truck tested higher speeds and Tom welcomed the fresh air. It was early morning but very muggy, and the temperatures promised to be in the triple digits by noon.

Emilio settled in behind the wheel and looked over at Tom, speaking for the first time. "So do you know what you're doing here?"

Tom contemplated an answer but realized he didn't have one. He was focused on the end result, but the in-between was blurred. He decided on complete honesty.

"Not really. I'm an ex-cop following a killer into your country. He's being harbored by a cartel in the south. The only name I have is Martel."

"You probably mean Marco," Emilio stated, knowingly.

"Yeah that's it," Tom said. "You know him?"

Emilio was expressionless. "I know *of* him."

The Venezuelan fell silent, looking at Tom, dubiously. "So you know what you *want* to do, but you don't know *how* to do it?"

Tom smiled, humbly. "No I don't."

Tom was introverted and never one for idle conversation, but information was crucial. He was in a foreign land on an illegal mission. He had no authority and was tracking an accomplished killer who was being protected by a dangerous drug cartel. Furthermore, he didn't speak the language, and despite his daily workouts and recent weight loss, he was still a sixty-year old white American, all but lost in an unfamiliar land.

Emilio explained that the bulk of the Venezuelan people were farmers, laborers, and tradesman. They were family-driven and good people. But the government was a dictatorship; run by militants and a loose police force that was quick to accept bribes and take care of themselves.

Venezuela's biggest export was oil and the land was rich with it. The oil revenues allowed for an elaborate infrastructure that fed into Venezuela's second biggest industry, which was the refinement and transport of cocaine.

The drug cartels operated mainly in Columbia, but much of the product was transferred into southern Venezuela, where it was refined and efficiently moved out.

"Do they have any weaknesses; anything I can exploit to get my guy?" Tom asked.

"Their strength and weakness are the same," Emilio said. "It's money, and depending on how much you *have*, you'll know where you stand."

Tom frowned. Jeremy had more money than he could imagine; and Tom could only guess what kind of deal he'd struck to buy a new life.

"So where are you from?" Tom asked, changing the subject.

"Originally Columbia, but now Caracas. My family was moved here by your CIA, and that's how they sent you to me."

"Really?"

"You could say that they owed me."

"How's that?"

Emilio relaxed and his tone became conversational. "Your DEA and military, in connection with the CIA, used to run field training exercises in Columbia. They would parachute in, burn raw coca fields, and hump back to a landing zone for extraction. Some of these operations happened near my home and I came into information that saved many American lives. Basically, I was able to avoid what would have been a very bad ambush."

"Wow," Tom started. "The Columbia government allowed the United States to do that?! Basically attack them within their borders?"

"No, but they couldn't protest, because in doing so they'd be admitting they were the source of more than 75% of the world's cocaine. Instead, they let the cartels handle it and the silent war goes on."

"Did the cartels know you tipped the U.S. off?"

"No, they wouldn't have suspected me, but to be sure the CIA set me up in Caracas and calls on me from time to time. We are mutually grateful for what we've done for each other."

Tom had so many questions but didn't know where to start. He was amazed at Emilio's story and the lawlessness that abounded.

"Do the cartels run *everything* down here?"

Emilio loosened his grip on the steering wheel. Then he rested his left arm on the interior door, casually. He smiled widely, looking over to Tom.

"Do you want a quick lesson in the ways of Venezuela?"

"I think anything you say can only help me."

"Then I must start with Simón José Antonio de la Santísima Trinidad Bolívar. Do you know of him?"

"I don't even know what you just said," Tom said, laughing.

Emilio was unmoved. "Simon Bolivar. Ever heard of him?"

"The name sounds familiar."

"He is known here as 'The Liberator,' similar to your George Washington. He was an intellectual and very well-traveled for his time; moving throughout Europe and the United States in the early 1800's. He saw the conquests of Napoleon and the early accomplishments of your founding fathers. He commanded armies throughout northern South America and freed Venezuela, Columbia, Ecuador, and Peru from Spanish rule."

Tom stared at Emilio, absorbing every word.

"The reason I'm telling you this, is that our current leader has adopted Bolivarianism. It's basically a type of socialism, where the government consolidates the nation's industry and infrastructure, and pushes the government into the everyday life of the people."

"Is it a good thing?"

"It's *meant* to be a good thing; in fact that's why he calls it Bolivariansim, because Bolivar's name adds historical significance and credibility. But Venezuela is known for two things: oil and cocaine. And both lead to greed and corruption, which is *never* a good thing."

"How do you know so much about this?"

"To quote Cicero, 'To know nothing of what happened before you were born is to remain forever a child.'"

Tom looked over in amazement. Suddenly he saw a different man than the one he'd met an hour before. Emilio was not just a simple guide sent to help Tom, but a patriot and an intellect. A good man that believed in doing the right thing.

"The only quote I know is something one of my police captains told me once. Vincent was his name."

"And what was that?"

"It went something like: 'Men are like dogs and women are like cats. Men just need food, water, and a warm place to sleep. And who knows what women are thinking?'"

Tom smiled at the memory but Emilio looked perplexed.

"I know there's a language barrier between us but what does that mean?" Emilio asked.

Tom erupted into a laugh. "I don't know but I don't think it applied to me. My wife ruled the roost and I put her on a pedestal."

Emilio concentrated on the road and Tom looked out the window, considering the land that was flashing by. Their present route was a two-lane highway that wasn't heavily traveled. Large oil refineries dotted the landscape, and occasionally he'd see a farmer working a field. The sun was burning away the last of the morning clouds and the bright blue sky was striking.

But Tom wanted more information. "Getting back to the cocaine," he began. "Columbia is the big drug operator, right?"

"They are, but with such a large and unchecked border with Venezuela, and our cozy government alliance, they are able to use our substantial infrastructure for manufacturing, processing, and eventual export. There's about four-hundred tons of cocaine passing through Venezuela each year."

"Wow," Tom said, genuinely amazed. "How's it all work?"

"The Colombian drug cartels airlift raw coca or refined cocaine into jungle strips inside southern Venezuela for processing, literally about eight-hundred kilometers south of here. From there it's driven by road to military-controlled airports and loaded onto long-range aircraft. It's flown to West Africa; usually Guinea-Bissau, Senegal and Sierra Leone, before being moved into Europe."

"All this just goes on without any problem?" Tom asked, incredulously.

"Yeah, and even with the help of Venezuela's military and our CICIP."

"CICIP?"

"Venezuela Secret Police. You don't want to run into them. In fact, if you meet *any* resistance and you feel things are going bad you need to shoot first. The aggressor always wins here."

They continued to speak for several more hours. Emilio was an effective counselor and guide and it was obvious he had a passion for life. Tom was amazed at the man's stories, all of which offered valuable information for what lay ahead.

Tom opened up about Jess and Kelly, and his career as a Chicago cop, and the two men formed a speedy friendship. In the late afternoon they pulled into a small town south of El Jobal for gas, food, and coffee.

When the truck rolled to a stop in a gravel parking lot, Emilio looked over at his passenger, studying him for a long moment. Emilio's smile was gone. His casual demeanor turned rigid and he was gripping the steering wheel tightly.

"What's wrong?" Tom asked, looking around, concerned about their safety.

Emilio frowned. "I like you Tom. I can tell you're a good man and this is the finest advice I can offer."

"Go ahead."

"I must stress that you should always shoot first. Don't take anything for granted here. You'll definitely live longer."

But the information did little to discourage him.

"Thanks for the advice, Emilio," was all he could say.

CHAPTER 43

Tom stood next to the truck, eating a bowl of chicken, rice, and mixed vegetables. He took a long pull from a water bottle and stretched his legs. Then he walked to the tailgate and looked at a large box that was covered and tied down. Peering in, he saw the supplies that were meant for him.

Emilio walked over with his own bowl of food. Then he slapped the box, proudly.

"This should be everything you'll need over the next several days. You have a seven-pound tent, bug spray, three changes of clothing, a hat, hiking boots, three pairs of light-weight socks, sunglasses, a small pot for cooking, flint, a machete, bowie knife, flashlights and batteries, a first-aid kit, and energy bars, among other things."

Tom looked over the supplies.

"And what's in those?" Tom asked, pointing to two boxes in the rear of the cab.

"Two 9mm handguns, plenty of ammo, and a large crucifix necklace."

Tom was taken back. "Why the cross?"

"From now on you're a Christian missionary on a pilgrimage and you've been separated from your group. You are humble, unassuming, and in need of help."

"Shouldn't I have a bible then?"

"No way," Emilio said, flatly. "If they catch you, they could quiz you. The men you'll encounter will not have access to bibles, trust me."

Tom remained quiet.

"Here's a little money for you," Emilio said, handing over an envelope. "It's enough to get a little help along the way, but not enough to arouse suspicion. It's about $300 U.S."

"Thank you," Tom said, accepting the money.

They ate in silence for several moments; each wondering what was in store for Tom, but neither bringing up the realities. The odds were clearly against him.

Suddenly a soccer ball landed nearby and Tom was delighted to see about twenty schoolchildren running over to retrieve it. He hadn't noticed, but next to the small eatery was a large farm house with a cross on top. There was a small, one-story extension shooting off to the right, and a playground beyond it.

Between chews, Emilio pointed to the place. "This is an orphanage that offers schooling for all ages of children. It's run by a group of nuns from Barista."

Tom nodded, greeting the children with smiles. He patted a few on the head, looking at each one. They were between the ages of five and fifteen and most were not wearing shoes. Their clothing looked either too large or too small, none of it matched, and everything was worn and dirty. Still, the smiles on their faces and the spark in their bright, brown eyes outshined it all. Soon Tom and

Emilio were surrounded and the children took great interest in the white stranger.

A nun appeared, touching a few of the younger children and speaking harshly in a foreign tongue. They quickly dispersed and the woman looked to Emilio.

"¿Cómo te va?" she spewed, hastily.

Then she looked to Tom and he met her with a genuine smile. He reached for the envelope and handed it to her.

"Sister, can you please take this for the benefit of the children?"

The nun was startled. She peered into the envelope and gasped. Tom was delighted to see her soften as tears streamed down her face.

"Gracias Señor!" she exclaimed, turning to the others.

Then she focused on Tom and took his hands in hers. "And may The Lord bless you," she added.

Tom smiled and the woman bowed and hurried back to the shelter.

They finished their food and were soon heading south again. Emilio patted Tom on the leg, beaming.

"That was a very good thing you just did. It'll help them more than you know. But why'd you give it all away, knowing where you're going?"

Tom looked to Emilio. "It'll benefit them more than me. Besides, I'm a pilgrim now and we don't think too highly of money and possessions."

"I think you're referring to monks," Emilio said, and the two men shared a hearty laugh.

But then they passed a sign announcing that Solano was only three-hundred kilometers away. Both men knew it was the drop-off point for Tom, and from there he would be completely on his own.

CHAPTER 44

The cecropia trees that lined the roadside were small, umbrella-shaped, and plentiful; extending well into the much denser and higher forestation. They were spaced well apart from one another, and Emilio was able to slowly maneuver the truck between them.

It was crucial to get out of sight from the road.

Emilio explained that the Azteca ants lived within and aggressively protected the cecropia tree, and the spacing was a credit to their efforts. Millions of ants worked to kill any insect that threatened the tree's growth and they even cut any vine that grew nearby. It was one of the rain forest's most amazing symbiotic relationships, and once again Tom wondered what other marvels he'd experience.

The sun was nearly down when they parked the truck and trekked deeper into the trees on foot. Tom strapped on an over-sized pack and Emilio carried a large cooler, a much smaller back pack, and a tent. They found a small clearing and set up camp. The air was moist and humid and the mosquitoes were swarming all around, but

Emilio made a central fire, with four other smoking fires to help keep the insects at bay.

While Tom assembled the tents, Emilio cooked chicken, beef, and rice in various pots and skillets.

During dinner, Emilio explained their current position was about fifty-five kilometers north of Tom's final destination. This was as far as they could drive, because the roads were patrolled and they would be discovered on their current heading.

The only way was on foot, directly south through unchartered rain forest and jungle.

Emilio produced a map of southern Venezuela and crudely sketched the route that Tom would take. He calculated it would be a three-day hike and detailed what should be expected. The map was hardly specific, as most of Venezuela's southern region was uninhabited jungle and rain forest that had yet to be explored.

Emilio explained the differences between the jungle and the rain forest, which were the two main environments that Tom would travel through. The first day would be the hardest, because the jungle surrounded the rain forest and it would be thick with brush, vines, and root systems.

Although it was estimated that Tom could probably walk about thirteen miles each day, the first leg would only cover about eight. Emilio showed Tom how to use a machete in a quick arcing motion to cut through the brush, and discussed the different kinds of vegetation he would encounter.

Emilio then spoke of the rain forest, which Tom would enter the second day. It would contain several distinct layers, with the upper canopy consisting of trees that could reach well over a hundred feet high. Then there was the lower canopy of trees about sixty feet high, and the ground level which had very little vegetation because the sun light couldn't penetrate to the ground. Emilio explained that the forest would be much easier to walk through, but that it would be extremely humid and that about 80% of the world's insect population lived on the rain forest floor.

This peeked Tom's interest and he became uncomfortable. Back in Chicago, there were spiders, ants, and bees, but he knew that things were much different here.

"So are those Aztec Indian ants or whatever you called them gonna be all over me when I sleep?" Tom asked.

"They are relatively harmless to humans."

"But I thought you said they kill everything that gets near that tree!"

"Yeah, but they don't travel too far from it."

With that, Emilio produced a small booklet with pictures of jungle life, many of which were circled. School was in session and Tom was an ardent pupil.

"First of all," Emilio began. "Forget everything you think you know about ants. Did you know that in Japanese the word 'ant' is written by linking two characters together?"

Tom remained quiet and Emilio persisted.

"One means 'insect' and the other is 'loyalty.' These little guys don't mess around and work more efficiently than any human military ever could. They are naturally selfless and cooperative; and have no fear in attacking anything—however big—that threatens the colony."

"But we're still bigger and can just stomp 'em, right?"

Emilio laughed. Then he looked to the sky, contemplating things. "Let me point out a couple of things. First, if you weigh all the ants and humans in the world, the weight would approximately be the same. They outnumber us more than a million to one! Second, a colony of army ants—and by the way they're all over here—can devour, dissolve, and eat an entire cow in a matter of hours."

A look of horror and disbelief overcame Tom's usually pleasant face, and he was visibly shaken.

But even as Emilio eyed Tom, he didn't slow down. He explained that the jungle and rain forest were home to an array of dangerous animals and insects; and they were as extensive and diverse as they were deadly. Emilio carefully detailed each one, from the alligators and piranhas in the water, the jaguars in the brush, and the insects and snakes that could be anywhere from the ground to the canopy so incredibly high above.

It was clearly something Tom hadn't given much thought to, and for several minutes he forgot about the perilous hunt for Jeremy and the deadly cartel that was harboring him.

To even get that far, he had to hike through three full days of wilderness.

But when the fire cracked loudly and broke his train of thought, Tom rebounded and regained focus. He thought of Kelly and Jess and then Dannie and Seargant. He knew what he had to do. He nodded appreciatively at Emilio and filed the information away in his mind.

"Speaking of ants," Emilio began. "You'll have topical steroid cream. I also worked hard to keep your pack under thirty pounds, but it's gonna feel heavier as you go. Make sure you carry it evenly across your back and maintain a steady walk."

Emilio passed Tom a note which inventoried everything. Tom perused it with great interest, and was thankful to see things he'd hoped for and others he hadn't even considered.

He knew the basics were there, from his earlier conversation, but he was happy to see three pounds of dried meats, a loaf of bread, water, peanut butter, and fruit. And he was especially grateful for the weaponry.

Emilio continued speaking for more than an hour; describing the danger, but also the drug cartel that awaited Tom even *if* he made it to the other side. But Tom grew weary and became detached.

Tom focused on the fire; with its brilliant orange and blue embers at the base, and the sharp flames that licked the air. A piece of wood cracked, sending sparks into the air, and Tom followed their ascent into the dark sky. Then he concentrated on the bright stars above and wondered if he'd ever see them again.

Emilio noticed Tom's mental disconnect. "I'm trying to save your life," he said. "Whether you know it or not, the odds are against you."

"I know. But sometimes you have to accept what life brings and hope you're equipped to meet the challenge."

Emilio stoked the fire, which proved a convenient distraction, then gazed at Tom. "So you're Mr. Courageous and not afraid to die?"

"Something like that, yeah," Tom said.

But Emilio was unmoved. "I'd rather you have the courage to try to live."

The comment hung in the air and Tom changed the subject. "You know you have a real passion for your country," he said.

Emilio explained that Venezuela was ripe with natural splendor that was rarely seen in the world, much less in one place. He talked about the coastal cities to the north, the beautiful forests, jungles, mountains, and waterfalls, and the proud and generous people that made up the diverse culture.

"Have you ever thought about running for office?" Tom asked.

Emilio became excited and Tom knew it was something he'd contemplated. Then the Venezuelan continued with a thorough diatribe that Tom had come to expect and admire.

"I would love to but I can't because I haven't been in country for fifteen years yet. Our legislative branch is represented by a national assembly that consists of one-hundred and sixty-five diputados. Three of these deputies are reserved for representatives of Venezuela's indigenous people and I hope to occupy a seat someday. The office can really bring positive change, because the position isn't political and can be occupied by *any* citizen with strong ties to the community."

"That's great," Tom said. "I think you'd be outstanding in any role that helps others. I have no doubt you'll do it."

Emilio grinned at his new friend. "Thank you, Tom. And I hope you achieve your objectives as well."

Emilio continued to stoke the fire and both men retreated inward to thoughts they didn't want to share. Each knew the dangers that lay ahead for Tom, but no more words were necessary.

For a long time Tom stared into the flames, mesmerized. His thoughts jumped at random. Images of Jess, Kelly, Seargant, Dannie, and even Olly and Elmer flashed in his mind.

He knew what he had to do and one thing was certain. Over the next week, either he or Jeremy would be dead, and probably many others.

Then he slept undisturbed for several hours.

CHAPTER 45

Daylight came quickly and Tom awoke to find Emilio working the fire and cooking a surprisingly hearty breakfast of eggs, bacon, sausage, and even coffee. Fresh fruit and nut bread rounded out the meal, and both men took in the food hungrily.

They ate in silence, knowing the time to say farewell was near. Tom finished first and wasted little time in packing his tent and meticulously inventorying and organizing his pack.

He changed into hiking boots, reapplied a generous covering of bug spray, and donned a straw hat. On his left ankle he strapped on a pedometer and on his hip a holster with a loaded 9mm. Then he took out the machete and palmed his compass, looking south, expectantly.

Emilio chewed slowly, eyeing Tom and hoping he'd change his mind. He'd given the American every bit of advice he could and supplied everything he'd need, but Emilio feared it wouldn't be enough.

Tom walked over to Emilio with confidence. "I'm ready," he said. "I think it's best to just get started so I can make it through the first part by evening."

Emilio nodded. "Are you sure? Is this what you really want?"

"I appreciate what you've done, and I don't fault you for not understanding. But it needs to happen."

Tom perused the make-shift camp site one last time and sighed. Then the two men shared a firm and extended handshake and Tom swiftly turned and walked away.

And for the second time in as many days, a concerned friend watched Tom Brightwell's back as the man headed into almost certain death.

Tom met his first difficulty around noon.

He'd been steadily moving through the trees until he came to the base of a large rock formation. It was several stories high and as wide as he could see in both directions. Climbing it was out of the question, as smooth and high as it was, and who knew what on the other side? Tom checked his compass and turned left, easing downward and south-east.

After nearly an hour, he came to a section that dropped off considerably and formed a natural path through the rock. His sight was limited. The trail twisted away and there was no way of telling if it dead-ended or how far it reached.

Tom sat to contemplate things. He was again reminded that although he needed to travel due south, his route was untested wilderness. There wasn't a clear path to his destination and everything could be a life or death decision.

He checked his compass and looked south-east to where the rock seemed to continue forever. He knew he had to eventually cut south and even south-west to compensate for the last hour and this could be the opportunity.

Taking a pull from a water bottle, he entered the rock formation, hoping it was the right choice. The walls eventually rose and seemed to bully him as the sunlight waned. Soon he realized he was in a cave, not just a pathway through the rock. The darkness swallowed him but his compass showed him heading south and his flashlight lit the way.

The path became increasingly narrow and he was forced to slow. Still, he maintained patience, using his gloved hands to balance against the rock walls.

He was keen to everything he stepped on. Emilio had warned that a broken or twisted ankle could mean a slow death. And not far from his thoughts were the fear that ants could get into his boots.

After two hours of hiking through the cavern, Tom was despondent. He looked to where the sky *should* be but saw the rock walls were even higher than before. His flashlight beam disappeared into the darkness high above, and he became anxious, as the close surroundings pressed him deeper into uncertainty.

But he kept going.

Soon he was entertaining every thought of doom. Where was he exactly? Would he ever get out? What would get to him first; lack of food and water, or any of the animal threats that thrived all around him?

He heard a crunchy sound beneath his feet and was amazed to see small pebbles. The rock walls on either side eased wider and he could see chalky white lines at eye-level. Tom guessed they were water marks from long ago; which made sense, because the stone was so smooth to the touch and he'd been walking downward for so long. He was able to pick up his pace.

The smell in the air turned moist and the rocky path gave way to vibrant green vegetation that sprang up from the soft ground. Tom took in deep, relaxing breaths and could taste the precipitation in the air. He used his compass to look south. He was thankful to be out of the cave, but a feeling of foreboding swept over him, as he saw the thick wall of green in his way.

He was definitely in the jungle.

He was amazed at how quickly things had changed. But without deliberation, he took out the machete and started swinging at the tall grasses, vines, and thin trees in his path.

Hours later, he came to a large tree, perhaps the biggest he'd ever seen, and decided to rest. The trunk was about fifteen feet in diameter and rose like a skyscraper, taller than his line of sight afforded. Loose vines hung limply from branches high above. He wondered how old it was and how many species of life called it home.

He thought he saw a dark form high above and moving fast, but before he could focus it was gone. He shook the thought, concentrating on the ground. He was far more concerned with snakes and insects.

One of the tree's large roots rose high and Tom sat on it like a bench. He took several generous swigs from a water bottle and nibbled on a granola bar. It wasn't substantial or incredibly satisfying, but he felt the rush in his head as his body welcomed the nutrients. He removed his hat and stretched his legs, breathing steadily.

Looking up, he saw the amazing branch systems that comprised the jungle's lower canopy, as each of the giant trees spread their branches, intertwiningly. He sat in awe, taking in the undisturbed jungle. Birds cackled from unseen places and the vibrant green plant life thrived all around him.

Tom enjoyed the solidarity of the moment. He was in the Venezuelan jungle, a day's walk from anything modern, and probably in a place that no one had ever been.

He became pensive, appreciating the true timelessness of it all. The chaos of man was absent in a place where things hadn't changed in thousands of years. He was witnessing a slow, unchecked balance; and was thankful to observe such natural splendor. Why couldn't the real world be as symbiotic?

But then his train of thought was broken as he heard movement in the immediate distance. He saw a small tree sway, as if something had just been there. His police instincts kicked in, along with a substantial amount of adrenalin, as he removed and leveled his 9mm Beretta. He silently stepped behind the large tree, scanning the area.

For several moments nothing happened and he was hoping he'd imagined the entire thing. Sweat poured from his body and stung his eyes. He could taste its saltiness on the corners of his mouth, but didn't dare make a move to wipe it away. In the empty moments he could feel his pulse pounding as his heart beat quickened.

Then, without warning a large jaguar stepped out about twenty feet away, eyeing him, and lifting one of its beefy paws in the air. Tom aimed his gun at the large cat, which held its ground. For what seemed like forever, man and beast just stared at each other.

The animal was absolutely stunning. Its coat was vibrant orange, with deep black spots that seemed to jump from it. Tom could see the lean muscles move as it breathed. There was no doubt it was built for speed and survival, and Tom wasn't confident he had enough firepower at such close range.

Then light noises sounded all around and birds called out from high above. A sudden rain began and the fat drops of water started falling faster. But Tom still didn't move.

The jaguar smelled the air, distracted, before running out of sight.

Tom sighed and holstered his Beretta. Not wanting to miss an opportunity, he quickly drank a bottle of water and positioned several large leaves to catch the rain. When the shower ended, he'd filled two of his empty water bottles.

He checked his watch and saw it was approaching evening. His pedometer showed that he'd gone more than ten miles and he was happy to be ahead of schedule. He set up camp; then removed his boots and socks and stretched out in the tent, with his machete and gun within reach.

Despite the heat and humidity, he fell asleep easily.

The city boy felt good about his first day in the jungle.

CHAPTER 46

Tom was dreaming of being hugged. It was an all-encompassing feeling that was pleasant and warm. But when it became tighter and his breathing was interrupted, his eyes flew open and he screamed in agony and terror.

The confusion didn't last long.

The green anaconda was the biggest snake Tom had ever seen. It was coiled around his mid-section at least twice and squeezing hard. Tom thrashed erratically to no avail. The snake constricted even more, leaving no doubt of its intentions.

He was in trouble and had to think fast.

Tom found the machete and brought it down hard on the snake, sawing as he did. But it didn't seem to affect things and only winded him further. Even as Tom curled and twisted, he could only afford short, erratic breaths which weren't enough to sustain him. He was starting to weaken and was only moments away from passing out. The snake persisted, as if sensing the end was near.

Then Tom reached for his Beretta. Leveling it at the snake's head, about six feet away and just outside the tent, he aimed and prepared for the loud blast.

He shot twice and the snake's head nearly disappeared. He felt the grip loosen, but he was still caught in the beast's post mortem squeeze.

Lifting a portion of the anaconda, Tom was eventually able to wiggle free. He scrambled out of the tent; dizzy and deafened by the gun blasts.

"Holy cow!" he yelled, barely hearing his muted words.

"What the hell was that?!"

He sat for several moments, gaining a mental foothold.

The snake's head was a bloody stump, but other than the initial wound, there was surprisingly little blood or splatter. Still shaky, Tom grabbed the tail. Like a long rope, he pulled the massive creature away from his tent and into the brush.

He took a moment to study the fully extended snake and even felt a pang of guilt for having to kill such a beautiful animal. It was at least fifteen feet long and about a foot in diameter at the center. It was truly remarkable; mossy green in color with yellow and black spots lining its entire body.

Tom could only guess how old the anaconda was, or even how many of them were still alive in the wild. Still, he had acted in self-defense and would never hesitate to do it again.

Then he started laughing. Whether it was out of complete elation for surviving the attack or to combat the anxiousness within, he didn't know. But it felt good and the moment ceded.

"Hell of an alarm clock, aren't you?" he said, still eyeing the snake's extensive mid-section.

"Who needs coffee when you provide at least a pot of excitement?"

Tom knew he couldn't go back to sleep. So he packed his things and began his second day in the jungle.

CHAPTER 47

By mid-day a feeling of nausea set in, and Tom began to feel the effects of his harsh journey.

He'd fallen into a comfortable motion that was both efficient and easy. He'd moved with an even gait and kept his breathing steady. But the heat and humidity was hard and unforgiving. He'd been covered with a thick layer of sweat the day before, but was now perspiring very little. Had his body adapted to the harsh environment? Had his blood thinned out? Or was he just not keeping himself as hydrated as he should?

Walking down an embankment, he saw the first of two rivers Emilio said he'd encounter. It was slow-moving, about forty feet across, and the blue water cast a striking view against the bright green ground.

Without hesitation, he removed his boots, socks, and clothing, and held them high as he treaded into the water. He instinctively looked for snakes and alligators, but kept moving; trying not to think of the things he *couldn't* see. He was concerned about piranhas, but

Emilio assured him that they were usually in low-lying, still water and not flowing rivers.

The ground underneath was slick and muddy, but he was able to maintain a slow and steady pace. The water became deeper and finally rose to his shoulders in the middle. He slowed to where he could only gain inches at a time and suddenly felt increasingly vulnerable, with only his head and arms above the waterline. The weight of the backpack was excruciating as he continued to hold it out of the water.

But then the ground rose beneath him and he happily approached the other side. He placed his things on a rock and retreated into the water to soak and bathe for a few minutes.

Then he set off once again. The topography of the land changed, this time giving way to dry soil and less vegetation, and the trees were shorter, thinner, and more scattered. He no longer needed his machete. There was no doubt he was in the rain forest and he moved ahead with confidence.

Tom allowed his mind to wander as he contemplated his life in total. He thought of his parents; two first-generation immigrants whom had come to the United States with nothing, and rose their only son in a one-bedroom apartment in Chicago.

He remembered being poor as a child, but not wanting for anything. His father was usually away, but he understood the man had worked three jobs, and sometimes slept only a few hours each night to provide for his family. His mother did well to attend to both home and child, and was a constant source of comfort.

Tom felt a lump on his throat as he remembered them both dying just weeks apart from different ailments, and attending their funerals as a numb eighteen-year old. But thankfully Jess had been there for him.

Then he was married and felt reborn. He got a job and excelled on the police force. Then Kelly came and life was more than he could have imagined.

But soon they were gone and he was left alone, again not knowing what to do.

A strange smile crossed his face as he thought of how far he'd come, with the help of Jack Seargant. He'd stopped his medications and quit drinking. He began exercising again, and found a new purpose in aiding in an international murder investigation!

But was it all for nothing? He had no illusions that he was the underdog; the only advantage being the element of surprise. Who would imagine that a lone sixty-year old American would attempt to ambush a drug cartel and take Jeremy out?

Although he knew it was a suicide mission, he'd never felt so good in his life. Should he survive—and he knew he probably wouldn't—nothing would ever impede him again. He made a silent promise to live every day to the fullest and never take anything for granted.

How he wished he could reach across both space and time and communicate his current thoughts to his family and friends, both living and dead. To connect on an even plane and apologize, celebrate, laugh, cry, forgive, and accept. He'd never been a philosophical man, but he had a renewed sense of living and he embraced it!

Then his mind turned to Dannie. What was she was doing? She was back in Alabama and he envisioned her sipping lemonade on her porch, reading a magazine, or tending to her garden.

He wondered if he'd ever see her again. Would he ever watch her lovely face launch another broad smile? He grinned, thinking of the three days they'd spent together in Saint Maarten. Those times, despite the situation that allowed them, had been the happiest he'd known for some time.

He quickened his pace as the memories fueled him.

Then he thought of Seargant. Hopefully he was with his wife and things had returned to normal. For him the Island Hopper case was over, with the only suspect having fled across international borders. Tom prayed they would have children and live happily ever after. He wished them the best.

Tom walked thoughtfully for several more miles and the woods continued to thin. He could see further into the distance now and was able to gain a better perspective. He was happy to leave the thicker trees behind, but missed the cover they'd allowed. His most treasured defense was anonymity. Looking to his right, he saw the sun cresting over the distant tree line.

Checking his pedometer and compass, he felt good about his pace and decided to establish camp.

He sat and ate some dried meats and canned fruit. His thoughts cut deep and he continued to feel a growing sense of harmony. When the sun cast the last of its light, he entered his tent.

The darkness consumed him and he drifted into a deep sleep.

CHAPTER 48

Tom awoke slower than the day before, taking a few minutes to stretch before climbing out of his tent. He felt the strain in his muscles, but found comfort knowing he was ahead of schedule.

He'd hiked twenty-four miles in two days, in harsh conditions and over uneven terrain. He packed his things and started off. *What dynamic would today bring?* Would he reach his destination by evening and face the final chapter in this awful saga?

The immediate future held such an array of possibilities that it was overwhelming. He bit into an apple and embraced the new day as he bounded down a narrow path.

Today's hike, Emilio had assured, would be the easiest of the three. He was well out of the jungle and the rain forest would soon give way to moderate forestation, prairies, and even active farmland. Emilio said there would be scattered homes by mid-day, and another river, which would mark the end point. It was on the *other* side of that river that he would find the drug cartel and Jeremy.

Thinking about the end lent him encouragement. He couldn't believe who he'd been just weeks earlier; a complete drunk, banged up and lying in a hospital bed. Then he was in the Caribbean and working with the FBI, only to run into his daughter's killer and track him through the Venezuelan wilderness!

He thought of Olly and Elmer at Captain's Pub back in Chicago. Would they believe what he'd done? Would he even live to see them again? He smiled as he jumped a small ravine and allowed his motivation to move him down a hill. Did the White Sox win or lose last night? What was the date?

The next several hours went fast. He took more extended breaks, but compensated because the terrain was much easier.

At noon he stopped for lunch, sitting on a large rock and removing his shoes and socks. The forest floor was soft and he exfoliated his tired feet on the ground. Still, he was vigilant about any ants in the area. Seeing none, he left his shoes off while he unpacked his lunch.

He finished the last of the dried beef and ham, ate another apple, and drank a bottle of water. Then he donned a new pair of socks and headed off.

After several more hours, the trees became even thinner and smaller. There were no more root systems or low brush to navigate. The land turned grassy.

He could see a great distance through the trees and noticed a large field up ahead. He slowed and carefully moved forward. An open field meant complete exposure. He palmed his binoculars and scanned the countryside from the safety of the tree line.

He saw considerable fencing, outlining large fields. There was livestock about a mile into the distance, and rooftops beyond that. It was the first sign of civilization he'd seen in days and a feeling of relief swept over him.

There were a few more hours of sunlight, so he took an extended break. He spread some peanut butter on the last of the bread and sat down, taking measure of his aching muscles. Then he napped and set off with the setting sun.

The ensuing darkness would only help camouflage his movement, so he continued slowly, in no hurry to best the waning daylight.

He was finally leaving the woods and he felt like an alien walking into a new, untested land.

The fields rose and fell and after climbing and descending several hills, he paused to check his heading. He decided to walk the perimeter of a crude fence that was no more than posts with uneven boards and tree limbs. He was moving up and down with the natural landscape when he heard voices and froze.

He was at the base of a small grassy incline, so he gently placed his pack down and eased up the hill on his belly to get a better view.

He saw a beautiful young girl, no more than sixteen years old, working in a field of low crops. There were several wheel barrels overflowing with non-descript vegetables. But there were also two men with machine guns, poking her and speaking harshly.

Tom couldn't understand the language, but their tone and demeanor left little doubt of their intentions. They were about to assault her and it was a bad scene. Tom saw a red pickup truck behind them and guessed they had ridden up on her, possibly from the very place he was heading to.

He took out his Beretta, gently moving back the slide. Then he retreated down the embankment, placing the gun out of sight in his rear waist band. He placed the crucifix over his head, making sure the cross was visible at the center of his chest.

Even from the other side of the hill, the voices became louder and more agitated, and he heard the girl scream. Tom leveled his breathing and walked into plain sight. Both of his arms were extended and his palms open. He closed to within thirty feet before one of the men spotted him and pointed a machine gun his way. Tom decided to be direct and non-combative. He raised his hands even higher as he slowed.

"May God be with you," he offered in a soothing voice. "I'm a lost missionary and I apologize for any intrusion."

The men stared at him in dismay, looking to each other. Tom seized the opportunity to establish a dialogue.

"Hello my child," he offered, looking to the young girl.

He could now see that she was about thirteen, with long dark hair and olive skin. She was wearing a plain black dress which had seen better days. Her large brown eyes were wide with fear. She looked at all three men and the moment seemed to last forever.

"Hola," she said to Tom, and she bowed her head to him.

The larger man stepped closer, his gun leveled at Tom's chest.

"Who are you?" the man hissed with contempt.

Tom saw pure ugliness; but remained calm and sized up his foe with smooth glances. He thought of what Seargant and Emilio had told him about shooting first. Darkness was coming quickly and he only had a few more minutes of good light.

He could almost smell the man's rancid breath as he spit his words over his crooked, yellow teeth. The outlaw was in his mid-forties, with an uneven dark beard that did little to hide his bad complexion. His clothes were old and dirty.

The other man moved next to the girl, cleverly guarding her from an elevated position. They had spread out and Tom's plan was in jeopardy. Still, the American's facial expression bore nothing but uncertainty and his body stance was awkward and disarming.

Tom's heart beat faster. He had to move between the two men in a V formation. He moved to his right, feigning an attempt to leave the situation behind him.

"I guess I'll be on my way then. Peace be with you."

Tom *was* able to take several steps before both men jumped forward to engage him. In the sudden movement, both had taken their fingers off their triggers and allowed their guns to sway from their neck straps. They had taken him for a wandering fool and softened. They were no longer spread out, the girl was now out of the line of fire, and Tom had earned a better position.

"You a long way from home," the taller man said in broken English, laughing heartily.

"Americano," the other called out.

Tom looked down to his cross and raised it for everyone to see. "I'm just a lost missionary, trying to bring hope to your country," he said.

Then he moved his hands behind him, while keeping an open dialogue. "You see, I have this bible here, and I—"

The gunshots were sudden and unexpected, and both men dropped before they even knew what happened. Tom had hit the man on the left first, because the angle of his gun was more of a threat. Then he'd shot the other in quick succession. Both were head shots and were instantly fatal.

Before the bodies settled on the ground, Tom pulled his Beretta back and dropped it. He walked to the girl who was even more terrified.

"It's okay; you're gonna be fine now," he said, kneeling in front of her and making eye contact. "Are your parents close by?"

The girl hugged Tom, sobbing softly. He instinctively kissed the top of her head and gently patted her back. Tom couldn't help but think of his daughter, and he held the little girl tighter.

In the distance another vehicle approached. Seeing it, the girl fell away and she ran to meet it. Tom felt vulnerable, both physically and emotionally, though he sensed there was nothing to fear. Still, he picked up his weapon, ready for any other surprises.

A large man spilled out of the truck. He held a shotgun in his left hand and scooped up the girl with his right arm. His concentrated stare never left Tom.

Tom stood his ground, raising his hands in surrender and feeling out of place. He was, after all, thousands of miles from home and deeply embedded in a foreign country. He didn't speak the language and had just killed two people.

But he knew the girl would convey their side of the story.

CHAPTER 49

The man's name was Javier and his only child was twelve-year old Anna. She was fluent in both English and Spanish and was an effective translator.

Anna spoke rapidly to her father; and although Tom couldn't understand, he knew her words were conciliatory. Javier's eyes flashed in anger as a range of emotions ran its course.

Then Javier turned to Tom and relaxed. He reached out and shook Tom's hand, before grabbing the American's shoulders and moving closer. Tom was surprised but didn't turn away, and for a few moments the two men just looked at each other.

Javier's dark eyes peered into Tom's, as if physically searching him for answers. Exhausted, Tom just looked back at the burly man that held him. Both were similar in height, and although Javier was a couple decades younger, the deep lines that cut into his leathery, unshaven face seemed to even the years.

Javier broke into a warm smile and patted Tom's back. Breaking away, he withdrew toward the truck, speaking to Anna. The girl walked to Tom's side and placed her small hand in his, leading him to the vehicle.

"Papa says he is thankful and you will stay with us for as long as you need. He also says we must talk more at the house."

Javier and Anna hopped in the front of the truck and Tom jumped in the back, eventually sitting between a bag of fertilizer and an old tool box. The truck leapt forward and Tom enjoyed the breeze on his face as they moved across the grassy field. Watching the landscape fly by, he was happy to be off his feet. He never so appreciated a motorized vehicle.

He sat with both legs extended and stretched his aching body, craning his neck to see the darkened sky. *What would the next part of this adventure bring?*

The house eventually came into view, as did several other structures, and Tom noticed they were the ones he'd seen from the tree line. They were different in material, size, and architecture; and Tom guessed they were built over long time periods with whatever material was available.

Inside, Tom was offered food and bottled water and he accepted both, humbly. They ate stewed vegetables, chicken, and rice; and the conversation was easy, even with Anna having to moderate. Tom was hungry, but he held back so he wouldn't upset his stomach. He still had a lot to do and didn't want to overwhelm his body.

It was clear that Javier was a loyal and hard-working man, and although not overly-educated, he was a skilled laborer and farmer that provided for his family. He told Tom that the cartels had never come onto his property before, though they knew of his existence. He was just a simple man who worked the land and was no threat to them. He looked to his daughter during the conversation, and Tom saw his expression soften at each glance.

Anna was petite but much stronger than her size suggested. She had an angelic innocence about her, but was also rigid. There was no doubt that she carried her weight on the farm.

Javier was very open about his life and family, while Tom held back and stuck to his baseline story of being a missionary. Tom learned that the family had farmed the land for several generations, long before the drug cartels had come. Thankfully, the river that edged his land forged a natural separation; and although they were just miles away in distance, they were almost two hours away by car.

Anna explained that she and her mother lived in Caracas full time, and Javier farmed and maintained the land for half the year, making several trips north to sell his produce.

The conversation continued and Javier and Anna remained interested in Tom. But the American was guarded and eventually excused himself, walking to the outside bathroom. The air was cooler now and the sky was clear, showing a bright moon climbing above the trees.

When Tom finished, Javier and Anna were waiting on the slanted porch. Anna held a pot of coffee and poured the dark brew into tall mugs. Tom took one, gratefully. Then he sat on an old chair, moving the coffee to his lips and blowing off the steam.

Javier spoke to Anna and she translated her father's words.

"Papa would like to thank you once again. He also wants to remind you that this land has been in his family for over a century and that no one knows it better than him. While he doesn't mean to pry, he finds it difficult to believe that you are a lost missionary, judging by the path you took and your knowledge of guns."

Tom remained silent, testing the coffee.

"If you don't want to tell us anything we will understand. You have no enemies here."

Tom nodded, looking to the sky as if seeking council. Then his eyes settled on Javier.

"Tell him that I don't want to get you involved for your own safety."

Anna spoke to her father and he shook his head, speaking back to Anna.

"He says that we owe you and you would be better off with our help."

Tom looked at Javier. "Are you sure?" he asked.

No translation was needed, as Javier bobbed his head. Tom regrouped and for nearly an hour, they sipped strong coffee as Tom told them everything.

Javier and Anna were good listeners. They learned about Tom's wife and daughter; and he was forthright about his problems with alcohol, and even his suicidal tendencies.

Then he spoke of the investigation that brought him to the Caribbean and his developing relationship with both Dannie and Seargant. He discussed his new-found perspective on life and how he'd never been so clear or self-aware. Finally he talked about Emilio, meeting the nuns and children near El Jobal, and his eventual path through the jungle.

When he was done, he pulled out a recent picture of Jeremy, which was taken at the Saint Maarten jail.

Shockingly, Javier had seen the man at the market just the day before. A white man this deep into Venezuela was uncommon, so he'd taken notice. When Tom showed the picture a second time, Javier confirmed it with absolute certainty.

Jeremy was just on the other side of the river.

CHAPTER 50

It didn't take long for a plan to be assembled.

Javier sketched a crude map of the area, showing the main route into and out of his property, and the central roads and main bridge that fed into the southern region. Like Emilio, Javier lectured about the cartels and how dangerous they were—especially to outsiders—as he drew a rough layout of their compound.

The cartel that received Jeremy was the largest and more dangerous of the three, and run by a man named Marco. Javier explained that they had a considerable infrastructure. There were two airstrips for transport and well-paved roads throughout their complex. They were well-supplied, embedded, and enjoyed every modern convenience of a small town. He likened them to a major military installation, with all the weaponry and manpower to wage a war.

Javier and Anna pleaded with Tom to stay the night and rest. But Tom was rejuvenated, knowing that Jeremy was so close. So father and daughter let him be. Javier left to dispose of the bodies and the truck, while Anna cleaned up in the kitchen.

Later they all drove south to the river. They stopped short of the trees and walked single-file, with Javier leading the way. Moving down an embankment overtaken by brush, Javier was quick to find his old metal boat. It was about six feet long and built for no more than two people, but Javier looked to it with pride.

In the night, the river looked ominous. The moonlight showed the rippling waves in the near, but there was complete darkness beyond. Tom was concerned about the depth, the current, and the distance to the other side. The river was over a mile wide at this stretch and the cartel was about three more miles west of the other side.

But Tom wasn't turning back and he eagerly awaited instructions. Anna explained the depth was no more than ten feet at any point, but there were alligators, piranhas, and snakes in the water. The current was actually a good thing, because all three threats favored shallower and slower moving water, and it would also aid him in moving downstream.

Javier cleared the boat of some brush, looking to Tom. He spoke to Anna firmly and used his hands to mimic a steady rowing motion.

"Papa says you must reach the other side in less than an hour. Anything more and you could over-shoot and arrive right at the compound. He says it's imperative that you land at least a mile east and then walk through the trees."

Tom nodded and moved to shake Javier's hand. Then he looked to Anna and gave her a quick hug. Getting in the boat and moving into the water, Tom gripped the oars and began rowing. But as grateful as he was for their hospitality and help, he concentrated on the task at hand.

Jeremy was the only thing on his mind.

CHAPTER 51

The water flowed steadily under the small boat.

Soon Tom couldn't see the river bank he'd just left or the one he was heading to; and although uncertainties abounded, he'd become used to the feeling.

Staring ahead and working his thick arms, he became lost in the steady rowing motions.

The air was mild and a steady breeze found him. Night had fallen and he was no doubt invisible in his movements. Although the stars were shining brightly, the only real light came from the moon, which was now playing hide-n-seek behind some modest cloud coverage.

But his eyes adapted well, and although he was rowing nearly blind, he knew he couldn't hit anything. So he continued to focus on his methodic rowing pattern and his destination.

Javier told Tom to land east of a large clearing. The cartel had cut down and used a tremendous amount of lumber in building their compound, and in doing so carved out several acres leading up to the water's edge.

Tom forward-thought to his arrival on the other side. It would be close to midnight; a perfect time to move under cover and approach. Would Jeremy be there? Would there be armed guards posted at the perimeter?

Tom suddenly felt vulnerable, so like many times before, he dug deep within himself. He imagined his wife, forever fifty-four years old, in a non-descript dress, smiling widely. Then he saw Kelly, so full of life. A multitude of memories and mental snapshots flooded him. In an instant she was a baby in his arms, then a small child climbing on his lap, and then a young woman with the same smile as her mother.

His arms burned as time wore on, but he continued rowing, lost in thought.

Dannie came to his mind. He smiled at their random encounter in Saint Maarten, and the deep and thoughtful conversations they shared in their brief time together. She was such an emotionally-charged and mentally-equipped woman. Like Jess, she was able to bring out the best in him. Would he ever speak to or even see her again? Or was he literally crossing a river just to end up in a shallow and forgotten grave?

Thinking about the very likelihood of his death was unsettling, though he didn't fear it. His existence in Chicago wasn't real anyway, and he *did* long for peace. But meeting Seargant and Dannie, and even Emilio, Javier, and Anna had helped his evolving perspective.

Although he'd only known Seargant and Dannie for a short time, they'd become so close. If he could just get through this, perhaps he could find happiness again.

After nearly an hour, he looked ahead to see a definitive outline of trees and forestation; and judging by the current and the speed he gained with each rowing thrust, the water beneath him was becoming shallower. The moon disappeared behind the trees and he hit land. Jumping out, he hid the boat behind some heavy brush and got his back pack ready.

He was drenched in sweat, his arms burned, and his legs were cramped. So he stretched before walking back to the river and splashing water on his face. Then he rested, catching his breath.

But then he grew impatient; and although he'd been awake for nearly twenty hours, he had never been more ready for anything in his life.

Tom hugged the water's edge for several minutes before hearing voices and the low rumbling of an engine. Stepping quietly through the trees, he saw three men standing by a truck, with at least two others inside the vehicle.

The conversation was in Spanish but it was upbeat and light-hearted, and the men were laughing, heartily. Whatever the circumstance, Tom was glad they were in high spirits and hopefully less engaged.

But they *did* look physical and much younger than him. They were trim, tall, and broad-shouldered, and Tom hoped he didn't have to fight them. Still, he had emotional strength and the benefit of surprise. There was no real way of retreat anyway, and no matter what his future held, at least it was forward and he would move swiftly to that end.

Tom saw a large tarp covered the rear of the truck. Could it be the cocaine the region was known for, or was it something more benign? Judging from the armed men in its company, he concluded the former.

Tom took off his pack and silently removed two 9mm handguns. Then he looked to the guards. The truck lurched forward and coughed as it moved out of sight, and the men entered a long single-story building.

He was no doubt at the edge of the compound. The building in front appeared to be a large dormitory, simple in both size and construction. It looked like a long metal box, about forty-feet wide and several hundred feet long. The walls were made of thin metal, and it was clearly meant for utility, not ascetics.

Tom carefully emerged from the woods.

He shrank to a crouch and lightly ran on the balls of his feet. Reaching the building, he peeked into a small window and into complete darkness on the inside. Wherever the men were, he couldn't tell.

He continued on, flanking the exterior wall until he saw a light inside. He peered in to see several wooden tables with simple fluorescent tube lighting overhead. The facility was empty, but it was clearly the main work area for a drug operation.

Continuing on, he reached the end and saw several small makeshift residences. They were constructed in the same simple material, but each had distinguishing characteristics. Some had porches and steps, while others were overrun with weeds. All looked to be tied into the large utility poles that lined the main road, and the humming of air conditioners were all he could hear. Most of the units were dark, but some had muted lighting inside. Tom estimated about fifty overall.

He moved left until he came to the end of the buildings at the southern side. A tall structure, much like a lighthouse showed in the distance. And he saw several vehicles, a helicopter, and a few single-engine airplanes sleeping on the far side of an airstrip. To the left was a farm, with a classic-looking barn, and simple fencing that probably corralled several animals.

Tom ran back into the woods and moved through the brush, choosing to study the rest of the perimeter under cover. He walked for several minutes until he came to the other end and finished his cursory look.

The place was simple in layout; and other than the river at the northern end and the dense forestation that hugged its perimeter, it lacked any real strategic defense. Maybe the cartel didn't feel it needed protection, other than the young and equipped soldiers in their employ. Who was stupid enough to attack them?

Then Tom remembered why he was here.

It was time to find Jeremy. His daughter's killer.

But before another thought could form, he felt an overwhelming force on his head. It numbed him and made him keel over. The shock didn't last long, as his legs gave out and he lost consciousness and hit the ground hard.

The tall soldier stooped to look at the older man's face before raising his walkie talkie to his lips.

Then a jeep appeared and Tom was whisked away.

CHAPTER 52

Tom awoke suddenly. He didn't know where he was or for how long he'd been there. He was in total darkness, but could tell he was in a very bad place. Thoughts of his recent past came slowly.

But one thing was self-evident. He was a prisoner.

The throbbing in his head was so intense that it almost sent him back into unconsciousness. The wound was left untreated, and without a bandage the blood flowed freely. He touched it gently, feeling his hair matted down with thick, sticky blood. He was covered in sweat, and the smell of his own body odor was throwing. He was also struck with a thirst he'd never known.

He tried to roll over but was immediately caught by leg and hand irons. A thick chain was wrapped around his mid-section.

Feeling overwhelmed, he closed his eyes and happily returned to a deep sleep.

When Tom opened his eyes it was daytime, and two armed guards were standing over him. There were several aluminum buckets at their feet. Without warning they poured them over his head and stepped back, looking at him as if he were an animal on display.

The guards began a hushed dialogue that Tom couldn't understand. But he was clearly the topic of conversation, as they shook their heads and scrutinized him.

Tom welcomed the cool water, and used his hands to capture some and run his fingers through his hair. At the same time his mouth was open, trying to catch any stray drops.

Another guard entered and left a smaller bucket of water, motioning with his hands that Tom should drink. Tom smiled weakly; nodding to the men in total as he drank, thirstily.

When he looked up another man entered the room.

He was well-dressed; with a crisp black suit, bright white shirt, and a yellow silk tie. He was a striking man in his mid-fifties, about six feet tall, with peppered black hair and a thin goatee. He carried himself with confidence and the guards were sensitive to his every gesture. Tom took in everything about him; keen that the man undoubtedly controlled his fate.

The man cleared his throat and spoke deliberately. "My name is Marco and you have come here uninvited. Who are you and what do you want?"

Tom had long thought of what to say if captured, but with his pounding headache and desperate situation, he decided to tell the truth. Even for his condition, Tom acted more hurt than he felt, hoping to gain sympathy from his captors and appear even weaker than he felt. Maybe they were family men or had some sense of honor he could exploit.

"My name is Tom Brightwell," he began in a low, pained voice. "I'm here alone, from Chicago, Illinois, on an extended search to find my daughter's killer, who I believe you know."

Marco laughed. "Is this a joke? Because I am not amused."

Tom shook his head, raising his shackled hands to wipe away the sweat and blood that stung his eyes.

"You expect me to believe that you came all this way, only to end up in chains?"

"Have you heard about the recent Island Hopper killings throughout the Caribbean?"

"Yes, I have."

"A man named Jeremy—my daughter's ex-fiancé—is to blame for those murders. He killed the most important thing in my life and I have tracked him here."

Tom watched Marco, and the ex-cop drew upon a study he'd read in his police days. He'd learned about spontaneous facial expressions and recognized a combination of understanding, concern, and then confusion.

But then Marco's cell phone rang and the man reached into his pocket. Before he answered he looked to the guards.

"Categorize his possessions and question him thoroughly."

"Where should we put him?" one of the guards asked.

"He's an American. Put him in the barn with the pigs."

CHAPTER 53

The Hoover Building
Washington D.C.

Seargant stared at his computer screen but saw nothing. He'd been back for five days now—to the concrete jungle of Washington D.C.—but he hadn't acclimated well.

He missed the clean, consistent air quality of the islands. He missed the open spaces and awe-striking colors of the Caribbean waters. He missed the care-free mentality. But most of all he missed his friend, Tom.

Was the man even still alive? Seargant had left him in such a precarious situation. Completely compromised. Even if he *had* survived the long and arduous hike through the wilderness, his mission could only end badly.

Upon returning, Seargant had thrown himself into his work. His team had been scouring every part of Jeremy's life, picking it apart layer by layer. They'd joined forces with the NSA, CIA, IRS and even Homeland Security; starting from Jeremy's childhood and dissecting everything up to the previous week. Jeremy's friends, business associates, and limited family were interviewed and then re-interviewed.

His wife had been visited by federal agents every day since Jeremy's arrest.

But even as Seargant read the reports and orchestrated the ongoing investigation, his thoughts always returned to Tom. Would he ever see him again?

Forcing his burning eyes away from the computer screen, Seargant sat back in his leather chair, his hands clasped behind his head. A clerk appeared and another report landed on his desk with a thud.

Seargant nodded to the messenger but didn't move to the paperwork right away. He'd spent the better part of the morning replaying every event and murder, separating each piece and analyzing it for anything that could help.

While every jurisdiction was satisfied Jeremy was the Island Hopper and had escaped into the bowels of South America, Seargant still had an uncomfortable feeling he couldn't shake.

He finally looked at the report, taking time to absorb every detail. The first segment was another rehashing of Jeremy's net worth, business dealings, and personal life. The second section showed another timeline of the killings, with the official autopsy results and photographs of each crime scene. Then there was an overlap of Jeremy's supposed alibis and assumed locations during the murders. Although Jeremy had lied to his wife about his whereabouts, there was little proof he'd actually been at the crime scenes either. The final tab detailed the methodology of each murder and several independent profiler composites of the killer. Seargant perked up as he read each opinion, but was at full attention when he finished the report.

Even though all six FBI profiles fit Jeremy, a pang of uncertainty still haunted him.

So Seargant decided to get out of the office.

He wanted to interview Jeremy's wife personally.

CHAPTER 54

Seargant enjoyed the drive out of D.C. Taking New York Avenue and then Route 50 into Maryland, he could actually *feel* the stress leave him with each mile of separation. A feeling of openness eclipsed him with every white line that flew by.

With his left hand resting on the downed window's ledge, and the steady air flow from the sun roof, he was lost in contemplation. A cold bottle of water layed untouched on the center console, and he slowly bobbed his head to the smooth sounds of Alicia Keys.

Driving over the Severn River Bridge in Annapolis, he looked in both directions to see an impressive display of sailboats. He smiled as he took in the view; with the high, white sails reaching proudly to the sky, moving in the wind as if waving a silent goodbye.

Minutes later he reached the highest point of the Bay Bridge's eastern extension and saw the vastness of the Chesapeake Bay. A large freighter moved slowly as smaller speed boats zoomed through its large wake.

In the moment he almost forgot the purpose of the trip.

Closing the windows and turning on the air conditioning, he silenced the music and focused on the very important interview he was about to conduct. Bunny Richards was Jeremy's wife; and because of his sparse family and friends, she was the only person who really knew him.

Seargant had read the reports of the previous interviews and could recite most of them by heart. Bunny was forty years old, well-spoken and kind. She was also now worth hundreds of millions of dollars—if not more—since her murdering husband had abandoned her for a life on the lam.

She was a southern belle from Memphis and was raised in a strict Baptist household with her three brothers. Her father worked at the local bank and her mother was a hard-working housewife; but Bunny reportedly hadn't spoken to her family in years.

Another account detailed Bunny's looks, noting she was drop-dead gorgeous and had a "special something" that was enthralling.

It was just one more thing Seargant was curious about.

Seargant had read what she'd said about Jeremy. He loved sailing and was a master at the craft. He had unlimited funds and didn't care who knew it. He was controlling, had an addictive personality, became hot-tempered at times, but could also be alluring and charismatic.

Their relationship had been more physical than emotional, and had deteriorated rapidly over the last few years. But most importantly, Bunny couldn't explain why her husband was in the Caribbean, along with items linking him to the murders.

She'd thought he was in London on business and was as confused as the authorities. Cursory analysis showed she was being honest and she was not considered a suspect or conspirator.

The traffic thickened, but Seargant maintained a steady speed and was soon in Easton. Before long, he turned right onto Route 322 and entered the quaint, historic town of St. Michaels.

Seargant's visit was two-fold. Of utmost importance was interviewing Bunny and either confirming what had already been gathered, or digging deeper into anything that had been missed. He trusted his men implicitly and technically didn't have to make the trip, but when he found that she lived in St. Michaels, he decided to walk the town's historic streets as well.

A student of history and a naturally curious man, Seargant had always wanted to visit the charming towns on Maryland's eastern shore. He'd read about the War of 1812 and had visited several points of interest in Baltimore, but had yet to visit St Michaels.

It was known as "the town that fooled the British," specifically for the early morning hours of August 10, 1813, when the townspeople had learned of an imminent nighttime attack by the British. The villagers kept their homes dark and hung lanterns on the tops of buildings and in very high trees. As a result all but one of the enemy cannonballs overshot their intended targets.

He remembered the story since grade school, and was looking forward to seeing the "Cannonball House" on Mulberry Street. There were still burn marks on the stairs that traced the projectile's path from the upper dorm window.

Seargant drove through St. Michaels slowly, admiring the shops and restaurants that lined the main route. He turned right onto Yacht Club Drive.

When he pulled up to Bunny's vast estate, near the Miles River Yacht Club, the large gate was already open. He drove the long driveway, shaking his head at the sheer magnificence of the grounds.

To say it was grandiose and impressive wasn't enough. Everything about the place was commanding and stately, with a presence that was arresting.

He'd read the report about the property. They had purchased it for eight figures four years prior, paying cash after yet another one of Jeremy's companies had launched a successful IPO.

But none of the pictures could do the place justice. Seargant tried to take in as much as he could but his senses were overwhelmed. He'd never seen anything like it and he hadn't even entered the house.

He parked in an area outlined by high hedges and a pond of exotic, colorful fish. He walked across the cobblestone driveway and peaked into a large fountain with water spraying high into the air. The portico was raised by large white pillars, accentuated by a tremendous chandelier.

Seargant looked at the house itself, impressed by the traditional English Bond brickwork that extended three stories high. The surrounding landscaping was immaculately kept, and the green grass and flowers held no evidence of the sweltering humidity that had pressed the area.

Seargant was impressed at the sheer decadence and was thankful he'd seen it first-hand. He'd always told his team that a study wasn't complete until a thorough application of every sense.

A good investigator smelled the air and heard the sounds where the subject lived. They took in every sight. Seargant especially liked to walk the exact paths a suspect took in their daily routine; from showering to getting the newspaper, from eating in the kitchen and lounging in the backyard.

This was another reason Seargant had come; to get a comprehensive sense of where and especially *how* Jeremy lived. He'd called in advance and was greeted by one of the staff. Then he was swiftly escorted to the rear patio where Bunny was sitting.

The descriptions of Jeremy's wife were accurate.

Bunny was a stunning and beautiful woman. Her hair was done perfectly, with long golden locks falling around her narrow shoulders. She had a naturally pretty face, with a small, pug nose, round lips, and high cheek bones that were accentuated by a modest covering of cosmetics.

Bunny perked up upon seeing her guest, offering an easy, welcoming smile and showing perfect white teeth. She was striking in a simple pink sun dress and white sandals, but Seargant guessed that she'd look great in anything.

The FBI-man brought nothing to the meeting; not the thick file his agents had worked tirelessly on, or even a pen and paper. He wanted the meeting to be as simple as possible; just to look into the eyes of a killer's wife to see if there was anything they'd missed.

"Mr. Seargant," Bunny began, smiling and taking his hand. "I welcome you to my home."

"Hello Mrs. Richards," Seargant said warmly, shaking her slender hand. "I have no doubt that my men have exhausted you in their questioning. Let me be very clear that it's not my intention to rehash this nightmare or cause additional headache. I just want to speak with you at the most basic level to better understand things."

Bunny took an instant liking to Seargant. He had a genial manner that was simultaneously authoritative, honest, and engaging. He carried himself with a great deal of confidence and she connected with him immediately.

Bunny motioned to the large patio table behind her. "These are my attorneys. They insisted on being here in case the conversation turns legal. And please call me Bunny."

"Certainly," Seargant said.

The lawyers rose to meet Seargant. They were all dressed in expensive suits and had million dollar smiles to go with them. They held a superior air that was off-putting, but each looked impressive and formidable. There was no doubt they were eager to protect their client from anything the FBI could muster.

But Seargant didn't mind them at all.

"Thanks again for having me," Seargant said. "I just want to be sure nothing's been left out."

Bunny looked at her attorneys, all of whom had their pens out, ready to document everything. They all perked up as her steady gaze washed over them.

"You guys can go," she said with a quick wave. "Mr. Seargant and I can talk privately."

Two of the men stood but the third remained seated, looking contemptuous.

"Mrs. Richards, may I remind you that Mr. Seargant is with the FBI and there is an active criminal investigation that could extend—"

"Donald," Bunny snapped. "I have done *nothing* wrong or *anything* I'm ashamed of. And if a simple conversation with Mr. Seargant can help then so be it."

Her lead attorney was unmoved. "A conversation is fine, but I implore you—"

Bunny shot the man a look and he was silenced.

"Very well then," he conceded. "I'll call you later."

Then he walked away with his team in tow.

CHAPTER 55

Seargant was impressed with Bunny so far.

"You know they could've stayed," he said.

"I don't need them to talk about Jeremy," she said, waving her hand casually. "Besides, that group charges almost two grand an hour for on-site council and I had to dismiss them on principle."

Seargant smiled in steady admiration. Even with unlimited funds, she was still grounded.

"First off, how are *you* doing with all this?" Seargant asked.

"I'm fine," she replied, flatly. But it was clear she'd given the same response several times in the last week.

Seargant studied her. "Bunny it's okay. I know this is difficult but it's all on him not you."

Bunny smiled for a few moments, before looking down and moving her dress over her knees. When she looked up, she blinked away a tear. Seargant reached for a napkin and handed it to her.

"I'm really sorry. I didn't mean to—"

"No it's really fine," she said. "I know there's nothing I did to bring this on, but it's just so surreal. I keep thinking back on our time together, wondering what went wrong with him. Do you think it was the money; that he just lost his mind?"

"Finances are actually a good place to start. Do you mind if we discuss it?"

Bunny poured Seargant a tall glass of Iced Tea and then casually sipped hers. "We always did things separately. I had a couple of bank accounts with about a million dollars each, and he had everything else. This may sound crazy but I don't even know how much money we have. I just hired a team of forensic accountants and they're working with our financial people. I also understand the FBI is working with the IRS to see what they can find."

Seargant nodded. "Everything is frozen and we're finding new assets daily."

"You know what's strange?" Bunny asked, rhetorically. "As chaotic as things are, it's never been so quiet and peaceful around here."

Bunny let out a nervous snicker and Seargant changed the subject.

"So tell me all about yourself," he said.

Bunny composed herself, looking to Seargant, thoughtfully. "When I was a little girl, I was very expressive and artistic. I loved to sit and draw. Sometimes I'd write a short fairy tale with exciting characters and a fantastic plot. I had a whole shoebox full of these homemade books."

Seargant smiled. "They say the best vehicle to get to a faraway place in the shortest amount of time isn't a car, plane, or a boat. It's a book."

"I like that," Bunny said. "It's so true."

"How did your stories end?"

"The princess *always* wins, of course. Almost every story I wrote had a prince and a princess and they lived happily ever after."

"What were your characters like?"

"I was only eight or nine at the time. The prince was always handsome, but had some sort of flaw that the princess would help remedy. They would face a challenge—like a dragon, thief, or a troll—and conquer everything. At the end they'd kiss on top of a grassy hill or beside a stream, and then walk into a happy future."

"That's beautiful," Seargant said, shaking his head. "It sounds like you have a true gift."

"I don't know about *that* but I certainly did enjoy it."

Bunny fell silent as her eyes glazed over and she stared into the distance. Seargant had conducted enough interviews to know he'd touched on something that ran deep. She was not just thinking of a passing memory. She was paralyzed in deep thought; an embodiment of pensiveness.

When she continued, her facial expressions softened and her look was indirect.

"Then puberty hit and I started to look like *this,*" she said, waving her hands, pointing to her body and face.

Although it could have been received as self-adulation, Seargant picked up on its mechanical nature. Like her beauty was a burden that she'd been carrying around. Bunny was clearly in turmoil, and although in control on most fronts, perhaps she was still a little girl inside.

"Then nobody cared what I said or wrote. My teachers let me get away with things that other kids couldn't. Things got easier; as if I were being protected and coddled. I felt like I was *physically* among others, but totally isolated.

"It sounds weird, but even in my mid-teens grown men would notice me and do whatever I wanted. Some of my girlfriends turned on me and women—even those many years older—would be jealous and catty.

"Moving on in time, all of my friends were beautiful and rich. We were the cheerleaders and athletes that ran the school. We had the best seats in the cafeteria and went to the coolest parties.

"My brothers and sisters grew apart from me, and my parents treated me like I was a slut and a stain on the family. But what's funny is that Jeremy was my first and I waited until I was in a long-term relationship to give my love away."

Bunny let out a small whimper and Seargant passed over more napkins, which she accepted, gingerly.

"Looking back I would trade everything to be part of the *other* crowd, not caring about my looks and what to say or do. I used to love playing kickball and tag; playing softball and just running around a field with my friends."

Seargant mirrored Bunny's demeanor as he sat patiently beside her. He saw discomfort in her expressions; anger and frustration in her body language. But he felt drawn to her, wanting to console her.

"So what did you do?" he asked.

"Went to USC with a full scholarship for cheerleading and dance, majored in political science, and graduated with a 4.0. I met Jeremy in my senior year and we became fast friends. But he was dating Kelly and I was dating someone as well."

Hearing Kelly's name, and especially from someone other than Tom, threw Seargant for a loop. He was taken back and turned inward, thinking of his friend.

Bunny's voice suddenly cracked. "Do you think Jeremy killed Kelly?"

"It's an active investigation, but what do you think?"

"Jeremy is many things, and the last week has been very telling, but I can't see him as a killer. I couldn't have been that naïve to be with someone like that."

"Did he ever speak of Kelly?"

"He rarely talked of her, but when her name came up, he became distraught and withdrawn. He said it was such a surreal memory and he would be forever numbed. Again, I can't believe he could've killed her or anyone else."

"What happened after college?"

"We found each other again. He sold his software company, started three more ventures and eventually sold them off as well. Then he did whatever he was doing up until last week. As you can guess we've drifted apart."

"What was he like, overall?"

"One of the coolest and commanding people I ever met, actually. He could socialize with the best of them and adapt into any situation. At a function, he would always have a drink in his hand, but would rarely finish it because he wanted to remain in control.

"He would tell captivating stories and always have people around him, like he was holding court. He remembered names and faces and everybody's hot buttons, to make them feel special. Jeremy would have made a great politician."

Bunny smiled as a memory of happier times flashed within her. "When we first met it was magical. Everything was first class, even in college. We'd talk all night. He was real sweet."

"What changed?" Seargant asked, casually.

"I think it was the money. He could suddenly travel anywhere and indulge in anything. He had handlers pop up out of nowhere and his future was limitless. I guess I became a liability; someone who was holding him back."

Bunny shook her head and Seargant could tell she was close to tears.

"Would you like a change of scenery?" Seargant asked. "May I have a quick tour of the house?"

"Sure thing," Bunny said, getting up and dabbing her eyes. "Follow me."

CHAPTER 56

They walked through the most amazing kitchen Seargant had ever seen. Then past the living room that took up almost half the lower floor. Bunny kept moving as he trailed behind her.

They entered the dining room, which was a big, rectangular room with the largest table he'd ever seen. He quickly counted over thirty ornate wood-carved chairs, lined perfectly around the table, and a beautiful chandelier hanging from high above. He looked at the two entry ways, which were much too small to allow the table to pass.

She sensed the ensuing question. "The table was imported from Brazil and is solid mahogany. It was brought into this room through the wall, and then we had the window made custom. It will never leave this room for obvious reasons."

Seargant and Bunny spent the next several minutes walking from room to room and talking. The exchange was effortless, with moments of laughter fitted into the more serious conversation. He was struck with how perfect and regal everything was; but also that the décor—while dramatic—had very little utility. There was little warmth or ambience. It was like a museum and he wondered if they'd ever really *enjoyed* the house.

But then they entered the master bedroom, with an enormous bed chamber and an abundance of cozy furniture. Large mirrors covered the north wall and it opened up into a small parlor with a leather sofa, some throw blankets, and a reading lamp.

A basket of novels and magazines lay next to a large chair and ottoman, and Seargant could tell that Bunny spend considerable time there. The biggest flat screen television he'd ever seen hung across from them, and with the small kitchenette and coffee station, Seargant wondered why anyone would ever have to leave.

He turned the corner to see that the rest of the room covered at least half of the third floor. There were twin soaking tubs on a platform, a sauna, and an over-sized shower stall. Like everything else, no expense was spared on having every luxury.

"Over here," she said, walking into a large closet. "This was his."

Seargant wasn't surprised to see that it looked more like a men's fashion store than a closet. It was well-lit, with a three-panel mirror on one wall and a variety of suits and shirts perfectly lining the other. Around the perimeter were scores of shoes and the air smelled of expensive leather. A huge chair sat in the center, with another television hanging on the wall. But what really struck him was the large fireman's pole in the corner.

"Is that what I think it is?" Seargant asked.

"You mean the 'bat pole?'" Bunny asked, laughing.

"Is that what you call it?"

"This is typical Jeremy. When he wants something he has to have it. He grew up loving Batman and Robin and wanting a 'bat pole.' It actually goes down three levels to behind the bar."

Seargant placed his large hands on the brass pole, feeling its sturdiness and looking into the darkness below. Then he turned to Bunny, who was studying him.

"You should see yourself right now. You look like a little kid on Christmas!"

"Do you think I could—"

"Absolutely," she said, cutting him off. "It's an easy and fast way downstairs and I use it all the time."

With that, she walked by him and grabbed the pole. "See you at the bottom," she said, disappearing below.

He waited a few moments, took one last look around and then followed her, smiling the whole way. He landed softly in a small room, where she was leaning against a wall, expectantly.

"This way," she said, walking through a door and into the basement.

"Wow," was all he could say.

Seargant took in the long granite bar with its dark mahogany cabinetry, the long glass shelving that held the high-end spirits, and the enormous mirror behind it that reflected the recessed lighting.

Opposite, he saw classic arcade games and counted at least ten televisions. Further down were more leather sofas and chairs. The lighting was plentiful and ornate, with sconces lining the walls under triple crowned molding.

"This basement is better than anything I've ever seen," he said.

"Again, this is Jeremy," she said, shaking her head.

They toured the gym, theatre room, poker room, and bathrooms; eventually walking back outside to the patio.

Seargant extended his hand, handing Bunny his business card. "I've taken up enough of your time. But it was an absolute pleasure meeting you. Please call me at any time for any reason at all."

"I'll do that," Bunny said, matching his smile. "It was really great to meet you, too."

Seargant spent another couple of hours walking the streets of St. Michaels. He strolled down Talbot Street and looked into several of the quaint shops, before walking by the old historic church to the "Cannonball House." Then he walked St. Mary's Square, pausing by the old Revolutionary War cannon and peeking into the St. Michaels Museum.

But soon he was on the road again.

Just before reaching Route 50, he stopped for a quick bite at the Old Mill Deli. He entered the low, red wooden building to find a moderate crowd, and knew it had to be popular with the locals.

He ordered a crab cake sandwich and bottled water to go. Walking across the gravel parking lot, he realized he was famished and ripped open the bag, eating as he stood. Then he started his car; but instead of taking the west exit for Route 50, he took a hard right.

The last few weeks had been mentally-draining and his personal life was in disarray. And although he had just spent considerable time in the Caribbean, he hadn't walked on a beach or felt the ocean for some time. Ocean City was less than ninety minutes away and he needed to sort some things out.

He always carried a duffel bag with a variety of clothes and toiletries, and he even had an extra suit and shirt hanging in the back seat.

He entered Ocean City from Route 90 and settled into a room at the Fenwick Inn. He'd called his wife from the road and told her his plans. She understood, but the conversation was terse, and he knew there were unresolved matters with her as well.

Then, like every night since he'd left him, Seargant thought of Tom Brightwell, and prayed for the man's safe return.

CHAPTER 57

Seargant didn't need an alarm clock. He'd been waking up before 5 a.m. since his high school work-outs.

But he felt awkward. He questioned his impromptu decision to drive to the ocean when so much was happening at the office. So he methodically did one-hundred push-ups and sit-ups. It wasn't as extensive as his usual workouts, but the simple motions were effective in getting his heart pumping and his mind sharp.

Then he enjoyed a hot shower and changed into shorts and a T-shirt. He packed the few things he had, picked up an apple and a bottle of water at the lobby, and left the hotel.

The late-August air was muggy, even before sunrise, and the temperature was firmly in the eighties. Making his way south on Coastal Highway, he turned left onto Pacific and then right, eventually parking on 89th Street, next to the Sea Terrace.

Walking onto the beach, he felt like an excited child. Feeling the rough, cool sand on his bare feet conjured up memories of his childhood. But seeing the faint orange glow on the skyline, and the promise of a new day's sun, made him shiver.

He thought of Tom Brightwell and remembered their conversation in Bonaire while looking at the stars. The exchange had been telling and full of philosophical talk that left Seargant wanting more.

He looked to the sky and traced the sun's eventual path. The east was royal blue while the west was still black. He could even see a thick ribbon of stars over the bay.

Seargant reached the water's edge, allowing the frothy white surf to run around his ankles. He smiled at the simple, sudden feeling that had been lost on him for too long. He looked up and down the beach to see he was alone. The feeling was whimsical and he knew he'd made the right decision in coming.

Standing next to the ocean, he was reminded that he was such a small part of the world; even as insignificant as any one of the grains of sand that comprised the beach. Also, that his actions—although seemingly relevant—we're just events between two ends of time.

He watched the orange glow of the rising sun bounce off the low cloud cover. It forced a pinkish hue to jump off the horizon. It was beautiful and he delved further into thought.

The sun had been rising and falling around the earth for millions of years, and would continue to do so whether he was alive or dead. But what really mattered was *what* he did and *who* he did it with, and his relation with God, his true father and life source.

Seargant suddenly had an epiphany; a deep yearning to speak to God about things he'd been harboring inside. He closed his eyes, feeling the first warmth of the sun's rays, as a gentle breeze washed over him.

Then he openly prayed.

"Oh Lord," he cried out. "I don't go to church and I'm not as familiar with the bible as I once was. Maybe chasing bad guys has dulled my inner core, but I'm here to reaffirm that I am yours to command. I have lost my way, but feel born anew as I say these words."

Seargant opened his eyes and sucked in the salty air.

"But may I ask two favors, God; one for me and one for someone else?"

"As you know my wife and I are very much in love and have been since we met. We have so much to share, and feel a child would bring us closer to each other and to You. It would be the most precious gift we could ever receive."

Seargant began a slow walk in the tide.

"I also pray that Tom Brightwell returns safely and finds the inner peace he so much deserves. I know his recent actions are suspect, but his heart is true and he *is* a good man."

Seargant fell silent, reflecting on his thoughts and prayers. He felt an overwhelming sense of calm, as if a large burden had been displaced.

Then he sat on the sand, threw his long legs in front of him, and quietly watched the sun start its climb into the early-morning sky.

CHAPTER 58

Coffee had never tasted better to Seargant, as he crossed the Choptank River in Cambridge on his way back to Washington D.C.

The car windows were down, which allowed for a virtual wind tunnel of fresh air to blow through, so he raised the volume on the radio to compensate. He could hear nothing but the wind and the music, and with the caffeine gripping him, he became pensive. There was a certain anonymity involved and the feeling was invigorating.

The sun continued to rise behind him and as the bridge tilted downward, Seargant saw the low ball of burnt orange in his side mirror. It hung just above the horizon like an ornament. Looking in both directions, he saw the early morning boaters on the sun-streaked water and fell envious.

He knew it would be another grueling work day.

He imagined himself pulling into a marina and renting a simple pontoon boat for a quick fishing trip. Then he visualized living the life of one of the boaters below. But he dismissed the thoughts as reality set in. He lived in a world at odds with evil, and it was his calling to seek justice.

But then he waged an internal debate. Was the life he carved out worth it? The Job provided substantial income, great health care, and the promise of a federal pension, but at what cost? He knew he'd lost a connection with his wife, most certainly over the last month, but it stung deeper than that.

At the heart of it was their inability to conceive and he knew it was gnawing at her. She took it personally and felt inadequate. Although he had tried so many times to tell her that *she* was all that mattered, she would only nod through her sobs.

Seargant would comfort her, but new tears would appear faster than he could wipe them away; and although he was eager for open conversation, it only led to more frustration. So they had drifted apart. When they spoke, it was cosmetic; when they touched, it was cold.

Arriving at the Hoover building, Seargant changed in the fitness center and headed toward his office, bringing another cup of coffee with him. He noticed four more crates of files had been delivered in his absence.

The folder on top was market urgent. He knew it was the final summary of Jeremy's interrogation and his likely path to freedom within Venezuela.

Seargant was happy to see no record of his *own* insertion into South America. No one could ever know that the FBI had escorted Tom Brightwell into Venezuela, or even provided him a guide and resources to go after Jeremy.

It was another silent reminder of his friend, and like so many times before, Seargant thought of Tom's safety. But he wasn't optimistic. His professional experience and sense of reality grounded any real hope. Still, he picked up one of the crates and tore off a fresh piece of paper from a legal pad.

It took him all day to read, dissect, and cross-reference the information. By late evening his mind was over-worked, his body numb, and his skin felt gray. He'd been in the same office for the better part of the day, and even after finishing the final review, he still felt uneasy about the finality of the case.

Whether it was due to the unknowns about Tom or something else, Seargant didn't know. He just internalized a sense of anxiety about the entire investigation.

He was tilting back in his office chair when the phone rang, shaking him out of his trance.

He moved to the handset smoothly, like he did several times each day. But he couldn't have known this time would be different.

"This is Seargant," he answered, mechanically.

"Honey, it's me," his wife countered.

Susan's voice was measured and flat. Her tone was direct. He'd never heard her like this and within moments everything changed.

"You need to come home right now!"

CHAPTER 59

The drive home was uncomfortable. Little else had been said after Susan's first words; and his inquiries were met with silence, which only increased the tension. But then her voice softened and she said she was okay.

Still, she needed to see him immediately.

The words kept ringing in his head. *You need to come home right now.* What did she mean? What was wrong? He knew her well enough to know things were fine, but he'd also heard something in her voice that was unfamiliar.

His mind was all over the place and he entertained all possibilities, as unlikely as they were. Was she being held against her will? Were they *both* in danger?

Seargant was home in half the normal time, arriving in the exclusive Potomac community of Downing Woods. He pulled in front of his house, choosing to pass it for a quick review. There was nothing unusual and he even saw Susan in the upstairs window folding clothes. This comforted him and he quickly turned around and parked in the garage.

He checked the alarm system control at the doorway. Nothing unusual had been triggered, and he even saw that no one had entered or exited for several hours. Then he heard the hypnotic music of Enya's *Watermark;* something he and his wife had listened to in college when alone late at night.

His mood relaxed as he moved through the kitchen.

"Susan?" he called out, but she didn't answer.

Then he saw the rose petals on the floor that led up the back stairs. Walking up, he saw candles were lit at the entrance to the master bedroom. He was all smiles now, certain nothing was wrong. Heading into the bedroom, he saw more rose petals and the source of the music. His wife was in a sexy nightgown, cut down the front, barefoot, and leaning against the bed.

"Babe, is everything all right?" he asked.

She moved directly toward him. Her almond eyes were wide and serious, never leaving his gaze. Then she took his face in her hands, stepping on her tip toes, and they fell into a long embrace.

"Everything is perfect, dad. I'm pregnant. Fourteen weeks."

He stepped back, holding her hands in his. Reality hit and they fell into another embrace, rocking back and forth.

"May God bless this child and continue to bless us," he offered.

They made love twice that night and spoke for hours, like they hadn't in years. It was a warm and open exchange, and erased all the anxiety between them. They felt like teenagers again, clumsily planning a bright future, and all too impatient for it to begin. They spoke of paint colors and baby furniture, feeding schedules and diapers, and then baby names and the pride of creating a legacy.

They laughed and cried together in an uninterrupted flow of emotion that kept them up until dawn.

It was the happiest time of Seargant's life.

It was also the first time in a week that he didn't lie awake thinking of Tom Brightwell and the Island Hopper case.

CHAPTER 60

South West of Esmeralda
Southern Venezuela

Not knowing the hour was strange. But not knowing the day was absolutely maddening.

Tom estimated that he'd been in captivity for about a week, but there was no real way of telling. The minutes, hours, and days had blended into a hellish nightmare and his deep sleeps and hallucinations only added to the confusion.

His constant thirst was intolerable. He choked when he breathed, as the air flowed through his dry mouth. He would lick his lips often, only to feel the tender blisters that had formed. The inside of his throat was raw from coughing.

He'd been interrogated, beaten, and starved. Sometimes he awoke soaked in sweat, with the hot, unrelenting sun beating down on him. Other times he found himself in complete darkness.

Occasionally he was lucid enough to produce a valid stream of thoughts, but for the most part he simply existed with his mind in a fog. Time was frozen; the only evidence of its passing being the differing degrees of pain and discomfort he felt.

In the beginning there had been an unrelenting stream of questions. How did he travel to them and for what reason? Who knew he was in Venezuela and what was his real purpose? To that end, he had been mostly honest, though he never mentioned Emilio, Javier, or Anna. He had hoped to spur some sort of compassion, but it hadn't come. These men had lived hard lives and a murdered daughter wasn't going to sway them.

But he had an alternative goal in telling the truth. He was aware of differing methodologies in giving and surviving torture and interrogation. As a detective with the CPD, he'd read the Irish Republican Army's *Green Book*, the anti-Soviet *Manual for Psychiatry for Dissidents and Torture*, the *Interrogation Experience* by the Iranian guerrilla, and even the CIA's own *Human Resources Exploitation Manual.*

He was keen in knowing if someone was being truthful or at least holding back information. And even in his diminished capacity, he'd been watchful of the facial expressions of his captors.

They had been very telling. They never answered his questions and usually dismissed him completely, but something stirred whenever he'd mentioned Jeremy's name. Tom was sure they knew him and that bead of hope kept him going.

Somehow he had to survive and get to Jeremy.

But things had gotten worse and he could tell there was waning interest in him. The well-dressed man, Marco, had never been back. The number of guards that monitored him had been cut in both number and formality. Recently there had been no one watching him. Had he been left for dead?

A few days before, Tom was moved to a barn on the far side of the property. It was an open lean-to, which was good for ventilation and mostly shaded, but he was handcuffed and tightly bound by a heavy chain that was secured into concrete.

His food and water had been steadily reduced, and nothing had been brought over the last couple of days. He'd been forgotten and chained like a wild animal, but even in his shaded pen, the heat was unforgiving and his thirst only grew.

Though bound, he could move several feet in each direction; but with the weight of the chains and his weakened mind, he usually laid on the ground, unmoving. Much of his time was spent in deep sleeps. When conscious, he just stared through half open slits.

Tom tried to keep his mind active by thinking about and analyzing anything he could. His thoughts, he knew, were his best ally and the only hope of escape. Thankfully his body had started to acclimate to his extreme surroundings. His body had regulated his temperature and hadn't been producing as much perspiration. His hunger pains had also ceded.

One of his mental exercises was replaying his immediate past in the form of a video diary. He remembered leaving Saint Maarten and arriving in Venezuela for his mission through the jungle. He envisioned the animal and plant life, and recalled the smells and the harsh terrain he'd traveled.

Tom worked hard to recall what Emilio looked like, and even smiled when he thought of the large anaconda that had nearly killed him. He recalled his encounter with the jaguar, and then thought of Javier and Anna and hoped they were okay.

He also formed random and far-reaching thoughts of his past, especially of his wife and daughter, and he thought of Dannie and Seargant and wondered how they were doing.

Then he was there.

Jeremy was standing above him, with a stream of light behind him as if he was being introduced by some heavenly force.

Tom didn't know if he was dreaming or hallucinating. But when he saw movement and then recognized the face, he perked up and slowly rose to a sitting position. He blinked away the stinging sweat, and took in the killer that had taken his daughter and so many others.

"Are you still here, old man?" Jeremy asked, moving closer.

At first Tom couldn't speak, and he realized it had been several days since he'd even tried. But then he moved and felt the sharp pain in his hands where the handcuffs had started to dig into his skin. He felt the tightness around his mid-section where the chains encircled him like a belt. He realized that the moment was real and his senses peaked, drawing on some auxiliary reserve.

Tom was in the present and this was happening. Jeremy was standing in front of him.

"So you *are* here?" Tom said, hoarsely. "You son-of-a-bitch!"

"Relax, Tom. This will all be over soon. I just had to come see you for myself. To be honest you really fascinate me."

"Why did you kill Kelly?"

Jeremy crossed his arms casually, as Tom looked him over. His former would-be son-in-law was wearing relaxed white, cotton pants, a thin blue button-down, and leather sandals. He was clean-shaven, well-kept, and looked like he was off to some high-end country club function. His entire being rang with confidence.

If the Island Hopper investigation had thrown a wrench into Jeremy's plans or disrupted him in any way, it wasn't apparent. He was a sociopath, Tom knew, but it was almost more disturbing seeing how easily the man could adapt.

"We'll get to that, Tom. You're not calling the shots. We are in Venezuela and you're an American trespasser, and even former law enforcement to boot. Things aren't really going your way."

"Tell me why," Tom persisted.

"How did you know I would be in Saint Maarten?" Jeremy countered.

Tom was taken back. Jeremy seemed to think the FBI was tipped off about his whereabouts in Saint Maarten. But Tom remained stone-faced. He buried his emotions and put his head in his hands, feigning exhaustion. It wasn't all an act. This was the most energy he'd spent in days. But his police instincts kicked in. Whatever Jeremy needed, he wasn't going to get it. So Tom tried to leverage the situation.

"You really don't know, do you?" Tom led, acting bewildered.

"Know what? What are you talking about?" Jeremy erupted, showing his first sign of agitation.

Tom shook his head. He was hoping the younger man would draw closer so he could strangle him with his chains, but he doubted Jeremy was that careless.

"Tell me why you killed Kelly and all the others."

Jeremy sighed and then lowered his head, thinking things through. Then his hard, piercing eyes found Tom's and a terrible grin played on his face.

"I guess it doesn't matter now, does it? I mean, you must know that you'll never leave here."

Tom remained quiet; absorbing every word like it was the cold water he so desperately craved.

"Okay, Tom. What the hell, right? My latest deal went through a couple weeks before the wedding. No one knew, not even Kelly, because of insider trading laws and the investment bankers, accountants, and lawyers were still involved in due diligence. But on paper it instantly put me into the list of Forbes billionaires, just under Paul Allen."

Jeremy paused to check on Tom. He was still sitting on the ground, pathetically staring through hollow eyes.

"Am I losing you? Do you hear what I'm saying? This deal literally made me a billionaire overnight. And then Kelly told me she was pregnant and I guess I kind of lost it. Not at first. Sure I acted surprised and happy, but then I thought about the whole thing. I knew we were being married in Jamaica and if you're gonna kill someone, it should probably happen where the investigation would be loose, the officials bribed, and any witnesses wouldn't want to get involved."

"She was pregnant?" Tom managed, the words barely escaping his cracked lips.

"Yeah and I was about to become a real player, a real force in—"

In the moment Tom realized that he'd not only lost Kelly and Jess, but also a dear, helpless grandchild that he'd never know. Suddenly his mind was alive and it flashed forward to a life unrealized.

He envisioned the child being born and was oddly convinced it would have been a girl. Pictures formed in his mind, like random fireworks that are gone before they can be distinguished. Memories that could never be came to him in an instant. Tom saw his granddaughter with big, brown eyes, laughing at some funny remedy. He saw her as a toddler, smiling and clapping her tiny hands; and he saw her as a grown woman on the beach holding hands with her *own* children.

Tom's anger swelled and his body trembled. Energy erupted from deep within and he launched at Jeremy. It was as if he wasn't bound by chains or even the laws of physics. He was going to kill Jeremy where he stood and there was nothing that could stop him.

Tom attacked like a starving lion, but Jeremy took a quick step back. Focused on Jeremy's throat, Tom's outstretched hand was within inches of its target when the chains jerked him back. His speed was unbelievable for his condition, but the chains were unforgiving. Tom was caught at his mid-section and thrown to the ground with a force that knocked the wind out of him.

Jeremy called to a guard, who came running and immediately kneeled on the broken prisoner. Tom was physically and mentally spent and couldn't resist. He just shut his eyes in defeat, breathing heavily and blinking away the tears that tracked down his dirty face.

Others rushed in to play witness, and Tom heard Jeremy speaking with some of the guards. After several minutes of hushed dialogue, Tom heard someone say "just get it over with."

Then he drifted off once more.

And like so many times before, he welcomed the darkness.

CHAPTER 61

Tom Brightwell awoke in the middle of the night. It was odd: the random time warps he experienced. Wasn't the sun just cascading down on him? Hadn't he been talking to Jeremy? Didn't he lunge at him?

But in what seemed like moments, day had turned to night and he was alone again. As usual he wore the darkness like a blanket and was comforted by it.

He always felt safer in the dark.

Tom looked at the far wall, where the slanted beams of moonlight showed through the uneven wall boards. He heard the low hum of the insect chorus just beyond that; a constant din he'd become increasingly accustomed to and even fond of.

At first he thought he'd dreamt the encounter with Jeremy. But the pain in his chest where the chains had caught him was real. He passed a gentle hand over his mid-section and repositioned himself slightly, breathing as deeply as he could afford. He'd reinjured his ribs.

Still, he knew it would all be over soon.

He recalled the heated exchange. Had Kelly really been pregnant? Did Jeremy actually confess to her murder? Tom was too incensed to press Jeremy for more information and he inwardly cursed himself for losing control.

But as much as he was deflated, Tom felt a small sense of victory and closure. He now knew the truth and was comforted, for the short time he expected to live. But he still needed more from Jeremy. He wanted to pump him for information on the Island Hopper killings. How did he move around so freely? How did he choose his victims and why were the methods of murder so different? What was the purpose of placing the coins on the eyes? Jeremy was a self-indulgent narcissist, but why all the games?

Then he heard a voice.

He stopped breathing and his eyes grew wide. His mind had been playing tricks on him from the beginning, so he couldn't trust any of his senses. When he heard the voice again, it was firm and direct, and he knew it was real.

Tom slowly moved to the wall on all fours. He exacted the posture of an animal that had been beaten into submission and was being called for some coveted prize. But it was also the only way he could effectively move and not have the chains impede him.

"Hello?" he called out.

"Tom Brightwell. It's Emilio, your guide from last week. Place your back against the wall and your hands through the loose board."

Tom recognized the voice and did as he was told. He heard and then felt the tension of the chains being cut, and the instant relief of a lighter burden. Then the larger body chain fell away and he gently rolled on his side, completely free.

But there was no time to rest.

"Now move to the far door and stop. On my command run into the trees directly across and stop again."

Tom's mind was suddenly acute. He moved to the barn door, stumbling as he adopted a clumsy walk. Stopping short, he leveled his breathing and awaited instructions. Blood rushed to his head and he felt dizzy, but his survival instincts prevailed. His entire future depended on his immediate actions, so he focused on his rescuer.

"Go now," the voice sounded.

Tom stepped out in silence and rushed into the tree line about ten yards away. A heavy arm found him and brought him to a crouching position.

"We have a lot of ground to cover and very little time," Emilio said, pointedly. "Take my hand and don't let go."

Tom nodded and the two men awkwardly, but steadily, made their way through the harsh terrain. The proximity of the encampment prohibited the use of light, and the dense canopy above prevented any moonlight to shine through.

After several minutes, Emilio produced a compact flashlight, and they picked up speed. The branches reached out and scratched them at random, and the untested path was unforgiving in both slope and obstacle. Thorns were pushed into their unprotected skin without warning, but no words were spoken.

The determined pair even gained momentum.

They reached a clearing and Tom saw the familiar pick-up truck. There was no reason in communicating that time was an important factor. They jumped in and were soon moving through the trees and eventually onto a narrow road.

Emilio spoke quickly. "I've been watching you for a couple of days. We probably have up to five hours until you're discovered missing. By then, we'll be well on our way to Caracas. The cartels rarely fly at night, so that's not an issue, but there's only one road in or out of here and the next hour is literally a life or death scenario."

"How did you know to come for me?" Tom asked. His voice was raspy and low.

"Your farmer friend was retrieving his boat and did some spying. He managed to get a communication to me and here I am. He said he was indebted to you and was committed to your safety."

Emilio looked at his passenger. Tom had shrunk into the seat, cowering like a wounded animal. He appeared confused and possibly hallucinogenic. It was clear he was trying to think things through, but he couldn't get a grasp on reality.

Emilio continued. "He was extremely motivated to help you. I must say that you certainly have an amazing effect on people!"

"But how did—"

"You told him about the orphanage near El Jobal. He went there and they knew who I was. They contacted me and said they owed you as well. Remember all the money you gave them?"

"But why—"

Emilio cut Tom off, curtly. "Look, you need to save your strength, because we have a long way to go. There's a cooler at your feet, with bottled water and plenty of meat. I have baked chicken, beef, and some fruit. When you're done, undress completely and put on the clothing in the bag on the dash. There's also a gun in the glove box. If there's any kind of road block or trouble, wait for my word and we'll take out as many as we can. You'll be dead if taken hostage, so try your best to get out of any struggle."

Tom perked up. He wasted no time in opening the cooler and gulping down the first bottle of water. He then opened another, and started to eat the beef and chicken, taking quick breaths and alternating between the treasures, greedily.

"Slow down; you'll make yourself sick."

Tom managed a quick grunt. "I can't. This is the best meal I've ever had. I can't thank you enough."

Emilio nodded, but didn't take his eyes off the thin roadway. The truck was steadily moving out of danger, and although the plan was progressing nicely, there was no denying his anxiety.

Emilio turned off the headlights as they approached an intersection. He peered in all directions for a few moments and when satisfied, turned the wheel left and punched the accelerator.

After several more miles Tom sensed his friend was breathing easier and it was obvious that some of the threat had abated. Tom put the food and drink down and undressed; eventually donning a completely different wardrobe, with sandals, relaxed tan shorts, and a button-down shirt. There was also a straw hat that remained on the floor. He could do nothing about his body odor or the scraggly beard that was almost two weeks old; but he realized that both could only help mask his American features.

"So was it a success?" Emilio asked, lightening the mood and drawing a quick look from Tom.

The food and water had been well-received and Tom was feeling much better. "I saw Jeremy and was able to talk to him."

Emilio tightened his grip on the steering wheel, remaining silent.

"He told me he killed Kelly. She was pregnant and he didn't want any part of playing daddy."

"I'm so sorry, my friend."

"I only wish I could have gotten my hands on him."

Emilio continued staring ahead and Tom could tell something had changed.

"What is it?" Tom asked.

"What do you mean?"

"What do you know about Jeremy? You twitched a little."

Emilio looked astonished. "What are you talking about? You should get some rest."

"Don't lie to me. After what I've been through, nothing will shock me."

Emilio drew a long breath, expelling it slowly. "I saw Jeremy come into the barn and heard most of what was discussed. I heard the commotion and you yelping in pain when you tried to attack him. I was there after you passed out and heard they were going to kill you this morning."

"Go on."

"Yes, I know where Jeremy is staying, at least right now. But *he* is not my mission."

Tom's eyes went wide. He couldn't get the words out fast enough. "He *is* the mission; not me! Where is he? I have to finish this!"

Emilio made no attempt to refute Tom or slow the truck. He continued eyeing the road.

"His house is ten minutes behind us, east of that last intersection. But we are not equipped, nor you physical enough to go after him. I'm sorry, but my goal is to get you to safety."

"Turn around, Emilio. Please. My daughter—"

". . . Is dead," Emilio yelled, finishing Tom's sentence and finally looking over. "And I'm very sorry for everything that's been taken from you. But my decision is final. Respect it and regroup. We are

260

not out of this by any means. We still have to get over the bridge to start moving north!"

Tom lifted the bottle of water and sipped it slowly this time. Defeated, he turned away from Emilio and stared out the window, trying to discern the landscape that was flying by.

Eventually, Tom's body gave in and exhaustion overtook him, as he slept unchecked for several hours. He awoke to find the truck had stopped. He heard voices and saw several men speaking to Emilio. He quickly went for the gun, but Emilio ran over.

"It's okay, Tom. I can't believe you were out for so long, but we're at the fishing boat that will take you to Aruba. In about an hour you'll be met by another handler, and soon you'll be safe."

Tom slowly exited the truck as several harsh-looking men scrutinized him. Emilio took him by the arm and maneuvered him onto the boat.

"Thank you, Emilio," Tom offered, humbly.

They shook hands, and Tom regarded the Venezuelan for several moments. The bright morning sun shined on the younger man's face, and it was the first time Tom could really study him.

Emilio's facial features were hard, but kind. A scar slid down his left side, from his ear to his neck, confirming he was no stranger to action. But what caught Tom's attention most were his light brown eyes. They resonated with a confidence that only came with years of training and experience. Tom suddenly realized that he didn't know his rescuer at all. This wasn't just a simple do-gooder that taught at a university. Had it all been a facade?

"Who are you, really?" Tom asked, softly.

Emilio bent at the waist as a long, slow laugh erupted from him. "I'm one of the best friends that you'll never see again."

Then Emilio moved back to the truck.

Soon the boat was off, slicing through the aqua blue water and heading north with purpose. When Tom situated himself, he looked to the shore and Emilio was gone.

CHAPTER 62

Oranjestad
Aruba

The arrival in Aruba was anti-climactic.

The boat ride took about an hour, with the six-man crew keeping their distance from Tom. They went about their duties with fervor—as if he wasn't there—speaking in foreign tongues and not including him in their lively banter. Tom wondered if they even knew anything about him. How they were saving his life.

The sun was strong and the wind blew hard, but Tom welcomed both on his face as the boat sliced through the open water. Occasionally he was hit with ocean spray and tasted the salt on his lips.

He didn't mind. It was just another reminder that he was still alive.

It was now late morning and Tom felt safer with each wave the small craft bested, and every bit of separation from the Venezuelan shore. But he couldn't shake the uneasiness entirely. He kept looking in every direction for a pursuer. A boat, helicopter, or plane. Anything that could thwart his escape.

But it didn't happen.

They approached Aruba from the south-west and entered an inlet in the heart of Oranjestad. The boat engines mellowed and they slowed considerably. Then they passed other touristy water crafts venturing out from shore.

Tom marveled at the huge bow of a cruise ship as they drew near. They were heading straight for it, but then turned hard right and into the inner workings of the Renaissance Marina.

They docked easily and several of the crew jumped out and Tom followed. He looked to the busy downtown area and substantial infrastructure, finally accepting his freedom. Could it be this easy? After what he'd been through over the last couple of weeks, could he simply step off a boat and melt into a crowd?

He regarded each of the men, trying to express his gratitude, but they seemed too busy to notice. So he moved to the end of the pier and stretched, taking measure of his injuries. He felt the burn in his mid-section where the heavy chains had caught him, but he still tested a steady gait.

He sucked in a deep breath and made his way along the uneven boardwalk, moving with a thick crowd. Most were walking fast and stepping past him, but he was in no rush. He saw a Starbucks and Häagen-Dazs, and scores of people enjoying their purchases as they sat in the sun.

To his right was the Seaport Casino. He slowly climbed the three green steps and was hit by a rush of cold air from inside. The table games were silent, but several of the slot machines were busy sounding their carnival-like hymns. He moved past them and turned right into the bathroom, relieved himself, and moved to the sink, thankful to splash fresh water on his face.

He looked in the mirror and saw a stranger in the reflection. He inched closer, not believing it. His blood-shot, yellow eyes scanned his unkempt beard and the deep lines in his face. The dirt seemed to be a permanent part of his sun-beaten, leathery skin. His face was much thinner and he estimated he'd lost another thirty pounds. He swallowed hard, tasting his wiry, acidic saliva. Then he breathed deeply, smelling his own harsh stink.

He moved a wet paper towel over his face and heard the bathroom door open. Then he felt the presence of someone next to him.

"Mr. Brightwell?" a deep voice sounded.

Tom looked to the source, frightened. The man was dark-skinned. He was dressed plainly and his demeanor was one of anxiety and anticipation. He smiled awkwardly, before seizing Tom's hand and squeezing it gently.

"I'm sorry I missed you out there," he motioned. "My name is Harlow and I'm to drive you to the Marriot."

Tom stared blankly, but managed a deep sigh. He recalled Emilio saying someone would meet him. Harlow exited the bathroom with Tom and soon they were driving out of the capital and into the high-rise hotel district.

Tom questioned Harlow on who had orchestrated his movements from Venezuela to Aruba, and about his itinerary. But it was clear the man had been hired for a specific task and wasn't privy to anything additional.

They eventually turned left into the Marriot compound and Tom marveled at the perfect rows of palm trees that danced in the brisk wind. Then they took a quick right and stopped at the entrance of the hotel side.

Harlow handed Tom an envelope and spoke evenly. "There's a paid two-night reservation under your name and you'll receive instructions later."

Tom entered the hotel lobby near Champion's Restaurant and found a sofa. He ripped open the envelope to find several hundred dollars in cash. Then he moved through the wide hallways, past Gandelman Jewelers and Stellars Casino.

Up ahead he marveled at the Ketsu Sushi Bar, with its sleek glass wall and platform floor. In the casing, he saw an assortment of desserts and ice cream and made a mental note to return the next day.

He found the check-in desk, leaning against the high yellow marble and looking to the dark wood back-drop. He received a hotel key card and nodded through the resort perks the enthusiastic receptionist was spewing.

Then he moved to the north wing and entered one of the small convenience shops, buying a handful of toiletries and a couple days worth of light clothing.

Soon he swiped his card for room # 768 and was in awe. The floor was dark hardwood, and he treaded on a pink rug as he threw his purchases on the large bed. To the left sat a desk and flat-paneled television; to the right a yellow couch and a high reading lamp. He was drawn to the balcony and he opened the high drapes, stepping out to consider the ocean-front view.

The terrace was huge and wrapped around the side of the building. To his right was the Ritz Carlton and several miles beyond it the California Lighthouse. To his left he saw the other hotels that made up the high-rise district. He looked to the sea, with the electric blue water extending as far as he could see.

He ordered room service; then enjoyed the most anticipated shower of his life, relishing the feeling of a clean-shaven face, a fresh mouth, and the comfort of the over-sized robe.

When his food came, he savored a light salad, chicken sandwich, a large bowl of fruit, and a couple bottles of cold water.

Then he focused on the king-sized bed, drew the curtains, and slept longer than he'd ever had.

Early the next morning the phone rang, forcing Tom awake. It took a few moments to adjust, but unlike recent experience, he felt instant comfort and security, as he rolled over in the warm sheets.

He felt the tenderness in his chest, but easily moved to the phone, breathing deeply.

"Hello?" Tom said into the receiver.

"Tom Brightwell. This is Jack Seargant."

"Seargant!" Tom exclaimed, grinning widely. "Do I have you to thank for this?"

"We'll get to that. I'm just happy you're okay. Tell me about your little adventure."

Tom fell silent, unsure of what to say. Though he trusted the man implicitly, he'd been so focused on getting out of captivity— and Venezuela altogether—that he hadn't decompressed or given thought to what he wanted anyone to know.

"We'll get to that," Tom countered, slyly. "What's my next step?"

"Have some good meals and get some rest. I took the liberty of booking you on a two o'clock flight to Chicago tomorrow afternoon."

"I have so much to tell you; I really do," Tom said, gaining spirit. "I just need to think things through a bit."

Seargant wanted to reach through the phone lines and shake Tom's hand. He wanted to look his friend in the eye and let him know he was there for him. He couldn't know the full extent of what Tom had been through, but gathered that it had been a horrible ordeal.

"No problem," Seargant said. "Your passport and plane tickets are at the front desk. Give me a call when you're ready."

The conversation over, Tom laid back and studied the spinning fan, finding comfort in the motorized whirring sound. It didn't take long for him to doze off once more, and he slept undisturbed until late morning.

Chapter 63

Tom waited to call Dannie. He wanted to be fully-rested and more mentality-equipped before their conversation. He was still reconciling things deep within himself, but growing stronger by the hour.

He'd felt a real connection with her in Saint Maarten and knew he could tell her anything; but because theirs was such a young and budding relationship, he was torn about what to say.

The next morning he watched CNN while doing morning stretches in his room. His mid-section felt better, and he was confident he hadn't broken any ribs when he'd lunged at Jeremy. The knot on his head was gone, though it was still tender to the touch and scabbed over.

He enjoyed another long shower and put on the clothes he'd bought the day before. Soon he was at the breakfast buffet at La Vista's restaurant. He sampled a yogurt, ate a vegetable omelet, and finished it all with a tall glass of fresh orange juice.

Tom was thankful to be back in the real world, though he was slow to the adjustment. Once again he walked the substantial Marriot lobby, feeling like a foreigner amongst the teeming modern conveniences. He stopped to eye a simple drinking fountain and considered the scene in total. It was a world he knew all too well, but one that had been out of reach for so long.

Simply treading on the white marble flooring, with the air conditioning pumping in from the walls, and the music playing from distant speakers, was surreal. He took it all in, appreciating it anew. He walked past the game room and into the open air, noticing the two-story fitness center to his left and the exclusive serenity pool to his right.

Lazy bodies surrounded the pool, lying in lounge chairs. Some were in the water, while others were already at the swim-up pool bar. Didn't these people know there was a place just a short journey south that was full of danger and poverty? Where all these modern conveniences were so alien and impossible?

But he didn't want to dwell on the fairness of it all. He'd been given yet *another* chance to reclaim his life and he vowed to live it slower, with wider eyes than before.

With a clearer mind, he thought about the morning before. He now realized that Emilio truly *did* save his life (again) when he'd refused to go after Jeremy. Being so physically-inept and emotionally-blinded, Tom would have ended up dead. Even worse, he would have put his rescuer at risk. Tom wished he could apologize to Emilio, but was strangely confident that somehow the man knew.

Tom ordered a large black coffee from the bakery shop and strolled back to the main pool area. He paused on the wooden bridge and sipped the steamy, hot brew; watching some boys tossing cherries to the iguanas on the rocks.

Suddenly the sounds of steel drums swept over the pool deck. Tom found himself surrounded by people of all ages, enjoying another day in paradise.

He found comfort within the throng. Children ran past their parents, trying to best each other; and their excited screams made him smile.

Tom found a lounge chair and enjoyed the freeing effects of the caffeine. He thought about the last couple of weeks, but focused more on his future.

An hour flew by and he was completely relaxed.

In an instant he found clarity and had a sure sense of what to do. He needed to call Dannie and tell her that he was okay. He needed to hear her voice. Gone were any thoughts of uncertainty or denial. He didn't care if he told her too much or too little. He just knew it would be alright.

Riding the elevator up, he felt giddy and foolish; like a school boy with a new crush. He couldn't get to his room fast enough. When the heavy door shut behind him, he darted onto the bed, picked up the phone, and started punching in digits. He eventually reached an operator in Alabama, who assured him of the number. He listened impatiently for the connection to take hold, and waited out the familiar ringing pulses.

"Hello?" her familiar voice sang, and his heart leapt.

"Danielle?" he offered, softly. "It's Tom."

"Oh Tom, I've been worried sick! Is it really you?"

Tom grinned, unable to control himself. His fears dissipated and the uneasiness in his stomach abated.

"It's me, Dannie. I'm in Aruba and will be in Chicago tomorrow night."

"Is everything okay?"

Tom breathed deeply and realized how much Dannie meant to him. They'd only shared those incredible three days together, but it felt like so much more. How he'd missed the feeling of needing someone and *being* needed! Wiping away a quick tear, he spoke evenly.

"Dannie, for the first time in a long time, I think things are gonna be just fine."

"I'm so glad, Tom. Tell me everything."

The flight to Atlanta arrived early and Tom got a quick bite before the easy hop to Chicago.

He'd used the time to his advantage, categorizing his experiences and deciding on what to disclose. He thought a lot about Dannie. Their phone conversation had been so fluid. It was as if no time had passed and their friendship had even deepened in the separation.

His affairs in Chicago were no doubt in disarray, and he longed to visit Jess and Kelly at the cemetery. He also yearned to formally organize his financial situation and perform some over-due house work.

Somewhere over the Atlantic, he'd stared into the blue sky; the space seemingly as open and unknown as his future. He knew he had all but wasted the last several years of his life, but now he was sober, focused, and determined.

He also recognized that he wasn't suicidal anymore. He certainly didn't feel like it or have any morbid thoughts.

He sat back and accepted the comfort of the first-class seat, enjoying a moment of contentment.

Tom Brightwell was all too eager to start living again.

CHAPTER 64

Morgan Park
Chicago's South Side

By noon the next day, Tom had gone through the mail and cleaned out his refrigerator and pantry; replacing the stale and unwanted goods with fruits, vegetables, and healthy foods.

He'd phoned Peggy at Captain's Pub and thanked her for looking after his home and taking care of his mail. She had nothing of interest to report, but told a few funny stories about Olly and Elmer's latest arguments.

Tom humored her and offered a few laughs in between the general conversation. Still, he told her nothing of what he'd been through. He also kept Dannie and his new-found sobriety to himself. He promised to stop by over the next few days.

After a quick lunch, he spent several hours weeding and pruning the garden, and mowing and edging the lawn. A mid-day rain caught him by surprise, but the cool drizzle felt good and he kept working into early evening.

He took a quick shower, dressed in an old suit, and made his way to the cemetery. The cloud coverage was moderate, painted against the royal blue sky, and the evening air was starting to snuff out the day's humidity. A light breeze shook the tall trees, and carried the fresh smell of the flowers from the graves nearby.

Soon Tom was standing over his wife and daughter. But unlike any visit he could recall, there wasn't a sense of desperation or hollowness within him. Looking to the sky and across the landscape, he was able to detach himself from the somberness the cemetery exuded. He appreciated the natural beauty in the distant sky; the orange streaking of the waning light.

Then he regarded the two graves for several moments, sitting on the grass, comfortably.

"Hello girls," he began. "I know it's been a while, but I want you to know that I'm doing much better."

Tears filled his eyes and he strained to get the words out.

"I'm sorry for how I've behaved, but I promise that until we meet again, I'll start living. For me, for you, for God—I don't know—but I'm gonna be okay.

"I've met a couple of new friends that I think you would like. Jack Seargant is a great man; honorable and thoughtful. We were working on a case together. Can you believe it? I dabbled in a little law enforcement . . ."

Tom smiled through tears but they kept coming, rolling down his cheeks, unchecked.

". . . Which leads me to what I've been through. I finally saw a good part of the Caribbean and even ventured into South America!"

He shook his head at the irony. His wife had always wanted to travel to the Caribbean and even South America and beyond.

"I also met someone, who reminds me of you, Jess. She's friendly, charismatic, open, funny, and trusting. Every time we speak, it's as if we've known each other forever. We engage each other in the deepest discussions and it's truly inspiring.

"Her husband has passed, so we've found common ground that's rooted in loss. I've started my work-outs again, given up drinking, and began a healthy diet. I've lost so much weight and my mind is as sharp as ever. I know I have a way to go, but I'm committed to making it happen."

Tom stood and paced the area, before moving to Kelly's grave. He bent to touch and then kiss the smooth, cool marble.

"I'm so sorry Kelly," he started. "I found Jeremy and he told me about your pregnancy. I don't fault you in your secrets and don't pretend to know what you were thinking. I just want you to know that I've never loved you more."

Tom backed up and sat in front of both graves, remaining silent for a long time. He traded thoughts of his past, present, and future, and then prayed.

When the sky darkened, he drove out of the cemetery. But instead of turning left to the Grove Sports Bar & Grill, he made it home in no time, ate a salad, and spoke to Dannie for a couple of hours.

When he finally went to bed, he did so with a smile.

CHAPTER 65

Annapolis
Maryland

Pat Sajak was the key note speaker of the annual charity event.

It was held at the Westin hotel near downtown Annapolis, and was attended by the who's who of the area. All of the proceeds went to the Anne Arundel Medical Center, nearby.

The popular game show host's wife was from the area, and each had deep ties to the community. The AAMC was close to their heart, which was why Pat Sajak was at center stage and doing a great job of keeping the crowd motivated.

William Monocacy was on his third vodka tonic, standing at the edge of the crowd and taking in everything from afar. Many of the area's wealthiest citizens were on full display, most draped in Versace, Prada, and Gucci; and accentuated by the best that Tiffany's and Cartier had to offer.

He thought it amusing to watch them, but was happier melting into the background. He didn't want to draw attention to himself, though he knew it was inevitable. He'd been a major donor to the facility over the last several years. But recently he'd made a contribution that was so enormous it couldn't be ignored.

Two beautiful blondes, each rail thin but curvy in the right places, made eye contact and seized the opportunity to come over. Both looked similar in their tight black cocktail dresses, stylish heels, and stockings that hugged their perfect legs. They were stunning, but William saw that one was taller and carried herself more confidently than the other, who looked just out of her teens.

"Are you William Monocacy?" the tall one asked playfully, eying him sensually and silently communicating her intentions. She had high cheek bones, pretty blue eyes and long blonde hair that fell casually off her bare shoulders.

"Did you really donate fifty million to the hospital?" the other added, and William turned to regard her for a long moment.

She was naturally pretty and communicated more of a girl-next-door look. She had short blonde hair and fair skin. Her wide smile birthed dimples that drew attention to her pleasant, round face. Her jewelry was modest, her make-up understated. She was probably the daughter of one of the many doctors in the room.

Feeling uneasy with the sudden attention, William turned to see if anyone had overheard, before smiling at the young women.

"Yes, that's me. What may I ask are your names?"

They were beaming, holding onto each other as if for support.

"I'm Gina," the tall one said. "And this is Ashley. We're nurses in the neo-natal unit and can't thank you enough."

William nodded. "It breaks my heart to hear about those preemies that come into the world only to start fighting for their lives."

Gina stepped closer, a serious look coming over her face. "The appropriations committee gave us ten new incubators and enough annual funding for five full-time specialists."

William continued to study both of the nurses. Gina seemed to be well-educated and committed to her work, and he guessed Ashley was barely out of school. He was unusually intrigued by the conversation and chose to keep it going, if only to avoid speaking to another one of the societal elite that were watching him.

"I read about that baby, Noel," William began. "She was born on Christmas last year at just over a pound and your unit was able to save her. If there's money to be given, I can find no better place."

Ashley decided to join the conversation, seductively bringing her left hand around William's neck and bringing him closer. She pressed her breasts into him and whispered in his ear; her body so close he could smell her sweet perfume.

"If you're not too busy later, we would love to personally thank you for your donation," she whispered.

William smiled, shyly, but then took her arm and gently released it, again scanning the room. He stood back and took a quick swig of his drink. Others walked by, regarding him, and he nodded, appropriately.

"I have no response to that, actually, but I appreciate the offer."

Both girls looked to each other and winked, as they giggled in turn.

Suddenly applause arose from the room and the lights dimmed. The band started playing "For He's a Jolly Good Fellow," and a spotlight bore down on William.

Pat Sajak's voice boomed over the drone. "Mr. William Monocacy is a very good friend of mine. He's showed me around the Severn and

Magothy Rivers, as well as the bay since becoming my neighbor in Severna Park. Though I must say that his boat is *a lot* bigger than mine."

This drew laughter from the crowd and William shifted, uncomfortably. Sajak allowed the crowd to settle down before starting again.

"This award is the biggest honor that AAMC extends each year, and goes to the most exemplary of all its annual donors. So for giving so much to AAMC and from the people they are able to treat, it is my privileged honor to present this award to Mr. William Monocacy."

More cheers rang out and the spotlight seemed to shine brighter. William instinctively waved to the audience, though he could see nothing through the flashes of light. Still, he moved to the stage, accepting several accolades along the way. Pat Sajak extended his hand, which William took warmly, and the two men cordially embraced.

Pat Sajak handed over a clear obelisk-shaped award and William took his place behind the podium. He studied it for a long moment. It was about two feet long and much heavier than it looked. The lights caught the sharply-cut edges, forcing a spectrum of different colors to shoot in all directions. It was as if it was electrically charged. Even *he* was impressed by the beautiful crystal piece.

Then William smiled acutely to the crowd. He was well-spoken, calm, and delivered his words with precision and timing. His posture and relaxed demeanor radiated confidence.

"You know I first met Pat Sajak at the Safeway on Benfield Road. We were both in the frozen vegetable aisle and I asked if he was buying some P's."

The crowd roared with laughter and many people began clapping. William turned to look at the famous game show host, who was smiling broadly.

"After finding out we were neighbors, we became fast friends, and it's my honor to share the stage with a true American icon and philanthropist."

William shook his drink, allowing the ice cubes to rattle within the tall glass.

"And although I'm truly humbled by this award, I am more inspired by the people who practice medicine at AAMC. It's each and every one of *you* that deserve the spotlight."

William raised his right hand into the air, holding the award tightly. "So I am giving this back to the heroes of AAMC. I feel it belongs on display among those who make it their life-long purpose to serve mankind."

More applause erupted and William stood like a statue, smiling like a politician.

"And because you've been so hospitable to me this evening, and as this is my third vodka tonic, I am doubling my donation."

Laughter and then thundering applause exploded in the room, and everyone stood to cheer.

Looking to the crowd, William Monocacy smiled along with them, but it was the irony of the situation that really gripped him. He was far more superior to these people. He looked down on them with bitter disdain. Sure he could shake hands, offer a warm smile or pleasing anecdote; but in reality people existed to either amuse or irritate him, and all too often it was the latter.

It was all a game to him and everyone was his play-thing.

But suddenly a piercing pain in his head hit him like a lightning bolt. He clutched the sides of the podium and maintained a smile, but he knew what would happen next. The headache that would follow would be massive and persist for several hours.

Feeling overwhelmed and tired, William waved to the crowd and shook Pat Sajak's hand before walking off stage. He quickly exited a side door and was alone in a wide hallway, though the cheers could not be muted. Moving fast, he stumbled erratically to the exit, swinging the doors widely and treading on the outside cobblestone sidewalk.

The sudden blast of humidity made him even more uneasy and he started to sweat profusely. His driver ran to open the door of the customized Bentley and William lunged into the vehicle, eager for the cool air and solitude the ride home would allow.

But then he heard yelling and he looked to the source, frowning.

"Mr. Monocacy!"

Gina and Ashley stood arm and arm, each holding a glass of wine and cooing. But when they looked to him they didn't see the man they'd just met; or even the one who had rallied on stage just moments before.

William stared back through dark, vacant eyes. He was breathing heavily, caked in sweat. His mouth was open and lopsided.

The girls stared in disbelief.

William shut the door and disappeared behind tainted glass. Before long he was moving down West Street, on his way to the Bluff Point community in Severna Park.

That was, after all, where the Island Hopper lived.

CHAPTER 66

Dr. Sinclair's office was on the third floor of the Anne Arundel Medical Center, ironically in the Sajak Pavilion. The Island Hopper was no stranger to it, having visited at least every week over the past year.

The doctor, as always, cleared most of his morning appointments for William Monocacy, and even greeted him in the waiting area.

There was no small talk or inane pleasantries and this pleased the killer. The doctor knew about his patient's idiosyncrasies and respected every one of them. Dr. Sinclair shook William's hand, but waited until they were in his office before speaking. William glided into a leather chair, before looking to his doctor, expectantly.

"How are you feeling, Mr. Monocacy?" Dr. Sinclair asked, cordially. There was no mistaking the genuine sense of pity in his voice.

William, conversely, was accustomed to his condition and had given more thought to death, dying, and the afterworld than the good doctor could imagine.

"I actually feel really good. How are you?"

Dr. Sinclair didn't answer. Instead he motioned to a white board holding three X-rays. He flipped a switch and a bright light flashed behind the screen. It illuminated the film and allowed William to see the inside of his head. Even with a limited knowledge of medicine, there was no mistaking the large black mass that was covering a good portion of his brain.

Dr. Sinclair studied his patient, folding his arms and exhaling deeply.

"I'm not so sure I believe you. The GBM has grown bigger and is now pressing on most of your cerebrum; all the way to your brain stem. You must have trouble sleeping, focusing, speaking, and even tasting. You have sudden, very painful headaches; many of which cause blackouts, fainting, and nausea. I'm not even going to ask if you drove here."

The Island Hopper remained unmoved as he stared into his doctor's eyes. An awkward smile played on his face, as if he was actually enjoying the exchange.

Dr. Sinclair continued. "Your condition is worsening by the day, but there are drugs to ease your pain in the time you have left. I think we need to have a time-line discussion and make sure your legal affairs are in order."

William nodded in understanding. Then he frowned, choosing his words carefully. "I'll take the drugs, Doc, as long as they don't immobilize me or inhibit my thought process. And I've made arrangements at my home, with medical support in a nice room that looks to the Severn River."

"That's good. And since you're progressing, I can come to *you* and visit as often as you want."

William became solemn. His voice changed and he looked to Dr. Sinclair. "How much time do I have, really? And don't sugarcoat it."

It was the question Dr. Sinclair dreaded most, but had been accustomed to answering for almost thirty years. He let out a long breath as an uncomfortable but knowing look came over him.

"Maybe a week of *real* living and another few days in bed. You'll eventually sleep twenty-two hours a day, with enough drugs that you'll feel no pain and just drift away. In the days to come you'll have spells of forgetfulness, confusion, shortness of breath, and speech problems; and everything you've already known will get a lot worse."

The Island Hopper accepted the information, studying the floor. He thought of what he'd done the week before. To think that the same thread of time represented all he had left was frustrating.

He scanned the office; focusing on the degrees, awards, and framed offerings that were so formally situated throughout the room.

"So all of your education and experience and all my money, and there's nothing we can do?"

Dr. Sinclair was used to the comments and questions. Especially the feelings of irritation and denial.

"As you know a GBM grows quickly and doesn't respond to treatment. Even if we *had* been able to remove it, the outcome would be the same. The transformation of normal brain cells into tumor cells continues even after surgery."

William remained silent and the doctor broke the tension by reaching for a pre-filled paper bag.

"This is a one-month supply of morphine pills and several fentanyl patches for pain control. Take them as needed; just follow the directions I've included. Also, my cell phone and contact information are on the bottle so don't hesitate to call me anytime."

William rose and the two shook hands. Dr. Sinclair followed his patient through the wide hallway and into the lobby, but William's stepping was quick and purposeful.

"I'll see you in a few days, perhaps at your home, right?" Dr. Sinclair called out.

The killer looked back, humored. "We both know we'll never see each other again."

"But I'm your doctor."

William was already out the door. "Not the type of doctor I need," he added, laughing uncontrollably.

As Dr. Sinclair and the whole world would soon find out, William Monocacy needed a psychiatrist far more than a neurosurgeon. Someone who could delve into the killer's mind and explore his fascination about life and death.

William slowed as he walked through the parking garage, feeling some pressure in his head. He closed his eyes, took in deep gulps of air and the sensation eased. Then he found his brand new Bugatti Veyron. It had arrived the week before, after being on order for over a year. He knew there were only twenty manufactured, with his being the only one in North America.

Soon he was driving east on Route 50 over the Severn River bridge. He took the north exit onto Route 2 at almost seventy miles an hour. He smiled as he worked the seven-gear clutch transmission, feeling the torque as the fourteen-inch tires gripped the road. He closed his eyes momentarily, capturing the moment. The rear tires were the widest sport performance tires ever produced for a passenger car and were supported by twenty-inch rims. The entire set cost nearly $40,000 and he regaled in knowing it.

William revved the engine on the downshift and passed an old Honda. Ironically he never felt so alive.

He recalled being at the Shanghai auto show the previous year and looking at several of the Bugatti models. He learned that while it went from 0 to 100 km/h in only 2.5 seconds, it took even less time—only 2.3 seconds—to return to a complete stop. This one feature intrigued him so much that even with the $1.5 million price tag he had to have one.

Passing the Arnold Fire Department, he was suddenly in a hurry. There were so many things to do in the short time he had left. Although he hated all of humanity, there were still a few more people that he was all too eager to play with.

The Island Hopper wasn't finished.

Not by a long shot.

CHAPTER 67

Ellie's Place is on Veteran's Highway in Millersville and wasn't too far from the Island Hopper's home. A classic family-owned pub, it's known for its simple ambience, the variety of beers on tap, and their outstanding buffalo wings.

The boneless buffalo-garlic, served extra-saucy with celery was one of William Monocacy's favorite cravings; and Stella in the kitchen knew exactly how he liked it. It was this simple delight, along with a tall draft beer, that made him one of Ellie's more loyal customers.

The Island Hopper had just finished his second Coors Light. He sat at the north end of the square, wooden bar, just in front of the small juke box that was thankfully dormant. He felt a rush in his head as the alcohol hit his system and warmed his core. The feeling held him and he embraced the sensation. It was such a welcome change from the paralyzing headaches that had been imprisoning him.

The killer leaned back in the bar stool, regarding the area in total. Leah & Cheryl were in the back room, Stella and Matt were in the kitchen, and Theresa was busy serving the moderate crowd that sprinkled the table area.

"Another one?" Steve asked, moving over to William and offering a knowing smile.

"Sure," William said, looking the man over.

Steve Winebrenner was his favorite bartender. He had a modest build, scraggly brown beard, sympathetic brown eyes, and a straight-forward way. He always wore his baseball hat backwards and William noticed the Makers Mark emblem on the day's hat of choice.

The killer found Steve genuinely interesting; always good for a story or to offer a considerate ear. Their discussions had spanned many topics over the years, but today William wasn't in the mood for conversation. He was there to think things through and had retreated within himself.

The Island Hopper smiled as he thought of The Plan. The doctor's visit had been eye-opening but not all together bad. He'd always known and respected that his time frame was shrinking, but with Jeremy out of the picture and Tom Brightwell properly monitored, he was reassured of his position.

The FBI thought Jeremy was the Island Hopper, and although it bruised William's ego, he was thankful there wasn't an active investigation focused on him. He was once again operating invisibly—which also meant he was invincible—for at least the next week or so.

His dealings with The Organization, his personal and very private handlers, had been well worth the cost. Not only had they helped get Jeremy to Saint Maarten, but they were instrumental in planting the necessary contraband that led to the man's arrest. Then the same people had helped Jeremy escape with the ex-prison guard and travel to Venezuela. William shook his head, wondering what they must be thinking; not that they would ever question a thing.

Furthermore, Tom Brightwell's phone was tapped and his home bugged. William had been receiving daily encrypted transcripts of the conversations between Tom and Dannie. Those coveted communications were so essential and the Island Hopper openly laughed at how well things had come together.

The beer arrived and William nodded a silent thank you as Steve retreated to the cash register. William took a pull from the large mug, taking in the banners that lined the bar soffit above him. A variety of beer logos and Baltimore Ravens flags hung down and spanned the entire upper rim. Then he settled on the picture of Johnny Unitas. He put the beer down on a coaster and placed his hands on the smooth, wooden bar top.

Out of all the luxuries the killer had at his disposal, time was not among them. He enjoyed the moment, knowing he would miss coming to Ellie's. Then he thought of his other local favorites in Severna Park, including Adam's Ribs, The Big Bean, and the incredible cheese steaks at Jeno's. He would also miss riding his Bridgestone RB-1 on the trail and hanging out with Rod at the Pedal Pushers bike shop.

His boneless buffalo garlic wings arrived and Steve poured him a large glass of ice water. William enjoyed them slowly, taking his time with each bite and closing his eyes to savor the explosion of flavor.

When finished, he pushed the paper tray away, swigged the rest of his beer, and called Steve over.

"What's up?" Steve asked, his eyes narrowing.

The Island Hopper smiled, knowing it was the last time he'd see him. "I just wanted to say thank you for your camaraderie over the years."

"My pleasure Mr. Monocacy," Steve said, looking at the long-time patron. "Is there anything else you need?"

William laid five one-hundred dollar bills on the bar, fanning them out like a winning poker hand.

"I also want you to know that everything you'll read about me is absolutely true."

Perplexed, Steve looked at William and then at the money. But before he could speak, the Island Hopper was out of his seat and heading for the south door. Then someone approached him about a Keno game and the day wore on.

CHAPTER 68

Morgan Park
Chicago's South Side

"Tell me something else about you," Dannie purred.

Her voice was calming. It was as if she were sitting right next to him, whispering in his ear, instead of on a phone hundreds of miles away.

Tom was lounging on the sofa, completely comfortable and at ease, wearing old cotton pajama bottoms and a worn White Sox T-shirt. He felt like a teenager, with his feet kicked up, a bowl of popcorn beside him, and the phone pressed against his ear.

He and Dannie were on the third hour of their nightly phone date.

"Let me see," he began. "I like warm sunshine on my face in the winter. You know when you're bundled up tight and you turn your face into the sun and feel its warmth, even though the air is freezing?"

"I like when I pour a can of Coke into a glass and it reaches the point where even though I continue to pour, the level doesn't rise because of the bubbles coming up."

Tom laughed. "I tell you I like the sun and you talk about pop?"

"No, I tell you about soda and you call it pop. What's that all about?"

"Tomāto, Tomäto," he countered. "I'm mid-west and you're a southern belle."

"I'm a little country and you're a little rock 'n' roll?"

"Something like that."

"Fine; what else do you like?" she asked.

"I like waking up on the first day of daylight savings time in the fall and having an extra hour."

Dannie reacted immediately. "I like finding money in the pocket of a pair of jeans I haven't worn for a while."

"I still enjoy getting the mail, even though most of its just bills or junk."

Dannie smiled. "I like the sounds of children playing at the playground. Their innocent laughs are the purest thing in the world."

"That's the best one so far. I'm with you on that," Tom said.

Since Tom's return to Chicago, they'd spoken each night, sometimes for several hours, starting at nine o'clock. Each call was substantial. The conversations were easy and often full of both laughter and tears.

One of Tom's deepest fears had subsided when he realized their time apart hadn't dulled their burgeoning relationship. But he was cautious. He'd spent considerable time thinking about and trying to overcome his feelings of guilt. There was no denying he felt a definite connection forming, but it was much different from his relationship with his late wife.

Was it because he'd met Jess in high school and he was now sixty and starting over? Or was it because he *wasn't* falling in love with Dannie? Was it just a welcome distraction from the mundane?

During the day he tried not to think about it, filling the void with the household duties he'd been neglecting for so long. But the thoughts always crept in and they were a constant burden.

By evening, he would be apprehensive and distracted; wondering if Dannie was having the same doubts. But hearing her voice each night lent him encouragement and always set him at ease.

They melted together so perfectly.

She was his warm hug at the end of each day.

He just hoped she felt the same way.

CHAPTER 69

Captain's Pub was about a mile from Tom's house, so after finishing up some light landscaping, Tom decided to walk over for a visit. He entered the bar just like so many times before. But this time was different. He felt alienated and strangely aware that he didn't belong.

Little had changed in the time he'd been gone. The pool tables still took over the far corner, the televisions hung on the walls, and the stale smell of spilled beer rose from the worn, wooden floor. An old country song struggled against the drone of the handful of patrons, all of whom looked at Tom when the door slammed shut behind him.

The sudden darkness was a steep contrast to the afternoon sunshine and it took Tom several moments to adjust. Looking around, he couldn't believe how much time he'd spent drinking and wasting away. He saw his favorite place at the bar and shook his head. It was both familiar and foreign, and he realized just how much his perspective had changed.

But he smiled. He had been nervous about being in a bar, but as he looked to the bottles on display, he knew he would never drink again.

Peggy had a dish rag in hand and was looking at him, puzzled. "Tom?" she asked. "Is that you?"

Tom walked over. "I wanted to thank you for taking care of my home."

She just stared, looking him over and shaking her head. Then she slid his house key onto the bar and he pocketed it.

"You look great!" she erupted. "New diet or something?"

Tom laughed, considering his choice of words. He couldn't tell her the truth; that he'd quit drinking, started eating better, began an exhaustive regiment of exercise, and had tracked a killer through three days' worth of wilderness in South America, only to be taken captive, beaten, and starved for over a week. Instead, he just waved off the compliment.

"I've been dieting and exercising," he said.

"Still, what are you down, fifty pounds in like a month? Are you okay?"

He saw Olly and Elmer were drunk as usual and arguing about something on the television. He strolled over and patted them each on the back.

"How are you gentlemen?" he offered.

Elmer smiled wide. He stumbled from his bar stool, spilling beer. "How are you, Tom? Wanna sit down and have a few?"

Olly looked back. He nodded, before returning to his drink and taking a selfish swig. Tapping the wooden bar, he silently ordered another, drumming his hands in anticipation.

"Anything new?" Tom asked.

Olly chirped in. "Government's screwing us again. Inflation's rising, medical costs are higher, and our social security's just not keeping up! Damn those pricks in Washington!"

"Same old stuff, huh?"

Olly grunted and Elmer finished his beer, letting out a satisfying belch.

"This is how they treat the greatest generation?" Olly asked, rhetorically.

Tom moved to speak, but Elmer was already revving up for a dissertation of politics and the legislative process. Tom remained silent for several minutes, uncomfortable in that both men were drunk and slurring their words. Elmer in particular was spitting with each outburst.

Tom waited for a quick stall in the conversation, seizing the opportunity to retreat and announce his departure. He motioned a friendly wave to Peggy and made a quiet escape.

Exiting the bar, he started a light jog, which eventually quickened into a steady run. The process lent itself to self-thought, and he once again pondered his future, which was so open-ended.

He returned home sooner than expected, so he continued to the far end of the block and kept going for over an hour.

It was now late evening and the waning sunlight spilled a pink streak across much of the sky. Pink was Dannie's favorite color and he was reminded of their time in Saint Maarten.

He recalled reading about Bermuda's famous pink beaches and a crazy idea formed in his mind.

If the night's phone call went well, he was going to ask Dannie to meet him in Bermuda for a quick get-away.

The nine o'clock phone date was much different from the others. It was as if they both knew their relationship was at a crucial point and they wanted to push through any untested barriers.

Every topic was discussed and every uneasy subject bridged. Tom admitted that although he was open to Dannie, he had feelings of betrayal to his wife's memory. He also completely confided to her about his ordeal in Venezuela; especially about the two men he'd killed in saving little Anna.

Dannie understood the impossible situation and appreciated Tom's honesty. She listened carefully, not judging. She offered unconditional support and he felt relieved.

Dannie also voiced her concerns about bringing *him* into her life. She wasn't sure how it would affect her two daughters and grandchild. She asked about his drinking and wanted to be sure he was still sober. He told her about going to Captain's Pub and his emotional detachment from the place. He had no desire to drink. He wasn't that man anymore.

The exchange was freeing at both ends.

Tom wondered why he and Jess weren't able to be as communicative in the years after Kelly's murder. But gone were the days of dwelling on the past or even over-thinking the present.

Maybe it was maturity, sobriety, or just the personalities involved. But living life, he decided, was better than analyzing it. So he made a decision to deliberate less on his place in the world and be happy with his new friend.

Caught up in the moment, and having complete faith and confidence in his feelings, he asked Dannie to spontaneously meet him in Bermuda the very next day for a three-day rendezvous.

She agreed immediately and they spoke well past midnight. Tom heard her tapping on a keyboard through the phone, as they excitedly planned their itinerary.

CHAPTER 70

The Pompano Beach Club
Southampton, Bermuda

Quaint, charming, eclectic.

That's what Tom Brightwell thought when the cab rounded the corner and ran down the hill to the Pompano Beach Club. After a thirty minute ride on Bermuda's windy, crowded, and sometimes harrowing roads—with no shortage of drivers passing and honking—he was happy to finally arrive at his destination.

Tom slipped the cabbie the fare and a generous tip; then exited with his only bag. To his left he noticed a row of mopeds and straight ahead was the entrance to the modest, closed lobby.

Inviting, spirited, exquisite.

The adjectives kept coming as he met the proprietor; one of two brothers who ran the place. Larry Lamb was an energetic, middle-aged man with a warm, encouraging smile and an easy, enthusiastic manner. Tom felt special as he listened to Larry reel off the amenities of the resort, and inquire as to anything he may need.

But Tom was more interested in getting settled and exploring things before Dannie's arrival. His flight from Chicago, though longer, was more accommodating and he was able to arrive a couple hours before her.

He'd used the flight time to his advantage, reading as much as he could about Bermuda and fine-tuning the agenda. He wanted to cater to Dannie, so he absorbed everything he could; reading with great interest about the shopping districts, historical hot spots, and unmatched sunsets on the island's west side.

He was enthralled by the pictures of Bermuda's pink beaches, reading about how the color came from the waves pulverizing the shells and coral with millennia of effort. He forward-thought to them holding hands and walking the water's edge.

The happy couple only had a few days and he wanted everything to be perfect! The conversation the night before had been a new high. There was the usual upbeat speak and feel-good banter; but there was also absolute candor and the spontaneity of a three-day excursion to relax and be together.

Still, they had discussed and agreed upon certain guidelines. To not place any pressure on their nascent relationship, they agreed that all expenses would be shared and they would reserve two rooms. There were no obligations; just complete honesty and companionship.

Tom was handed a key card to room # 81. He thanked Larry and exited in a spirited walk. His room was two buildings away and he bounded up the exterior stairs, happily.

He was pleasantly surprised with his suite. It had a homey charm that was different from the Caribbean accommodations he'd seen of late. There was a large four-post bed, with several pillows and a fluffy comforter. To his left was a simple wooden desk and to the right a sofa and a large chaise facing a flat screen television. He placed his bag on the floor and walked to the balcony.

He sucked in the salty air and exhaled, triumphantly. It was the exact view he'd wanted. A true look across the Atlantic, facing west to ensure a great view of the next three sunsets.

He regarded the two lounge chairs and simple table between them, imagining where he and Dannie would sit in just a few hours. He removed his shoes, sliding his bare feet on the smooth, orange tile. Then he stepped to the railing and looked out to the sea and directly below.

He was amazed that the resort was literally cut into the side of the limestone hillside and it was almost a vertical drop to the water. He saw the pinkish tint of the beach to his far left and then several parrotfish fish swimming in the immediate surf.

Then his line of vision floated to the horizon. It was the most magnificent view he'd ever seen, bar none. Like in the Caribbean, the sea was fluorescent blue. But here it stretched at least a mile before merging with the cool, royal blue of deeper waters.

Feeling excited with their choice, he left to explore the rest of the resort. He strolled back to the main entrance and considered the small, wooden bar off the lobby. All four stools were taken and Larry Lamb was pouring a citrus concoction across several tall glasses.

The main restaurant was straight ahead, but he turned and walked down the three stairs to a sitting area, with a television, bookshelf, and several pieces of furniture. The flooring caught his attention, and he smiled at a white fish that was sketched right into the green-tile flooring. Then he paused to read the plaque about John Cabral above the fireplace.

Tom found the outside patio and moved to the stiff white railing, again looking out to the ocean.

"It's something, huh?" a low voice sounded from behind him.

Tom turned, startled to see a man he hadn't noticed. He was Caucasian and in his mid-forties; with a strong, defining look that complimented his confident manner. His green eyes were piercing, his dark hair perfectly combed, and his smile was energizing. His dress was business-casual, with relaxed beige pants, a thin white button-down shirt, and a pair of loafers. He was well-tanned and handsome; his overall look one of leisure and success. He swirled a drink in his hand, allowing the ice cubes to rattle around the glass, before taking a long sip.

"It sure is," Tom said, turning back to the sea.

The man continued. "You know that's a sand bar that goes for about a mile. You can *literally* walk out that far before it gets deeper than your waist."

"Are you serious?" Tom asked, already thinking about attempting it.

The man continued. "It's like that all around the island. That's why there are so many shipwrecks off Bermuda. The shelf-line and coral are so scattered and unpredictable."

"Have you been here long?" Tom asked.

"Yeah, about a month this time. I'm actually staying closer to Hamilton, but I sometimes come here for the view. You can't do any better than the Pompano Beach Club for that, especially the sunsets."

"Sounds like you know the island pretty well."

"I should. I trade time between Virginia and Bermuda. I just finished up some business at the Navy Yard and decided to stop here for a drink and a view."

301

Tom reached over and shook the man's hand, hoping to gain some information. "I'm Tom Brightwell," he announced. "Complete novice to Bermuda but in search of some ideas to better enjoy my stay."

"Chris Reyes," the man announced. "Are you here solo or with someone?"

"My girlfriend—at least I *think* she's my girlfriend—is arriving in a couple hours and we're just looking for some neat stuff to do."

"Well you got the Navy Dockyard, which is historic and a pretty cool place, though a bit touristy. It's one of two ports for the cruise ships, so it can be crowded, but it's a must-see. There's Hamilton, which is the biggest town and capital, full of everything you'd expect. Then there's St. George's on the other end past the airport, which is smaller and more quaint and historic. In between, there's no shortage of scenery, restaurants, history, and some great beaches."

"What's the best way to get around?"

"That's the tricky part. There are no rental cars, so either you cab it—which can get expensive—or you rent a moped and conquer the island on your own terms."

Tom frowned, unsure if Dannie would ride a moped.

"But there's also another choice, which may offer more flexibility and be more affordable."

Tom perked up. "What's that?"

"Hire a personal car and driver. Because your time is limited, rent a two-person moped for your first day and then a car to explore the island on the second day. St. Georges is on the other end of the fish hook and your butts will be hurting if you attempt it on a moped."

"What do you mean by fish hook?" Tom asked.

"Bermuda's shaped like a fish hook and we're almost at the top end, facing the west side of the hook."

"Gotcha" Tom said. His eyes moved to the left and the man followed his gaze.

Chris rose, rattling his ice cubes once more and pointing to where Tom was looking.

"There's a cove down there where the surf comes into the rocks. During low tide you can walk that stretch and there are pools of water you can swim in. But beware of the golf balls coming off the eighth hole right above it. It's a par three and people always over-shoot it!"

Tom looked up to see a distant golf course he hadn't noticed.

"That's Port Royal. Not sure if you're into golf, but that track is one of the best on the island."

"So you really know you're stuff, huh?" Tom asked, rhetorically. "What's a great place for a romantic dinner?"

"The Waterlot Inn, no question about it. There's a substantial outside area that looks out to a marina and the bay. They have amazing food and the place is like three-hundred and fifty years old. If you want great food *and* atmosphere, with a little history to boot, that's your place."

"How far is it?" Tom asked, painting the image.

"Just go out to the main road, take a right and it's about three or four miles on the left. Actually now that you got me thinking about it, I'll probably be there tomorrow night."

Tom nodded. "Thanks for the advice."

"No problem," Chris said, turning. "Nice to meet you but I've gotta run."

The men shook hands and Tom was alone. He noticed the sharp stone stairway to his left and decided to continue his tour. He quickly ducked in and out of several rooms, including the main upper restaurant, the lower eatery, and the pool. Then he passed through the free arcade and into the fitness center, where several machines were placed in front of windows that looked directly to the sea. He smiled, looking forward to his work-out the next morning.

Then he walked to the resort's second bar and ordered Iced Tea, before moving to the pool and finding a lounge chair. He looked to the high thin clouds that did little more than hide the sun for a few moments at a time.

A gentle breeze found him and he breathed deeply. He was a picture of contentment as all the stresses of life seemed to leave him. He closed his eyes and napped before being awakened by the smells of the outdoor grill behind him. He stood to stretch and saw Dannie trying to sneak up on him.

She wore white sandals and a simple yellow sundress that accentuated her slender figure. She smiled wide and he grinned back at her. She emanated so much positive energy and beauty that it was distracting. Her gaze held him for a moment and he looked her over in awe.

"Hello Beautiful," he said as they hugged. "I was just thinking of you."

"You're sweet," she said, and they fell into a relaxed embrace.

For a short time, they felt alone in the world. All trepidations melted away as they searched each other's eyes. Tom wanted to tell her how much the moment meant—how much *she* meant to *him*—but he couldn't produce the words.

She broke away, looking him over. "I can't believe how much weight you've lost. You look fantastic and toned!"

Tom grinned. "Yeah, but I wouldn't recommend the weight-loss program I took in Venezuela!"

Dannie took Tom's hand and they began a deliberate walk. "I'm in room # 82 right next to you. I'm going to check it out and call the kids. How 'bout I knock on your door in an hour and we'll have dinner?"

"Absolutely," Tom said, enjoying the feeling of Dannie's small hand in his. He gently swung her to the right, as if they were in a ballroom dance. She laughed, finishing elaborately by raising her hands like a ballerina.

"I'll see you in an hour, Mr. Brightwell."

It was a moment that Tom swore he'd never forget. He couldn't take his eyes off her as she walked across the pool area and up the narrow roadway in the rear.

And it *would* have been perfect if he was alone. But there was a man watching them. He was in plain sight and seemingly innocent to the casual glance.

But he wasn't innocent.

And neither were his intentions.

CHAPTER 71

Tom & Dannie dined at the main restaurant, where all the outside tables hugged the terrace in a crescent-shaped arc. It was the highest view the resort allowed, and they were able to look down to the pool and beach, and across the sea to the horizon.

Both took time with their meals. Tom enjoyed one of the best steaks he'd ever had, while Dannie munched on her salad and ate a baked chicken dish. They were so wrapped up in each other that time seemed inconsequential. Like always, the words came easily and they talked and laughed as if they'd known each other for years.

Both declined dessert but they accepted the carafe of coffee that was placed on the table. Tom poured the strong, steamy brew into their cups and they held hands, as everything around them seemed to melt away.

They paid little attention to the other patrons and couldn't hear the excited children playing in the pool. They hardly noticed the wait staff that cleared the table and didn't acknowledge the illumination of the exterior lights as daylight waned.

They just looked into each other's eyes, lost in the moment.

The sun fell lower in the sky. They turned to see it disappear from sight, leaving a stretch of burnt orange splashing up from the water. But soon the light faded; replaced by the cooler report of evening.

Darkness rushed in and the first stars appeared high in the sky. Another waiter came over and asked if they needed anything else, and Tom realized they were alone. They laughed, wondering just how long they'd been there, before quickly paying the bill.

They cut through the pool area and carefully maneuvered the narrow stone stairway that descended to the beach. Once there, they kicked off their shoes to feel the cool sand on their feet.

Dannie broke away and walked into the surf, lifting her hands high in the air and twirling around. Tom moved beside her, cradling her back. Then they looked back to the resort, which was bathed in a pinkish hue.

"This is perfect, Tom. I'm so happy right now."

"I know. I feel giddy."

She turned to him. "I feel the same way. Everything about you makes me feel safe, happy, wanted, and real."

"Don't forget invigorated, understood, validated, and excited. Because that's what you do for me."

"Okay, then let me add content, joyful, and alive."

"Alive," Tom repeated. "That's perfect. For the first time in so long I feel I'm living again."

Dannie stepped closer and she gave him a warm hug. They moved in a slow dance as the incoming surf ran around their legs.

"I feel it too, Tom."

After a few moments, Tom pulled away and looked into her eyes. "One thing that I've really appreciated is our ability—and want—to be absolutely open with each other."

"Of course, Tom. It's crucial in any relationship."

"I was just thinking that when I lost Jess and Kelly it was like night fell and it's been dark for so long. I've been walking through life; seeking shelter in my sleep and comfort in my drinking. But when I met you the sun started shining again. The filters are off and everything is clear. I know that Jeremy is still out there, but at least I know the truth and there's *some* consolation in that."

Dannie formed one of her contagious smiles and they hugged again.

Tom took her hand and guided her back up the stone stairway. But when they neared the outdoor grill, Tom rushed over to a stone archway. He touched it in several places and then stepped back to consider it from a distance. It was substantial, but simple in both design and structure.

He turned to Dannie, who was confused. "This is one of those Bermudan moon gates!" he said, excitedly. "I read about them on the plane."

"What's a moon gate?" she asked, moving next to him.

"It symbolizes peace, happiness and good luck for couples. It originated in China but has become an icon of romance in Bermuda."

"Romance, huh?" Dannie quipped.

"Yeah," Tom said. "In the mid-1800's a Bermuda sea captain brought home a plan for a moon gate he'd seen in a Chinese garden. He drew the design and then built one, but made of stone, not wood like the Chinese. The result looked something like this and other Bermudians quickly adopted it."

Tom moved through it, continuing to examine it. "They say that when a couple makes a wish as they pass hand-in-hand through a moon gate, they are guaranteed everlasting happiness and good fortune."

Dannie began to giggle. "You never cease to amaze me Mr. Brightwell. You and your romantic notions!"

But when she turned to study him, he was distant. He hadn't even heard her. He was entranced with the stone work and perfect symmetry of the design. His eyes were wide and his demeanor resonated with calm excitement.

It was one of the things she admired most about him. He was a capable and proven tough guy, but he was also deeply romantic and thoughtful.

"Well, then," she started. "What do you say we try it out? Is it like a birthday wish that you keep to yourself?"

He snickered, turning to her. "I don't know about that. Maybe newlywed couples openly say their wishes, but how about we just keep it to ourselves and walk through?"

"Sounds good. I'm ready when you are."

They held hands and walked slowly through the arch, pausing on the other side. Suddenly it was as if the air was charged and no words were necessary. They shared a long, gentle kiss, before peering into each other's eyes.

"That was nice," Dannie said.

"I agree," Tom said, and they walked up the road to their rooms.

"Just leave your door open," Dannie said. "I'm going to change and be over in a few minutes."

Inside his room, Tom retrieved some snacks and water bottles from the small refrigerator, then lit a candle on the balcony.

Dannie walked in shortly thereafter. She wore pink workout attire and her hair was tied back in a ponytail. She moved past him and onto the balcony, where she looked to the sea, with the moonlight glimmering on the still water.

He met her there and slid the door shut. They kissed again and talked on the outside lounge chairs for several hours.

But then they grew tired as jet lag set in.

So they moved to the large bed and slept, holding each other until morning.

CHAPTER 72

Tom awoke first, leaving Dannie in favor of a morning workout. He changed into exercise shorts and a T-shirt; then sat to put on his running shoes.

He gently leaned down to tie them, always worried about his mid-section, but found he could move freely without any pain. Testing it, he rose and began light stretches, happy to be healthy.

In high spirits, he quietly left the room and ran to the lobby, maneuvering the place like a pro. There was no one in the fitness center, so he took his time examining the different pieces of equipment.

He chose the treadmill at the center of the row and ran eight miles, the whole time looking out the large window to the sea. Exercise always relaxed him and he became lost in thought. His mind settled on Dannie and how grateful he was for her. But as happy as she made him, he couldn't help but think of the ordeal he'd been through.

He shook his head, trying to release anything negative. Then he moved his right hand across his mid-section, where the chain had dug into him when he'd lunged at Jeremy. Though healed, he knew he would forever feel the phantom pain of that exchange. Then, with borrowed energy, he added some speed to the machine and finished the last mile in record time.

Stepping off, he grabbed a bottle of water and a towel. He walked to the beach, sat on a lounge chair, and enjoyed the fresh breeze. Then he hit the buffet for some fruit and coffee and returned to the room to find Dannie on the balcony, finishing the last bit of her room-service breakfast.

"Looks like we both need showers," she said, looking to him. "How was the run?"

"Absolutely amazing. The fitness room is set up so everything looks out to the sea. It's really something."

"This place continues to impress," she said. "So what do we do next?"

Tom sat beside her and took her hands in his. "I say we rent a moped and just get out of here. I've studied a map of the island. Let's explore everything!"

"Is it safe? We're not young you know."

"We can try and if we don't like it we'll just get a cab."

Dannie looking down in contemplation. Then her eyes met Tom's. "Okay. I trust you."

"Great. I'm going to take a quick shower and set it up. Just wear something comfortable and meet me in the lobby when you're ready."

Dannie rose and walked to her room while Tom showered and dressed. Then he went to the lobby and inquired about a moped. Larry Lamb was at his post and eager to help.

"Just walk right outside and talk to Randall. And watch out for the road toads."

Tom turned to leave but then looked back. "Road Toads?"

"In Bermuda we don't have squirrels but we have enormous toads, literally bigger than your hand. You'll see them flattened all over the roads. They just shrivel up from the sun and eventually blow away."

Tom was about to counter but thought against it. "On a separate note, do you have any recommendations for a nice restaurant close by? The dining was great here last night, but we'd like to try something new."

Larry grabbed a few pamphlets and a map. "The first place I'd recommend is the Waterlot Inn about three miles to the south. Great food and a phenomenal place. It's been operational since 1670 and is the second oldest restaurant on the island. Then there's the—"

"That's it!" Tom interrupted. "You're the second person to mention it."

"Very good then," Larry said, marking the restaurant's spot on the map and handing it to Tom. "Let me know if you need anything else."

Tom thanked him and headed outside. In no time, he was on a double scooter and doing test runs up and down the hill. After some light paperwork, Tom felt invigorated and optimistic about the day. With perfect timing, Dannie arrived; wearing comfortable pink Capri pants, sandals, and a white blouse.

Tom rose to greet her and opened the back hatch for her purse. He placed a helmet on both of their heads and held the bike as she climbed on. Then he eased forward to release the kickstand and they sped up the hill and to the right, with Dannie leaning into him and holding him tight. He felt her stiffen as the moped jerked, but found encouragement in her touch.

Tom immediately counted five "road toads" and shook his head at the discovery. Then he checked on Dannie's comfort level.

"How are you doing so far?" he yelled over the drone of the motor and wind.

"This is so fun!" she yelled back instantly.

"Good! Now don't freak out but they drive on the other side of the road. Just yell or squeeze me if you want to stop."

"What are you talking about, old man?" she chided. "Let's go faster because we're not getting any younger!"

They came to a stop at Middle Road, before turning left on the way to the Royal Navy Dockyard. They stopped at the Somerset Bridge and took pictures of the world's smallest drawbridge, only eighteen inches wide.

They spent several hours at the Navy Yard, shopping for souvenirs, walking the docks, and exploring the history within the Casemate Barracks and the Royal Navy Cemetery. Then they stopped into The Frog & Onion Pub, where they each enjoyed a lunch of fish and chips.

Afterward, they ordered coffee and walked the wooden plank floor, studying the artifacts on the walls. They treaded slowly, taking in the atmosphere of the old salty pub that was so steeped in history and tradition.

They strolled through the old munitions building and stopped at the Dockyard Glassworks and Bermuda Rum Cake Company. Still, with everything around them, they were just happy to be with each other. Tom walked outside while Dannie ambled through the mall stores. When she exited, she found him studying the large clock on the watch tower.

"What's up, Babe?" she asked, looking at the clock through the brilliant sunlight.

Tom shrugged his shoulders and started a deliberate walk toward the water. He didn't require any prodding.

"Just thinking about time," he started. "It's a constant reminder that we're not here for that long."

Dannie remained silent, wanting him to go on.

"I know I've told you everything that happened in Venezuela. But there are two dead bodies somewhere down there that I'm personally responsible for. I'm not saying I wouldn't do it again, just that I don't know what to think about it."

Dannie grabbed Tom's hand. They sat on the dock, facing a cruise ship in port. Her face relaxed and she chose her words carefully.

"Well that's one way to think about it," she began. "But I see a man who stood up for what he believed in. He made the courageous and impossible decision to travel through the unknown in search of answers, and saved a little girl from an unimaginable ordeal. Probably even saved her life. You did what you had to do and I *hope* you would do it again."

Tom smiled, uneasily. "I'm not seeking self-adulation. It's just that—"

"Tom," Dannie stated, firmly. "Do you even know who you are? Do you know how you make me feel? I haven't felt this happy and sure of anything for so long and you're the reason!"

"Yeah but I'm—"

"No. I won't let you get away with it."

Dannie turned her body and leaned into him, cupping his face with her tiny hands. Her big blue eyes stared into his and he fell silent.

"*You* are a good man. *You* are a decent person. *You* saved that girl and did what had to be done. And forgive me but Jess and Kelly knew you were a great man too."

Tom shook his head, looking away. But she was unrelenting and gently shook his face within her firm grasp.

Dannie continued. "You're worried that you fell into a dark place and hit the bottle. But who wouldn't forgive you, given the circumstances? You're just a man Tom Brightwell!"

"I just need to know that they *are* proud of me, however impossible it is now."

"The only way to do that is to be proud of *yourself* and take control and responsibility for your actions and the consequences."

"But I'm not sure I can."

"I think you already have. You haven't had a drink in over a month, you've been focused and determined, and you were very helpful to Jack."

"But Jeremy's still out there!"

"Yeah he is. But maybe you should focus on what's right here."

Tom looked to Dannie as her hands fell away from his face. He drank her in, with his senses peaking. He smelled her perfume, felt her warmth, absorbed her words, and eyed her natural beauty. She was striking and he peered into her eyes, finding comfort within them.

"You know on the police force, as part of training and ongoing education, they require you to write your own obituary. It allows for an inward perspective on how you think you're perceived."

"When was this? What did yours say?"

"I wrote several of them. The last of which was about six months after Jess's death. I stated the obvious, just general facts about who I was and what I enjoyed. Then I went into the pride of my life—Jess and Kelly—before quickly finishing with my final resting place and the pre-paid chicken dinner at Captain's Pub."

Tom laughed but Dannie remained stoic; searching his mindset and wanting more. It was the same lineage of conversation they'd had since meeting, and she respected how deep and forging their talks were.

"And what would it say now?" she asked.

Tom looked at her through moist eyes. "It would double in size and be a lot more cheery. I'd say that I was given a second chance at life and it's all because of Danielle Sullivan."

Dannie moved to kiss Tom. They fell into an easy embrace, before considering the water that was lapping at the wooden planks below.

Then Tom changed the subject. "You know what we have to do now, right?"

"What's that Mr. Brightwell?"

"I say we bypass Hamilton and save it for tomorrow. Let's go all the way to St. George's."

Soon they were back on Middle Road. They stopped on the north side of the airport bridge to stretch their legs, but eventually arrived at St. George's, walking the historic square and surrounding cobblestone streets that spilled out from its center.

Then with the sun favoring the west, they decided to head back to get ready for dinner at the Waterlot Inn.

The killer lost them twice. Once at the Navy Yard and then again at the turnabout, mistakenly thinking they would turn left into

Hamilton. Still, he found them in St. George's and followed them back to the Pompano Beach Club.

It wasn't that he *had* to trace their movements. He only did so out of curiosity. All of his preparations were already finished and he didn't have much left to do.

It didn't matter where his prey was going, as long as he knew where they would eventually end up.

CHAPTER 73

St. Michaels
Maryland

Bunny was devoid of any feelings toward Jeremy.

The media circus that had landed in St. Michaels—with her at the epicenter—had thankfully ended after a press conference by Jack Seargant. He'd explained that while Jeremy was the prime suspect in the Island Hopper killings, he'd fled the country and an investigation was ongoing. Seargant was very adamant about a double-life scenario; and that the killer's wife was just another victim in a string of horrific happenings.

Meanwhile, a senator had been accused of sleeping with a couple of his aides, and the national spot light had shifted elsewhere. After a few more days of camping out in St. Michaels and getting the cold shoulder from the locals, the media numbers eventually reduced and faded to zero.

Bunny was happy to be left alone; though she lived the nightmare every day and knew the story would never really end. But she found comfort in her daily routine; and with her recent filing for divorce going smoothly, she was feeling much better.

She'd been concentrating on her financial affairs; spending considerable time with her husband's personal assistant, Rodney. He was a small rat-like man with dark shifty eyes, perfectly parted hair, and a crisp and direct way of speech that grated on her. She didn't know too much about him, but Jeremy had trusted him implicitly, which alone drew suspicion.

Her previous encounters with Rodney had been brief. He'd always snubbed her; either ignoring her completely or being exceedingly abrupt. But with his job in jeopardy, he was overly-interested and cordial to Bunny, and she didn't know which was worse. But she *did* need to know where the money was, so she was being patient.

The FBI and IRS were also interested in Rodney, which only helped her cause. Seargant's team had deemed him innocent in any involvement of the murders, but the forensic accountants at the Bureau had uncovered plenty.

Rodney had been paid handsomely and in some cases illegally. The SEC joined the investigation after they'd found evidence of wash trades, stock option backdating, and insider trading.

Now Rodney was singing like a bird. His toothy grin was long gone and his curt and pompous manner nonexistent.

Bunny and Rodney worked tirelessly with her personal legal and financial team, aided considerably by Seargant's oversight and the cooperating government agencies. Still, everyone knew the situation was dynamic. Jeremy was very much alive, which was evident when they found so many recent outgoing distributions across many of his accounts.

The FBI was tracking the transactions but few were optimistic. Jeremy was too smart to leave a trace, and even if he did, international financial affairs were tricky and would most certainly lead to a non-extradition country. What they *had* uncovered was now frozen.

The entire process had been eye-opening to Bunny.

But what was more extraordinary was what she found in one of Jeremy's business offices in Easton.

While the others were tracking Jeremy's operations in cyberspace, Bunny had been concentrating on the physical aspect of things; visiting his local business offices and rummaging through everything she could find.

It was late one night when she found the file and it sparked her interest immediately.

It was within a thin folder, tucked among the inane. But it contained information about a safe deposit box that was opened about ten years prior.

It was located at a Bank of America in Severna Park, Maryland, about forty minutes away. The next morning she visited the bank and was greeted by Cathie Campbell, one of the account specialists; a petite, friendly woman with long blonde hair.

Bunny brought the necessary paperwork and was soon in the small rectangular room. Cathie pointed to a nearby table and chairs, with a computer, phone, and a small lamp, before leaving her alone with the key. Box # 1748 was on the left side; a plain metal compartment at her eye level. It looked innocent enough, though she noticed it was a bit larger than the others stacked all around it.

Bunny eyed the simple lock and stole a quick glance at the key in her sweaty palm. She became anxious and uncomfortable; dwarfed by the high walls of metal shelving that surrounded her.

Why did Jeremy own a safe deposit box and what was he hiding? And why here, so far away from where he usually banked? She envisioned him standing in the room and another feeling of betrayal swept over her. But then her misgivings were replaced by anger and curiosity.

She inserted the key.

The box slid out easily. It was light, but there was definitely something inside. She eagerly moved to the table, spilling the contents. There were several letters bound with a rubber band and a DVD in a case. She pivoted to the computer and inserted the disk. Then she unraveled the bundle of papers, waiting for the screen to come alive.

She began reading the first of many letters and her mouth dropped open. She gripped the edges of the papers tight as a feeling of sickness and unchecked emotion eclipsed her.

Then the DVD began to play and her senses were suspended. She was drawn to the images on the monitor. She became nauseated but couldn't turn away.

Bunny couldn't believe what she was seeing!

Could it be true?

With her thoughts fighting for consideration and her mind in turmoil, she went into shock and fell to the floor.

CHAPTER 74

Seargant got the call and headed to the roof of the Hoover building, where a helicopter flew him and Agent Hartley north-east into Maryland.

He was briefed en route; coordinating with his men on the ground, and speaking to the manager of the Bank of America. He was informed that Bunny was awake, but had a bump on her forehead from a fall. She'd refused medical attention and would only talk to Seargant in person.

It appeared that Bunny had uncovered very important and sensitive information about her husband's affairs—and quite possibly the Island Hopper case—and soon he would have access to it all.

It took less than a half hour to arrive and land at the Severna Park Middle School; and only a few minutes more for Seargant to enter the Bank of America across the street.

Bunny was still in the room, sipping coffee and looking exhausted. She had been taken outside several times for fresh air, but had always returned, feeling too weary to stand.

When Seargant entered the room, she ran to him, swinging her arms around him. "Thank you for coming. I just watched this DVD. It's awful!"

Seargant accepted her easily and held her until she let go. He remembered their substantial and charged conversation at her estate, and appreciated her willingness to help.

"I know it's hard, Bunny. You did the right thing in calling us."

She shook her head, wiping away a few stray tears. "I just feel so betrayed; so terrible for what he's done!"

"You *know* that none of this is your fault. It's all Jeremy."

Seargant offered a small smile that lent her confidence and she nodded, regaining some composure.

"Bunny, do you mind stepping outside and allowing me to see what you've found?"

She was escorted out gingerly, and soon Seargant and Agent Hartley were in the room with the door closed. Wasting no time, the DVD was played and they watched in silence as an image of a tropical beach appeared.

The view originated from just off-shore, perhaps from an anchored boat in the immediate surf. It showed a beautiful stretch of white beach, with aqua blue water all around. The image was jumpy and amateur, seeking to capture the broad extent of a perfect scene. Then it focused on a resort setting, with plenty of sun bathers and a busy volleyball game near a beach-side wedding chapel.

The camera dramatically focused on a young woman in a wedding gown as she walked along the shoreline, away from the resort. Her gait was hurried, the expression on her face haunting, and the camera stayed with her. Seargant no doubt shared what the operator saw; that the young bride looked out of place, both in spirit and dress.

Then, as she eased out of the resort beach area and moved along the high grasses, an arm grabbed her and a gloved hand plunged a knife into her chest several times. The image jumped, as if the cameraman was part of the violent clash. But then it steadied. The woman kicked and screamed, throwing her body to the side and forcing her attacker to move into sight.

It was brief, but Seargant paused the frame; and even though the screen was small and the resolution average, there was no doubt the killer was Jeremy.

In silence, the FBI men moved to the stacks of letters, donning latex gloves and using tweezers to handle them. For almost an hour, they poured over each one, sharing the relevant details and then discussing them in total.

"So it was blackmail," Seargant finally said. "Someone shot this, found out who Jeremy was, and then extorted who knows how much money."

Agent Hartley sighed and moved back in his chair. He was Seargant's # 1 and was respected for his attention to detail and knack in deciphering things.

"But what concerns me," Hartley began. "Is why didn't the person go right to the police? They *couldn't* have immediately known the killer was so wealthy. And how could they have planned such an elaborate plan so quickly?"

"I have an address and phone number right here," Seargant said. "It seems that the supposed blackmailer wasn't afraid or even shy about Jeremy knowing exactly who he was."

"And that alone begs even more questions," Hartley said. "What's the address; where is he?"

"William Monocacy is the name. Incredibly, he's right here in Severna Park."

"I don't think that's a coincidence," Hartley whispered to himself.

CHAPTER 75

Seargant stepped out of the bank and into the narrow parking lot. The fresh air felt good after being in such close confines. He moved to one of the FBI cars, a less conspicuous SUV, to check the GPS for directions.

He'd requested a warrant and it was pending, but he wanted to make a quick pass of Monocacy's house to be ready when the order was issued. He made a left on Benfield Road, heading east for a half mile. Then he took a right into the Bluff Point neighborhood and slowly rolled past several nice homes, taking note of the wide interior streets and large yards. But when he reached the rear of the private neighborhood, there was a gate and he called his assistant.

As usual, Carrie picked up on the first ring and he recognized the enthusiasm in her voice. "Hey Sarge," she sang. "What da' ya' need?"

"I'm in the field, outside the Bluff Point neighborhood in Severna Park, Maryland. It's near the Truck House Road/Benfield Road intersection. The in-road is Severn Road. I need the contact information for the HOA board to get through a gate after a warrant is issued."

"I'm on it," she said, and he ended the call. He knew the conversation was recorded and Carrie could replay it as she worked. Within moments his cell chirped and she was back on the line. He could hear her busy computer keyboard working its magic on the other end.

"I've got the HOA board right here," she said, listing the members, starting with the president."

"Send it to my phone. I'll wait for the warrant to call."

The conversation over, Seargant swung back to the bank. He reviewed the DVD once more and re-read the letters, running through the possible scenarios. He grew impatient, feeling each tick of the clock. He could think of nothing else but getting to the man who'd taken the video.

Then he heard the fax come to life beside him and saw page one of the warrant appear in the tray. Looking to Hartley, he nodded and the team was off.

Three SUV's turned into Bluff Point. They eased left and dipped into the tree line, before coming up to the small marina at Forked Creek. Then they came to the monitored gate.

But as they approached, a jogger was doing her best to run in place, while punching numbers into the key pad, and as she glanced over at them, the wide gate swung open and she gestured them in.

Offering a quick wave, Seargant smiled at the woman and looked ahead, expectantly. Vast estates appeared on both sides of the street, as a breath-taking view of the Severn River showed on the south side.

The address they were looking for sat proudly at the point between the Severn River and Rock Cove, and there were two vehicles in the circular driveway. The house was made of stone on all sides, with large pillars stretching up to an arcing roof that seemed to reach into the trees behind it. The driveway was cobblestone and it framed an impressive marble fountain. At its center, water gushed up like a soaring, moving ornament.

With utmost efficiency, everyone emptied and flanked Seargant at the front door. No one answered the multiple knocks, so a ram splintered the heavy door on the second attempt. The FBI swarmed in and fanned out, and within minutes the house was cleared. Nobody was home and a check of the grounds confirmed it.

Seargant concentrated on the great room in the rear of the house. There was a massive stone fireplace to his left and a wall of windows to the south, where he looked out to the massive lawn that stretched to the river.

In the far corner, he saw several pieces of expensive furniture—both antique and modern—stacked up and moved to the corner, haphazardly. Instead of being furnished in the beautiful décor that adorned the rest of the house, there was a large king-sized bed, a bookshelf with several periodicals, and a large television in the middle of the room. A telephone sat on an end table; along with a medical dictionary, several bottles of pills, and phone numbers scribbled on a pad.

"It looks like someone's planning to die here," Seargant said to Hartley.

For several minutes they picked through the stacks of medical journals, pain medications, and the assembly of notes. Hartley read a report on brain tumors, while Seargant slowly walked the main floor, taking it all in.

Suddenly a young FBI agent ran into the room, grabbing a pillar to steady himself.

"Sir, you need to see this right away. It's in the basement."

"What is it?" Seargant asked.

"William Monocacy isn't just a blackmailer. I'm sure he's the Island Hopper."

The words hung in the air and were emphasized in the silence. Stone-faced, Seargant looked back to the bed and medications, before looking to Hartley.

"What?!" Hartley exploded. "There are *two* killers and Jeremy is *not* the Island Hopper."

Seargant grimaced. "And I don't think they're getting along, considering that Jeremy is on the lam."

"Yeah, I guess serial killers don't play well with others, especially *other* killers."

"But we also have something more dangerous on our hands," Seargant said, grimly.

He waved at the room and pointed to the furniture that was discarded in the corner. "We have a serial killer that is dying, and he's trying to take some people with him."

Hartley surveyed the room in complete agreement. Then he gathered all of the medications.

"I'll call his doctor and see what's up."

CHAPTER 76

Every serial killer had one, and it never ceased to amaze Seargant. They called it by different names—their lair, operation center, office, or even dungeon—but they *all* had one. It was the one safe place they planned their killings, celebrated their efforts, and indulged in that special something that only they could know.

It didn't take long to find the Island Hopper's special space. The FBI agents scoured every bit of the enormous home and knew exactly what they were looking for.

Despite the seemingly unlimited wealth at William Monocacy's disposal, or how ornate and lavish his home was, *his* lair was at the far end of the basement, behind an ordinary wooden panel, and unusually small.

A computer and phone sat on a simple desk, with a worn orange chair that had seen better days, tucked underneath. The walls were covered with photographs of the Island Hopper's victims, a map of the entire Caribbean, and thumb tacks dotting many of the islands. There was a short file cabinet against the desk, with papers and pens scattered across it, and a single light bulb hung from an exposed rafter.

Seargant gaped at it all, a feeling of bitter sweetness eclipsing him. He was ecstatic that he finally found their killer, but sad at the extent of the criminal mind; how cruel and calculating another human being could be to another.

A technician was busy typing at the computer monitor. His hands moved furiously across the keyboard, and he squinted at the small screen between bursts of typing.

"Anything yet?" Seargant asked him.

"This is definitely our guy," the agent said, flatly. "I can't get into some of the programs and a lot of it's encrypted, but there's a *ton* of travel information that I'm sure will correlate with the murders. I also see internet searches on methods of death and dying, and a ton of photographs of Caribbean destinations."

"Good work; keep it up," Seargant said.

Then he spoke to his agents, succinctly. "Let's remain focused. We don't know where William Monocacy is, so time is of the essence.

"First I want our vehicles moved off-site and a loose perimeter established. Move the front door back in place so it looks unscathed to the cursory look. Maybe we'll get lucky and he'll be coming home soon. I also want all of his cars inventoried and an A.P.B put out for any that are not here."

Two agents immediately ran off and up the stairs.

"I want a list of his bank assets and holdings and want all of his credit cards and bank accounts accessed."

Another agent left, punching numbers into his cell phone.

"I need a complete background check, including any known aliases and where this guy's been in the past five years. And call the TSA and U.S. Customs to see if he's on travel now."

Another agent left.

"This house is our operation center until we catch him. Double our force inside—full forensics and tech squad—and call the press. I want this guy's picture everywhere!"

Seargant's phone chirped in his pocket and he moved to answer it.

"Go ahead," he said, calmly.

"Sir, this is Hartley upstairs. I have Dr. Sinclair on the phone. He's the specialist that's been treating Monocacy for over a year and I'm gonna three-way him in."

Seargant walked out of the cramped space and sat in an over-sized sofa in the plush basement. He heard some clicks before the line was established.

"Doctor? This is Special Agent M. Jackson Seargant of the FBI. What can you tell me about William Monocacy?"

"Agent Seargant," Dr. Sinclair started, evenly. "Agent Hartley has filled me in and I understand your position. But I must also respect my patient's right to privacy and the law itself."

"Dr. Sinclair, I'm going to get right to the point here. This man *is* the Island Hopper, the guy that's been killing people all over the Caribbean. Not allegedly; not possibly. He's not a suspect; he *is* the killer and time is something we do not have."

The doctor exhaled loudly. Silence ruled as he weighed his choices.

Seargant continued. "Again, I have a warrant for the premises here and I can subpoena you and your office as well, but frankly we just don't have the time. We don't know where he is and we're sure he'll strike again. I just really need to ask you some questions."

Dr. Sinclair let out another sigh and then conceded. "What do you need?"

"Did he ever mention anything that was germane to our case or something that could help us locate him?"

"No; I only knew him by treating him. He's a very sick man with a stage four brain tumor. It's a Glioblastoma tumor; the same kind that killed Edward Kennedy. I don't think he has more than days to live."

"What does that look like, Doctor? I mean is he walking around hunched over in pain or does he have full use of his faculties?"

"It varies by patient and depends on several factors, mainly how fast the tumor is growing, what it's pressing on, and the patient's tolerance for pain. In William's case, he's probably drugged up pretty well but fully lucid and capable, in between spells of Absence Seizures and unconsciousness."

Seargant was absorbing every word. "What's he like?" he asked.

"Confident, intelligent, and arrogant. But he's very likeable and charming if he wants to be. He's definitely carved out a world that he controls though his wealth and ego."

"What are his hobbies? Where might he be?"

"I never saw him outside the office and each visit was about his condition. The conversations were full of the common 'what if?' and 'when?' questions. He rarely mentioned anything of a personal nature, though I know he's an avid sailor and loves to travel."

"What boats did he have? Do you know his favorite ports or marinas?"

"He liked the BVI's, but not for their ports I remember him saying."

"The British Virgin Islands?"

"Yeah; he liked the currents and the waters there. I specifically remember him talking about sailing around Virgin Gorda. He said the pastel-colored homes looked to be thumb-tacked into the steep hillside. I'll always remember that image he described."

"What else?"

"That's the only conversation we ever had of a personal nature, and that's only because we discussed the Annapolis boat show last year."

"Thank you, Doctor," Seargant, said. "Hartley, please finish up the interview."

Seargant continued to sit, tapping his cell phone against his temple, as if it would prod his mind into revelation. Then his eyes wandered to where he'd just come from.

The room that held all of William Monocacy's deepest secrets.

The Island Hopper's lair.

Seargant re-entered and his stare floated to the wall of photographs. His eyes grew wide. Why hadn't he seen it sooner? To the far left were several photographs of Tom Brightwell and Danielle Sullivan. Seargant moved closer, eyeing a piece of paper with circled words and dates.

Searching the desk, he opened a folder and saw a detailed itinerary—one from Chicago and one from Montgomery—and information on the Pompano Beach Club in Bermuda. Looking further, he saw detailed transcripts of what appeared to be recent phone conversations between Tom and Dannie.

"Oh my God," Seargant said to himself.

In the last couple of hours Seargant had learned that there were two killers not one. He'd also uncovered the true identity of the Island Hopper.

But now he also knew the killer's immediate intentions.

He stabbed at his cell phone, hoping he wasn't too late.

CHAPTER 77

The Pompano Beach Club
Southampton, Bermuda

Tom and Dannie enjoyed long, hot showers; each feeling the full effects of the all-day moped ride. But when Dannie knocked on Tom's door, all the aches and pains seemed to fade away and the happy couple walked arm in arm toward a waiting taxi.

Dannie wore a long white sun dress with matching flat sandals. Her jewelry was understated, with a single string pearl necklace and matching earrings. On her right wrist she wore a purple gemmed bracelet that stood out, no doubt a special gift from one of her daughters. It was just another thing he was drawn to about her. She shined, and always did things her own way.

They walked by their moped and Dannie smiled at Tom, with a look of amazement.

"I can't believe we took that thing everywhere today!"

"Wait until tomorrow," Tom said, proudly. "We still need to hit Hamilton for some shopping and more exploring."

"That's fine as long as we take a car tonight!"

Soon the taxi was heading to the Waterlot Inn. They were dropped off to the north and entered near the second floor bar. Tom checked on the reservation, finding they were early, so they held hands and descended the black hardwood split staircase.

They walked past the piano, pausing to notice the elegant décor that enveloped them. The furniture was historic and charming. Vintage Windsor Captain's chairs surrounded the tables. Crisply tucked tablecloths, lit candles, and fine china made the consummate look almost too elegant to disturb. Oil paintings of nautical themes hung on the walls, and exposed wood beams protruded from the high, white ceiling.

"This is some place," Dannie said. "One of the most exquisite restaurants I've ever seen!"

Tom squeezed her hand. "Nothing but the best for you."

They strolled outside, feeling the warm, balmy air that blew off the bay. The outdoor area was elaborate and eye-catching as well. The high hedges that formed the perimeter were cut sharply, and an ornate, cobblestone path forged through the pristine gardens. Dannie paused to absorb the splendor of it all. Every color was represented in the flowers that appeared to be painted onto the ground.

Tall palm trees swayed above them, and they moved to the bar to order a couple of Iced Teas. Dannie quickly paid, winking at Tom, who had been distracted by the view.

"Remember we're going Dutch," she said, teasingly.

They started walking away when a man's voice called out from a bar stool. "Tom, is that you?"

They turned to see a man jump up, excitedly. He and Tom shook hands and Tom introduced Dannie.

"This is Chris," Tom explained. "The guy who told me about this place."

Tom turned to him. "So how are things?"

"Everything's great! I'm just meeting some friends who are a little late."

They made idle chit chat for a few moments, before Tom and Dannie walked onto the dock to look out at Jews Bay. The sun had set and they turned back to the restaurant, noticing the salient red against the white limestone rooftop. The Gibbs Hill Lighthouse peeked up from the hill against the royal blue sky.

Water lapped at the dock and they could hear the muted sounds of outside music. Tom took Dannie's hand and they began a slow dance that finished with a long kiss.

Dannie spoke first. "I want you to know that I'm falling for you, but we can take this as slow as you want. I'm not here to compete with Jess, or do anything that makes you uncomfortable."

"Nor I in regard to James. I was thinking the same thing."

"Are you as nervous as I am?" she asked, blushing.

"You make me feel like I did in high school, and there's only one other woman who had that effect on me."

Dannie exhaled, loudly. "Well I'm glad that's settled then."

She started walking back to the restaurant. "I'm going to freshen up in the ladies room. I'll be right back."

"Don't be too long," Tom said, playfully. "We have so much to talk about."

She waved as he watched her go. Then he took a long drink from his Iced Tea and smiled in the solidarity of the moment.

A place where nothing could go wrong.

CHAPTER 78

After nearly ten minutes, Tom was getting worried about Dannie. It had been some time since he'd been around a woman, and he knew she took her time, so he tried to dismiss any negative thoughts.

But after several more minutes, he walked back to the restaurant with an uneasy feeling. He found the bathrooms on the second floor.

Several women entered and exited, and he asked a woman if she'd seen someone resembling Dannie. She said the bathroom was empty and Tom darted inside, checking the stalls.

Then he ran to the front of the restaurant. The hostess remembered Dannie immediately, saying she'd left with another man several minutes before. Tom swung around and bolted outside.

He ran to the windy road, looking in both directions. But night was falling fast and he only saw a couple of red taillights in the distance. He stood feeling helpless, until several cars zoomed by so close that the air pushed him back and he choked on exhaust. Then he ran to the lower parking lot, making cursory glances into the rows of cars.

A well-dressed couple rushed passed him, looking to him, quizzically; but Tom continued on. Finally, he walked back into the restaurant. The hostess was on the phone, but she excitedly motioned to him.

"Are you Tom Brightwell?" she asked, confused.

He felt relieved, grabbing the phone.

"Hello? Dannie?!"

The voice was low; the tone direct. "Tom, it's Seargant. Is Danielle with you and are you both safe?"

"Seargant, how did you know that—"

"Tom! Are you both in a safe place?"

A feeling of dread washed over him. The temperature in the room seemed to rise exponentially and he became flush. He suddenly felt uneasy and his legs almost gave out.

Tom grasped the phone tightly. "Dannie just left with a guy and I don't know why. What's going on?"

Seargant sighed, heavily. "We know who the Island Hopper is. It wasn't Jeremy like we thought. It's complicated. I'll be there in the next few hours."

Tom stared blankly, trying to process what he'd just heard.

"If Jeremy's not the Island Hopper? Then who—"

"I'll be there by midnight and we'll—"

Tom cut Seargant off, spewing a quick description. "Is he white and handsome, in his mid-forties; with dark hair, green eyes, well-spoken, animated, and crafty?"

"Sounds like our guy."

"Then I know who he is and he's got Dannie."

"Okay Tom, listen. My team is already in contact with the police in Hamilton. The airport and marinas are shut down and road blocks are going up. The police are en route. And by the way this man tapped your phone. I have hundreds of pages of written transcripts from every phone call you and Dannie have had in the last week or so."

"But how is that possible?"

"Just want you to know in advance of me getting there. Start thinking of what this guy wants and what he knows about you."

Seargant paused, hearing nothing but his friend's frantic breathing.

"I'm so sorry, Tom. I'll be there soon."

CHAPTER 79

It was the hardest phone call Tom Brightwell had ever made.

As a homicide investigator, he'd often talked directly to the families of the deceased; many times being the first to inform them. It was an ugly but necessary part of it all, and he'd adopted a sense of detachment.

But this time Dannie was the victim; not that it was homicide yet. He was personally involved and felt an overwhelming sense of guilt. He was in love with her!

Dannie had two daughters and he'd reached Abby, the oldest, first. He explained the situation as honestly and directly as possible. After the initial shock, came worry, confusion, and anger. The usual questions were asked.

Was she *definitely* kidnapped? Is the now-famous Island Hopper killer to blame? Where do you think he took her? What's being done?

Tom sighed in between the questions, but maintained control. He felt helpless to the events of the hour, but was resolved to do everything to get Dannie back safely.

The FBI was on the way, and Tom was already working a composite and hypothesizing all outcomes. But he was certain of one thing, which he shared with Abby. This went against the Island Hopper's previous Modus Operandi and Tom perceived it as a sloppy act of desperation.

Abby had asked the most difficult question, which was also the first on Tom's mind. Do you think she's already dead? Although Tom could not guarantee anything, he believed she was alive. That Dannie was being used as bait for a final confrontation. She was a small piece in a much bigger puzzle. Time was their friend, and every minute that they didn't find a body, was one step closer to a happy conclusion.

But then Abby started hurling insults. She'd been against her mother dating a man with a drinking problem, someone involved in a murder investigation. Her mother was a simple, genuine person. She deserved the best from life and Abby knew the relationship was reckless.

Tom received the impact easily. He understood that his resume didn't read well. He *was* an alcoholic and broken from the deaths of his wife and daughter, and even hardened by his life's experiences in police work. Were Abby's accusations and summations of him that off-base?

Yes, he decided. The man he used to be would have thrown himself into a bottle to self-medicate. Instead, he was patiently explaining the situation to Dannie's family, helping the authorities, and working on his own theories.

Cindy, the younger of Dannie's daughters, was subdued. She asked the same questions, which he refuted affably with the same measure of calm. But she internalized it all, happy to defer to Abby.

Both calls over, Tom sat at a conference table at the police station with a notepad, writing his thoughts freely. Gone were the feelings of helplessness that had paralyzed him earlier.

He was going to find Dannie.

He'd never been so sure of anything in his entire life.

Seargant and his team arrived as promised. They set up operations in the fourth floor conference room of the Hamilton police station. Tom was still there; having gone through every detail he could with the local detectives.

He'd been over the story a dozen times and nothing of consequence had been gained, even as the police swarmed the Waterlot Inn. There were no security cameras, no real witnesses other than Tom and the hostess. The road blocks had proved fruitless.

Dannie was gone.

Tom learned quite a bit about the Bermuda police. Most of them, save the detectives, didn't even carry guns. There were no protocols for this type of scenario, and they were all too eager to have the FBI take over the investigation.

Tom was visibly relieved to see Seargant. He hadn't seen him since the drop-off in Venezuela, and they embraced before finding an empty room.

"Wow," Seargant began. "You've really lost a lot more weight."

Tom shifted uncomfortably. He was in no mood to talk about himself.

Seargant picked up on it, speaking evenly. "As I told you, Jeremy is *not* the Island Hopper, but they were definitely in communication."

Tom was hanging on every word.

"I don't know how to tell you this, but we uncovered a secret lock box at one of Jeremy's banks. Inside was a DVD that showed your daughter's murder. It was definitely Jeremy."

Seargant put a heavy hand on Tom's arm to steady him. "We think that the Island Hopper, a.k.a. William Monocacy, was filming the beach from a sail boat, and accidentally captured the killing. Then, for unknown reasons he traced Jeremy's movements, began blackmailing him, and the two were involved in some sick game."

"So there are two of them," Tom said, concentrating on the floor. "And you don't think they are working together?"

Seargant frowned. "Based on what we've found, I don't think they are in contact anymore."

"Working together or separately, either one is bad news," Tom said, sighing.

Seargant remained stoic.

"Tell me everything you know about this guy," Tom said.

"Like Jeremy, he's worth hundreds of millions, if not more. He's a loner who thrives on control and extravagance, and he's a very sick man."

"You think he's sick?" Tom snapped, sarcastically. "He's been on a killing spree throughout the Caribbean! He even enjoys it enough to film it!"

Tom stood, moving his hands to his face and rubbing his eyes, forcefully. He breathed heavily and then peered down at Seargant.

"That's not what I meant," Seargant said. "I mean he's *literally* dying of a brain tumor and only has days to live."

Tom sat down and took a long sip of coffee, thinking through this last bit of information.

"So we have a very wealthy serial killer who's dying of a brain tumor. He's broken from his MO and is on the run with my girlfriend on one of the smallest islands we've been on so far."

"That's a good summation."

"So what are we doing?" Tom asked.

"Everything's shut down and there's no doubt he's still on Bermuda. I've given a press conference on the developments and his photograph has been broadcast everywhere. The local police are canvassing the entire island."

"So we suffocate him until he pops?"

"What else can we do?"

"I say we get inside his mind and poke around. Let's brew another pot of coffee, get your best profilers on board, and see what we can come up with."

CHAPTER 80

Dannie awoke abruptly, kicking off the blankets that covered her. Her eyes flew open—her face frozen in horror—as she looked around the dark space that swallowed her.

The immediate past was a blur.

The headache hit like a hammer and it was the worst she'd ever known. The pounding was constant and unforgiving; the pain so cutting that it nearly sent her back to sleep.

But as impotent as she was, she knew she was in a very bad place.

Dannie tried to move but was instantly caught. She saw shackles on her feet and a chain extending into the darkness.

She forced herself to concentrate; to try to understand her surroundings. She was alone and it was quiet. She picked up a distinct smell—medicinal and antiseptic in nature—but couldn't determine the source.

She looked around to get her bearings. There was no natural light and she couldn't judge how big the space was. A single light bulb shined in the corner, and as her eyes adapted to the faint light, she started to decipher things through the darkness.

To her right was a table with several tools and chemicals; to her left were stacks of canned goods and cases of bottled water. The sofa she laid on was old and worn. It was the only hint of furniture.

Coughing through a dry mouth, Dannie swallowed hard and tried to exercise her vocal cords. She struggled to speak but only managed a few moans. She had to figure this out; make sense of what was happening. She rubbed her eyes to help ease the pain in her head.

A dark figure appeared at the far end of the room and she froze. It approached slowly and deliberately. It was the man Tom knew from the restaurant! He peered down at her, looking her over as if she was a prize he'd just won. He was calm and measured, which made her even more uncomfortable.

"Look who's up?" he purred, enthusiastically. "How's the headache?"

Dannie squinted up at him, staring blankly.

"It's okay," the man continued. "You're experiencing some unfortunate side effects from one of my favorite drugs. Quite honestly, I don't envy you."

"Who are you? Where am I?" Dannie asked in a low, scratchy tone, finally finding her voice.

"Dannie, Dannie, Dannie," the man, sang. "Do you really not know? And after all the thought and preparation I've dedicated to you?"

The man continued staring at her and she fell back into the sofa, her energy nearly spent. The last thing she remembered was walking through the restaurant lobby and seeing the man who Tom had spoken to. He took her by the arm, speaking to her softly, and gently guiding her to the exit.

He had a surprise for Tom that he wanted to show her. He had spoken with him about it. But when she turned the corner in the parking lot, he had shoved her into his van. A rag was placed over her mouth. She was thrown into darkness until she'd awoken. There was no telling how long she'd been asleep.

"I don't know what's happening. Please just—"

"Oh Dannie," the man said, kneeling in front of her and gently touching her cheek. "I guess formal introductions *are* in order. I am the Island Hopper and you are my guest."

He rose, still watching her. It was the looks from his victims he cherished most, and he had a litany of them frozen in his mind. Every human expression had been witnessed over the course of his murderous past. He found honesty in them, especially the ones just before and during death.

It was the purest look into human nature and the Island Hopper treasured them all.

CHAPTER 81

The Island Hopper glanced at his watch before scribbling a few more notes into his journal. He pushed the pen across the paper delicately, taking his time with each entry.

After filling a page he stopped. He paused in contemplation, closing his eyes as if pained. Then, with a flash of enlightenment, he wrote some more and finished by emphatically signing his name.

He turned to Dannie, who was sleeping on the couch. He regarded her for a long moment, taking time to notice every detail. The whole time he smiled, beguilingly. Then he picked up a syringe, attached the proper tubing and bag, and without deliberation plunged the needle into her arm.

Bright red blood instantly coursed through the clear tubing and began to assemble in the bag on the floor. His eyes moved to hers and his hand gently caressed her cheek, moving some stray hair away.

Too weak to take any real notice and too befuddled to care, Dannie slowly opened her eyes, staring vacantly at her captor. She could hardly see him through her delirium, but she didn't have to see evil to feel it so near.

She realized he was taking blood from her again—the third time in two days—but she showed little emotion. He had withheld food and water as well, and seemed to be sucking the life from her little by little. Parched and weary, she managed to rise a few inches before bringing her weight down at a slightly different angle.

"What are you doing to me?" she asked, her voice deep and rough.

The killer smiled at her, as he always did, sending more chills through her limp body. Then he checked on the bag and squeezed her hand to help the flow.

"I'll discuss the more pertinent details, seeing as you're playing the starring role."

Confusion swept over her, but it was nothing new. The man always spoke in riddles and loved playing mind games. But information was essential to survival. She now accepted that she was being held by the serial killer known as the Island Hopper. The same man Tom had been tracking. But to what extent she played a part still eluded her.

The killer withdrew the needle and wrapped her arm tightly with tape. Then he stood above her.

"Because I know so much about you," he started. "And because time is of the essence, I feel it only mannerly to tell you a little about myself. I am your friendly neighborhood Island Hopper and I am dying of a brain tumor. And while I may be on limited time, we still have so much to do.

"You have no doubt heard of my recent activities. I've killed because I'm naturally curious. I will be at my end soon and want to see what it's like first-hand. Certainly you understand, don't you?"

Dannie just stared at him, taking shallow breaths.

"You were a natural fit, because it all started with your boyfriend ten years ago. I—like he—was at the very beginning, and now I have his prize to make sure that he and I will be at the end. It's actually poetic if you think about it and I couldn't have planned it better.

"Anyway, I can't kill you like the rest. I mean, where's the fun in that? I simply wouldn't have anyone to enjoy my last days with."

Dannie's mind was foggy, every one of her senses dulled, but she was starting to understand. She was bait to bring Tom and the killer together, though she wasn't sure to what end.

Her frustrations grew and a fire ignited within her. Hearing Tom's name flow from the killer sent her into a rage. She kicked and screamed against the chains.

"You leave Tom alone!" But even before she finished the words, she fell light-headed and dizzy.

The killer looked at her, amused.

But suddenly his face went white; his expression frozen. He stumbled backwards and his arms fell to his side. A murmuring sound erupted and was caught in his throat. His entire body convulsed as if he was being shocked. Then he fell sideways, splayed out on the floor, unmoving.

Dannie's eyes followed his fall. She was bewildered at the exchange and the man's sudden collapse. But before she could process the information, she became even more somnolent.

So she closed her eyes and gave into her body's need for rest.

CHAPTER 82

When Dannie awoke, she looked to the floor but her captor was gone. She raised her head slowly but heard nothing. It was still dark, which she was accustomed to, but things were eerily silent.

She forced herself to remain awake, re-thinking her brief exchange with the Island Hopper and trying to piece together the puzzle. Strength and coherence, she knew, were her only way out.

Like each time she awoke, she recounted the recent past, making a mental journal. By her count, this was the third day she'd been held hostage. Food and water had been given in select quantities and timing, and he'd been taking blood from her.

With her deteriorating strength, her chains had been reduced, and she was able to crawl to a bucket a few yards away for bathroom breaks. Still, she'd only managed to go twice the day before and she had no inkling to now. Her body was shutting down and she felt it with every waking moment.

Like several times before, her mind shifted to happier thoughts, and a montage of random and colorful memories came to her. She remembered meeting her husband for the first time, and then thought of their wedding and their two daughters. Then there were diapers, feedings, bath times, reading, schooling, sporting events, and holiday celebrations. She smiled at the images but then frowned as she tried to see their faces. As hard as she tried she couldn't concentrate.

Frustration mounted, but she forced herself to remain calm. Then she thought of the last words she'd heard from the Island Hopper. He was going to use her to draw Tom in, and she had no doubt that Tom's life was in danger. She suddenly realized she loved Tom and could envision spending the rest of her life with him. The thought of anything happening to him made her sick and she sank deeper within herself.

Then the killer came into the room, flipping on lights that had not been used over the last few days. The room turned bright and she buried her head into a pillow against the shine.

"Today's the day, Dannie! Get ready because your man is coming!"

Testing the light against her eyes, she peered out at him and for the first time was able to survey the room. It was a basement for sure, but she saw stairs at the far end that were carpeted and promised nicer accommodations above.

The Island Hopper remained focused on Dannie, palming a cell phone, and looking down at her with menacing green eyes. He held a handgun in his other hand.

"What do you say, Dannie? Is it time to call Tom?"

CHAPTER 83

It had been three days since Dannie's abduction and Tom had felt every moment of it. He'd been thinking of her nonstop, and although the uncertainty was agonizing, it was the only way to feel close to her. He just hoped that wherever Dannie was, his positive energy and thoughts of comfort could reach her.

Tom had been sleeping in chairs, eating random offerings of food, and erratically moving in all directions. He was completely disheveled and always uncomfortable. Concentration had abandoned him; and although he tried to posture confidence, he was deflated and exhausted.

His duties had been torn in several directions and all had proven futile. He had promptly yielded to the authorities and patiently given them every bit of information he could. But after meeting with so many for so long, with each wanting to recount what he'd already repeated at nauseam, he was despondent.

Still, he *did* trust Seargant and his team. They had been unbending; working around the clock and drawing on every resource.

And Seargant had just told Tom some good news.

Using the NSA, they'd confirmed that the Island Hopper and Dannie were *definitely* on the island. Backdated satellite images had concluded that no boat or aircraft had left the island since the abduction.

Seargant had shut down Bermuda, and with increasing global intrigue from the media, the world's spotlight had turned to the tiny island. With the killer unmasked, the authorities knew that it was just a matter of time.

But while it was comforting to know Dannie was still close, with the area spanning less than twenty-one square miles, Tom didn't rest. He'd launched his own search, mostly in the form of on-the-ground intelligence.

He'd retraced his and Dannie's steps from the resort to the Waterlot Inn, and spoken to everyone he could. No one had ever seen or heard of Chris Reyes or William Monocacy, and no one recognized his picture.

Tom had gone to the government and utility offices and met with the management. His message was simple; knowing all too well that even the smallest thing could blow the case wide open.

He wanted the utility personnel, trash collectors, beat cops, and everyone who worked among the populace to be keen to anything out of the ordinary. Tom believed that the Island Hopper was holed up in a high-end rental home, and although the killer had surely changed his appearance, he was possibly walking among the people. Tom also went to the public records office to obtain a list of rental properties and a demographic breakdown of the residences.

He was encouraged by what he'd found. There was a national law allowing only a couple hundred homes to be owned by non-Bermudians, and there was a strict rental policy.

Every officer was canvassing these houses and many others, but Tom had sensed that Dannie was in Tucker's Town. Being the most high-end part of the island, it was consistent with the Island Hopper's taste, and something Tom was eerily sure of.

So he'd driven his scooter, tirelessly.

He'd scoured every bit of Bermuda's residential areas and spoken to everyone he could. He knocked on so many doors that his knuckles hurt and he could mutter his short message without thinking.

On the third day, though exasperated and without any credible leads, he still pushed on.

Tom was on Tucker's Town Road, snaking up the hill toward the golf clubhouse, wondering if Dannie was being held in any of the gated homes. This was where Ross Perot, Michael Bloomberg, and many others of Bermuda's societal elite lived.

Was the Island Hopper among them as well?

The hot shower felt good. But even as the steam rose around him and the spray washed over his weary body, Tom thought of nothing but Dannie.

Was she even still alive?

The day's excursion into the more affluent neighborhoods had again been fruitless. He'd been through all nine Parishes and talked to everyone he could, but he still had nothing to show for his efforts.

But Tom pressed on.

He continued to check in with Seargant every hour, but there was nothing new. The airport had been reopened, though the security checks had been increased considerably. So while the FBI and local police worked the official investigation and the media angle, Tom persisted on his own.

Am I missing something? Tom wondered, letting the warm water massage the back of his neck. *Is there something in the other crime scenes or in my own past that I'm missing?*

Tom left his room and walked to the car the police had loaned him. But before he could get in, a taxi pulled up and Dannie's two daughters exited. Surprised, he rushed over and helped them with their bags.

Tom was confused; his voice strained. "I was just heading to the airport to pick you up. I'm so sorry I thought—"

Abby spoke first. "We got an earlier flight, no big deal," she said curtly. Then she pawed at her bags and started carrying them to the lobby with her younger sister, Cindy behind her.

Tom slid some money to the driver and followed them. Larry Lamb was there and all too aware of the situation. He offered two free rooms, but the girls refused, wanting to stay where their mother had been.

"It's just that we would feel closer to her if we were surrounded by her things and could smell her perfume," Cindy offered, meekly.

Larry made additional keys and then helped Tom carry the bags.

Tom remembered Dannie speaking reverently of Abby and Cindy. Abby was extremely bright, motivated, and mature. She was like her father, with a personality that was direct and honest. Her younger sister, Cindy was more emotional and reserved; and although as sharp as Abby, it took longer for her personality to shine.

Dannie had shown Tom pictures of the girls, and even Sara Ann, Abby's ten-year old daughter from a broken marriage. They were all pretty, tall, and thin; and Tom could see a younger version of Dannie in them all.

Dannie's descriptions of her daughters were spot on. Abby ignored Tom's pleasantries, while Cindy retreated inward and allowed her older sister to take control. Tom asked about Sara Ann and Abby abruptly said she was staying at a friend's house.

They arrived at room # 82. Abby and Cindy entered slowly, taking time to walk the room, as if searching for their mother's essence.

"We'll be down in about five minutes to talk with you," Abby said, turning to Tom for the first time.

"Absolutely," he said, closing the door and leaving them alone.

CHAPTER 84

"Nothing new?" Tom asked, breathing heavily.

Seargant sighed on the other end of the line. "It's been less than an hour since you called. When's the last time you even ate or slept?"

Tom remained quiet.

"Look, we're doing everything we can do."

Just then Abby and Cindy walked into the lobby.

"I just hope it's enough," Tom said, ending the call.

It had only been minutes, but the girls were already unpacked and had found Tom. He guided them to the outside veranda where Dannie and he had eaten the first evening. A waiter rushed over with menus and filled their water glasses.

Tom eyed Abby and Cindy. "I know this is hard," he began. "But every effort is being expended; every resource deployed."

Cindy avoided eye contact while Abby looked to Tom with a penetrating stare. And he felt it; like it carried every bit of energy within her.

Abby was direct. "With all due respect Tom, I have no time for pleasantries. I understand that my mother is quite taken with you and that's good enough at this point. But I cannot ignore my feelings of contempt that it's because of *you* that she's involved in this. I need to know the truth and quite frankly I *expect* it. Time is short and so is my patience. What's the *real* story and where do we go from here?"

Tom nodded. He understood Abby's frustrations and knew the pain she felt. He didn't internalize her comments or take them personally. He took a long drink of water and set the glass down.

"Ladies, the conversation we need to have cannot be done over a meal. Food would be wasted on me anyway because I have no appetite. Unless you're hungry can we move down to the pool? I think the open air and space would better suit us."

The girls rose without a word and Tom turned on a quick heel, indicating them to follow. They moved past the moon gate, and though he instantly recalled walking through it with Dannie, he chose to harbor the memory.

They sat at a table overlooking the beach. But the girls didn't comment or even seem to notice the beauty that abounded.

Tom spoke first. "To be straight with you, I'm a retired homicide detective from Chicago and not officially on this case. The FBI, in cooperation with the local—"

"We know that," Abby interrupted. "And that's exactly why I want to speak with *you* first. You don't have to follow protocol and are not subject to any red tape. You are operating off the grid and I hope you can exploit the obvious freedoms that come with it."

"Well said," Tom offered. "While they've been working up profiles, monitoring the airports and marinas, and giving press conferences, I've been working on my own. But to be honest, I haven't been very successful."

Cindy placed her hand on Tom's, surprising him, but he didn't recoil. Abby was taken back as well, but knowing her sister's frail state, she remained silent. Cindy spoke quietly, obviously uncomfortable in talking about something so unsettling.

"Tell me about you," she inserted politely, looking into his eyes.

Tom softened and took in a deep breath. Her eyes were pale blue, but surrounded by the redness that comes from constant crying. Her facial features were subtle and he found her naturally pretty. Her hair was long and straight, colored auburn like her mother's.

"I met your mother in—"

"I mean about *you*, Tom. *Before* you met our mother. From what she's said you're a very decent man and you have a lot in common. In the absence of her, I have a strong need to know the last person she was with."

The words came easily. Tom had no problem with Cindy's request and even appreciated the inquiry.

"I was born and raised into a working class family on the south side of Chicago and never left the area. I was an only child of Irish descent and always worked odd jobs to help my much-older father with the bills.

"Right out of high school I met and married Jessica, the only *other* woman I've ever loved, and we had a daughter named Kelly. Those two girls were everything to me, and for a while, we enjoyed a very simple but wonderful life."

Tom paused, knowing he'd just openly admitted that he loved Dannie. But the girls remained tacit, transfixed on Tom's every word.

"I'm not sure if it was my faith or strong moral code, but police work called to me, and I never felt so comfortable doing anything in my life. There was something about trying to fix an injustice or outwit an evil that surged through my entire being. My team shared the same resolve, and we worked some of the worst crimes on the city's south side.

"My daughter was supposed to be married about ten years ago in Jamaica. But just before the wedding, I witnessed her murder. It wasn't solved, and through the emotional distress, Jess and I grew apart. She was diagnosed with melanoma a few years later, and having lost the will to fight, she passed away soon after. I took a quiet retirement, withdrew inside myself *and* the bottle, and that brings us to almost six weeks ago.

"The recent Island Hopper killings caught my attention, because they were similar to Kelly's murder. Island destination; coins on the eyes. With help from the FBI, most notably Jack Seargant—who you know from the press conferences—I was able to tag along on the investigation.

"Consequently, we now know there are *two* killers. One is Kelly's former fiancée, a man named Jeremy Richards. And the second is the Island Hopper, who we now know is William Monocacy. It seems that he witnessed Kelly's murder and had an undefined relationship with Jeremy that we're still looking into."

Abby could no longer remain quiet and took advantage of a lingering silence.

"In your experience, Tom. What does this killer want with my mother and where do you think she is? How will this play out? It's been three days!"

Tom's eyes floated back to Abby, as his tone became more controlled. "We know that William Monocacy has a brain tumor and is close to dying himself. To be frank, it's a very *good* thing that it's been three days and we haven't found a body. The timing breaks the killer's MO, so your mom is special to him."

The girls nodded and Tom continued.

"I truly think she's safe within a home somewhere. The authorities were quick to shut down all transportation off the island and we know she's still on Bermuda. I think he's just waiting for something to finish this."

Cindy spoke again. "My father died too young, much like your wife. It sounds like you and mom went through similar things. What was Jessica like, if you don't mind me asking?"

Abby shot a glance at Tom and then to her sister, silently chastising her. Tom noticed and was quick to speak.

"That's a very good and well-deserved question and I appreciate it," Tom said, more upbeat. "My wife was an amazing person, much like your mother. She was so full of life and all too eager to share it. She was deeply involved in the community, the church, and every part of mine and Kelly's life.

"She made things so comfortable and took care of everything. She especially loved the holidays. It was her excuse to triple up on the decorations and inject personality into our lives."

Tom stopped abruptly, as if remembering something long lost within him. His face flushed and his tone changed.

"Jess loved the holidays so much, that in her last couple weeks when hospice was called in, I would decorate during her naps. She died on Father's day. But in those last few weeks, I hung up Valentine's Day hearts and St. Patrick's Day shamrocks. We carved watermelon jack-o-lanterns, dyed Easter eggs; and I even covered the inside and outside of our home with every Christmas light and decoration I could find."

Cindy softly cried as Abby reached for Tom's hand. "What did she think of the Christmas lights in June?" Abby asked.

"Actually, I finished them on Father's Day during her morning nap. Jess wasn't well enough to come out to see them, but she would have loved them.

"That entire day I played Christmas music, and she died that evening after hearing Celine Dion's version of "Oh Holy Night." It was her favorite song. That final 'Noel' at the very end is so uplifting. I'm thankful that it was the last word she ever heard. I was kneeling next to her, praying and crying and gently touching her face. I remember her smile as the song ended and her breathing relaxed. Then she was gone."

Tom's words trailed off and he blinked away tears. Cindy stood and hugged him, tightly. Then Abby rose, her arms touching them both. After several moments, Tom withdrew and looked steadily into their eyes.

"I will not rest until we find your mother," he said, pointedly.

Abby looked at Tom, but her hardened expression was gone. As tough as she was, she couldn't find any reason not to trust him.

Then Larry Lamb appeared. He was out of breath and carrying a phone. "Tom there's a call for you!"

Tom grabbed the phone. "This is Tom Brightwell," he said, anxiously.

"Hello Tom Brightwell. This is the Island Hopper."

And that's when everything changed. Larry, Abby and Cindy all looked to Tom, expectantly.

He listened intently and then repeated the instructions he'd just heard. "'18 Tucker's Town Road in one hour; just me, unarmed. You and Dannie will be downstairs.' Is there anything else?"

But there was only silence.

"Is she alright?" Tom added, quickly.

But the line went dead and Tom handed the phone back to Larry. Then he turned to the girls.

"It was him. We need to act fast. Please run along side me."

They began a light jog to the car. Tom was already punching numbers into his cell phone and soon Seargant was on the line.

Arriving in Hamilton twenty minutes later, Tom found Seargant and his team strategizing. The trace had been ineffective, but an advance team was en route to secure a distant perimeter, and the FBI was assembling crisis gear, weaponry, and organizing communications. Local police had already accessed the tax records on the home and the utility company was being notified.

Tom looked to Seargant. "I know how I'm going to play this and I want no interference," he said, flatly.

CHAPTER 85

The kevlar vest was placed over Tom's shoulders, with Seargant making the necessary adjustments.

"I hear what you're saying," Seargant said, trying to remain calm. "I just don't *like* it."

Tom was expecting the response but he didn't care. He was trained for the task at hand and all too motivated.

He even considered himself expendable.

Tom remained stone-faced. "He *did* ask for me to come alone and I don't want other lives in danger. If that door's wired to blow or it's just an ambush, I want to be the only casualty."

Seargant let out a deep breath. Then he turned to Tom and narrowed his stare on the man he'd come to know and respect. In the ensuing silence, Tom stepped closer and placed his hand on Seargant's shoulder. Tom spoke softly, as if tending to a child.

"I'm going in armed and wearing a vest. You can wire me to see and hear everything. But I *am* going in alone. It's what he asked for and Dannie deserves every chance, however slight."

Seargant nodded in slow agreement. "I just don't want to lose you to a small error that my men are trained to adapt to."

"And *I* don't want another officer dead; another widow wondering why the bad guys took another hero away. Remember our talk in Bonaire? This is me doing it. It ends here and now and I'm ready."

Seargant stood, addressing his men. "I want Tom to have everything he needs. Microwave the house to see what kind of heat signatures we can pick up. I want the schematics so he's not going in blind and I want the utilities on line to cut power on my command."

Seargant stopped and looked at everyone on his team, taking several moments to regard each one.

"Is there anything we're missing? Are there any questions or does anyone have anything to add?"

The men nodded a collective "no" as they looked to their leader.

"Then this is it. We all know what we have to do."

The FBI agents cleared the room, leaving Tom and Seargant alone; and they looked to each other with everything on their mind but nothing more to say.

The Island Hopper paced the room, impatiently.

He wanted the clock to move faster.

Time was not in his favor.

The headache struck just after he'd spoken to Tom and the searing pain had persisted since. The initial distress had rendered him unconscious, but he'd awoken minutes later and rose on wobbly legs.

Now he was forcing himself to stay awake.

But it wasn't easy.

He was sweating profusely and his breaths came in short gasps. His nerve endings felt like they were on fire and his body ached all over. His mind was overwhelmed; jumping to every conclusion, real or imagined. It felt like the brain tumor was alive and physically rotating across his head, as if trying to explode out of his skull.

He fumbled with the morphine pills; not even counting them as he threw a handful into his mouth, swallowing hard.

The killer had to concentrate on the matter at hand.

The final act of The Plan.

His eyes darted everywhere. He staggered around the room, using his arms to steady himself. Dannie was still on the couch. She was probably dead but he didn't have the energy to confirm it.

He scanned the deposits of C-4, before concentrating on the table in the far corner. It was where he'd spent most of the previous day. The canisters of cyclotrimethylene trinitramine, diethylhexyl, polyisobutylene, and motor oil were empty; now perfectly mixed— along with several pounds of nails and screws—into the C-4 that was so strategically placed around the room.

Then his eyes settled on the detonator.

No matter what happened in the next several minutes, there would definitely be an explosion.

The Island Hopper picked up the device. He was standing in the middle of the kill zone and he regaled in it. Checking the clock, he picked up his Sig Sauer 9mm and leaned into a large chair, moving the gun across his head trying to wipe away the pain.

Thankfully, it would all end soon.

With a very loud bang.

Everything was different now. Gone were any questions about Dannie's whereabouts and the why behind it all. All Tom's feelings of doubt, anxiety, remorse, and even rage, were replaced by a channeled focus of confronting the Island Hopper and extracting her safely.

Just minutes earlier, he'd been surrounded by FBI weaponry experts and the head of Seargant's tactical team. Bare-chested, wires were connected and taped to his body. Protective padding was added to his arms and legs and then he donned an over-sized shirt to cover it all. A camera and microphone were attached to his collar with a direct feed to Seargant.

Tom was coached on close-contact strategy and combat, but he knew his 9mm Beretta would be his first line of defense. Easily concealed and very manageable, it would provide enough stopping power and the fifteen-round clip was more efficient in a shoot-out scenario. He also carried a .380 Smith & Wesson Bodyguard in an ankle holster and two smoker grenades dangled from beneath his shirt.

Just before Tom left, Seargant squared off against him. "We've only got another minute, but I want you to know that I'm proud of you."

Tom smiled at his friend and Seargant continued.

"This is different from your experience on the force. This time you *know* the guy is a killer. He's been planning this for quite some time and we had less than an hour to prepare. He's also dying and you know he's not there to surrender, so drop him if you get the chance."

"I will and thanks for your help."

The two men embraced, not unlike they did in Venezuela. But this time it lasted longer and the emotions ran deeper. When they separated, Seargant straightened to his full height.

"Now go get this bastard and tell me all about it. I'll be minutes behind you."

Tom sped out of Hamilton.

He reached Paynters Road and slowed; snaking through the luxurious golf course that hugged both sides of the narrow road. But he paid little attention to the elegance that abounded; even as he turned right on Tucker's Town Road and moved past the large gated homes that dotted the bay.

He stopped at # 18 on the left, atop a hill that looked out to the water. It was a considerable single-floor L-shaped house, with a beautifully-maintained yard that covered at least two acres. The entire structure was bright white, except for the blue shudders across the windows, but Tom instantly took note of the black wrought iron gate that was ominously open.

Local tax records had traced it to Reginald Gateau, a wealthy Frenchman who had not been on the island for several years. A management company verified the rental was organized several days ago. A floor plan was found and Tom had memorized the layout. Still, he knew the killer was entrenched and at full advantage.

Tom cut the engine, looking to the large home. His eyes traced his given path, onto the curved red-brick driveway and to the covered porch. He counted the seconds it would take him and closed his eyes in mental preparation.

Suddenly Seargant's voice rang in his ear piece.

"No heat signatures on the street level sweeps, which could mean a no-vacancy or they're downstairs in the walk-out basement. We cannot penetrate the ground from the street angle. We're right behind you and can advance on your signal. Good luck, Tom."

"Roger that," Tom said, as he rolled out of the car with every one of his senses peaking.

Here I come, Dannie, he thought. *And Jess, I may be coming to you as well.*

CHAPTER 86

As Tom approached, the house seemed to get bigger as it rose in perspective. Evening wasn't far off and the perimeter lighting shined around him.

He'd never felt so vulnerable in his life.

He was quickly at the front porch and a heavy oak door. Touching its handle, he leaned away and pushed it, gently. The door opened slowly and he pressed it further, crouching and ready for anything. Perspiration gathered on his forehead and he stopped breathing altogether. His heartbeat quickened and he felt its rhythmic pulse in the empty silence.

He peered in. All the lights were off, but the rear of the home was a sheet of glass, and the fading sunlight illuminated the interior.

Entering the foyer, he flattened against the wall with his Beretta aimed at his forward progress. Taking measured steps, his head turned in every direction as he cleared the area.

"We're on the street Tom," Seargant chirped in his ear.

Tom stopped, straining to listen. But he could only hear his own breathing and the cracking of the hardwood flooring as he stepped.

Turning the corner, he saw light coming from the basement and an open door leading downward. He swallowed hard and began descending.

The steps led to a landing, before turning, and Tom craned his neck to see around the corner.

Tom saw a man standing behind a couch. His right hand was high in the air and his left was hidden behind the furniture.

There was no immediate danger, so Tom approached with his gun leveled. The man remained eerily still; standing proud and looking omnipotent.

But Tom stopped when he saw the detonator.

"No need to stop, Tom," the Island Hopper said. "You're already in the kill zone, so you may as well keep coming. Will you be a dear and check on Dannie for me? She hasn't moved for some time and I'm getting worried."

Tom remained steadfast, with his gun pointed at the man he'd known as Chris Reyes. But he now knew him as William Monocacy. The Island Hopper.

Tom saw the killer had a gun pressed against Dannie's head. She was lying on the sofa, wrapped in blankets. Any shot he took would put her at risk and could also result in an explosion, if there were any bombs.

"I'm here, just as you requested," Tom said.

"You are. Armed and with a battery of police outside, just as I had *not* requested."

"What happens now?"

"We all go out together."

Tom blinked away any sign of fear. Remaining calm was his goal; beginning a dialogue to gain information and stall time was vital. He hoped the killer would want to talk. Tom knew that Seargant was hearing and seeing everything.

"I just don't get it," Tom said, acting confused.

"What Tom? I'm so eager to help."

"Tell me everything."

"Actually, I really don't think I have the time. But I can tell you a few of the more important details. First, you should know what I learned as a star engineering student at MIT. My *passion* was wiring and frequency, along with a natural fascination of chemistry."

The Island Hopper pointed his chin at his right hand. "This detonator is very special. I created it myself and it includes anti-handling and jamming detection and an altitude meter. It's tied into the C-4 that's surrounding us; and will trigger when I hit the button, if it moves erratically, or if it drops below two feet local in height. Technically, eleven feet because it's based on sea-level.

"In other words, you can put your gun down."

Tom scanned the room, seeing several placements of C-4. He swiftly counted at least ten but knew there were probably more. There was no doubt the bombs were real. The Island Hopper's demeanour spoke loudly. The killer wouldn't lie about it.

Tom's mind went wild with possibilities. Could Seargant jam the frequency? Should he take his chances and shoot now?

But Tom lowered his weapon. He looked back to the Island Hopper, who stepped to the right and now pointed his gun at Tom.

"I meant what I said," the killer said. "Feel free to check on Dannie. I've removed her chains for you."

Tom moved to the couch and knelt in front of her.

"Dannie?" he called out, gently touching her face.

Her eyes flickered but didn't open. He checked for a pulse but couldn't feel one. She was warm to the touch but he sensed she was close to death. What had this maniac done to her? While tending to her, Tom touched the base of the couch and snaked his hand underneath. He felt a substantial metal frame and was thankful it was a sleeper sofa.

An idea formed and he glanced at the Island Hopper. "Tell me everything."

The killer eyed Tom. His finger was on the detonator and for a moment Tom thought it would all end. But then the man softened.

"I guess you *are* entitled to *some* information," the killer began, casually. "It all started in Jamaica. I was on my sleuth, about to launch. I was video recording the beach and happened to capture Jeremy killing your Kelly. I was initially taken back, but then became strangely intrigued.

"I tracked Jeremy to learn more about him and Kelly, and eventually even you and Jessica. When I was diagnosed with a terminal brain tumor I had an idea. Why not test death; see what it's like first-hand?

"What's interesting is that Jeremy—and I confirmed this with him later—actually put the coins on Kelly's eyes to make it look like a ritual killing or something. Anything that would create a distraction for the police. So I did the same thing to make it more interesting."

Tom looked down, shaking his head. "So you befriended my daughter's killer?"

"It started like that, actually. It turns out we both had homes in Maryland, so we got together and even sailed the Chesapeake a few times. We are uncommonly wealthy and shared some resources. It wasn't really blackmail, though we both understood I could've destroyed him at any time. He also knew that killing me wasn't an option, so it was an interesting dance for sure.

"Then I decided to frame Jeremy for my recent work, which stung my ego, but it was a necessary evil. By the way congratulations on you and Dannie. She's quite a catch for someone like you!"

Tom looked down at Dannie and frowned.

"So are you ready, Tom? If you've done your homework you know I *literally* don't have time for idle chitchat."

Tom looked to the man. He saw the Island Hopper take a deep breath and close his eyes. An eerie calm swept across the killer's face and Tom knew he had only seconds to act.

With a burst of energy, Tom sprang up and flipped the couch toward him, so that he and Dannie were on the floor and tucked in the void underneath.

Simultaneously, a deafening blast rang out and Tom felt like the floor would give way beneath him. He felt an inferno of heat and a bombardment of pressure, as all the air was sucked out and they were thrown sideways. He tried to breath but smoke filled his lungs. He was suddenly coughing uncontrollably.

In the darkness he hoped the metal under-workings would offer some protection, but then he felt the flames and realized the couch was on fire. Tom quickly rose on all fours, feeling the sofa heavy against his back. Then he stood and moved it to the side.

Looking around, he couldn't believe what he saw. The room was gone. The walls were blown away and he could look up through the ceiling. Items that had been on the second floor had fallen all around him and nothing was discernible. It was as if he was standing in the aftermath of a tornado; with jagged pieces of wood, concrete, and plaster all around him, and exposed wire and plumbing hanging down.

A high-pitched ringing sounded in Tom's ears. His eye sight was limited, with the black smoke swarming him. He pressed his shirt to his mouth as he fought to breathe, knowing he only had a few more moments of consciousness.

Without another thought, he scooped Dannie up and ran through a hole in the rear of the home. He dodged burning debris and sidestepped random obstacles, moving swiftly and taking in gulps of fresh air. Soon he was treading on grass and could see the bay directly in front of him, but he kept moving.

Tom laid Dannie down and looked to the house a couple hundred feet away. It was now engulfed in flames and the second floor was tilting downward about to fall.

But only one thing was on his mind. "Dannie?! Are you still with me?"

Tom shook her small body, unleashing the full range of emotions he'd been holding in.

"Dannie! Please God!"

His eyes searched for any signs of life, as he grabbed her neck to feel a pulse. Seconds felt like hours as he steadied himself. He closed his eyes and shut out his surroundings. Then he felt it, however faint, and he knew she would be alright.

He gently touched her cheek. To his dismay, her eyes slowly opened and grew wide with recognition. Her lips moved to speak but nothing came.

"Don't talk. Help is on the way."

"Is it really you?" she strained.

"I'm here. It's all over."

Understanding resonated within her and he breathed a sigh of relief.

Then Tom heard yelling and saw Seargant and several others running down the hill. The EMT's swarmed Dannie and Tom slowly backed away.

Tom turned to Seargant, only to collapse into the larger man.

"I've got you," Seargant said, catching Tom and holding him tightly. "You did great and I've got you."

Then Tom looked into his friend's eyes and wept.

CHAPTER 87

The hospital waiting room was lined with green and blue plastic chairs, and Tom, Seargant, Abby, and Cindy occupied four of them. The fluorescent lighting buzzed from above and spilled sharp rays of light that bounced off the shiny floor.

They sat quietly, waiting for the doctor's initial assessment. Although everyone was happy Dannie was safe, they *were* in a hospital and had been for over an hour. The ticks on the wall clock were audible and Tom felt each one of them.

When the swinging doors opened, everyone looked up. Dr. Carrington smiled broadly at the group.

"She's going to be just fine. She's a real trooper," he said.

Abby and Cindy hugged, as Tom and Seargant exhaled, triumphantly.

"After a couple bags of saline she's been able to talk more, and we'll continue to rehydrate and replenish her electrolytes. She was borderline anemic, with her hematocrit level under 25%, so we transfused two units of whole blood. She's on a liquid diet until tomorrow and should get exponentially better. We can release her in a couple of days, provided she gets a lot of rest and fluids."

Smiles abounded as Tom shook the doctor's hand, vigorously. Then he hugged Abby and Cindy and looked upward to mouth a silent thank you to God. All of his anxiety left him in a long, emphatic breath. Cindy turned away as tears came, and she fell into another embrace with her older sister.

"She's asking for you, Tom," the doctor said. "She's right through those doors. Just a few minutes, though. Then her daughters can go in."

Tom looked to Abby and Cindy, uncertain of what to do.

"Go ahead, Tom," Abby said. "It's okay. Doctor's orders."

Tom darted through the doors, pausing on the other side when he saw Dannie lying in a high bed, a host of machines buzzing around her. She was resting comfortably, and looked much older than she really was. But when he approached, her smile widened and he saw the woman he'd known.

"Hello Dannie," Tom said, softly. Then he bent down, brushed her hair with his hand, and peered into her big blue eyes.

"Hello Babe," she said, reaching for his hand.

They held hands for several moments, taking each other in.

"The doctor says you're gonna be okay. How are you holding up?"

"I'm freaked out by the whole thing, but I think I was asleep most of the time."

Tom nodded, still looking her over, and Dannie continued.

"But I *do* remember thinking of my family and of you. Then you were there and I'll never forget that vision for as long as I live."

"I wouldn't know what I'd do if I lost you," Tom said.

"We don't have to worry about that. I'm not going anywhere."

Tom was unmoved. His stare was fixed and trance-like; his eyes wide and glassy. Dannie focused on him, realizing something had stirred deep within him. He wasn't the same man he'd been just moments before, and even for her weakened state, she assumed control.

"Tom?! What's wrong?"

Tom looked to Dannie and wiped away the tears. His face was flushed with perspiration.

"I lost Kelly and then Jess. They were the two most important people in the world to me. I was just thinking that I couldn't stomach the thought of losing you."

Dannie inched up in bed and managed to wrap her arm around Tom's back, gently rubbing him.

"Again Tom, I'm here. I'll be okay and I'm not leaving you."

"Dannie. I'm completely in love with you. I'm sorry for saying it that way, in this place, and under these circumstances. But you need to know it."

Dannie's eyes flashed as a smile replaced her frown. Despite her condition she seemed to glow.

"There's no bad time, place, or circumstance to say 'I love you,'" she said. "In fact those words are spoken too infrequently, if you ask me."

Tom forced a quick laugh.

"Well, I only had a few minutes," he said. "Abby and Cindy are eager to get in here so I'll let you be."

Tom kissed Dannie on the cheek, gently pumped her hand, and then ambled away. But before he got to the door, Dannie called after him.

"Tom I need to tell you two very important things before you go."

He turned back, again leaning in next to her. "Anything you say."

"First, I know you've been working non-stop and haven't been sleeping, so I want you to go back to the resort and go to bed. Tomorrow I want you to unwind and do something selfish for yourself. Workout, relax, watch television, or just lounge around the place."

"What's the second thing?"

"I love you too."

Tom took her hand and gently kissed her on the forehead.

"I'll see you tomorrow after a long sleep," he said.

CHAPTER 88

The dream was as real as any waking thought Tom could recall.

First he was standing in a long white corridor that was so obscure it didn't allow for a peripheral view. His stare was fixed straight ahead. He was paralyzed in his perspective and couldn't look away even if he wanted to.

Then he was in a large room, though he couldn't see any walls or borders. The brightness was blinding; a screaming white that was like looking at the sun. But he didn't have to turn away or even squint. It was the most comfortable and reassuring warmth he'd ever known.

Tom was completely transfixed as he concentrated on the magnificent, awe-inspiring light. There was no doubt the source was God himself; a large, ambiguous figure standing on a great platform. Tom tried to speak but couldn't make a sound. But he felt the presence of God and a feeling of calm resonated within him.

Tom fell to his knees. Was he dead; finally home and at peace, or was this a dream?

Then two figures emerged from the light and became more defined as they drew near. He silently cried out as he saw his wife and daughter, both wearing simple white gowns. They looked down at him and smiled, and he felt instantly connected. It was as if they'd never died and the last several years didn't even exist!

No words were spoken, but it was conveyed that he had to go and live his life. *They* were at home in a different place, but *he* still had a life to live. With tears in his eyes, he was told, albeit silently, that it was okay to be with Danielle.

Abruptly he awoke and found himself in his room at the Pompano Beach Club. He was clear-headed and well-rested. He moved to the balcony doors and opened them wide. The thin, white drapes blew in like a flowing dress in a fairytale, and he stepped onto the terrace.

The Atlantic looked the same as it had for the last several days; an electric blue expanse that seemed to go on forever. He breathed deeply as his mind deciphered recent events.

Was it all over? Was the impossible mess he'd been embroiled in at an end?

Then he remembered the dream he'd just awoken from. Was it a sign that Jess and Kelly were at peace? Was it a blessing for him and Dannie?

Cheerful laughter broke his concentration and he saw Abby and Cindy in the distance, running along the surf. He stole another glimpse at the sea, with the sun's morning rays dancing on the water.

Then he decided to begin what he hoped was a long, happy, and loving future.

And it had to begin with a thoughtful conversation with each of Dannie's daughters.

CHAPTER 89

Tom found Abby and Cindy at the pool.

Abby was chewing on a piece of toast at a far table and working on some paperwork. Cindy was lounging in a chair; her sunglasses perched on her face as she listened to her iPod. Tom decided to talk to the easier of the two, first.

"Hi Cindy; may I join you?" Tom asked, motioning to the chair next to hers.

She stiffened but then relaxed, shielding her eyes to get a better view of him. Then she removed her sunglasses and ear buds.

"Anything for the man who saved mom."

"Well, there were a lot of people involved but thanks."

"It's true, Tom. We owe you everything," she said, reaching out to squeeze his hand.

Tom smiled, shyly. "What are you listening to?"

"It's actually a compilation playlist of my favorite songs. Stuff that's not really on the radio or even popular, but really speaks to me."

Tom didn't know what an iPod was, much less a playlist, but didn't want to impede the conversation. He knew Cindy had difficulty opening up, and could be even harder to reach after what happened. He needed to connect with her and even saw it necessary for his future with Dannie.

"Anything I may know, something by the Rat Pack, possibly?"

"I've got about ten-thousand songs here and I've broken down four-hundred or so that mean a lot to me. They stretch from The Beatles to Metallica; Pearl Jam to John Denver. I've got rap, R&B, metal, rock, country, thrash, pop, blue-grass, freestyle, and yes even some Sinatra.

"Sometimes, I just listen to the first ten seconds or so before switching to another song. It brings back memories that span every turn in my life. I can't fully explain it, but music grips me in a way nothing else does. It kind of allows me to step outside of myself."

Tom nodded, realizing it was the most he'd ever heard Cindy say. She was meek, but was genuine and thoughtful.

She continued, eagerly. "In a moment I can hear a song that brings me back to driving in the car as a child with my dad. Then I'm a teenager, heart-broken over some dumb boy that I can't even picture. Next, I've got my license and I'm blasting Bon Jovi in my old convertible going down a country road. Music really opens me up."

"It's great to have that outlet," Tom said. "Can you let me listen to a song or two?"

Cindy beamed, grinning enthusiastically. Then she worked her iPod, pressing and turning the dial with practiced motions. She nodded upon coming to a selection and then offered Tom the small unit.

"I think you'll appreciate this. Listen to the words and passion of Martin Gore from a band called Depeche Mode. It's a live recording of "Somebody" at the Pasadena Rose Bowl in June of 1988.

"Let me set the scene for you. Martin Gore was bare-chested, wearing suspenders and a white hat, bearing his soul through this song. The arena was a dark bowl lit up with thousands of cigarette lighters. And he just stood there with hand on hip, bathed in a single spotlight, completely alone. I've watched it a hundred times on YouTube and it gives me chills every time."

"I can't wait to hear it," Tom said, settling in to listen.

The song started and he closed his eyes, trying to decipher the lyrics. Cindy eyed him, but he was lost in the simple melody.

When it ended, he looked to Cindy. "Can I hear it again?"

"Of course, but tell me what it's about first. What's it say to you?"

"Other than the 'perverted' part, I think it could be about your mom and me, or any relationship that's open and honest."

"That's exactly right," Cindy said, grinning. "And have you ever heard of Depeche Mode before?"

"I guess I haven't."

"See? There's so much out there. You just related to a band you've never heard of; hearing a song that was recorded live decades ago. I know I sound strange, but that's one of the coolest things ever."

"You're not strange, Cindy. But can I ask you a question?"

"Anything at all."

"What do you think about your mom and me?"

"I support anything that makes mom happy and that's you. Nothing more needs to be said."

"Thanks Cindy. Really, it means a lot to hear that."

She pressed some buttons and Tom listened to the song again. When it ended, she played Queensryche's "Anybody Listening?"

"Geoff Tate is the lead singer here. Recently the band broke up and now there are two versions. You should also hear 'Silent Lucidity,' which is about waking up from a nightmare and getting a second chance with the people you love."

"That sounds familiar," Tom said.

Cindy continued. "In that song he sings about living in parallels. Once in the physical while sleeping, but also simultaneously within your dreams."

"I think I know what he means there," Tom said, thinking of the dream he'd awaken from earlier.

Tom gave the ear buds back to Cindy. Then he excused himself and walked over to Abby in the far corner. Her demeanor was much different and Tom wondered if the girls had anything in common.

Abby wore reading glasses as she stacked paperwork in neat piles. Several pens and pencils were neatly arranged to her left, and she was busy working a calculator when Tom approached.

Without looking up, she started writing in a notebook. "Did you enjoy the music tour inside Cindy's little world?"

"Actually, she has a passion that I really admire. She's very artistic and pensive."

"That she is, though sometimes it doesn't translate well into the real world."

Tom let the comment hang in the air as he looked around the pool area, feigning interest. Abby slid the calculator away and offered Tom a seat.

"So what's all this?" he asked, sitting down.

"I'm a medical billing rep and I'm catching up from the past few days. A few more hours here and then some more on the flight home and I should be okay."

Tom nodded. "Do you like it?"

"I think you'd be crazy to *like* it but I happen to be very good at it. I was born with my father's attention to detail. This job requires exactness; especially because money is on the line and I deal with insurances that are sometimes complicated."

"Is it difficult?"

"It can be. Right now I'm swamped because of the new compliance procedures. All insurance claim forms must now have a *physical* address for the medical practice and not just a P. O. Box, so most of my electronic claims are being rejected.

"Then last week I was told to start generating reports for my doctors based on the percentage of their patients that have Medicare versus all other insurances, and they even want it broken down by each doctor!"

Tom remained silent. He knew that Abby was probably less enthusiastic about him than Cindy, and probably still blamed him. She was a rigid individual and he couldn't read her. But he also knew she was an intellect and should know his intentions were pure. True to her nature she took control, removing her reading glasses and easing back in the chair.

"Look, Tom. I assume you want my blessing. To be honest, I think you're a good person, though I have reservations about your past drinking problem. I also think it's a little soon, because you're both still emotional about losing your spouses and you've both just been through hell."

Then Abby spoke softly. "But I also understand that you make mom happier than she's been in years, so I approve."

"I appreciate your honestly," Tom said.

Then his demeanor changed and he stiffened. She remained fixed on him, knowing that what he had to say was very important. Tom's face tightened and his voice became thick with emotion.

"I am a man of principle and honor and do not take my commitments lightly. I promise you two things. First I will never drink alcohol again, and second I will take care of your mother and her interests for as long as she'll allow it, without exception."

Tom's voice trailed off as he searched Abby for common ground. Then, breaking the stare, his eyes floated up to the sky and he felt the sun's warmth on his face. Abby got up, grabbing Tom's forearm as she rose and they embraced.

"Welcome to our world, Tom. I invite you to stay for as long as you like."

The next day Dannie returned to the Pompano Beach Club. Abby and Cindy had visited her in the hospital before leaving for home; and Seargant and his team were long gone.

Tom thought of buying flowers and a simple gift but decided against it. Any effort, he knew, would be well-received, but would also be a reminder of what happened. So he took a cab to the hospital, just like the day before, and upon her release they took another cab to the resort.

But although they had so much to be thankful for and discuss, the ride was somber and silent. Tom respected Dannie's condition and let her rest. He looked out the window; seeing the beautiful Bermudan landscape fly by, but not feeling it with the same sense of wonder he'd known before.

Tom helped Dannie to her room and made sure she was comfortable. But before he could inquire further, she was asleep and he let himself out.

The next morning they had breakfast at the main restaurant, sitting at the same table they'd shared the first night. Tom hoped it would bring back better memories, but Dannie didn't seem to notice. Tom tried to remain upbeat, but she seemed withdrawn. The spark that Tom cherished about her was gone.

Afterward, they packed their bags and shared a cab to the airport. His flight was a few hours after hers, but he checked in and sat with her. She smiled feebly and rested her head against him as they waited. But when her flight was called, she simply looked to him and kissed him on the cheek.

"Gotta go, Tom," she offered, easing away. "I'll call you tonight."

He shook his head in understanding and watched her leave. He moved to the large window and stood for several minutes, even watching her plane taxi down the runway and eventually lift off.

"Goodbye Danielle," he whispered against the glass. "I love you."

CHAPTER 90

Morgan Park
Chicago's South Side

Back in Chicago, Tom fell into a rhythm that was both productive and self-serving. He maintained his daily workouts and healthy diet, but also focused on some well-needed home repairs. He embraced both charges with vigor, and as the days merged together, he fell into an easy routine.

He would awake early, do his morning stretches, and then choose one of three pre-planned jogging routes, depending on whether he wanted to run five, seven, or nine miles. All of them took him near the Tinley Park Elementary School and through the back lots of the shopping center, but he would sometimes run around Lake Lonin before circling back.

He always met people along the way and offered smiles and simple pleasantries. He found happiness in his steady, tested strides; happy to trade the treadmills of late for a true run through the neighborhood landscape.

He'd been experiencing a wide range of emotions and knew of no better activity to direct his focus.

But it wasn't only his mindset that was different. He favored the morning chill in the air to the persistent, balmy breeze of the islands. He enjoyed hearing the sounds of the children's laughs as they ran to catch the school bus and liked the brisk winds that shook the heavy leaves from the trees.

It was now late September and a full three weeks since he'd returned from Bermuda. But although he was happy to be back, his home seemed foreign, almost like he'd never been there before.

He knew it was his sobriety but the feeling was surreal. Just two months before, he was a used-up drunk with death on his mind; living in a blurred, mechanical existence. The days seemed so short then. He wouldn't rise until afternoon and the alcohol would carry his last lucid thoughts by evening.

Now he was astounded at how the simplest things seemed so different. He'd never noticed the weeds around his once well-kept garden, how the old shabby draperies were covered with dust and pulled tight against the sunlight, or even the stale smells that ran up from the basement.

Some things were easy fixes, while others required planning and thought. So after each morning run, he would enjoy a healthy breakfast and plan his afternoon work detail, while sitting on the outside patio and sipping strong coffee. His list was substantial and spanned every degree of hardship and detail, but he was adamant in attacking each one.

In the first several days he'd cleaned out the basement, attic, and garage of nearly everything; calling a variety of charities to donate the items to and a hauling service to clear the rest.

He black-topped the driveway, cleaned out the detached garage, and painted its interior walls white and the flooring a deep gray. He built shelving on the back wall and placed hooks to organize his tools and light machinery. Finally, he washed away years of dirt from the garage windows and was surprised to see how bright the effect was. After washing and waxing his Oldsmobile, he took it out for a ride around town and felt pride as he glided it into his newly-refurbished garage.

Next he'd focused on the exterior of the house. He'd hired a handful of contractors and worked with them as they examined and fixed stray roofing shingles and cleaned out the gutters. They painted the house a brighter shade of white and installed new shudders and trim work that framed it nicely.

At the same time a landscaping company over-hauled the entire yard. They re-seeded the grass, put down a fall fertilizer, weeded and mulched; and even created several new beds throughout the yard. They planned for the long term by planting several trees to better outline the property and create more personality with the coloring. A new stone path was forged to the front door and a sprinkler system was installed to maintain the lawn.

Inside, he cleaned out every room and put in new carpeting throughout. He started a list to renovate the bathrooms and kitchens, but wanted to get Dannie's advice before advancing any further.

Finally, he'd finished off a significant space in the basement for his inside workouts. He'd bought several pieces of equipment and weights, even installing a wall of mirrors, a flat screen television, and a simple sound system to keep things interesting.

He was in awe of what he'd accomplished in the last few weeks. In his labors he'd become lost in self-thought and had taken yet another step in finding inner peace.

He was happy the Island Hopper case was over and William Monocacy was confirmed dead, but he was still upset that Dannie had been involved. He would never forgive himself and became emotionally deflated whenever the thoughts crept in.

Still, he tried to concentrate on his workouts and household duties and always found contentment there. But as happy and fulfilling as both were, the best part of his day were his nine o'clock phone dates with Dannie.

Tom was relieved to find that as her health improved and she settled into the comforts of home, she'd come back to him. She'd seemed so distant and cold on their last day in Bermuda, but that was over; and although they were apart, their talks continued to be invigorating.

One evening he was outside grilling a couple of tilapia filets and asparagus. Flipping the food over, he took a moment to appreciate the new gardens and fresh landscaping. He swelled with a pride long forgotten and smiled at his accomplishments.

But a car took him by surprise as it drove by and sped around the corner. His senses heightened and he turned off the grill and moved to get a better view of the vehicle.

A few moments later, it turned down the street again and stopped directly in front of his house. He could see it was a taxi cab, which he thought odd, as he moved closer.

Suddenly the car door flew open and a shadowy figure emerged and rushed up the driveway. Squinting through the darkness he readied himself for anything. But then recognition came and Dannie ran into his open arms.

The embrace lasted several moments, before he pulled away and took her in. The cabbie followed with her luggage and she handed the man a wad of cash.

"I packed my suitcase in less than ten minutes, took a stand-by flight and here I am. I thought we'd have our phone date in-person."

CHAPTER 91

That night, Dannie wore pink sweatpants, a matching Nike sweatshirt, and fluffy white socks. When Tom reached out to hug her, she fell into his arms and they melted together.

Tom breathed in her sweet perfume, so happy to be holding her. But then she broke away, taking his hand and leading him to the sofa.

"Okay, let's talk. Is it really okay that I'm here? I don't want to disrespect the memory of your wife and be in the home that you shared if it's not okay."

Tom looked at Dannie, thoughtfully. He had similar concerns but he grinned, remembering his vivid dream in Bermuda.

"I was wondering about that too," he said. "Not just now, but for as long as we've known each other. Jess is gone. I know and respect that now and I *truly* believe she'd want me to be happy. Your being with me doesn't replace her memory, whether it's here or anywhere else. I love your spontaneity and you are absolutely welcome here."

Dannie let out a visible sigh and sunk into the sofa, finally accepting its comfort.

"Then sit next to me," she said. "How are you? Are you getting back to your old routine?"

"First let's talk about you. What's the doctor say?"

"You're worse than the kids, Tom. They're all over me, especially Abby."

"You *have* been through a lot," Tom said, still looking her over.

Dannie looked incredulous. "What about you? You were held prisoner for a week in Venezuela!"

"Yeah but—"

Tom cut himself off. Dannie was right, as always, and he couldn't form the words.

"That's what I thought," Dannie said. "Anyway, I've gotten a lot of rest and I'm fully hydrated. My doctor says I'm fine and I feel great."

Tom nodded, still not fully convinced. "What about the mental aspect of it? I mean you were forcibly taken and experimented on for days."

"I'm not going to lie and say I don't think about it several times each day, but I also take comfort in the end result."

"Your resolve is tremendous."

Dannie spoke evenly. "'Reflect upon your present blessings of which every man has many; not on your past misfortunes, of which all men have some.'"

Tom thought through the words. "Your optimism continues to inspire me. Who said that?"

"Charles Dickens. Now show me around your house."

"I still can't forgive myself, though. It was me who put you in that awful situation."

Dannie took Tom's hands in hers and squeezed them. "As I remember it, a hero came in, put his life on the line, and rescued me. He even sheltered me from a bomb blast and carried me out of a burning house."

Tom looked down at their hands, shaking his head slowly. "But I was—"

"Tom!" Dannie interrupted, raising her voice and visibly jolting him. "You *cannot* take responsibility for other people's actions. But you *can* accept my appreciation in saving me. Do you think I'd be okay if the FBI rushed in there instead of you?"

Tom softened and looked into her blue eyes. Then she moved her hands to his face and gently touched him.

"I'm okay and I don't want to talk about it anymore. Is that understood?"

Tom nodded, like a small child being chastised.

"Then give me a tour," she said, changing the subject and jumping up, excitedly. "Or I'll start quoting William Wordsworth. You know, 'The child is father of the man . . .'"

Rising, Tom walked Dannie through the dining room and kitchen, then to the basement and to the three bedrooms upstairs. He explained the things he'd recently worked on and the paint colors and crowned molding he was thinking about.

"I've always loved painting and remodeling, Tom. If you'd allow me, I'd like to help, at least with the color selections."

"Really?" Tom asked, happily. "You know the paint colors are the last thing on my list. I'm good at cleaning things out and doing the big jobs, but I'm not into color schemes and décor."

Dannie laughed. "Well *I* am and I'd absolutely love to help."

"Great. Then first thing tomorrow we'll plan it out and go to the hardware store."

Tom showed Dannie the guest bedroom where she'd be staying. Suddenly the clock downstairs began chiming; sounding off that it was nine o'clock.

"Looks like we're right on time for our date," she said, playfully.

He guided her back downstairs, where they made popcorn and poured a couple of Iced Teas. Then they fell into the sofa, covered themselves in a huge Chicago Bears blanket and talked for several hours.

Sometime in the dark night they fell asleep, holding each other until morning.

CHAPTER 92

The days passed and Tom & Dannie were lost in each other. They were energized in their emotions and forward-thinking in their perspective. Time seemed inconsequential, with its only measure of passing being the newspaper headlines, the cooler weather, and the dramatic changes to the house.

Tom continued his work-outs, and Dannie joined him every other day for a brisk walking session. He showed her the neighborhood; the schools he'd went to, the local shopping center, and the large park nearby.

They'd walked to the cemetery twice to visit Jess and Kelly.

At first, Tom was unsure of how to react. But when Dannie knelt to place flowers on each of the graves and then wiped away her own tears, his trepidations eased.

Watching Dannie as she lowered her head in silent prayer, Tom couldn't help but smile. She was an amazing companion and gave him a sense of contentment that had long abandoned him.

Each afternoon, they would diligently work on renovating and decorating the house. Dannie had completed the color scheme, and within the first week they'd painted most of the interior. Tom hung crowned molding and new light fixtures, with matching door knobs and hinges.

In a week's time their duties were complete and Tom met Dannie in the living room, where she was organizing a screwdriver set.

She looked up and smiled. "The faceplates have all been changed and the new curtains and window treatments are up."

Tom looked to the front bay window in awe. It had been closed off for so long; with the old draperies closed tight and clutter collecting against the wall. On the outside, he could see that the stray bushes and high weeds were gone.

Now the large window was thoroughly cleaned and visible. Flowing blue drapes outlined the edges. Two perfect bows fell to each side to accentuate the original wood framing. A simple end table was tucked underneath, with several pictures of Tom, Jessica, and Kelly in happier times. On the outside, Tom's landscaping was easily visible, as was the newly-laid stone path that led to the driveway.

"I hope you don't mind the pictures. I found them in a box in the basement and re-framed them."

Sunlight streamed in and lit up their accomplishments like a spotlight.

"It's absolutely breathtaking," Tom said. His mind was reeling; his eyes moving from one wonderful accent to the next.

"Thank you," Dannie said. "I think it turned out nice."

Tom placed his hands in hers. Then he gently put his right arm around her back and led her in a slow dance, moving to a silent melody.

"What are you doing, Casanova?"

"Everything you do invigorates me, Dannie. When I'm with you I hear music. When I close my eyes I see fireworks."

Dannie gently placed her cheek against Tom's chest, and they danced for several moments. Finally, Dannie broke the silence with a small giggle.

"What's so funny?" Tom asked.

"I was just wondering what song we're dancing to. If there's a sudden dip coming, I'd like to know so I don't break a hip."

She expected a laugh but heard nothing. He just continued a deliberate sway that became unsettling. Suddenly she tore away to study him. His eyes were moist and a strange expression played on his face.

"What's the matter, Tom?" she asked, concerned.

Tom blinked and a tear fell to the floor. "Actually," he began. "For the first time in as long as I can remember, absolutely nothing."

"Then I don't understand. Why are you—"

"Will you marry me, Danielle?" he asked, flatly.

Silence reigned and neither of them breathed. Then she smiled, before erupting into a full laugh. She searched his eyes, producing her own tears.

"I will, Tom. I mean I do."

SEVEN MONTHS LATER

MAY 8

Chapter 93

Holtville
Alabama

The wedding took place at Dannie's home at Jackson Manor. It was a sprawling ex-cotton plantation that sat proudly at the north-eastern extremity of Lewis Road, edging Jordan Lake.

Family lore had it that Andrew Jackson spent two nights in a smaller house on the property after the Battle of Horseshoe Bend. And Dannie's great grandfather had attached that piece of history to the estate, though the main house had been built almost a century later.

The mansion was three stories high, with a long upper balcony and large windows that looked directly to the lake. A considerable stone patio extended from the middle section, with stairs that emptied out onto the huge lawn.

In total, it resembled The White House in its neo-classical federal style, with all the accentuating details of classical Greek ionic architecture. Still, as impending and masculine as it was, there was no mistaking Dannie's feminine touch, and it showed in the colorful gardens and prolific landscaping.

It had been seven months since Tom and Dannie's engagement.

She'd used the time to plan the wedding, along with her over-zealous but well-intended daughters. She'd also prepared her home to include Tom, who had agreed to move to Alabama permanently. He'd put the final touches on his house and had successfully sold it to an eager, young couple.

Now sixty-one years old, Tom was in better shape than he was eleven years before. As he ran each day, his thoughts would inevitably return to the man he'd almost become. The dichotomy between the two was overwhelming, and he drew strength in the thought of the life he'd avoided. Now he was trim and energized. He was about to be married and very much looking forward to his life with Dannie.

Late in the morning Tom took a quiet stroll around the yard to check on the final details of the day. The event company was busy erecting the tent and a local florist had transformed the place into a fairy tale garden.

Tom looked to the long white carpet that stretched to the edge of Jordan Lake. There, several pedestals and candles were carefully placed, along with a sundry of flowers. On the groom's side there were pictures of Jessica and Kelly, along with roses and stargazer lilies, their favorites. Tom smiled at Dannie's attention to detail.

Then he looked past the alter to the lake and the high blue sky. The sun was rising steadily, and a gentle breeze promised to hold the temperatures in the low seventies. Tom heard a shout that cut through his thoughts, and he turned to see a well-dressed man running to him.

"Seargant?!" Tom yelled. "Is that you?"

Jack Seargant quickly closed the gap and the two men embraced for several moments.

"Dannie called me as a surprise."

Tom was glowing. "I wanted you here but didn't want to ask, with you being so busy with the baby! How are Susan and Hailey?"

"They're both great. Sorry they couldn't make it, but it's just too early to travel."

"I'm so happy you're here!"

"Like I said before, Tom. We've come a long way and I want to witness the next step in your life."

"How about being my best man, then?"

"I would be honored," Seargant said.

Then the two men started a slow walk around the lake to catch up on things.

CHAPTER 94

Reverend Kipp was a lanky man, wearing a flowing white robe that hung on his thin shoulders. He had short, peppered hair and close, dark eyes; with an easy and charming smile that lit up the room. He was an excellent speaker and his voice was conciliatory in its southern drawl.

After welcoming the guests and introducing himself, he discussed the sanctity of marriage and God's blessing on holy matrimony. Then he turned to the happy couple, looking to Tom and Dannie with revered esteem. He paused as a warm smile swept across his face.

The reverend had gone to elementary school with Dannie and her late husband, James. He'd even performed *their* wedding ceremony over thirty years before. He had eulogized James after his passing and was now honored to be part of Dannie's second marriage.

He looked to the guests and announced that the couple had written their own vows. Then he placed a gentle hand on Tom's shoulder, gesturing for him to begin.

Tom took a deep breath and held Dannie's hands, looking into her eyes. "First and foremost, Danielle, I must say that I love you and that's all that matters. I am not an orator. Everything that follows are just words. But I feel compelled to say to you again—and in front of all of these people—that you have saved my life."

Dannie continued to look at Tom, her blue eyes wide, as she tried to stay composed.

"The person I used to be is gone and the man I am is because of you. I simply cannot wait to share the rest of my days with you. When I proposed, I feared that it may have been too soon. I always frowned upon people making life-long decisions without going through the seasons with their prospective mates.

"I thought that a husband should know what color Easter egg his wife would dye first. Does she carve pumpkins with a happy or scary face? What kind of fireworks are her favorite? What kind of candy does she hand out on Halloween? On Christmas, does she rush to her stocking or unwrap the largest gift first?

"But every day kept getting better. I love you and I can't wait to go through the seasons as your husband."

Tom looked down shyly, as Dannie dabbed her eyes with a handkerchief.

"That was beautiful," the reverend said. "Now Danielle would you like to say a few words to Tom?"

Dannie squeezed Tom's hands, tightly. "You are a wonderful man and I love you, too. I also think you sell yourself short. You are the man you are because of *you* and you've also saved *me*.

"I chose this spot next to the lake for a reason. We are like the water, ever-changing and in constant motion. We are the ice, the rain, and the mist. We are the cool blue, the dreary brown, and the crystal clear; but constant in our love and commitment to each other."

Dannie wiped away a tear and refocused.

"When two people find each other and become greater together than apart, that's something special, particularly in today's world. I love you Tom; and I can't wait to go through the seasons with you, too."

The reverend smiled and asked Tom and Dannie if they took each other as man and wife. They both nodded eagerly, each saying a hurried, "I do."

Reverend Kipp beamed. "Then with the power vested in me by the state of Alabama, I *proudly* declare that you are man and wife. You may kiss the bride, Tom."

After a simple kiss, Dannie moved to the left and uncovered a large structure Tom hadn't noticed. He smiled wide as he looked at a stone moon gate she'd secretly had erected.

"It's permanent, Tom, so we can walk through it as often as we like."

Tom reached for Dannie's hand and they slowly walked through the moon gate and kissed again on the other side.

The crowd rose to applaud but the happy couple couldn't hear a thing.

Tom wasn't much of a dancer. So after a few obligatory twirls with his new bride, and two more with Abby and Cindy, he sought refuge at a far table with Seargant, as they enjoyed the cool breeze coming off the lake.

Dinner was over and the DJ was playing some light favorites. Several couples took the opportunity to move to the lawn and enjoy their coffee in the open air. Tom saw Dannie's granddaughter—Abby's daughter—sitting alone. Sara Ann looked uncomfortable and sad, and Tom walked over to her.

"What's the matter, honey?" he asked, looking at her thoughtfully.

Her big, brown eyes lit up when she saw him, but the excitement ran away just as fast.

"I was just looking at all of those presents," she started, pointing to the table. "They're so elegantly-wrapped and I have nothing to give. I'm just a dumb ten-year old kid."

Tom frowned, regarding the small child in her blind naivety. Her beautiful innocence. Her words were so sincere; her feelings shining through like the evening sun that streamed all around them. But although her message was illogical, she was genuinely distraught.

Tom had spoken to her many times, but not in such an emotional state. He hesitated, trying to exact a dialogue that would cheer her up. Sara Ann had a small voice that spoke more in questions than statements. She was a tiny, fragile girl; very much unsure of the large world around her. Tom also recognized that she'd lost her Grandpa James—Dannie's late husband—and was probably confused about accepting him.

Tom was about to speak when she surprised him. "I saw you dancing with my Nana and was wondering if you would like to dance with me."

Tom rushed to a stand and then bowed, ceremoniously. He formally extended his hand and she took it, excitedly. With perfect timing, a slow song began and Tom and Sara Ann moved to the center of the floor.

Others moved away and soon they were dancing in the spotlight, unaware of the smiles all around them.

Sara Ann's demeanor had changed into elation, as she spoke fervently about the decorations and the bright lights. She loved parties and had never been to one so grand. The ceremony was like a fairy tale and she was so happy to be dancing with the groom!

But as the song waned, she stopped her easy sway and looked up to Tom, thoughtfully.

"May I ask you a question, Mr. Brightwell?"

Tom knelt to her level and looked her in the eyes, oblivious to the applause. "Anything at all, sweetheart."

"Can I call you my Papa?"

Tom grinned uncontrollably, then hugged her tightly for several moments.

He glanced at the wedding gifts and shook his head, wiping away tears.

"Sara Ann, you just gave me the best wedding present of them all," he said.

CHAPTER 95

Playa Mujeres Excellency Resort
Playa Mujeres, Mexico

Tom and Dannie had decided against a honeymoon. They didn't fit the traditional composite; and with Tom transitioning to Alabama, and the travel they'd done in the past year, they just wanted to be together and catch their breath.

But Seargant wouldn't hear of it. He argued the contrary, saying they needed an escape to celebrate the next chapter in their lives. So as best man, he'd given the new couple a wedding present they didn't really want, but were happy to take.

They flew first class to Cancun. Then a private car took them through the three front gates and into the lushly manicured inner-workings of the Playa Mujeres Excellency Resort. They checked into a suite on the coveted club level, and Miguel, the concierge manager, personally escorted them to room # 9352.

It was the most luxurious place Tom and Dannie had ever seen.

They descended the flowing marble staircase, which was the center-piece of the open three-story lobby. They craned their necks, trying to absorb every minute detail, as Miguel spoke of the amenities. The high ceiling was a swirl of red, blue, and yellow stained glass panels framed by royal blue edges. Ahead and above them, exposed brick abounded and spanned out to the far end.

They paused at the lower lobby tan-stoned bar, marveling at its sharply cut edges and substantial structure. They ordered cold bottles of water, which they each drank, greedily. Tom ran his fingers on the curious, smooth top, which had internal lights that reflected through the stone. Dannie noticed the shops in the adjacent hall.

"This is quite a place you've got here," Tom said, still looking around.

"Thank you, sir. Your comfort is our number one priority."

Then Miguel took out several brochures and fanned them onto the bar.

"Here are some things to consider when you have time," he began. "We have wave runners, couples para-sailing, boating, scuba diving, snorkeling and many other activities. We also have excursions off-site to Isla Mujeres, the Mayan pyramids, zip lining, and a host of other things.

"I hope you enjoy all of our twelve bars and nine restaurants; and lounge at your private beach, where you can have anything brought directly to you. You are club level guests, so you have your own section of beach and may enjoy any of the private cabanas."

Miguel led them through the double doors and into the balmy breeze. They trailed lazily, enjoying the fresh air and relaxed feel. Miguel continued his dialogue, but they each fell silent and heard very little. They retracted deep within themselves. They were finally married and just happy to be together.

For the remainder of the day, they relaxed in a private cabana on the beach, where they read magazines, napped, and enjoyed each other's company. They ordered food and drinks directly from the beach waiter, and then held hands while wading in the clear blue water.

Straight ahead was Isla Mujeres—the Island of Women—and in between there were no shortage of boats, wave runners, and snorkelers to watch.

Looking across the water, with the sun casting sparkles on the sea, Tom breathed the salty air in complete satisfaction. Then he looked to his new wife. She took his hand and smiled, as if they'd just conjured the same thought.

"I love you, too," she said.

"It's amazing how you read me so well."

"I also want to say that Jack was right."

"About what?" he asked.

"About this trip. My hesitations were unfounded."

"I just want you to relax and enjoy yourself," Tom said. "You deserve it."

She tightened her grasp in his hand and moved closer for a kiss, before falling into him for an embrace. Small waves lapped at their ankles and they swayed in each other's arms, lost in the moment.

A loud scream erupted from the pool area and they both looked over. It was nothing unusual though, and they just laughed at the source. The resort was all-inclusive and adult-only, and the "younger kids" were their fellow newlyweds and those celebrating early anniversaries. Most of them were several decades younger and usually stayed at the main pool and swim-up bars.

Music started to play on the pool deck. It was accented by Latino sounds and was upbeat, flowing freely over the Lobster and Grill House and to the people on the beach.

Tom walked Dannie back to their cabana, happy to see that the towels had been folded in their absence. Another round of lemonades poked out from the ice bucket.

The happy pair sat down in silence. Dannie reached for a book, while Tom poked at the pre-populated iPod that Cindy had given him as a wedding present. The sounds of Sinatra filled his ears and a broad grin swept across his face.

Tom Brightwell felt like a teenager again.

CHAPTER 96

They were lost in each other. Not only in the deep conversations that *still* lasted well into the night, but also in the many activities they took full advantage of.

Tom hit the gym each morning and alternated between yoga and swim aerobics. After each workout, he'd shower and find Dannie on their open air balcony, relaxing on the outside bed and reading. The last remnants of her breakfast would be on a discarded plate and she would look up with the brightest of smiles.

"What do we do next?" she'd say each morning, and Tom took great pleasure in the planning.

They spent the second day relaxing at the resort spa. They enjoyed a couple's massage and then went to the pool area, where they visited each station in the water, with the targeted and pulsating spray hitting their different body parts.

Tom laughed as his unsuspecting bride walked through the different pools with surprisingly cold/hot/warm temperatures, but she exacted revenge when the bucket of ice was released on his head for the ice bath portion.

On the third day they took a boat to Isla Mujeres and explored the entire island in a golf cart. They climbed the top of the lighthouse, looked to the ancient ruins, and watched the younger generation on zip lines, flying through the air high above the sea.

They bought souvenirs in the marketplace. Tom marveled at his new wife, as she connected with the natives and played with the small children whom worked alongside their parents in the shops.

Next they took a boat nearly twenty miles off the coast in open water to swim with the whale sharks, where several hundred were migrating. They spent considerable time in the water as the largest fish in the ocean swam all around them.

Coming up for air and clearing his mask, Tom looked at Dannie. She treaded water carefully, grinning, with her pink mask on her forehead. It was one of the most incredible experiences of their lives. Like swimming with live submarines.

Finally, they explored the Mayan pyramids, walking in the steps of history and appreciating the ancient structures.

It happened when Tom was walking down the sandy slope to the tour bus. It was incredibly hot, with a high sun and no cloud coverage, and the stepping had been harsh and unforgiving.

He was getting a couple cold bottles of water, and on the descent the thought hit him like a hammer. He wasn't sure, but something was very unsettling and he couldn't shake the feeling.

Still, he grabbed the bottled waters and hurried back to where Dannie was taking pictures. As always, she could read him instantly. She grabbed a water bottle and wiped his sweaty face.

"What's the matter, Tom?"

"I don't know," he said, flatly. "I can't put my finger on it."

"Are you okay; do you need a doctor? We could just—"

"No it's nothing like that. I just can't shake a feeling I have. Like there's something important that I can't quite comprehend."

"Well it's almost time to head back. Why don't we hit the beach and see if we can think it through together."

Tom nodded, approvingly, and they both drank their water. On the bus ride he was quiet and closed his eyes as the bus jumped along the road. He wondered what had triggered the thoughts. Was it that he'd finally let go of the stresses that had burdened him? Was his mind now free to explore other things? Or had something he'd *seen* triggered it?

At the resort, they found a cabana right on the shore line. Dannie walked the beach and Tom stood staring out to Isla Mujeres.

Suddenly he came to a realization.

He gasped outwardly and threw himself onto the powder white sand. He held his head in both hands, massaging his temples as if he could force the information out.

But it came naturally, and he sat looking out to the sea, deciphering it. Then he moved to the cabana and worked his cell phone to call Seargant. Several painstaking moments passed, but his friend finally came on the line. Tom explained the situation and his complete confidence in what to do.

Seargant agreed to meet Tom at the Montgomery Airport the following day. They were going to be taking a very important trip together.

Tom knew *exactly* where his daughter's killer was.

He was going after Jeremy again.

CHAPTER 97

Seargant reluctantly agreed to Tom's plan. He gave in on certain points and shut him down on others. He'd pulled strings across department lines and called in some inter-agency favors; but as promised, the FBI was at the airport waiting for Tom and Dannie's arriving flight from Cancun.

Tom spoke to his new wife the night before. She didn't like him leaving so soon after their marriage. There was no denying he was placing himself in danger, but she knew they could never *truly* be together until he found inner peace.

He'd promised Kelly he'd bring her killer to justice and Dannie knew nothing could stand in his way.

So she had conceded, though her mind was racing with every imaginable consequence. What if she never saw him again? Tom said he and Seargant had a plan, and as clandestine and illegal as it was, there would be loose support from the FBI.

Seargant met them at the gate and directed them to a private security office nearby. Dannie was pleasant and cordial, but Seargant knew she wasn't keen to the idea, so he concentrated on her.

"How was your honeymoon?" he asked, moving to Dannie for a warm hug.

"It was great," Tom said, trying to keep things upbeat. "Just what we needed and we can't thank you enough."

But Dannie was unmoved. "So what's this look like, Jack?" she asked, pulling away from him.

"We'll all walk to the baggage area to get your luggage. My men will drive you home and Tom will bring his bags with him for *our* trip. We have a jet standing by with cleared flight plans to Praia International Airport. We should return in a few days."

"Tell me about Cape Verde," Dannie said.

"It's a series of islands about four-hundred miles off the west coast of Africa. It's remote and deeply cultural, but has all the influences of its European and South American roots. It's an arid, volcanic island, heavily stumped in boating and fishing, but most importantly for *any* fugitive, there isn't an extradition treaty with the United States."

Dannie exhaled, shaking her head in exasperation. "So you're going into some country illegally; and this place has no relations with us? Are you crazy?"

Seargant straightened. "That's not exactly true," he began with his palms up, defensively. "There's a U.S. embassy in the capital of Praia and the country is modern in all the right places.

"Although we don't have an extradition treaty with them, we maintain a presence to protect our own interests, support their democracy, and aid in humanitarian efforts. Cape Verde is a relatively young country in their independence, but they *do* belong to the United Nations and World Trade Organization. They are certainly not third world."

When Seargant finished, Tom jumped into the conversation. "Did you find anything more about what I told you?"

Seargant nodded. "What you remember hearing in Venezuela when you were slipping in and out of consciousness is very credible. We used the information to track a piece of property that's being rented to one of the aliases known to Jeremy and it checks out. We agree that Cape Verde is perfect for him. It's big enough to get lost in, yet has a cozy island feel. It's modern where it has to be and again, there's no extradition treaty with the United States."

Dannie was incensed. "So you're just gonna bust in unannounced and take Jeremy?"

Seargant deferred to Tom, who reached for Dannie's hand and held it.

"I'll be right outside," Seargant said, leaving them alone.

Several minutes later, Dannie left the room and walked directly to Seargant. She had obviously been crying, but still conveyed strength and control. She held the man's broad shoulders in her tiny hands and moved him close to her. He was accommodating and leaned down.

"Take care of him, Jack. I mean it. I just got him and I want him back. This is an unfair request, I know, but I'm holding you *personally* responsible for him. Is that clear?"

"Danielle, I—"

"Jack!" Dannie interrupted, her voice shaking, her small body trembling. "I *need* him back."

Seargant nodded, straightening up to his full six-foot-four inches. "I'll bring him back safe, Dannie. I swear it."

Then she walked to the baggage claim area, with everyone else trying to keep up.

◄O►◄O►◄O►

They landed unceremoniously via private jet at the Praia International Airport. They were whisked away by a common cab under cover of darkness, and checked into the Hotel Tropico on de Julio Avenue near the U.S. Embassy. The location was crucial if they needed to seek asylum, and the university nearby promised a busy crowd that could provide anonymity and cover.

After getting settled, Tom entered Seargant's room for a quick meeting before bed. Seargant was sitting at the small desk, typing vigorously on his laptop. He nodded at Tom, but kept working.

"Open the briefcase on the bed," Seargant managed, pointing to it with a quick flick of his hand.

Tom did as he was told, surprised at what he saw. It looked to be an ordinary briefcase in every way, well-used and beaten in normal fashion. But the inside was pristine, with deep cushioned pockets and an impressive display of weaponry.

Seargant joined Tom, speaking evenly. "I need to review the fragile *legal* aspects of this exercise. Although *I* can manufacture any number of reasons for being here on official business, there are very *few* to explain your presence, and especially in the possession of firearms."

Tom remained quiet, still eyeing the briefcase.

"Also, I know we've been over this a dozen times. But tell me everything you remember hearing about Jeremy's safe harbor here."

Tom looked to Seargant. "I'm not sure what caused the sudden realization in Mexico. But when I was being held captive by the cartel—all but dead and delusional—I *definitely* heard 'Cidade Velha' and 'Cape Verde.'"

Seargant nodded. "That *also* confirms what our satellites have seen. I've just received confirmation that Jeremy is about twelve miles east of us right now."

CHAPTER 98

The next morning they approached the chalet from the south, parking in a clearing a quarter mile away.

To the casual glance they looked like tourists; dressed for the clement weather and enjoying a casual stroll on a beach road. But they were each carrying a small arsenal in the simple, worn backpacks they slung over their shoulders.

Seargant's contacts at the NSA had pinpointed Jeremy's exact location. In their efforts they also found several more Swiss bank accounts that had previously eluded them. They confirmed that as current as ten minutes prior, Jeremy was alone in the beach-front home.

The stretch of land they were approaching was coveted and had been built on sparingly. The cumulative effect favored Tom and Seargant. It was out-of-the-way and security was non-existent. The house had perimeter walls but was open to the beach. Barring a couple of locked doors, they didn't expect any resistance.

As they moved closer, Seargant turned to Tom. "Don't forget the plan and don't allow your emotions to dictate your actions. As hard as this is to say, this is *not* personal. We are apprehending an international fugitive and suspected murderer. *You* don't act unless *I* act. I have no authority here and you have negative authority."

"Understood," Tom said, a little too eagerly for Seargant.

They walked directly to the beach, choosing to access the house from the rear to get a real time view. From the water, the villa looked harmless enough. It was modern in its architecture, and could have easily sat on any movie star's cliff in Malibu. The entire backside was comprised of glass. Several decks stuck out from the three-story unit, and a capacious stone patio poured onto the beach.

Seargant held out what looked like a video recorder, moving next to a tree and "microwaving" the house. On the monitor, the blackness was filled with different shades of yellow and orange, which showed the variance in temperature inside. Then a red blur appeared at the top of the north-east corner. It was stationary and it looked human. Seargant punched a few buttons and locked into the heat signature, which was bright red, with pinkish white at the top.

"What do you have?" Tom asked.

"He's in the third floor master bathroom. It looks like he's taking a shower, judging from the difference in colors coming off his head."

"Then we're a go, right?"

"Remember what I said, Tom. And I go in first with you right on my tail."

They each put on thin latex gloves and in the silence, Seargant took a deep breath. Then he glanced around once more and hard-lined it with Tom in pursuit. Seargant slowed only to try the door, which slid open, easily. Then he quickly moved through the kitchen and up the rear stair case.

Quietly and efficiently Seargant moved to the third floor, hearing water running in a shower. Stepping into the master bath, his eyes darted in all directions, clearing the room. He looked to the sounds at the far end.

Seargant treaded lightly. Steam encased him and the temperature rose significantly. His capillaries dilated and his clothes seemed to tighten on his body. With the stress of the moment and his adrenaline testing all-time highs, he felt on fire. He saw a body in the shower, leaning against the clear glass. But his view was muted by the steam and the water spraying down.

As Seargant moved closer; however, all of the air escaped him. There was something wrong. It was a mannequin.

Suddenly there was a shout. As Seargant swung around, Jeremy rushed from the closet. His eyes were wide with anger; his face contorted in rage. But what concerned Seargant more was the Smith & Wesson Sigma the man was holding.

Seargant jumped in front of Tom just as the gun fired its first shot. The two men crashed to the floor, destroying a small table and sending a potted plant airborne. Seargant felt an explosive pain in his chest and curled over. A second shot erupted and a decorative vase next to Seargant's head exploded.

Tom absorbed the impact from the fall and was able to move his right arm. He squeezed off a shot from his Beretta and Jeremy's face flashed in pain. Blood poured from his mid-section and he stumbled backward.

Tom moved from under Seargant and was on top of Jeremy in seconds, pinning him with his knees. Jeremy was decades younger, but Tom was in much better shape, and adrenaline—fueled by revenge—pulsated through every bit of him.

Tom repeatedly punched Jeremy into submission, as the wounded man groaned beneath him. With the sudden revelation that the life he'd known was over, Jeremy stared wide-eyed, gasping for air and coughing up blood. His look had quickly changed to desperation and confusion.

Tom swiftly handcuffed Jeremy and scooped up the Smith & Wesson. Then he rushed over to Seargant, who had managed to stand to check his wound.

"Are you okay, Seargant?" Tom asked, monitoring Jeremy from his peripheral.

"Looks like the vest did its job, but it'll leave a mark."

"Just one more souvenir, huh?" Tom said, between heavy breaths. "Thanks for stepping in front of me. With your height, and judging from the elevation, it would have gotten me in the head."

"Let's just get Jeremy and us the hell out of here."

But when they turned, Jeremy was trying to stand. The handcuffs were dangling from his left wrist, while he palmed a much smaller .22 in his right hand. His condition forced him to crouch and hold his chest, and the direction of the gun didn't show an immediate threat. Tom and Seargant trained their weapons on Jeremy as time seemed to stand still.

"Drop it," Seargant yelled; his voice loud and full of authority.

"I was blessed with small hands," Jeremy said, looking at the handcuffs.

Tom approached Jeremy. He stopped a few feet away and pointed his Beretta directly at the man's face. Jeremy recoiled, falling backwards and into a fetal position. His gun fell away, harmlessly.

"We saw the video that showed you killing Kelly," Tom yelled, still training his 9mm on Jeremy.

Jeremy stared blankly, seeing two guns pointed his way. "So you're here to take me in? Have me sent to some hole-in-the-wall prison for the rest of my life?"

"Something like that," Seargant said, still leveling his gun.

Jeremy managed a quick snicker between the small moans of pain. "But didn't you know that this is a non-extradition country? That you can't touch me here?"

Tom sneered, a strange contrast to the feeling in the room. "There are two pieces of information you should know Jeremy. First, no one knows you or even *we* are here. And second, we're *not* here to arrest you."

Fear flashed in Jeremy's eyes and he reached for his weapon. The room exploded in gunfire and the acrid smell of sulfur joined the steamy air. Jeremy slumped against the wall, dead.

Tom stooped to verify his death, while Seargant methodically inventoried the shell casings. The FBI-man closed his eyes for several moments, recounting how many shots had been fired. Then he retraced their steps and reviewed everything that could link them to the scene.

Meanwhile, Tom patted Jeremy down and removed the man's wallet. Curious about his life, he flipped through the different forms of identification and credit cards. There was nothing unusual, until he removed and unfolded a single piece of paper. It had been scribbled on with a place, date, and time. He pocketed it and returned to Seargant.

"I have his wallet; maybe it'll help the Feds in learning more about him."

"You didn't have to antagonize him," Seargant said, rigidly.

Tom looked down, faking a look of distress. "I'm sorry, Seargant. I had no idea."

Seargant knew Tom was being impudent, but there was no time for conversation. "Just keep your gloves on until we leave the property," he added, tersely.

Then the two men left as easily as they'd arrived.

CHAPTER 99

They de-briefed each other in Seargant's room. They each gave their perspective of the operation, and then summarized the threats that could expose them.

Seargant had planned for many outcomes. One was to use his credentials as a means of explaining things, but with the cleanliness and finality of it all, he decided against it.

"This is over Tom. We weren't here; you *especially* weren't here."

Tom paced the room. He exhaled and stretched, feeling the tension leave him. "I'm fine with that, Seargant."

"Are you going to Chicago to tell Jess and Kelly?"

"You bet. I also have to tell them about the wedding and where I finally am in my life."

Seargant nodded as he contemplated their relationship. "You know we've been through a lot over the last year," he started. "Remember when I first met you, a big bundle of a mess in Bonaire?"

"I was so nervous," Tom said, shaking his head.

"Remember our deep conversations; especially the one on the hill with all those stars?

"How can I forget? But I liked the one pool-side after that dinner at Sassy's."

"My point is that you have to accept that it's really over. You're only remaining task is to take care of Dannie and yourself. You've got a second family in her two daughters and the little one. Don't ever take life for granted again."

Tom moved his mouth to speak but stopped. There was nothing more to say about that or anything else. Seargant was right and Tom had found a best friend in the most unlikely of circumstances.

"There is something else, though," Tom trumpeted, pulling out a piece of paper from his pocket. "I found this in Jeremy's wallet."

Tom tossed it to Seargant, who read it aloud. "'6 o'clock, Genelle's Café, June 10, F.' What is it?"

"I don't know," Tom said. "But whatever it is, it's happening tonight."

Seargant sat on the bed, contemplating the big picture. They were supposed to be heading to the airport where their team would meet them to fly back. But what if this led to something bigger than just Jeremy?

Tom sat next to Seargant. "Jeremy was probably into a lot of stuff that we don't even know about. He could be meeting anyone: an arms dealer, drug or human trafficker, or maybe just a counterfeiter to establish a few more aliases. You know that mobility and anonymity were his best friends."

Seargant frowned. "Don't forget about the money. He was accustomed to having a ton of it and we've frozen every one of his legitimate holdings."

"So maybe he was meeting a money launderer?" Tom asked.

Seargant was a statue of concentration.

Tom pressed on. "With this new information, we have a *responsibility* to find out or at least pass it to the authorities."

"But we're not even supposed to *be* here and I'm not sharing anything with the officials here."

"Okay, then we'll go and have dinner or coffee at this Genelle's place and see what happens."

"Let's get some rest. I'll inform my team of a possible late night departure. Knock on my door in a few hours and we'll talk more about it."

CHAPTER 100

Genelle's Café turned out to be a bustling, mostly-outdoor restaurant that served the best of the local cuisine. Every kind and style of fish was available and perfectly married to an adequate wine or frozen livation.

It appeared to be made of bamboo, but the interior structure was designed to weather the wet season. There were odd knick knacks on the wall—deposits from the guests whom had visited over the years—and the cumulative effects were random and dizzying. The simple furnishings and décor were well done and nicely represented the English, French, and Brazilian influences that helped shape Cape Verde.

Judging from the modest line and the thick perimeter at the crescent-shaped bar, it was a hit with the tourists and locals alike, perfect for a meeting that required anonymity. As the evening progressed, the high blue sky changed colors. The sun hung lower and a reducing stretch of orange tried to hold on in the west.

A hostess escorted them to the rear of the outside deck. Passing a table, Seargant glanced down and thought he recognized an old colleague he hadn't seen in years. He paused to take in a second glance. The man appeared a little heavier now. He was wearing glasses and a baseball hat, but he was unmistakable.

Seargant knew it was Steve McCallister from the CIA, who he had consulted with on international cases. They hadn't spoken in years, but Seargant had followed his upward momentum with admiration. McCallister had always been an honest, decent, and hard-working operative, and Seargant was excited to see him.

Seargant slowed as his mind processed the information. What was McCallister doing in Cape Verde? He was currently the Director of the CIA!

Looking ahead, Seargant saw Tom being seated at a table in the corner, but Seargant couldn't help himself as he swung back to greet his old colleague.

Seargant had no way of knowing that McCallister and his team were intently watching *another* patron several tables away; a stout and serious man who was casually picking at the remains of a salad.

Seargant couldn't have known that the man was the most wanted fugitive in the world—the international terrorist known as Falby "The Chameleon"—and that there were other embedded agents in the crowd.

And Seargant *never* could have imagined that Falby was Jeremy's contact; and that while the CIA was following one piece of a very dangerous puzzle, Seargant and Tom had been carefully tracking the other.

And here they all were.

Except for Jeremy.

Seargant closed the gap with a few confident steps, gently tapping McCallister on the shoulder and offering a warm smile. The CIA-man looked up and recognized Seargant immediately. Throwing another look Falby's way, he was content to see the situation hadn't changed. But when Seargant turned to Tom and loudly introduced him to McCallister, Falby glanced their way.

Seargant saw McCallister's face freeze in uncertainty and knew things were very wrong. Seargant also looked to Falby and a flash of recognition crossed his mind.

Only a handful of people knew that Falby had been sentenced to life as a ghost within the clandestine CIA network of prisons; and that he'd been locked away for the past several years. It was classified that Falby had killed five agents in a successful escape and had found passage into South America, where he'd established a relationship with the same drug cartel that had protected Jeremy.

In the aching seconds that passed, Falby responded the fastest. He had a certain sense about him; and as he stared into Seargant, a knowing smile played on the killer's face.

Falby rose quickly.

His hands moved furiously in his jacket pockets.

And that's when all hell broke loose.

EPILOGUE

Montgomery Airport
Alabama

Just after midnight, Dannie stood on the tarmac, waiting for the jet to touch down. It had rained most of the evening and was now misting, with a thick fog falling all around her. Although the temperature was still in the seventies and she wore jeans and a jacket, shivers ran through her at random.

She was told nothing by the FBI agents that escorted and directed her there. And even as she looked to them now, they remained silent—even defiant—seemingly as uninformed as her.

Dannie looked into the distance, seeing the wet mist in the lighting that edged the runways. Airplanes took off and landed in turn, as she patiently waited, trying to focus on the good. Was Tom coming to her? Had everything gone as planned?

From behind her a cell phone rang and Agent Hartley sprang to attention.

He walked to Dannie and took her gently by the arm. "This way, ma'am," he said, walking her toward the runway.

She heard a jet but couldn't see it through the dense fog. Finally it emerged like a ghost, coming to rest about a hundred feet away, with its engines still roaring. Several moments went by before the small forward door opened and heavy stairs folded outward.

Suddenly she saw Seargant. He descended the steps and ran to her. She received him with open arms; tears filling her eyes as she hugged him.

"Tell me what happened, Jack. Where's Tom?"

Seargant started to speak but was muted as she screamed and ran to the plane. Another man appeared, descending the stairs much slower. He had a bandage on his face and his arm was in a sling. He walked with a limp as he bested each stair.

"Tom!" Dannie shouted, as he hobbled toward her.

The couple kissed, holding each other tightly in the dark, wet night.

"I'm so sorry we couldn't call and explain things," Tom said, hurriedly. "Seargant didn't want to risk any communication being intercepted."

"I'm just happy you're here!"

Seargant gestured to his team and they all moved back to the jet that would take them to D.C. At the top of the stairs, Seargant looked back and smiled at Tom and Danielle Brightwell, knowing they would be okay.

Then he set his intentions on seeing his own wife and new baby girl.

He had his own fairy book story to live.

And he was all too eager to begin the tale.

ACKNOWLEDGMENTS

Thank you to everyone who has been so supportive of this project over the last several years.

And a big thank you to everyone who offered their expertise throughout the story: Kimberly Hilliard and our children who continue to inspire me, Donald and Barbara Hilliard, Mark Licht, Steve Barker, Ken Reed, Larry & Dana Cate, Chester & Chris Craig, Dean & Stacie Zarriello, Vivian Brandt, Diana Landergren, David Kushner, Jim & Carrie Hilliard, Mike Miller, Dr. Eric Carr, Dr. Rebecca Middleton, Jeff Kolodin, William and Mary Lou Hooper, Steve & Jackie Hilliard, Linda Wood, Rob & Grace Gangler, Jim & Pam Middleton, Tyler Brown, Richard Osman, Cathie Campbell, Patti Murphy, Steve Winebrenner and all my friends at Ellie's Place, Tom & Larry Lamb, and the staff at the Pompano Beach Club, Rod Reddish, and Krystal-Rose a.k.a. "Doc" at On Target in Severn.

And finally, a very warm thanks to all of my friends at AuthorHouse.

CPSIA information can be obtained at www.ICGtesting.com
Printed in the USA
BVOW07*0147231213

339750BV00001B/1/P